OF KENNEDY & KING

A NOVEL

ROB CARPENTER

OF KENNEDY & KING

Of Kennedy & King is a work of fiction. Many of the characters are inspired by historical figures; others are entirely imaginary creations of the author. Apart from the historical figures any resemblance between these fictional characters and actual persons, living or dead, is purely coincidental.

Grateful acknowledgement is made to Dr. Candice Danielle Carpenter for editing this work.

RMC Lit
Los Angeles, CA

ISBN: 978-1-7366155-9-1 (hardback)
ISBN: 979-8-9906383-2-7 (paperback)
ISBN: 979-8-9906383-3-4 (eBook)

For information about this title, bulk orders, or to get in touch with the author email talktodrrob@gmail.com.

Publisher's Cataloging-In-Publication Data

Names: Carpenter, Rob, 1985-author.
Title: Of Kennedy & King/ Rob Carpenter
Description: Los Angeles, CA: RMC Lit, [2025] | Includes bibliographical references.
Identifiers: ISBN: 979-8-9906383-1-0 (paperback) ISBN: 979-8-9906383-0-3 (eBook)
Subjects: 1. Historical fiction. 2. Political fiction. 3. Civil rights movements. 4. Race relations. 5. Historical figures. 6. Bobby Kennedy. 7. Martin Luther King Jr. 8. Black Panther Party. 9. Ku Klux Klan. 10. FBI. 11. Political thrillers. 12. Assassinations.

*To Carol, my mother who has loved me,
cared for me, protected me, educated me,
and encouraged me to be my best.*

OF KENNEDY & KING

A NOVEL

APRIL 4, 1968

He has one thought and one thought only: *kill the nig*er preacher.*

He packs his Remington Model 760 Gamemaster in his light-colored duffle bag, hops in his 1966 white Ford Mustang, and takes off for Nashville in the dead of night.

In the life of James Earl Ray, a handsome, dark-haired fugitive on the run, only the future matters—and his future was about to cataclysmically collide with the Reverend Dr. Martin Luther King Jr.

It didn't matter that nothing Ray had ever done in his life succeeded. It didn't matter that the love of his life—a prostitute named Estella he had tried to wed—had left him. It didn't matter that his hopes of becoming a famous porn director flamed out with a whimper, not a bang. And it didn't matter that his life of crime always ended with the same emphatic conclusion as it began: a long sentence in the slammer.

He had to succeed this time. He needed to succeed this time. For his economic survival. For the survival of White Supremacy.

Ray speeds past the Great Smoky Mountains and into Nashville's hilly terrain, where the rain and hail are furiously spanking the city and its rugged highlands like they're simultaneously angry and disappointed with it. Like they're knowingly trying to do their part in helping to ward off tragedy.

He drives past a milk truck, America's easiest and most popular way to have milk delivered straight to their door from local dairies and creameries, and Elvis's home, "Graceland," which inspires him to take out the newly invented "cassette tape" and put on his favorite tune, "All Shook Up." He bobs his head back and forth to the beat of the music. He's eagerly anticipating the salvation he is going to bring to his beloved Jim Crow—and the salvation he is going to bring to his future as a rich man who can now call the shots in his own life.

He remembers that his "Contact" told him that when he arrived in the wee hours of the morning King would be asleep in his favorite motel—The Lorraine, room 306. He remembers that he told him to book a room 50 feet away at the nearby Bessie's Brewer's Rooming House which would give him a clear shot at the trouble-making Reverend.

Ray did exactly as he was told. Though he was dishonorably discharged from the military while fighting the Nazis in World War 2—something he was quite proud of given his fondness for Hitler's master race nonsense that he thought would take over the world—he knew how to take an order when money was on the line.

Ray exits his car, takes out his light-colored duffle bag, and walks inside of the Rooming House, a third-rate shack no respectable person would stay in.

"Well hello there sir, what's your name?" a white Motel Attendant with a strong hillbilly accent asked.

"John Williard," he responded, lying.

"And how long will you be staying, Mr. Willard?"

Ray looks at the Motel Attendant for a few moments, thinking how to respond, and then calmly says, "until I become the most celebrated man in America."

"You see, I like that. You must be in Nashville to pursue your music dreams. Lots of boys like you come through here for the same reason. Well my take is that a little confidence never hurt nobody."

"Except for when coons use it to hurt us," Ray retorts, a scowl edging the left side of his lip slightly upward.

"You know," the Attendant said, his cow-like face imitating Ray's, "I was just thinking the same thing. I saw Martin Luther King across the street earlier tonight and I think he's making all the nig*ers get a little too big for their britches if ya know what I mean. They're low-life monkeys if ya ask me."

"Couldn't agree more."

"They just need to accept that they are the inferior race and stop causing good white people all over this great white land so much trouble," the hillbilly Motel Attendant said as if his statement was self-evident.

Ray nods his head, takes the room key from the Attendant, and goes to his suite, a small room with a large window. He pulls out a pair of high-powered binoculars and spots room 306 at The Lorraine. His mind starts racing.

Will I kill him with one shot or two?

Will white America embrace me not as an assassin, but as their hero?

Will Estella take me back once I'm a rich man?

As he continues to think, Ray is getting giddier by the moment like a mischievous little boy with little sense and even less empathy. He takes his Remington out of his duffle bag, sets it up, and points it right at King's room.

Hour after hour goes by. But there is still no sign of King or anyone else entering or exiting The Lorraine.

Ray's giddiness turns into worry. He decides to call his Contact from the room phone, who picks up right away.

"It's James."

"I know. Have you done your job yet?" the Contact asked in what seemed like a deliberately muffled voice.

"I don't think he's here."

"Of course he's there," the Contact said, "I've got boys all over who know his every move."

"Do I still get paid if he's not here?"

"No."

"But we had a deal," Ray responded in disbelief.

"Deal is only good when Martin Luther King is in a body bag."

Ray hangs up the phone, furious, concerned only with the potential wasted money he fronted for gas and bullets, not about the life he so desperately wants to take.

But then he starts to smile.

"That's it nig*er."

The door to room 306 opens.

It's King.

King steps out onto his balcony and surveys the area, a habit he developed when daily death threats began a dozen years earlier. From King's estimate, he had probably received tens of thousands in his life making him nearly numb to them. He smiles at well-wishers in the parking lot below.

"Thank you, Reverend!" a black man shouts who is positioned near King's Cadillac.

"I'm just trying to do God's will."

"You are, Reverend, you are!"

Ray grabs his rifle and places his hand on the trigger as King moves around. *Stand still nig*er! Stand still!*

Ray's heart is throbbing, greedily thinking about the money he's about to receive for his act of cowardice, for his act of evil, for his act he has convinced himself is righteous. King then pauses for a moment, giving Ray the perfect opportunity to do something he has never done before in his life: succeed.

ONE

Fall 1960

"JFK is one slick son of a b*tch," Richard Nixon said to his sultry female secretary, whose Cover Girl makeup was overdone to the point of near-blinding distraction, in one of the conference rooms of his heavily-armed New York City-based presidential headquarters. "He's been secretly meeting with blacks like Jackie Robinson to try to steal the Negro vote from me."

"What should we do, Mr. Vice President?" the secretary asked, knowing that her boss always had a trick or two up his sleeves whenever he had *that look* on his face.

"Get my old friend Martin Luther King on the phone."

The secretary disappeared for a few minutes before quickly returning and gesturing to Nixon to come to the phone.

"I have him, sir," the eager secretary said, who was wearing a trendy and shortish Mary Quant-designed knickerbocker dress, enough to reveal her sexy freshly shaven legs to her boss, which he gazed at periodically, hoping to impress Nixon with how quickly she had tracked King down.

Nixon put down his favorite meal, cottage cheese and ketchup, and marched into his office, an opulent large room full of political memorabilia from his nearly two decades in Washington. There were the usual items a politician likes to keep around like photos with heads of state and newspaper clippings of his meteoric rise in American politics, items not just to stroke his own ego, which was simultaneously massive and insecure, but to remind everyone of how important he is. To remind everyone how powerful he is. To remind everyone never to think about crossing him.

But there were some unusual items in Nixon's office too. There was the poker set that became his daily obsession. There was his growing enemies list which included, among other people, several friends, family members, and even a children's book author. And, of course, there was his framed note from the FBI Director himself, J. Edgar Hoover, who personally thought Nixon would have made a great double agent in the Bureau if he hadn't chosen politics.

"I'll take the call in here," Nixon said, his widow's peak hairline looking like devil's horns with his desk lamp light bouncing off of it the way it did each time he stood at this spot in his office, his physical appearance as mischievous and disturbing as his sometimes crooked behavior, which he had a knack for concealing. He then picked up the black Western Electric rotary phone sitting on his oversized mahogany desk.

"Martin, how the hell are you?"

"I'm doing well, Mr. Vice President, I'm just getting back from a short vacation with my wife and kids," King responded in his baritone-like voice shaped by thousands of sermons he had preached.

"Oh, that's great, Martin, that really is. How many little ones do you have now?"

"I have two sir, with a third on the way."

"Great, you're keeping your wife quite busy. You know there's nothing better than a woman who submits to her role as a baby chute," Nixon said, to disgusted silence on the other end of the line, *that look* becoming more distractingly painted all over his face. "Hey listen, Martin, I need you to do me a favor."

"And what's that?"

"Well, you know that nobody loves Negroes like I do," Nixon said almost convincingly, his ability to smooth talk and bullsh*t behind-the-scenes being legendary, sounding like a Hollywood producer who gushes over the "talent" of a pretty girl he just met at the bar, promising to make her a star but in reality planning on making her something else entirely.

"You have been exceptionally progressive when it comes to race relations," King responded.

"That's right. The President and I carried the Negro Vote in the 1956 election and you know how hard I fought to pass the 1957 Civil Rights Act."

"We are grateful for your leadership on the bill, Mr. Vice President."

"So now I need you to do something for me," Nixon said with an increasingly eerie grin. "I've never asked anything of you. But you're such a dear friend and so now I need you to publicly come out against that son of a b*tch JFK."

"Well, I got a phone call from—"

"He called you!?" Nixon responded forcefully, expressing a little too much outrage that JFK would even think about calling the Reverend, much less actually do it, who everyone knew, at least in Washington D.C. circles, that Nixon supported.

"Not quite, I got a call from Bobby Kennedy and he wants to arrange a meeting between me and his brother."

"Listen Martin, let me tell you about that son of a b*tch Bobby Kennedy," Nixon exclaimed, clearing his throat to sound more stately, trying to break things down for King so he knew who the real Bobby was, at least through his filtered lens. "They call him Good Bobby and Bad Bobby because one minute he'll smile in your face and the next minute he'll be serving your balls to you on a silver platter—"

"Sir—-"

"And have you thank him while he does it."

"But, sir, I—"

"Yeah, I know Martin, it's really hard to believe, especially because he looks so sweet and innocent. But he's a nasty man who is trying to use you plain and simple. He only wants the Negro votes you can bring his brother."

"Sir—"

"And everyone knows I own the Negro vote," Nixon said emphatically, with a sincere laugh belching out afterward.

"Mr. Vice President, with all due respect, Negroes are not owned by any one candidate," King responded. "Or political part—"

"For Chrissake, Martin, I know that. But remember, it is my party, The Republicans, that freed the slaves, it is my party that passed the '57 Civil Rights Act, and it's my party that your old man, Daddy King, and most Negroes, support."

"I understand that sir, but my father and I do not always see eye to eye on every political issue," King said.

"Listen, I respect that you are your own man, Martin. That's one of the things I like about you the most. Really I do. But I just need you to be pragmatic and be Nixon's man this time."

"You're asking a lot," King replied, the irritation he felt disguised by practiced diplomacy.

"Come on, Martin? Once I win I'll pass all the civil rights bills this country can handle. It'll be you and me against the world. We'll be like the second coming of Abraham Lincoln and Frederick Douglass."

But King said nothing in response to Nixon's exaggeration. He knew the Vice President had the power to back up his talk—he had always kept his word to King by supporting him publicly and privately—but he just didn't know if the Vice President had the sincerity, or the heart, to bring true equality to blacks. No white politician ever had, even one with as strong of a record as Nixon's on civil rights issues.

As the silence slowly turned into discomfort, Nixon was unfazed. After all, he specialized in creating these types of moments; they were his strategy; his tool; his special weapon he could politically manipulate or dismember people with.

"As tempting as the offer is—"

"Alright, alright," Nixon said abruptly, feeling he had laid it on a little too hard for the Reverend. "I understand you're not committing today. But if you can't be my man, you sure as hell shouldn't be that son of a b*tch Kennedy's man. Can you at least promise me that, not to get in cahoots with that pretty boy and his ballsack-destroying little brother?"

TWO

A black stretch limousine pulls up to the mansion with the most feared Kennedy in America: Joe Sr.

The seventy two year old looks like money. He smells like power. And tonight he needs to make sure his wishes will be executed exactly as planned.

He steps out of his black Mercedes-Benz 600 vehicle and slowly enters the eight thousand square foot white-brick residence that his ambition built.

Within the elegant 13 bedroom, 12 bathroom McLean Virginia-based manor, Hickory Hill, the inside of which was a contemporary Mount Vernon if there ever was one, its interior luminescence spectacular but understated with a whiff of old-world palace charm, was a home full of rambunctious children, a presidential candidate, and the property's official owner, Robert Fitzgerlad Kennedy, also known as Bobby.

"Father," the blue-eyed Bobby said in the distinct and formal Boston accent he shared with his family, while holding an empty journal, which he almost never wrote in, "it's good to see you."

"Get Jack, we need to talk."

Bobby, who was accustomed to his old man's impolite manners, shook off the rudeness and started to make his way through the post-Civil War era estate. He passed photos from the children's pet shows he occasionally had there featuring real bears and elephants; he passed multiple statues of Mary and crucifixes—he had one in each room given his devout Catholicsm and days as an altar boy; and he made his way up the long Colonial Revival staircase in the house from which his Senator brother wrote his famous book, *Profiles in Courage*.

"Jack, it's Father," Bobby said to his hero, calling JFK, short for John Fitzerald Kennedy, by his everyday nickname, who sat playing with his itsy-bitsy three year-old daughter Caroline, while listening to his pal Frank Sinatra's most recent album. Jack's wife, the beautiful, charming, and voluptuous dark-haired Jackie, was resting with her feet up, glowing as bright as a Christmas tree, her aura emanating a warm kaleidoscope of colors, especially an enchanting red, in anticipation of her second child due in just weeks, a boy they had decided to name John Jr.

One of Bobby's seven children ran into the room, little Robert, chased by his younger brother, David, after stealing David's birthday present from him: 1960's hottest new toy, an Etch A Sketch.

"Kids!" yelled Bobby, "calm down!"

Bobby hated yelling at his kids—they were his life, they were his weakness—but at their ages they could act like little monsters. Although he hated saying so, he knew it; so did his wife, Ethel, the irresistibly sweet, cute, and down-to-earth woman who had captured his heart ten years earlier, who was sitting nearby petting Bobby's beloved dog Freckles.

JFK's exceptionally handsome, olive-toned six foot one inch frame got up and walked with Bobby downstairs, revealing that Jack's favorite blazer hardly had any wrinkles in it even after playing with Caroline. They entered the dining room where their ethnically Irish Father was waiting alone, which was out of character because it was usually the center of social and political life. Not only did it have a long, carefully crafted dark cherry wood table as its focal point, right underneath a rare Baccarat multimillion dollar chandelier and several exotic-looking crystalware decorations, items a few of their more covetous but less ruthless neighbors wanted, but it featured floor-to-ceiling windows that added a regal charm to a political family that seemed destined to become the closest thing America anoints as royalty.

"Sit," their Father said, his power-hungry eyes vigorous and resolute behind his black round glasses, "this election is closer than it should be."

"Polling shows us dead even with Nixon," Bobby responded, brushing his thick light brown hair away from his face, which always seemed to be drooping over his eyelids, given how he styled and parted it, allowing it to frequently sag to the left side of his face, and set his journal down.

"If you don't win the Negro vote, you will lose this election and bring disgrace to our family," their Father remarked, looking sternly at JFK, whose light blue-green eyes quickly darted away.

"Father, we've been courting every prominent Negro who will return our call," JFK said in his defense.

"Jackie Robinson turned you down," their Father said coldly.

"But he's a Republican—"

"Who turned you down," their Father repeated.

"We just put in a call to Martin Luther King who has agreed to meet with us," Bobby uttered, trying to rescue the conversation from the inevitable abyss it usually led to with his old man, typically a one-sided tyrannical tirade about how they were screwing things up, like a couple of jack asses.

"He has a lot of sway with Negroes, Father," JFK said to second Bobby.

"Everyone knows he's a Nixon man," their Father responded, tilting his head to the right, his eyes studying the sons he had bred to be the extension of his oppressive will.

"He hasn't endorsed Nixon yet and I think Jack can really lay on the charm in the meeting," Bobby said.

Joe. Sr. didn't seem convinced.

"Here's what you need to do. Meet with him and make any promise you can to get his endorsement," their Father declared before adding, calculatingly, "but don't be seen publicly with him."

"I'm not afraid to be associated with blacks," JFK said flatly, the war hero in him asserting himself, pushing back against his larger-than-life progenitor ever so slightly, pushing back as much as his Father would ever allow him to.

"But most whites are," their Father replied, interested only in objective facts, an ex-banker exclusively concerned with the hard numbers of millions of whites who would reject his son if he was caught, even in name or appearance only, associating with blacks.

"And most Southern whites hate blacks," Bobby echoed, trying to appease his old man, who was a "my-way or the highway" type of guy in general, and more so when it came to this election.

"That's why you need to privately balance securing King's backing and publicly securing the backing of Southern Segregationists," their Father said. "If you want to win, that's the only way you can do it."

Bobby's head swirled with thoughts, with political calculations, with how much moral compromise he could muster, with how much "Bad Bobby" he had to unleash, to get his brother elected President of the United States.

"I have an idea," Bobby said hesitantly. "Let's promise King that we'll create a civil rights division in the Justice Department to legally go after Jim Crow and let's promise Southerners we'll give them a federal judgeship or two so they'll feel the Courts are on their side. That way everybody will be happy."

"That's brilliant, Bobby," their Father said, proud of Bobby's willingness to be as ruthless as necessary, as ruthless as he usually was, to help his brother win—and to help Joe Sr. solidify his greatest aphrodisiac: power.

"This way we can neutralize the civil rights issue," Bobby said.

"And stop a potential second civil war," joked JFK.

With his Father's approval and brother's tacit support, Bobby knew exactly how they needed to handle King. But he didn't exactly know how King would handle them.

THREE

"Spit in her face!" shouted The Reverend James Lawson. "Spit!"

Diane Nash, the light-skinned black beauty-queen who successfully led a Nashville sit-in to desegregate lunch counters there a few months earlier as a leader for the Student Nonviolent Coordinating Committee (SNCC), nodded her permission.

"I can't Reverend, she's a lady," protested Jermone "Big Duck" Smith, a giant of a young man towering over six feet four inches in height.

"Do it Big Duck," demanded Lawson, "Spit!"

Next to Nash stood a 19-year old radical white girl from Berkeley, Carol Davis, along with 50 college-aged Southern black women in a cold, nondescript Tennessee warehouse side by side. Each of them had a bib under their chins purchased from the local Kroger store, placed unevenly across their various assortment of modern-chic styles they were wearing, with some donning brightly colored clothes, some African dashikis, some Gelé headwraps and big earrings, and some more utilitarian dress. They stared into the eyes of the 50 college-aged Southern black men standing directly in front of them, including the gentle-souled John Lewis, bookish Bob Moses, and spirited Stokely Carmichael, many of whom were wearing Kaftans and Kufi hats, in the fashion that was becoming emblematic of their people.

James Lawson, their fearless black on-the-ground leader who had spent three years studying nonviolence in India and who was one of Martin Luther King's deputies and his chief protest mastermind, looked like a man possessed as he orchestrated the clandestine training operation.

"Spit! Spit! Spit!" shouted Lawson. "Spit!"

One by one, the black men spat in the faces of the ladies of SNCC, oral liquid flowing like runaway lava, a domino of fluids splashing and splattering every which way.

As Nash looked to her left, she saw some of the women who appeared disgusted as the saliva dripped down their faces onto their grayish-white bibs. As she looked to her right, she saw other women appearing stoic, trying to hide their feelings of gross humiliation and ignominy. Looking around even further, she saw others standing there shaking, crying, as reality had kicked in to the fact that they had agreed to face any indignity that came their way to try to secure equality for their race—and to try to secure equality for every generation that came after theirs.

"Do you think these segregationists are gonna go easy on you?" demanded Lawson.

"No Reverend," the men and women of SNCC responded.

"Do you think they care about your feelings?"

"No Reverend."

"Do you think they're just going to let you desegregate their cities without a fight?"

"No Reverend."

"You're right," Lawson replied, "they don't care a damn thing about you and won't think twice about demeaning you, about harming you. That is why you are being prepared to fight back, but not with your anger or with your emotions."

Several of the students looked confused, even agitated.

"You are being prepared, " Lawson continued, "to fight back with your dignity."

At this statement, Stokely raised his hand in exasperation.

"Yes, son?" Lawson asked.

"Reverend, I don't understand. Why do we need to fight back with our so-called 'dignity' when no white person has ever treated us with any dignity at all?" Stokely questioned.

Several of the students shook their heads in agreement, their afros bobbing up and down. But Lawson was unmoved.

"You fight back with your dignity because this is what differentiates you from the White Supremacists who have been terrorizing your families," Lawson said. "This is what differentiates you from the people who think you're inferior, from the people who deny you education, from the people who over and over again have lynched, murdered, and mutilated thousands of your brothers and sisters with complete impunity. You fight back not by returning insult for insult or blow for blow; you fight back by showing how much better you are than them."

Ella Baker, the official founder of SNCC and godmother of the growing Civil Rights Movement, watched quietly from the warehouse corner.

"Ladies," Lawson said, turning his attention to the women, "I now need you to show your brothers what Jim Crow wants to do to them."

"Yes Reverend," the Ladies of SNCC responded in military-like unison.

Lawson walked over to a record player, pulled out a vinyl disc, and put on some music by Sammy Davis, Jr.—"Once in a Lifetime," his favorite song. He told the Ladies of SNCC to sing along as they went through three specially designed training exercises meant to provoke a violent response from the men, meant to see what they were really made of.

Exercise one. "For once in my lifetime, I feel like a giant," the Ladies sang in unison as they slapped their brothers in the face multiple times, to audible murmurs of anger and discomfort.

Exercise two. "For this is my moment, my destiny calls me," the Ladies sang in unison as they punched their brothers in the stomach, to groans of pain.

Exercise three. "And though it may be just once in my lifetime, I'm gonna do great things," the ladies sang in unison as they threw mildly hot coffee on their brothers, some of whom screamed violently.

Lawson then yelled, "stop and stand still!"

All of the students, including the women, stood still, some looking terrified at how harsh their trainer seemed to be. Despite being the only white person there, Carol Davis stood still too, trying not to let the fear she felt register on her face.

Lawson disappeared to a side room as the men looked beat, coffee dripping from their bodies, bruises starting to percolate on their dark skin. He reappeared with a vicious-looking female German Shepherd named "Dixie."

"Son," Lawson said, pointing directly at Stokely, "walk out ten feet in front of the group."

Stokely looked around, uncertain, and stepped ahead of his peers.

"Sick 'em," Lawson said nonchalantly to the German Shepherd.

Dixie then started barreling straight for Stokely whose face turned as pale as snow. The others looked on, hearts racing, eyes bulging, in complete disbelief at what they were witnessing.

Dixie was 250 feet away from Stokely and getting closer by the millisecond.

Then she was 100 feet away.

Then 50.

Lawson immediately scanned the room to see if any of the men— or women—were heading for the exits.

Nobody flinched.

As Dixie was racing closer and closer to Stokely and about to attack him, her fangs out, Lawson yelled, "Dixie, yield!"

The dog did exactly as she was told.

The students'—still wide-eyed—looked relieved. Stokely looked irritated.

"Ladies and gentlemen," Lawson said, "congratulations. You have just completed your first non-violent training workshop. These exercises were designed to be real-life simulations of the things you will be experiencing in our upcoming civil rights campaigns. If you can't handle it in here, then you sure as hell won't be able to handle it out there."

Ella Baker joined Lawson. She said, "Reverend Lawson is right. If you get spat on, assaulted, or arrested, you must not fight back—and you must not run away."

"If you are tempted to do either, let us know now," Lawson said, "because Dr. King will not permit you to protest if you cannot do it non-violently."

Stokely raised his hand again and said, "but what if they murder one of us, can we fight back then?"

Lawson, whose face looked as stern and uncompromising as a battlefield commander's, answered with an emphatic "no."

FOUR

"It's a mistake, Martin," Daddy King said to his son as he stepped on the gas of his stylish turquoise Cadillac DeVille, which reached an impressive 0-60 miles per hour in 7.4 seconds, en route to his Atlanta megachurch, Ebenezer Baptist. The Church stood resolutely tall despite its mere two stories, amidst the growing Atlanta skyline, skyscrapers popping up like whack-a-moles every which way in this former rural slave colony.

"I agree with your Daddy," Alberta King echoed while she sat in the back next to her pregnant and medium-brown complexioned daughter-in-law Corretta Scott, and her grandchildren, five year old Yolanda, who exuded radiant cuteness, and the adorable three year old Martin Luther King III, who was holding a teddy bear named "Love" that his dad had given him. "Meeting with those Kennedys will just stir up too much trouble."

Corretta, the elegant and diplomatic soul that she was, tried to change the subject. "So, I'm reading this new book called *To Kill A Mockingbird* that was just released this week. It's very good and causing quite a stir."

Martin, who was sitting in the front seat next to his pops, turned around and gave a loving smile, and said, "It's okay, honey."

"Really, Martin, don't do it," the elder Martin Luther King Sr. protested again, emphatically, shaking his large head in disapproval, his dark round face and white hair uniting in a distinguished and intimidating look that gave his statements seemingly more force, like some sort of wise owl mixed with a roaring lion, demanding to be listened to as much for his sagacity as for his power.

"Now Daddy, we have nothing to lose," King Jr. said, his words passing gently through his plump lips and past his well-groomed mustache, as he usually hated personal confrontation with anybody, especially his father, despite his calling that required him to publicly confront many, one of several glaring contradictions he struggled with.

"They're Catholics, Martin, and we're Protestants," Daddy King said, "Don't you understand? We don't mix."

Of course, Daddy King was referring to the long-standing feud between the Catholic and Protestant Churches, a feud he was all-too willing to enter when he personally re-named himself and his 5 year old son after the Protestant reformer Martin Luther, a feud that kept Christians around the world in an on-again, off-again civil war for centuries. For Daddy King, if there was one thing America got right, especially compared to Europe, it was that Catholics and Protestants remained separate but equal, in nearly all that they did. And he wanted to remind his son of this.

"Daddy, they're Americans who could help drive the Civil Rights Movement forward."

Daddy King, looking flustered, pulled his car into his personal parking spot at Ebenezer Baptist and abruptly turned off the engine. Several deacons and elders waved as they walked by and into the multi-story brick church that the senior King had turned into a spiritual and political powerhouse, one of the finest churches in all of black America.

"Listen Martin," Daddy King said in shifting his argument against the Kennedys, exasperation haunting his face. "JFK voted against the 1957 Civil Rights Act."

"Do you really think he's going to suddenly change his mind on it?" seconded Alberta King, struggling to hide a "duh" look on her face, her beautiful big hair concealed by the equally beautiful Southern black church hat she was wearing.

"Besides, I've already endorsed Nixon and his Republican ticket," Daddy King said, proud of himself.

"Most Negroes have," echoed Alberta King again.

"Hell, Martin, even Bobby Kennedy voted for Nixon for Vice President in '56," Daddy King continued. "Everybody knows he's the real deal who can bring political muscle to this fight, not some Catholic Johnny-Come-Lately who is trying to use your influence with Negroes to buy votes in his losing campaign."

King Jr. looked back at his wife, hoping for sympathy, for reassurance, for the emotional validation she had always provided him. After all, she was his rock, his confidante, the wife who had stood by his side even when things got tough for him—and for her. Not only had she nursed him back to health when he was stabbed to within an inch of his life, but she had also encouraged him not to quit when a white terrorist tried to blow her and her baby up by setting off a bomb at their house just a few short years ago. To her, Martin was her soulmate who she would support, for better or worse.

"Don't get Corretta involved, Martin," Daddy King said, unsympathetically. "She's got to focus on singing for my choir today."

Corretta looked at Martin with her dazzling brown eyes and gentle, inviting face but didn't say a word. She knew her husband and exactly what he would do.

"Now listen to me, Martin," Daddy King said with a spirit of control that had defined his personality. "Don't rebel against me. I don't want you meeting with those Kennedy boys now or ever."

"Daddy, I love you and am grateful for the man you have helped me become," King said with a defiance that contradicted his respectful tone. "But I will not rebel against my conscience. The meeting is set for tomorrow and I'll be there."

FIVE

Fresh off of his Grammy win the night before, Emmy and Tony award winner Harry Belafonte strutted into the upscale Park Avenue Apartment where his friends, John F. Kennedy, and his campaign manager Bobby, were strategizing about their imminent meeting with Martin Luther King.

JFK, who was putting on a slim blue necktie over a white button down shirt, said, "congratulations, Harry, you're a bonafide star," as Belafonte held his 9 inch tall, 5 pound zinc alloy trophy plated in pure gold triumphantly in his left hand.

The debonair and quick-witted Belafonte shot back, "Senator, the real star is your hair," referring to the beautiful thick locks JFK—and all of the Kennedy brothers, including Bobby—sported as their namesake trademark. "Does it have its own insurance policy?"

"Actually, it has two," JFK joked.

"Very funny," Belafonte said before he set down his Grammy and removed his haute-mod, Italian-cut outer coat, revealing a tight turtleneck that struggled to hide his muscular black arms perfectly proportioned for his tight, athletic frame.

Bobby, not wanting to waste any time as he always seemed to be in such a hurry, his expression matter of fact, blending in perfectly with his wiry body, opened up a manilla folder he had with King's photo in it along with a stack of papers. The papers revealed copies of King's speeches; interviews he had given to the press; newspaper clippings of King's successful Montgomery, Alabama bus boycott that desegregated the city and made him an overnight celebrity with blacks; and several quotes of King's like "Let no man pull you so low as to hate him," "Injustice anywhere is a threat to justice everywhere," and "A genuine leader is not a searcher of consensus but a molder of consensus."

But the papers revealed other things too. There was King's substantial arrest record. His tax fraud trial for which he was charged for felony perjury and tax evasion. And, of course, his long history of openly and defiantly disobeying numerous laws, something a "law and order" attorney like Bobby—who was held in contempt in some liberal circles for his work as the lawyer supporting the infamous communist witch hunt known as the McCathy Hearings—just couldn't understand, despite Bobby's penchant for bending or breaking a law or two if it helped his brother get ahead.

"Harry, thanks for setting up our meeting today with Dr. King," Bobby said. "You're a friend of his, what's he like? Anything important we should know?"

Belafonte made his way over to the brown Mid Century sofa in the middle of the room, sat down, and began to contemplate. He sat for a few minutes without saying a word, which caused the Kennedy brothers to give each other a puzzled—and concerned—look. Belafonte was known for being a chatty fellow—after all, he was an actor and singer, the ultimate extrovert—but he really seemed to be chewing on his thoughts carefully, calculating his words with precision.

As he looked at the luxurious furnishings of the Midtown New York City dwelling, twinkling with splendor like one of the shiny stars all of the new NASA telescopes had been discovering lately, Belafonte said, "Dr. King doesn't care about all of this. He doesn't care about opulence and extravagance, or even about power."

Bobby was scribbling notes as JFK finished tying his necktie and grabbed a seat in an arm-chair across from Belafonte, seemingly more curious than he had been a second ago.

"Really?" JFK asked, dumbfounded.

"Yes. In fact, King has taken an unofficial vow of poverty and donates his earnings to the Civil Rights Cause," Belafonte said.

"How does the man eat?" Bobby interjected.

"His wife, Corretta, is a singer and often performs professionally to help pay the bills around the house."

"So he's a true believer?" JFK said in a remark that was more a statement than a question, surprised at the financially unorthodox life Dr. King seemed to be living—and surprised at the idea that somebody of his stature could be genuinely altruistic.

"Yes Jack, he is a true believer and he believes God has raised him up for a time such as now to bring true freedom to Negroes all over America," Belafonte said.

"So he's a believer and a nutcase?" JFK said in a joking tone to try to keep things lighthearted. It's not that JFK wanted to appear anti-religious, he was a 'nominal' Catholic, as he puts it, it's just that his political secret to success had always been keeping things easy going: keeping things and people and ideas emotionally distant so he didn't have to get too close. After all, American politics tended to attract extreme individuals and ideologies and, for him, closely aligning himself with somebody who might have a messianic complex, especially a black man who could have a messianic complex, could spell all sorts of trouble.

But Bobby was still scribbling notes while Belafonte was speaking, trying to understand the man who in moments would walk through their front door. Trying to understand the Reverend who was causing so much fuss in the South. Trying to understand the convicted felon who could be the deciding factor in whether or not his brother became the President of the United States.

"Harry, anything else we should know?" Bobby asked.

"Well, there are a few things," Belafonte said, clearing his throat.

But before he could speak anymore, the doorbell rang: it was King—and he had brought his entourage.

SIX

Bobby's nerves suddenly felt like they were being ripped out of his body. And his face showed it. Unlike his smooth older brother who was self-assured and always acted as cool as a pleasant summer breeze, Bobby was never good at hiding his sometimes mercurial emotions from anyone. And for some reason meeting King made him look and feel anxious.

It wasn't that he was intimidated by King who, at only five feet seven inches tall, was actually one of the few people in American politics slightly shorter than him. And it wasn't that he was second guessing his politically self-serving, and some would say ruthless, plan to get King's endorsement. It was something else. But what?

But before he could sink further into his ruminations, his brother jumped to attention, put on his favorite blazer, and made his way to the door without showing any sign of the Addison's Disease he had been diagnosed with that ravaged his body and required him to privately use a cane, an act of deception he needed to keep far away from the public. "Reverend!" JFK said, sporting as enthusiastic a tone as he could muster, "welcome to my home!"

King, who at just 31 years old had the gravitas of a man twice his age, like a young Frederick Douglass, poised and dignified, his features measured by the existential seriousness of his purpose, his presence projecting grace and authority, walked past two stoic-looking Secret

Service members and politely greeted the candidate. He introduced his team which included his amiable best friend The Reverend Ralph Abernathy; his politically ambitious sidekick The Reverend Andrew Young; and his trusted photographer, Ernest Withers, who for years had captured all of the iconic images of the Civil Rights Movement and who insisted on trying to get photos of the meeting for posterity.

"I'm sorry, Reverend," Bobby said somewhat harshly, remembering his Father's wishes not to allow photos to be taken with King or any black person, "campaign policy is that we don't allow any photos of private meetings."

But King was used to what he perceived as political games from white politicians and their allies, so he nodded nonchalantly, despite being peeved on the inside with Bobby's tone, to Photographer Withers who was escorted awkwardly outside by the Secret Service.

JFK, looking to quickly change the subject, jumped in and said, "Reverend, I'd like to discuss how a Kennedy Presidency could benefit the Civil Rights Movement."

"Thank you, Senator," King said as he and his entourage sat around the elaborate dining room table. "First of all, we appreciate the invitation to be here today."

Looking at Bobby, JFK said jokingly, "it was Bobby's idea."

"Then this meeting should include him too," King deadpanned in an authoritative tone, looking over to Bobby who was standing by himself on the other side of the room, in what was a highly uncharacteristic move for King: confronting somebody personally.

Bobby walked over and pulled up a seat, a bit agitated by how King had so forcefully spoken to and looked at him. *Who does this guy think he is?* he thought. *Talking that way to me in my brother's home?*

"As you know, Senator," King said, "my people are hurting."

JFK nodded in agreement.

"In most cities across America, Negroes are denied the right to go to white hospitals down the street from their own homes even when they have a life-threatening emergency," King said.

Ralph Abernathy said, "That's right, Reverend."

"In most cities across America, the average Negro child goes to sleep hungry because white business owners refuse to employ their parents," King said.

"Yes, Reverend, yes," Abernathy testified.

"And in most cities across America, blacks are subjected daily to vicious white hatred in worst case scenarios, and to complete white indifference to their suffering in best case ones," King said.

"Amen," Abernathy shouted, ready to belch a "hallelujah" too.

Bobby, who from his research on King knew that King was the Civil Rights Movement's best communicator, though he and his brother had never personally heard the Reverend preach or speak publicly, decided to cut him off before he broke out into a sermon.

"Thank you, Reverend," Bobby said, curtly cutting him off, "but we know all of this. We just want to figure out reasonable political solutions for it."

But King didn't look like he appreciated Bobby's seemingly dismissive comment in reaction to all that he said. To him, it felt like it lacked empathy; like it lacked humility; like it was being filtered through a privileged white lens that claimed it "knew" all about the suffering of black people, even if it only knew about it in the abstract, even if it only "knew" about it when black votes were seemingly on the line. To King, even if Bobby "knew" the faceless and abstract statistics that black people were doing much worse off than whites, with black unemployment being 300% higher than white unemployment; black poverty being nearly 200% higher than white poverty; and black illiteracy being dramatically higher than white illiteracy, it still felt like Bobby "didn't know" about black pain, especially black pain directly caused by White Supremacist action and inaction.

JFK interjected, "if we can work with you, Dr. King, and pick the battles we can win, we can gradually chip away at segregation."

"With all due respect, Senator, Jim Crow doesn't need to die by a thousand cuts," King said, feeling the need to confront JFK's easy-going thinking, "it needs to be lynched and hung for all of America to see."

"Reverend," Bobby said, "that's a bit extreme."

"Bobby, the only thing I see here as extreme," King said in his baritone voice, "is that you think Jim Crow can be handled 'quote' reasonably."

"Says the convicted felon," Bobby shot back in a gratuitous low-blow, drawing the disapproving looks of King's entourage but not King himself.

"I am proud that Jim Crow has entered a guilty plea against me," King said with a thoughtful look of rebellion on his face.

The room was silent for a moment as King and Bobby stared at each other, their gazes growing cooler and cooler by the second, a standoff that felt as big and uncomfortable as the showdown of the Cold War the country was in, with Americans unabashedly on one side and Soviets unabashedly on the other.

"Listen, we have no other choice than to be smart about how we deal with this," Bobby said, looking irritated that King didn't back down from him. "Polling shows that 75% of both Northern whites and Southern whites oppose civil rights for Negroes. Don't you understand this?"

"I'm familiar with the numbers," King responded, his face imprisoned by agitation that Bobby thought he was revealing damning information, information that would be impossible to change, or overcome.

"Then you should know that we need a piecemeal approach," Bobby said. "One that targets segregation in the Court of Law and not the Court of Public Opinion. We just don't have the numbers."

JFK jumped in hoping to lighten things up a bit and said, "Reverend, I think the best way we can be allies is if I establish a new civil rights division in the Justice Department."

King's entourage looked on, curious about the proposal the Senator from Massachusetts had in mind.

"That way," JFK said, "we can build on landmark cases like *Brown vs. Board of Education* by legally confronting segregation in a strategic way."

"That won't be enough," King said flatly, continuing to stare at Bobby, searching his face for a reaction, testing the sincerity of the Irishman like a seasoned coach tests the resolve of a know-it-all rookie player.

"Then, what would you suggest would be enough, Reverend?" Bobby asked with slight exasperation, feeling he was being condescended to.

"The only way for a Kennedy Administration to make meaningful progress on civil rights," King said, "is to publicly enact a Second Emancipation Proclamation."

JFK and Bobby, frozen in their chairs, both looked stunned. *Is he really suggesting this? Didn't he know about the violent death the last president suffered who backed a black man's Emancipation Proclamation? Is he serious?*

"But that will create a new civil war," Bobby said incredulously, his eyes sprinting to Harry Belafonte for moral support. But Harry, his friend and adviser on all things related to black America, remained unusually quiet.

"Bobby, in case you haven't noticed," King said, "Jim Crow has been in a civil war against Negroes since the end of the last Civil War."

"Reverend, your language is just too much," Bobby countered, his irritation ricocheting throughout his body. "And so is your idea."

"It's not an idea," King said, looking straight through Bobby, "it is a moral struggle your conscience should obligate you to support."

As King went into the details of his 3 point plan he called the Second Emancipation Proclamation—which included legal desegregation, voting rights, and economic empowerment for blacks—JFK's heart sank. This was exactly the type of thing he wanted to avoid.

But while JFK was thinking about how impossible the politics of this would be, with balancing King's demands with the demands of Southern Segregationists, Bobby was thinking something else entirely: he was starting to see why he was so anxious about meeting King in the first place: he realized it was because King was, just like him, extremely stubborn and unreasonable, the kind of person who didn't mind being hated so long as he advanced his cause; the kind of person who would not back down from a fight even if he knew he'd probably lose; the kind of person that you disliked because they reminded you of the best and worst parts of yourself, revealing the shattered two-faced contradiction within that incontrovertibly defines you.

"What happens if politics restrains us from backing your Proclamation?" JFK asked, fishing for some type of olive branch from King.

"Then we will use every tool at our disposal to destroy Jim Crow in the streets of America," King replied, "even if that means going to war."

As JFK sat and mulled over King's statement, as he mulled over his Father's suggestion to say anything to King to get his support, as he mulled over his dream of becoming the most powerful man in the world, he remembered advice that Bobby once told him: politics was nothing if not a thorny bouquet of temporary bedfellows that you had to, at times, discard at will. So, in light of this, he said, "Reverend, if you give me your endorsement, I just might be able to support your plan."

Bobby, in complete disbelief at what he was hearing, nevertheless chose not to voice his opposition to his brother—and especially his opposition to King himself. That could come later, after the endorsement, after the election, after he could throw this chapter with this bedfellow out and into the fire, its ghost being but a faint echo of the past, once it was safe to. So instead, he simply decided to be "Bad Bobby" and echoed JFK by saying, "Reverend, we'd be grateful allies."

SEVEN

"My informant tells me that the nig*er Martin Luther King met with John Kennedy last night," FBI Director J. Edgar Hoover said as he sat in his hand-crafted red leather chair framed between a large American flag on his left and right.

"What do you think they discussed?" asked Hoover's top deputy, Clyde Tolson, who liked to wear identical suits as his boss, liked to vacation alone with him, and whom some accused of being his undercover gay lover, which Hoover denied claiming he preferred the vastly superior position of being the celibate virgin that he was.

"I don't, whatever nig*ers and Catholics discuss," Hoover said, in his typical tone that belittled his aide as much as the targets of his condescension.

Hoover's office, housed in the neoclassical-looking Federal Triangle collection of buildings including the U.S. Justice Department, was small and smelled like cream of chicken soup, his favorite. But that didn't matter; as far as he was concerned, he was the most powerful man in the federal government and whoever didn't like it could just shove it, completely unconcerned that power tended to corrupt, and that continuous uninterrupted power corrupts absolutely.

As the founder and leader of the FBI for the last 40 years, the old fossil Hoover exercised a political authority that even presidents didn't possess. He fired all female agents from the FBI's predecessor organization as soon as it merged with his, without so much as a hint of pushback. He kept dirt on anybody he considered dangerous—or in disagreement with his conservative, reactionary politics—including The Beatles, Charlie Chaplain, and other "unacceptable" movie stars and musicians. And he had politicians, Supreme Court Justices, and anybody in his orbit groveling at his feet in fear of avoiding getting put on his hit list: The Confidential Files he maintained in his personal office, currently running about 164 people in total, that could ruin careers, lives, and families in equal measure, a level of totalitarian control that would draw the admiration, and the ire, of Stalin's KGB, if they knew about it.

"I need more information on Kennedy," Hoover's fat mouth barked to his aide. "Just in case King has deluded him into attempting to tear down what I've fought hard to preserve."

Of course, Hoover was talking about law enforcement's dirty little secret, the "Iron White Wall," that since Reconstruction a century earlier kept blacks in fear of and submission to the legal system. Hoover knew that if he could keep the FBI 100% white, which it was, and if he could keep police forces around America 100% white, which they were, blacks wouldn't dare stand up for their rights because nobody would be there to protect them from the inevitable violent backlash of the KKK and their White Supremacist allies.

But Hoover also knew that this Iron White Wall was comprised of more than cops who would just ignore, or even assist with, widespread white violence on a retail level: he knew that it was comprised of the 100% all white judges in America's judiciary who regularly sentenced blacks to harsh penalties, even for crimes they didn't commit; that it was comprised of the 100% all white juries who would never convict a white person for attacking a black one; and that it was comprised of Jim Crow laws that were put exclusively in place by white people to keep black people, whom he thought had 20% smaller brains than whites, in their place, a place of social and economic powerlessness that even the great Lincoln couldn't undo.

"Shall I request authorization to wiretap Senator Kennedy from the Attorney General?" Tolson asked.

"I am the authorization," Hoover said arrogantly, knowing that he had supreme power within Washington, D.C. to do this—and supreme power outside of it too; his popularity with white America was near record highs, and the Bureau of 441 Special Agents he oversaw spread across 50 field offices throughout the country made him the only person who could easily get into any home in America with impunity, including a Senator's who was running for the highest office in the land.

"The presidential race is close and if Kennedy wins, he might try to do something stupid with that nig*er Martin Luther King," Hoover said, "and we need to make sure he doesn't."

With that order, Colson began drafting the paperwork that would wiretap all of JFK's phones, bug his rooms, and allow the FBI Director to collect any dirt on the would-be president that would keep him under his tight control—and that would help him maintain his insidious Iron White Wall if JFK got out of line on civil rights or anything else he disapproved of.

"Is there anything else you'd like me to do, sir?" Colson asked.

"Oh, and send the Senator a puppy," Hoover said playfully, confirming that he was in fact the conniving cop who loved to play hardball with others—even if they didn't know they were playing it with him.

EIGHT

———

With the presidential election just days away, Bobby was in Alabama trying to shore up support from the White Supremacists JFK would need if he wanted to beat Nixon, the Republicans' civil rights darling.

Though Bobby, at 34 years old, had traditionally handsome features, a virile jawbone, full cherry lips, and a nearly perfectly symmetrical button nose, he looked like a disheveled mess in his gray tailored suit as he waited to be introduced by the staunch segregationist John Patterson, the Governor of Alabama with horrible breath and an even worse comb-over. Bobby was stressed not only because Martin Luther King had failed to give his brother his coveted endorsement—King told them he was sitting out the 1960 race despite the Kennedys' vigorous solicitations—but because he was uncomfortable in the South.

"Gentleman," Patterson said to the all-white Montgomery Chamber of Commerce, "please welcome Bobby Kennedy to the stage."

Bobby flashed an on-demand smile, the same one he had learned from his Father who had served as President Franklin Delano Roosevelt's Ambassador to Great Britain twenty years earlier during World War Two, a time when you had to offer hope on your face even when it wasn't there in your heart. But Bobby's smile, like most political smiles, was counterfeit; he only used it because he wanted something from these men and he wanted it badly, like a man who lusts after a sexy but dangerous Jezebel, obsessed only with getting one thing from her, whipping himself into a melody of desire, his emotion assaulting and assassinating his logic and integrity in the process.

"There's no place I'd rather be," Bobby lied to the congregation of sweaty, overweight onlookers who listened with glee, their faces a creamy canvas of White Supremacist contentment. "You have no idea what you all mean to me and my brother."

But these Dixiecrats, the Southern Democrats who proudly opposed civil rights and saluted the Confederate flag as if the South had actually won the Civil War, in historical revisionism they called "The Lost Cause," didn't mean anything to him. In fact, these people couldn't stand him—and Bobby couldn't stand them either. How could he? They were anti-Northern, anti-Irish, and anti-Catholic, the very DNA The Kennedy's epitomized, and were only for JFK because he had voted against the '57 Civil Rights Act.

"The election is close but with your support, we'll beat Nixon and put a Democrat back in the White House," Bobby continued, brushing his thick light brown hair out of his face, his voice weak and uncertain at times, his ability to speak publicly not one of his natural gifts like it was Martin Luther King's or his brother's.

Although Bobby's speech was boilerplate—he spoke in platitudes like this for the next 45 minutes with the exception of promising the Segregationists a judgeship or two if JFK were elected—the Dixiecrats ate it up, though not everyone was convinced the Kennedys would, or could, help them maintain their Iron White Wall and way of life.

For one, there was Bull Connor, the pudgy, white-haired, no-holds-barred ex-baseball-announcer-turned Birmingham-Police-Commissioner, who was in town on official business and who doubted the youthful JFK had the balls to stop the civil rights assault. Then there was George Wallace, the boxer turned Alabama state Judge who believed desegregation would lead to intermarriage between blacks and whites—and, as he saw it, the destruction of the white race at the hands of 'mongrel Negroes'—who felt JFK needed to publicly put blacks in their place to prevent white "racial suicide." And, of course, there were several KKK members who invisibly blended into society as undercover police officers, school teachers, business owners, and medical doctors, who believed the fall of the Iron White Wall could only be prevented by a true-believer, not a one-term Senator from the North like JFK who seemed to be a little too-charming—and a little too smooth and nonchalant and Yankie-like—for their taste.

But despite their doubts, they remained cordial toward Bobby who was just finishing up. To them, their cordiality wasn't Southern manners or the hospitality their Sunday Schools had taught them; it was simply unadulterated political calculation that wagered that, between Kennedy and Nixon, Kennedy would be the person least likely to break up the status quo that helped them maintain social, political, and financial power over blacks, and keep them drowning in a shipwreck of despair.

"Thank you, gentlemen," Bobby said, flashing his counterfeit smile again, "Now let's win an election!"

As Bobby received a few cheers and polite applause, he quickly left the room, not wanting to stay behind for small talk or even to eat the complimentary rubber chicken lunch they had provided him. He was eager to get back to the campaign, to see how Jack's campaign speech had gone in Illinois, to see if the polls were going more in their favor.

But when Bobby made his way back to his hotel suite, something wasn't right; there were 4 urgent messages from his brother to call him back immediately.

"Jack," Bobby asked in a hurried voice as he finally got through to his brother after several calls, "what is it?"

"It's Martin Luther King," JFK intoned seriously, "he's been arrested at a sit-in in Atlanta with dozens of students."

"Was anyone hurt?" Bobby asked, not surprised by the news given King's arrest record and history.

"No, it was nonviolent," JFK responded. "But I've spoken to his wife Corretta who told me that the judge has sentenced him to 4 months in prison without the possibility of parole."

"What?" Bobby questioned incredulously, thinking the sentence incredibly harsh. "For a peaceful sit-in?"

"Yes. And you're not going to like this Bobby, but Corretta wants me to help bail him out," JFK said with a sigh of desperation. "If we don't, she thinks he's going to be killed."

Bobby paused for a moment, his thoughts in ten different places at once. As he brushed his hair once again out of his face, he simply said, thinking only of his and his brother's self-interest, thinking only of their political ambition, "but if word gets out that we did this it will cost us the election Jack."

NINE

Reidsville State Prison held 1,000 inmates, including convicted murderers, rapists, armed robbers, and now, the nonviolent trouble-making Reverend Martin Luther King Jr. Georgia Judge J. Oscar Mitchell had deliberately ordered King to the maximum security prison for, of all things, having an expired driver's license, which should have only merited a financial fine.

Mitchell was a proud enforcer of the Iron White Wall even if he denied its existence. To him, American justice was blind and impartial and, if Negroes were going to be stirring the pot like King, even if that pot was peaceful and nonviolent, then they needed to experience the consequences that "respectable" judges like himself felt they deserved: judicial lynchings and legal ass kickings. He believed it was the only way law and order could be 'fairly' maintained—and the only way that millions of blacks wouldn't rise up in revolution.

Inside the penitentiary, which was the largest local employer of white residents, a fortress of justice they liked to call it, King was stripped of his clothes and belongings and stood stark naked, profoundly humiliated, in front of two white prison guards, Orville and Tanner. The guards, whose buffoonish faces and throwback looks expressed hardened resentment, looked dumber and more out of touch with modern America, and the 20th Century, than the Fred Flinstone and Barney Rubble characters of the recently debuted Hollywood hit cartoon *The Flintstones.*

"This is the little nig*er trying to inspire all the other nig*ers?" Orville asked, looking over to Tanner as his Southern accent echoed throughout the dilapidated building.

"Looks like it Orville," Tanner responded, his fat blockhead face smirking from right to left at King who just stared at him, covering his fully exposed genitals to try to maintain any shred of dignity he could somehow search out in this position, to try to maintain a shred of manliness, to try to maintain whatever tiny morsel of pride he had left that he could latch onto.

"What are you looking at, boy!?" Tanner said, his hand forming into a tight fist that threatened to punch King, who reflexively put both his hands in front of his face to protect himself, accidentally exposing his genitals, causing a laugh to belch out from the hillbilly blockhead who was pretending to represent American justice.

King then put his hands down, covering himself once again, and said, after composing himself rather matter of factly, "I'm not a boy," deliberately using his otherworldly deep, baritone "preacher" voice, and said, "and no matter how much hatred you show me, I will choose to love you."

"Bullsh*t," Tanner responded, once again threatening King with a punch, who didn't flinch this time, as the rounded chubby fingers of the guard hung in the air like an impaled pig's head on a stick.

"Now put these on," Orville said, tossing a cheap prison suit at King's feet, "and get out of my face."

King slipped on the plain shirt and denim blue jeans, the uniform popular with penitentiaries that had replaced the black and white ones so common decades earlier, and was cuffed at his hands and ankles. He was led by Tanner down a long dark corridor in the 5 story prison that smelled like sweat, grime, and human misery.

"This is where you belong, nig*er!" a white death row inmate who had raped and murdered his next-door neighbor shouted at King. "As soon as I'm out of this cell, I'm gonna kill you!"

But even though King tried to ignore the comment and pretend as though his heinous circumstances didn't affect him, it was almost too much. Sure he was strong, but he hated prison; he hated being stripped of his freedom; he hated being stripped of his dignity; he hated being humiliated and being put in an environment where he could be murdered in a blink of an eye by a White Supremacist, something they took pleasure in doing to blacks, while white prison guards looked the other way, something Judge Mitchell knew all too well when he sentenced him there. And who wouldn't hate such things? King was only human after all, not a robot who didn't have emotions or experience worry or doubt or immense, terrible, God-awful fear. But for the sake of the Civil Rights Movement, for the sake of his deep love for black people, he felt he had to voluntarily endure it; that he needed to voluntarily endure it. If he didn't step up and put his life on the line, he thought, who else would?

"Here's your cell," Tanner said, harshly shoving the Reverend in, slamming the door on him, and locking it loudly with a key.

King looked around at the rusty 8x6 cage that would be his unwanted home for the next 100 days—if he survived that long, which, given the number of murders of Negroes here in the last week alone, didn't seem likely. He then looked at a germ-infected cot, a partially cleaned toilet bowl, and a thin wool blanket, all ironic representations of the sewer of sh*t that Jim Crow proudly stood for.

But then he saw, to his surprise, a King James Bible in the corner, which he studied from a distance, and studied some more, before finally walking over to it, picking it up, and opening to the place where his fingers led him, to the 5th chapter in the Book of St. Matthew. He began to read it aloud.

"Blessed are those who are persecuted because of righteousness, for theirs is the Kingdom of Heaven," he said as crescent tears started to fill his brown eyes. "Blessed are you when people insult you, persecute you and falsely say all kinds of evil against you because of me," he continued, his right hand wiping the water flowing down his face and onto his mustache. "Rejoice and be glad, because great is your reward in heaven, for in the same way they persecuted prophets who were before you."

King then closed his Bible, got on his knees, and did something that had become his daily practice since he began leading the Civil Rights Movement years before: he fought his formidable negative emotions and prayed for the courage not to give up. For the courage to forgive his imprisoners. For the courage to love white people even if, in his lifetime, they would never love him back.

TEN

"Get the hell out of here!" Richard Nixon yelled to his beautiful female secretary who had come into his campaign office during what looked like a stressful meeting with a few advisers.

"But sir, Corretta Scott King is on the phone for you again," the secretary said. "She's hysterical and saying that white klansmen in prison will murder her husband at any moment if he's not released."

"Tell her I'll call her back," Nixon replied in exasperation, his face crippled by annoyance.

But Nixon didn't know whether he would actually call Corretta Scott back. She had already called him seven times yesterday and twice today only to be met with the same perfunctory, heartless response from the Vice President.

"Now gentlemen," Nixon said, huddling with several male members of his campaign team, "we have to do something about this Martin Luther King situation."

"Sir, it's too risky," one white aide who looked like a real pencil pusher said, geeky with scars from his adolescent acne still evident on his skin, who was literally wearing a pocket protector, a popular Mac's 13 brand, with some No. 2's and ball point writing devices protruding out.

"Agreed," echoed another nondescript white aide who appeared trapped in an ad from the 1950s given his baggy suit, narrow tie, and cookie-cutter Levittown-seeming physical appearance, handing a stack of polling data from the Gallup Organization to his boss. "If you help him this close to the election, moderate white voters who support you but not civil rights might stay home—or they might even vote for Kennedy."

"Plus," the pencil pusher-looking aide said, pushing his thick glasses up his oblong nose, "there's no way you'll lose the black vote if you don't help him. Those people are loyal to a fault."

Nixon paced back and forth in the room like a neurotic peacock, stepping over "I like Nixon" lawn sides littered on the floor as well as spilt cottage cheese and ketchup. As he finished listening to arguments from his advisers—they had listed twenty four arguments against helping King and exactly zero arguments for helping him—he knew exactly what he would do.

"Look," Nixon said, sitting back down, "there is to be no public or private campaign involvement in King's imprisonment."

The advisers looked at each other, their faces marked with relief that they had persuaded the Vice President from trying to intervene in a matter that to them was foolish at best and political suicide at worst—after all, their boss already had the black vote in the bag and they didn't need to remind white voters of his "progressive" stance on race relations and risk their backlash.

"Nor will there be any communication with his family," Nixon said. "They're all just going to have to figure things out on their own."

"Sir," the nondescript aide said, looking stoically at Nixon, but excited on the inside knowing he was persuading his candidate, "it's what's best."

"And," said the pencil pusher, "it's the only decision you could have made under the circumstances."

Nixon's posture perked up a bit, inflated by the politically self-serving justifications his sycophantic aides made that helped him rationalize his decision; that helped him rationalize his cowardice; that helped him rationalize betraying his "friend," which seemed to come a little too easily to him. Even though he knew a single call from him could bail out Martin Luther King from prison—and prevent his suffering or potential death—he could only salivate on himself, on furthering his own career, on advancing number one, like most politicians, despite their rhetoric of entering politics as a "noble calling," as a "public service," or the other dubious phrases they use to conceal their toxic hunger for power and control over society, their motivations and rationale for "wanting to help" as ridiculous and paper thin as the "meritocratic" notion of the NBA and NFL banning black players from their leagues, which they had done just a few years ago, labeling them as "inherently unqualified to play."

As Nixon moved on to other campaign business over the next few hours—the Soviet Union, fiscal responsibility, and things politicians talk about—he pulled out his favorite poker set. He looked at an aide and ushered him to come over and play him.

"You see," Nixon said, shuffling the deck and dealing cards to his aide like a professional dealer, "politics is a lot like poker."

"I can see that," the 1950s aide said, flipping through his set of cards, realizing he had the worst hand possible: a high card.

"And do you know what the most important rule of poker is?" Nixon asked.

"Um, I–"

"Showing no sympathy for your opponents," Nixon said, his eyes greedy with victory, revealing a royal flush. "Or your allies. Ever."

"Yes, sympathy is for the weak," his pencil pushing looking aide agreed who was observing the game as Nixon flashed a large grin.

But before he could gloat too much over his poker win, his female secretary suddenly came running back into the office.

"Sir," the female secretary said, "there's been a development with Dr. King."

"What is it?" Nixon asked quizzically.

"Southern Negro media outlets are reporting that King has just been released from prison," the secretary said.

"What? How?"

"Bobby Kennedy bailed him out," the secretary responded flatly. "And lots of Negroes have now been spotted wearing John F. Kennedy For President buttons."

As Nixon sat in complete shock and disbelief, his eyebrows and armpits heavy with anxious perspiration, all he could say was, "that son of a b*tch!"

ELEVEN

Bad Bobby had struck. *Like lightning.* But he still had unfinished business as far as Martin Luther King was concerned.

"Good work, kid," JFK joked as Bobby arrived back from Alabama to his Hickory Hill estate, which was quieter than normal given the late-night hour, and which, despite being Bobby's home, was also JFK's unofficial campaign nerve center day and night, a 24-7 "war room" they had set up that made the beautiful home seem like an unsightly battlefield command outpost, with paper and people organized in a way that made no sense to anyone looking in from the outside, but perfect sense to those in it.

"I have an idea, Jack," Bobby said, a look of intensity forcing its way through his ever-creasing face and sleep-deprived eyes.

Bobby approached the table in the center of the room and cleared items off of the red and blue electoral map he had built his brother's entire presidential campaign around, the electoral map that seemed frozen in a virtual tie with Nixon. He looked at blue Texas, historically Democratic territory, and crossed it off as winnable, along with the Dixiecrat states. He then looked at red California, a historically Republican territory, and crossed it off as unwinnable, along with most of the middle of the country.

"This election is going to come down to one state," Bobby intoned, his Boston accent thicker than usual, the concern on his tongue growing stronger with each word he uttered. "And one state only."

JFK grabbed an orange from a fruit tray and pulled up a chair at the table to listen to Bobby.

"If we can drive up the Negro vote in Chicago," Bobby continued, drawing a circle around the Windy City, "you can win Illinois. And therefore the Presidency."

"But Democrats have lost the last two presidential elections there," JFK shot back attempting to play devil's advocate, to test his little brother, the mastermind who had engineered all of his electoral wins in the past, "and polling there doesn't look good for us."

"I know," Bobby said, "that's where my idea comes in."

JFK, still peeling his orange, looked intrigued but skeptical, knowing his kid brother was always thinking 10 steps ahead but also wondering if the bail out of King was too little, too late, to win over black voters in the North.

"After I called Judge Mitchell and forced him to release King—"

"Forced him?" JFK abruptly interrupted, an orange slice half in his mouth. "Is that legal Bobby?" he said, partly wanting to know the answer, and partly not wanting to know.

Bobby hesitated for a second and said, "I don't know, Jack. Probably not."

JFK looked at him, let out a small chuckle, and said, hoping to cheer him up, "well, if you go to jail for threatening a judge make sure you don't drop the soap in the shower."

But Bobby knew that his brother was only joking; he knew that his brother would never let that happen to him; he knew despite JFK never telling him as much, that he was impressed at the transparency and ruthlessness he demonstrated; impressed that his little brother, nearly a decade his junior, was his political hatchet man who always took care of business, even if he wasn't sure exactly how he took care of it.

"But as I was saying, after I called the judge and Southern Negro media outlets broke the story that the Kennedys bailed King out of jail," Bobby said, "countless Negroes who listened to it were seen wearing your campaign buttons."

"Bobby, I know this," JFK said, wondering why he would be repeating such obvious information. *Was Bobby just tired?* He thought. *Didn't he realize that the Negro media outlets who covered the story were in the South, not the North, the place he needed the votes to win? Didn't he realize that, in 1960 America, news travels very slowly and that Southern Negroes don't vote in Northern states, and usually don't vote at all given segregationist intimidation tactics and lack of voter registration?*

But Bobby bulldogged past his brother's concerns and said, "most Negroes in Chicago haven't heard about us helping King."

"And what's your point?" JFK said, not knowing where Bobby was taking this.

"My point is, we need to get the story out to as many Illinois Negroes as possible that you, the man who voted against the 1957 Civil Rights Act, bailed King out of jail."

"But Bobby, all of our campaign advertising dollars have been spent," JFK said discouragingly, "and even if we had the money, we can't risk going on the media with this story. It'd get out to white voters too who would punish us at the polls."

"We don't need to go on any media," Bobby said spiritedly. "We only need to go to Negro churches."

"Churches?" JFK asked.

"Yes," Bobby said, "churches."

Bobby picked up a folder near the electoral map, reached inside, and handed a couple of sheets of paper to his brother, who had just finished eating his orange.

"Negroes are the most religious group of people in America," Bobby said while JFK skimmed the papers which showed incredibly high church attendance rates among blacks. "If we can distribute flyers and leaflets on the ground to as many of their churches in Illinois that Kennedy bailed out King–"

"And by extension, wants to bail out Negroes?" JFK asked.

"Yes," Bobby said, his political instincts operating in full gear, a man endowed with both strategic and tactical prowess, his mind the electoral equivalent of a forensically accurate sniper. "Then we may be able to drive up the vote in Chicago, a heavy Negro population center, and win this thing."

"Bobby, that's brilliant," JFK said before he paused to think for a moment. "But we didn't get King's endorsement. Doesn't that feel like going behind his back? Like cheating?"

"It doesn't matter," Bobby said dismissively, not caring if it felt like it was cheating or not, "all we need to do is appear as if we got it, and it'll have the same effect."

He saw JFK nodding his head in agreement, seemingly trying to rationalize what Bobby was saying, before he put the paper he was holding down. After yawning, JFK got up from the table, put on his favorite blazer and navy blue Cashmere overcoat on top of it, and started heading toward the exit before he looked back at his kid brother.

"I got this, Jack," Bobby said, his eyes turning toward JFK, who looked just as exhausted as he felt, their bodies crippled by fatigue and running on campaign adrenaline.

"I know you do," JFK responded. "I know you do. But what happens if your idea doesn't work?"

Bobby thought for a moment, and then thought some more, before he simply said, "then you don't become President."

TWELVE

"Oh Martin," Corretta blurted out sympathetically as she peered out of her kitchen window and spotted her unkempt and traumatized husband exiting a cab in front of their Victorian-style Atlanta home.

"Is Daddy home?" Yolanda shouted, observing her mom's relieved expression, whose eyes were starting to well with tears of repose, before setting down her Play Doh Fun Factory.

King made his way from the sidewalk up his driveway, which housed his dark-blue Chevy Impala and his wife's off-white Ford Thunderbird, and stopped for a moment to take in his four bedroom brick residence that was his safe space. His refuge. The place where he didn't have to be The Reverend, or the civil rights leader or the man who had to act like nothing ever bothered him, but could instead just be himself: a husband to a wife who adored him, and a father to a growing family who adored him even more.

"It is Daddy!" Yolanda shouted, watching her dad come to the white screen door. She quickly ran down the steps of the front entrance, where her hair, which was done up in two cute pigtails, and her white polka dot dress, started flapping in the wind, a little girl full of hope because daddy, her daddy, was home.

"Hi baby, daddy's missed you," King said while Yolanda jumped in his arms and held him as tightly as her five year old frame could muster, her body wrapped so closely around his like a hand being snuggled into a perfectly fitting glove.

"I missed you too!" Yolanda responded, watching King struggle to hold back the tears bubbling up inside of him. Not only was he happy to see her after getting out of prison, but he was happy to see her period. Leading the Civil Rights Movement required him to spend most of his time traveling and seeing his daughter reminded him how blessed he really was in life. Reminded him how much he craved the gentleness of his child's touch. Reminded him how much he needed the joy of his child's laugh. Reminded him of what true love really felt like.

King and Yolanda made their way up the steps into the front of the house, where Corretta, whose belly was as round as a basketball in her third trimester of pregnancy, was holding their three year son, Martin Luther King III, who smiled, while holding his teddy bear "Love." He blurted out, "Papa."

"Oh Martin!" Corretta said again, emotion climbing up and down her voice, the wattage in her words high and low like a high school marching band, "I thought they were going to kil–"

"Honey, not in front of the kids," King said gently before kissing his son and tenderly embracing his wife, reminding her of the agreement they had made years earlier when he consented to lead the dangerous cause known as the Civil Rights Movement: not to talk about the harm he was in regularly, the hazards he faced daily, in front of their children.

"Oh, I understand my love," Corretta said to her husband, quickly thinking about what to change the subject to. "Guess what? I've made you your favorite dinner."

"Really?" King said, in a way that was more teasing than questioning, trying to keep things as lighthearted as possible, trying to refrain from thinking about the horrors of the hellscape he had just experienced.

"Yes," Corretta said back with a smile. "Salsbury steak and pickled eggs."

King's eyes lit up like a pinball machine. He licked his lips and said, "honey, you speak my language."

"But that's not all," Corretta replied, teasing her husband in return. "I've also made you some macaroni and cheese."

"And?"

"Collard greens."

"And?"

 "Peach cobbler."

"And?"

"Pecan pie."

"And?"

"Ok, Martin, now you're starting to sound like a pig," Corretta laughed, cutting her husband off mid sentence, knowing that the man she married would always eat more than his waistline could handle if he had his choice in the matter, a proud black man from Georgia who was unafraid and unashamed to indulge in Southern comfort food any time he could, one of the few treats from heaven he felt he could enjoy in this life.

King chuckled and said, "Honey, you're so good to me," before he embraced her and gave her several smooches on her soft auburn lips, taking in the cinnamon of her taste, the proximity of her heart inhaled by the love of his.

"Yuck!" Yolanda said as everyone started to giggle.

"Wash up, Martin," Corretta said, her soul smiling on the inside, happiness dancing across the twinkle of her eyes, "and I'll set the table."

King picked up his briefcase, walked past the piano in the family room, and went upstairs into his master bathroom. He removed his wrinkled coat and tie and then took off his shirt. He stared in the mirror at his messy hair. Then at the bags under his eyes. And finally at his chest, which revealed a jagged scar from an assassination attempt two years before.

The scar on King's chest wasn't just any scar, though. It was both ugly and beautiful and, to him, confirmation of his calling, as his attacker had carved the wound in his flesh in the shape of a deeply creviced cross. Right over his heart.

King then washed his face, put on a new polo shirt and fresh pair of slacks, and went to the dining room. As the family was eating, with King smacking loudly in delight from his meal, licking his fingers here and there during the entree, Yolanda asked him who he was going to vote for tomorrow on election day.

"Baby girl, given all of the trouble Mr. Nixon went through to bail me out, I think I'm obligated–"

"Martin," Corretta said with a look of surprise and disappointment, trying not to let her resentment boil to the surface and ruin the moment, "Nixon didn't bail you out of jail."

"Wait. What?" King asked. "The prison guards told me that a very powerful man had gotten me released."

"Well, they didn't lie," Corretta responded. "But that powerful man wasn't Nixon."

"Then who was it?"

Corretta paused for a moment. King had told her about his uncomfortable meeting with the Kennedys and how much he didn't like Bobby. How much he didn't trust him. How much he didn't think his heart was in the right place as far as civil rights were concerned. But she couldn't keep the truth from him, even if the truth rubbed him the wrong way.

Hesitatingly, Corretta said, "it was Bobby Kennedy."

"Are you serious?" King shot back, completely dumbfounded, salisbury steak almost flying out of his mouth.

"As serious as I can be," Corretta said regretfully. "I called Nixon a dozen times to help you but he wouldn't return my call."

But before King could say anything—he felt speechless and discombobulated about both Nixon and Bobby—Yolanda piped up. She said, like only a child could, "Daddy, does that mean you're voting for Mr. Kennedy now?"

THIRTEEN

It was well past midnight on election day and Bobby looked like a complete trainwreck in his Hickory Hill home—his unshaven face, bloodshot eyes, and wrinkled attire all revealed a man who hadn't slept, or bathed, in the last 72 hours. But it didn't matter; he had always insisted on being the guy who would only rest when he was dead and, for now, it was do or die time.

Just a couple of days prior, Bobby had launched his ruthless leaflet campaign targeting black churches in Chicago—and other parts of the country for good measure. He called his campaign the "Blue Bomb," all the literature was printed on blue paper, and he had done the unthinkable with it: distribute over two million flyers to blacks across countless churches completely unbeknownst to the media, and completely unbeknownst to all of white America.

At first, blacks were taken aback at seeing so many young white volunteers, mostly students, approach them. Some of them thought, *why the hell would a white person approach me about trying to get my vote? Was this some sort of trick? Did Kennedy, as the flyer claimed, really help bail out King?*

But after some convincing by the eager and sincere volunteers, including the Student Nonviolent Coordinating Committee's Carol Davis, blacks dropped their skepticism and word began to spread like wildfire among the people: that Kennedy, reversing his original opposition to the '57 Civil Rights Act, was not only for King, but that he was for them.

Despite hearing media reports on election day that voter turnout was higher than usual in black precincts, Bobby didn't want to take any chances with what could be unreliable information. He knew that reporters, while mostly good people, didn't always get things right and he didn't trust their facts. Hell, he didn't really seem to trust anybody's facts. Too much was on the line.

"Give me the numbers again," Bobby demanded as he phoned the head of JFK's Illinois presidential operation.

"Bobby, they haven't changed," the local campaign aide replied sheepishly.

"Just tell me again," Bobby insisted while his Father, who was sitting in the corner with a glass of brandy, peered on.

"Our state numbers are Nixon two million, three hundred and sixty eight thousand," the local campaign aide said. "And Kennedy, two million, three hundred and seventy seven thousand."

"Are you sure?" Bobby questioned, brushing his light brown hair out of his eyes.

"Yes."

"Ok," Bobby said.

Bobby then hung up the phone and looked at his old man. While neither of them said anything for a moment, the looks on their faces said it all—they knew.

"Gather Jack and the family in the living room," Joe Kennedy Sr. said, "and turn on Cronkite."

As Bobby sat everyone down in front of the television—his little brother Ted, his wife Ethel, Jackie, his mom Rose, scores of Kennedy children, and various campaign aides, who were brimming with anticipation—JFK was unusually quiet and reflective, a mode he slipped into from time to time. He thought about how it had been a hard fought campaign, and about the idea that even defeating an incumbent Vice President who was the Number Two man to a popular sitting President was still no easy thing to fathom—even if his good looks and quick wit had allowed him to own the incumbent Vice President in the eyes of the American people during a live national debate. He also thought about how his nominal Catholicism—which was being weaponized against him by Nixon and the Republicans—was playing a big role in why the polls were so close; every Catholic nominee for President had been defeated before him and what would make him any different?

Bobby turned up the volume on the television, which was set to the CBS Evening News.

"Ladies and gentlemen," CBS anchor Walter Cronkite announced in his pitch perfect media voice, "this is the moment we've all been waiting for."

Jackie squeezed JFK's left hand as their three year old daughter, Caroline, tightly clenched his right.

"The closest election in American history is finally over," Cronkite said. "Carrying the swing state of Illinois and winning by a margin of just 0.2% nationwide is America's new President Elect."

But before Cronkite could say anything further, he paused briefly for dramatic effect, America's favorite newsman being a bit of a show-man too, his trustworthy face belonging to the performance arts record books like no other, his eyes able to reveal the contours of a story by bypassing the camera and connecting directly into the hearts of his viewers.

"Come on, Walter!" Bobby screamed, "say it!"

As Cronkite looked into the camera he continued to pause before saying, "Mr. John Fitzgerald Kennedy!"

With those words, a thunderous roar erupted from the Kennedys. JFK had done it. Bobby had done it. Joe Sr. had realized his lifelong dream.

"Congratulations, Mr. President!" Bobby said, hugging JFK in a way that only a little brother could: with pride that his big brother, his hero, had just won the biggest lottery of all time.

JFK, who was grinning from ear to ear said, "Bobby, you made this happen!"

"No, Mr. President, you did!" Bobby shot back, again brushing his light brown hair out of his face, as the entire family began hugging Jack, high fiving each other, and allowing themselves to be overwhelmed by this moment.

Although Bobby wasn't trying to be modest, he really was selling himself short. After all, it had been his idea to bank on blacks to be the swing voters who would put them over the top, something no other campaign, including Lincoln's, had ever done. It had been his idea to flood black churches with pro-civil rights campaign literature, something that no other campaign had ever done. And it had been his idea to do it in the state that ultimately won his brother the Presidency.

As call after call came in congratulating JFK on his election—and as JFK was getting ready to address the nation—a call came in from Martin Luther King who had, earlier in the day, defied his own Father, and according to Corretta possibly his own conscience, by hesitatingly voting for Kennedy.

"May I speak with the President-Elect?" King asked, professionally.

"I'm afraid he's not available," Bobby said, gruffness filling his lips as he recognized his voice.

"Oh, it's you Bobby," King said, a little startled and guarded when he recognized his counterpart's voice too. "Well, I just wanted to thank you for what you did for me."

"Don't worry about it Reverend, it was Jack's idea," Bobby responded in an attempt to deflect praise and hide his lingering irritation at King from their meeting a few days ago, a feeling that, for Bobby, wouldn't wear off anytime soon; he built resentments fast and if he didn't liked you, that was just your bad luck and he couldn't give a hoot either way.

"Well then," King said, "can you thank him for me and have him return my call at his earliest convenience?"

"I will let him know you called," Bobby said. But Bobby didn't mean it: he had no plans of telling JFK that King had called and no plans of doing more than the bare minimum he had promised King on civil rights. To him, they had to focus on the "bigger" political issues now: the Soviet Union, getting a man to the moon, cutting taxes—and not on marginal election issues like Negro rights, even if it was the thing that made his brother president, as the issue promised no political upside given the near unanimous white opposition to blacks—and given the near unanimous white opposition to King himself. It wasn't that

Bobby was deliberately trying to be two-faced; it was just that he was trying to be pragmatic in the midst of his volcanic emotions about the election, and growing resentment toward King—and trying to protect his brother from losing his Presidency to a contentious issue before it even began.

"Great," King said. "I will look forward to speaking and meeting with him so that we can work together on a bold civil rights strategy for America."

"Sounds good," Bobby said. But Bobby didn't mean this either. Now that the election was over, there was no way he was going to let his brother near the radioactive King—and no way he was going to let King's Second Emancipation Proclamation near him either. But he damn sure wasn't going to let King, who he knew would stop at nothing to bring Jim Crow to its unholy knees, know this.

FOURTEEN

The Ku Klux Klan was furious, and so was their most powerful anonymous benefactor whom they only knew as "The Contact," whom some believed, without certain proof, was a White Supremacist don of the mafia—or possibly a 'higher up' at the FBI, CIA, or even the Soviet Union's KGB, which had a long-standing interest in destabilizing U.S. politics. The Klan had been tipped off by a local Chicago judge, one of their proud and inconspicuous Northern members, that JFK was supporting King. The judge had come across one of Kennedy's campaign flier's when he was walking by Quinn Chapel A.M.E., Chicago's oldest black church, and was completely outraged.

As the leadership of the Klan conspired over what to do about a potential budding alliance between Kennedy and King, numerous suggestions began to fly.

"We could bribe a district attorney to trump up criminal charges against King," a 56 year-old police commissioner said who was proudly wearing his wolfish white robe and pointy white hat, the standard KKK uniform designed, they believed, to symbolize the purity and holiness of being a member of the master race—and to conceal their identities whenever they capriciously persecuted and murdered innocent black people, their favorite pastime.

"Or we could have one of our boys in Washington give Kennedy a real kick in the ass," said a medical doctor who, of course, was referring to the hundreds of influential Klansmen who were U.S. Senators, Congressmen, and lobbyists who could pummel Kennedy with hardball political tactics and force him to be a do-nothing President on civil rights.

"Or we could—"

"Enough," said the newly elected head of the national KKK, the Imperial Wizard himself, the black-haired and thin-muschaed Roy Davis whose steely, parasitic eyes revealed a kind of dark, soulless quality about him, a viper of a man whose actions magnified his coronation as a Demon King. "We don't need to poke the bear unless the bear first pokes us."

The Imperial Wizard, who was an original co-founder of the second KKK and co-author of its constitution and alternative "Kalendar" system, oversaw a loosely held confederate organization that had once boasted a membership of four or five million, which was roughly half the size of the entire black population in the United States. He had built this organization from scratch—he was inspired by Hollywood's first blockbuster film, 1915's *Birth of a Nation*, which glamorized White Supremacy as the greatest gift ever given to America, to the delight of the majority of Americans—and so he had developed instincts about the best time to manipulate race relations. And, to him, this wasn't it.

"We what need to do," the Imperial Wizard said, standing theatrically in front of a Georgia church pulpit that was their meeting headquarters, and that he used as a pretend "minister" of the Gospel in his non-Klan time as a con man, "is wait until they do something first."

Of course, the Imperial Wizard hadn't always been this patient. As a younger man, he had gotten into all sorts of trouble for his lack of patience—and lack of discretion. He was convicted of forgery and grand theft for wanting to get rich quick. He had trafficked an underage blonde minor because he had to have her—he needed to have her, the lust inside him detonating like a crippling land mine inside him—and despite the gross illegality and oppressive perversion of doing so. And he had done lots of other atrocious things revealing who he was at his core: a white man who believed he was entitled to whatever he wanted—whenever he wanted it—simply because of the color of his skin. After all, most powerful Southern white men of his generation had been taught the same and, to them, it was the only 'truth' everyone else just had to accept—or else. And the 'or else' wasn't an empty threat;

these powerful white men were from a spiritual lineage that had used it to bring trauma, pain, and unnecessary evil on a group of people for centuries just because they could.

But what the Imperial Wizard had learned from all of his impatience and abhorrent racial ideology was something that he was now leading the Klan by: namely, that sometimes it's better to, like a snake lurking in the shadows, bide your time until you strike so that you don't give your prey any warning you're out there, allowing the messenger of death and defeat to arrive when it's too little, too late for its victims.

"Kleagles," The Imperial Wizard said, referring to the 45 leaders and recruiters of the KKK in attendance, men, and a few women, who were all pillars in their communities, and substantial fundraisers too who brought in other new dues-paying members in a financial pyramid scheme that kept their coffers bursting at the seams, "we have just received our largest donation yet from our anonymous donor. He believes that Kennedy will launch civil rights lawsuits to threaten our way of life."

The Kleagles, sitting in their pointy white hats, looked on with contempt, their collective eyelids stapled shut from the larger truth of their own needless hatred, with self-deception being the poisonous de rigueur by which they chose to arrange their lives.

"And he believes that King will launch more boycotts like in Montgomery," the Imperial Wizard said to audible groans. "When they do, we will be ready to fight them in the courts, fight them in the streets, and show them that no Catholic and no nig*er will take our country from us—or take it from the millions of white people God has promised this great land to. If they get too ballsy, just know we have the resources to do whatever it takes to snuff them out."

FIFTEEN

Joe Kennedy Sr. stood in the dining room at Hickory Hill and said, matter of factly, "Bobby is to be the Attorney General of The United States," as JFK, who was wearing a blue button down, and several excited-looking and fashion-sensible aides sporting unisex bell-bottoms listened. "And he is to be put in charge of civil rights."

"But Father, Bobby's not qualified to be Attorney General," JFK protested incredulously. "He's never practiced law—"

"I have spoken," the elder Kennedy said with chilly and intoxicating resoluteness that let the President-Elect know he had made up his mind—and that there was no way this rainmaker was going to change it.

"Ok, Father, I will let him know," JFK responded, not wanting to challenge his old man who had built the empire, who had built the pampered machine originally designed to elect his deceased brother Joe Jr. President, that made his second born son's presidency possible in the first place.

"That's a good boy," the elder Kennedy said paternalistically, ushering over a brown-haired house servant to pour him a glass of brandy.

JFK got up from his seat and walked through five rooms of the estate until he reached the living room. Bobby was interviewing candidate after candidate to be placed in his brother's Administration. He had just finished with Robert McNamara, his Republican tennis buddy and the

CEO of Ford Motor Company, whom he was recommending to become Secretary of Defense. He had also interviewed Dean Rusk, whose daughter Peggy was covertly dating a black man—a criminal offense in the United States—to be Secretary of State; Theodore Sorenson to be his "brain," speechwriter, and historian; and several others, including Washington-outsider John McCone, whom he was considering to recommend as director of the CIA.

"Bobby, I need to talk to you privately," JFK said. "Father insists."

Bobby excused himself from the room—he had dozens of people waiting in the queue to be screened by him and several of his deputies—and went into the hallway, next to one of his many Catholic statues of Mary that were sprinkled throughout the house, which looked like an American Annex of the Vatican itself.

"Father wants you to be Attorney General," JFK said flatly. "And he wants you to oversee civil rights."

"Is he nuts?" Bobby screeched, brushing his light brown hair out of his face. "I've never even stepped foot inside of a courtroom. The press will call it nepotism—"

"I know, Bobby," JFK said, looking increasingly resigned, worry blossoming gingerly upon his complexion, his mind's eye picturing the house of cards this unorthodox arrangement could become, his presidency potentially turning into a temple of ridicule, a canvas for which his political enemies could mock and crucify him day and night.

"And he wants me to oversee civil rights?" Bobby protested. "It's a political loser."

"I think he wants you to handle Dr. King," JFK said.

"But I've already handled him, Jack," a frustrated Bobby said. "We're going to create a civil rights division in the Justice Department to help him litigate segregation. That's really all we can do."

"Bobby," JFK said, looking into his brother's light blue eyes, "is it?"

Bobby thought for a moment, not wanting to search himself or his clever intellect for difficult answers. "I mean, I think so."

"You know King won't accept us just assisting his Movement with launching lawsuits against segregationist laws," JFK said. "You heard him in the meeting."

"Jack, civil rights has so many enemies," Bobby complained.

"I know it does," JFK said. "But Father thinks you're the one who can navigate the minefield."

"I think Martin Luther King is just a little too big for his britches," Bobby said, agitatedly, letting his real opinion about King trickle out loud for the first time, his diplomatic mask removed so that his wells of indignation could flow freely.

But JFK knew his highly emotional brother. He knew that he had the remarkable ability to set aside personal feelings to accomplish a task. He knew that he was a loyal soldier who would commit to a cause even when he didn't want to. He knew that Bobby, for all of his stubborn independence and ruthlessness, just wanted to please him—and just wanted to please their insufferable Father, whose respect he had desperately tried to earn all of his life, like a hopeful hamster spinning within a caged wheel that never went anywhere.

"Why does Father think I'm the one who should do it?" Bobby asked, fishing for both an answer and possible compliment.

"Because you got balls bigger than the state of Texas," JFK said.

Of course, JFK was referring to Bobby's bold civil rights election ploy. But he was also referring to something else about his little brother. Bobby had, JFK remembered, previously overseen the largest anti-mob investigation in U.S. history. He had launched over 250 investigations, subpoenaed 8,000 witnesses, and had gone after the mafia with an intensity that bordered on holy fanaticism. His little brother, when push came to shove, was the only person with the guts to dive into trench warfare that took casualties with impunity—and, make no mistake, JFK felt civil rights was about to claim some lives if he didn't traverse the situation carefully.

"Look Jack, I strongly disagree with being Attorney General and overseeing civil rights," Bobby said. "But I'll do it for you," he said as he started to hesitate, "and I'll do it for Father."

"Good," JFK said, "we're going to need your toughness. And your ideas. We need to offer King something else besides a civil rights division to mitigate the tension on this issue."

But Bobby already knew that. He just didn't want to admit it—and he sure as hell didn't want to accept it. But if giving King an olive branch to keep him away from his brother—and to keep civil rights out of the headlines—was what Bobby had to do, then he would just suck it up and do it. *Whatever it takes*, he thought. *As long as it gets the job done and helps protect Jack.*

As a voluptuous female aide who looked like Miss America approached JFK with a highly sensitive box—containing the ceremonial keys to the 55,000-square-foot White House, a getaway retreat known as Camp David, and a brand new Boeing C-137 presidential plane now being called "Air Force One"—Bobby was finishing his thoughts while JFK gave her a quick once over with his hungry eyes.

"Jack, let's appoint several Negroes to your Administration in low and mid-level positions," Bobby said. "That way we can show King we are leading by example on desegregation and keep him at bay for a while."

JFK placed his right hand on his chin and said, "Do you really think that'll be enough to placate him?"

Bobby shot back, "It'd better be."

SIXTEEN

January 20, 1961

Martin Luther King stepped into the parking lot of Ebenezer Baptist Church, reached into the pocket of his gray wool overcoat, and pulled out a red pack of Pall Mall cigarettes, America's #1 cigarette brand. He took out a gold zippo lighter and cigarette, lit it up, and began puffing away, the wet of his tongue on the lightly blazing butt relishing the best tasting sauce in the world.

"Careful, Martin," his best friend Ralph Abernathy said from a distance, "you don't want to let the children see you smoking."

"I know. I wish I could just kick the habit," King responded as bundled-up black school children walked by through sleet, "but it's too hard."

Abernathy gave King a look of understanding as he approached him, knowing all of the pressure his friend was under because, like King, he was under it too. So were all of the civil rights workers. America seemed united against them, seemed united against black people, a tradition it fiercely clung to since its founding in 1619, and working full time in the 'Freedom Movement,' as civil rights insiders called it, was no psychologically or emotionally easy thing. So if King had to smoke a cigarette to calm his rocky nerves, and to distract himself from his recent imprisonment as well as the fresh death threat he received this morning, then so be it. Each man is a labyrinth unto himself, with his uniquely creaky mental-fissures and eggshell thin emotional cracks requiring customized elixirs to medicate his pain, and this was among King's.

But King had other things he wanted to be distracted from. There was the snub of not being invited to attend JFK's Presidential inauguration, despite many of his black friends being asked to participate behind the scenes. There was the scolding lecture his Father, Martin Luther King Sr., had given him a few minutes earlier when he found out his son had secretly gone against his wishes and voted for Kennedy. And there was, most of all, the heavy guilt that was increasingly weighing on his heart that Corretta, who was due to give birth to another baby boy within the week, was raising their kids as a de facto single mom, given his travel schedule and workaholism.

As Abernathy noticed the distant look in King's eyes, he asked him, "Everything ok?"

"Sometimes," King said, taking a long puff in the chilly winter air, "I wish things were easier."

"If it were easy, Martin," Abernathy replied, blowing warmth into his hands, "then somebody else would have already done it."

"I want to be with my family," King said somberly. "When I know I can't be."

Abernathy put his hand on King's shoulder and squeezed it, trying to comfort him as best he could, his reassuring embrace overriding the dizzying depths of his friend's melancholy.

"I know," Abernathy responded.

"But in my heart I know the only way for us to stop the evils of racism," King continued, "is if I get crushed, and my family gets crushed right along with me."

"Martin, don't talk that way," Abernathy replied, rebuking him.

But Abernathy was just trying to be strong for his friend because, in reality, he felt the same way. He was there with King as they had successfully desegregated the Montgomery bus line and he knew the trauma they had gone through taking on White Supremacy. He knew that, for them to make it to civil rights heaven, they had to go through Jim Crow hell. And he knew that Jim Crow was a sadistic torturer of not only them as willing individuals, but also of their wives and children and families who never signed up to be immolated in the first place, who never signed up to be the pupils of bitter recrimination. In other words, Abernathy knew that King was torn between being a father on the one hand, desperately trying to preserve his family, and being a prophetic revolutionary on the other, desperately trying to change his country.

Before King could respond to Abernathy's gentle reproach, a green Cadillac full of fellow civil rights workers arrived. They pulled into the church parking lot, the official meeting headquarters of King's Southern Christian Leadership Conference (SCLC), a black nonprofit he had launched to take on segregation and enact his Second Emancipation Proclamation, to watch the Presidential inaugural address on their brand new RCA color television.

After the car parked and the music turned off— they were listening to 1961's hit song "Will You Still Love Me Tomorrow" by the all black female group, the Shirelles—the doors started to open. Out of the Cadillac stepped Andrew Young, the handsome executive director of the SCLC who had been at the meeting a few months earlier with the Kennedys; Bayard Rustin, King's closest adviser who had previously been arrested under anti-gay sodomy laws in California; Ella Baker, SCLC's only paid staffer; and James Lawson, who had just finished training another batch of students for imminent mobilization should King give the order to strike nonviolently.

"Reverend," Rustin opened, his smile as wide and as long as the Mississippi river, "it's a great day to be a Negro." King's sullen face suddenly wore a smile.

"Everyday is a great day to be a Negro," Abernathy interjected in a moment of black optimism that fueled their resilience, and fueled the way they saw themselves: as beautiful black human beings who could be proud of their heritage, and not ashamed of it, despite the subjgated identities many whites wanted them to internalize about themselves, a historical brainwashing that had been the icing on Jim Crow's exploitative cake.

"Come," King said, "let's go inside and see what Kennedy has to say."

Although he didn't show it, King was hopeful about JFK despite feeling like he had been used to winning the election and then snubbed immediately afterward. But he was hopeful because he knew human nature and JFK seemed like the kind of person who could be pushed to do the right thing—if he could only get the hardheaded Bobby out of the way to do it.

But his hope was also a fear. It was a fear because, if he could bend JFK toward the arc of justice as he liked to say publicly, civil rights success for the many almost certainly meant personal defeat for the few: in the form of an assassination of his life and possibly martyrdom of the lives of those closest to him. In other words, he was *damned if you do*, he thought. *And damned if you don't.*

SEVENTEEN

King and his team went inside of the church, walked across the polyester red carpet, and sat in the front pew. They turned on the RCA color television that was wheeled in front of them and sat transfixed in anticipation of history: the first Presidential Inaugural Address they were hoping would make civil rights a key issue in America.

JFK's 1961 Lincoln Continental pulled up to the Capitol escorted by a motorcade of vehicles and phalanx of security. He was wearing a black top hat and dark Brooks Brothers overcoat paired with a Jacques Fath navy suit, white button down shirt, and a baby blue, narrow necktie. Jackie, who had just given birth to their son John F. Kennedy Jr. a few weeks earlier, was by his side donning a dazzling pink Chanel jacket and knee-length pencil skirt along with a matching pink Halston-designed pillbox hat that was sure to turn heads.

The first couple exited the vehicle with shouts of "Camelot! Camelot!" being hurled at them referring, of course, to the glamor that they symbolized as the best looking and most elegant couple ever to make 1600 Pennsylvania Avenue their home, a veritable runway show for an America that was becoming an increasingly visual society, with television morphing into the default entertainment and leisure medium, arcade games coming online, and the corporate marketing of sex, drugs, and rock 'n roll in full swing, the "60s revolution" as commentators were calling it changing the country in ways it had never seen before.

"This is something," JFK remarked to Jackie, who smiled and waved at the throngs of well-dressed people they were passing as they made their way into the Capitol and through its Rotunda.

Just moments earlier, a bitter-looking Richard Nixon had arrived and was mingling with Washington's DC's new kids on the block: Kennedy's vice president, Lyndon Johnson, the new Secretary of Defense Robert McNamara, and the man who had outplayed him on election day, Bobby. As JFK entered the East Portico of the Capitol, Nixon mumbled, "that son of a b*tch" under his lips before he faked a smile and shook the new President's hand.

Nearly one million people had come out to see the 35th man to be sworn in as president, including a family of four from coal country in West Virginia; tie-dye inspired hippies from California; and a handful of blacks from Chicago who were wearing "Kennedy for President" buttons.

As the dignitaries sat down on the terrace of the Eastern Portico that was decorated in red, white, and blue pomp and circumstance, JFK started to experience something unusual: he was feeling butterflies. *This is it*, he thought. The moment he had been waiting for. The moment his Father had fought for his entire life: to install a Kennedy in The White House. And he was that Kennedy.

The Chief Justice of the Supreme Court, Earl Warren, who had written the decision to strike down segregation in schools in the *Brown v Board of Education* case, administered JFK's oath of office. He took out the leather-bound Fitzgerald Family Bible dating back to 1850, asked Kennedy to place his right hand on it, and then asked him to repeat the Presidential Oath promising to preserve, protect, and defend the Constitution of the United States.

"Congratulations, Mr. President!" Warren said as a cheeky Kennedy finished his oath and extended his hand to the Chief Justice.

But underneath it all, as King and his team sat there watching the television, there was still a lingering question they were hoping Kennedy would resolve in his forthcoming address: would JFK actually defend the Constitution as he promised? For Negro Americans? After all, every president since the Civil War of the 1860s had promised—and failed—to do so in their time in office. So would JFK be like all of them, Democrats and Republicans alike? Or would he, as King hoped, usher in a new era through his words that had been a hundred years in the making? An era of truth? An era of justice? An era of genuine equality between blacks and whites?

Kennedy began speaking, showcasing his majestic oratorical abilities that were second in America only to King's, well-honed through nightly debating matches and rhetorical battles of wit his Father strictly enforced between his sons at the dinner table growing up, an informal tradition the rich and powerful use to groom their children to rule, a verbal investment in preserving and extending the crown of the prep-school elite: their right to exist at the top of the aristocracy, mercilessly fought for and mercilessly defended, by shaping their ability to communicate, and think, in the most eloquent and sophisticated of ways.

"Let every nation know," JFK said, power thundering out of his voice, "that we shall pay any price, bear any burden, and meet any hardship to assure the survival of success and liberty!"

So far, so good, King thought.

"This much we pledge and more," JFK said. "United there is little we cannot do!"

Good too, King thought.

"And so, my fellow Americans: ask not what your country can do for you, ask what you can do for your country!" JFK said as he ended his dazzling 14 minute speech to rapturous applause. People in the audience, who were moved to both tears and excitement, began hugging and high-fiving each other; the news media declared the speech to be the greatest inaugural address of all time; and JFK, who had hoped to win over skeptical Americans who didn't vote for him, had done his job.

But in the midst of all of JFK's elocution and the surrounding palpable excitement, King only had one thought sitting there watching the speech through the RCA television screen: *what the hell was that?* The new President had said absolutely nothing about Negroes. Or civil rights. Or what he was planning to do about the Second Emancipation Proclamation.

"Kennedy said in our meeting that he would support us," Andrew Young said angrily. "Instead he acted like we don't even exist."

JFK, like all of his predecessors before him, had simply ignored the biggest domestic issue of all time, race relations, because he could—

and because Bobby told him to. And he simply ignored the hopes of King, and other black people, who were looking for a crumb of acknowledgement that their existence in the country mattered too, that their rights meant something to somebody somewhere. But, like many times before, King and his team realized that their hope had again been deferred by a President. But there was a difference between this time and the times before, they decided. And the difference was this: that, unlike the past, they would not wait until a white President, no matter how popular, made civil rights a central issue in America; instead they would make civil rights *the* central issue.

"If they want to play checkers," King said ruefully as he anticipated a nonstop onslaught of marches, campaigns, and innovative activities he now knew he needed to launch to hold the South, and the Kennedys, accountable to blacks, "then we'll simply play chess."

EIGHTEEN

As JFK settled into his first 100 days of office, Bobby was beginning to practice law for the first time in his career: as the 34 year-old "kid" Attorney General of the United States.

In his role as the nation's top lawyer, he oversaw all of America's legal affairs, a department of 100,000 lawyers, and the FBI, J. Edgar Hoover's domain.

"How are you Mr. Hoover?" Bobby asked, walking bristly past the pudgy FBI Director, his neighbor in the Justice Department Building, located a few minutes from the White House at 1425 New York Avenue.

"I feel like it's practically Christmas," Hoover said smirking, holding a thick manilla envelope in his hand.

"Good for you," Bobby said, making a sharp left turn and walking into his office. He sat at his desk which featured an oversized Snoopy portrait hanging above it and began playing with his cuddly office pal: Freckles, his black and white English Springer Spaniel who accompanied him to work everyday.

"Sir," Bobby's top aide on civil rights, Burke Marshall, said as he entered the room, "Dr. King has called yet again to request a meeting with the President."

"Tell him he's all tied up," Bobby said, the usual refrain he uttered. Since the inauguration, King had called him at least 10 times wanting to discuss civil rights with JFK to which Bobby always responded with a big fat no, not only because he wanted to protect his brother but also because he personally didn't like King. But he had another reason to say no too: he didn't want to get an ear full from the Reverend about why JFK had appointed segregationist judge Harold Cox to a federal judgeship in Mississippi as part of Bobby's ruthless plan to win the Presidency.

But while he was playing Dixiecrat politics and keeping King away from his brother, and therefore civil rights, out of the spotlight, Bobby was also slowly working behind the scenes to desegregate the U.S. Department of Justice and the broader federal government. He recommended JFK appoint 47 blacks to various roles in the Administration, which he did, and he dispatched several federal attorneys through his newly created Civil Rights Division across the South to begin litigating segregation cases against Jim Crow.

"Sir, I understand that you don't want to speak with King," Burke said with urgency, "but I really think you should this time."

"Why's that?" Bobby said, nonchalant.

"It seems that King and his students are threatening the Administration to see if we will enforce the recent rulings on bus desegregation," Burke said.

"You mean *Boynton v. Virginia?*" Bobby questioned, referring to the Supreme Court case that on paper desegregated interstate bus terminals but in reality didn't change the status quo one bit.

"Yes," Burke responded.

Oh no, Bobby thought. This is exactly what they didn't need: King interfering in the legal progress his brother was making on civil rights, even if that progress was minimal and in name only.

"What exactly are they planning?" Bobby asked as he pushed his light brown hair out of his face.

"Freedom rides," Burke said.

"Freedom what?"

"They're planning on riding interstate buses straight into the heart of Klan territory," Burke said. "And daring segregationists to kill them—unless you and The President protect them."

NINETEEN

J. Edgar Hoovver slithered into his office and closed the door. Then the drapes.

He pushed aside his empty bowl of cream of chicken soup and began looking into the manilla folder in his hand.

"My, my, my," Hoover said as he sorted through compromising image after compromising image. "Just what I was hoping for."

Hoover, who claimed that he was a lifelong virgin despite rumors to the contrary and who lived alone with his mom until he was nearly 50 years old, had a penchant for looking at sexual images—the more forbidden the better. As FBI Director, he had, as a part of his Confidential Files, gathered up some real doozies: white Congressmen's wives who loved to sleep with well-endowed black men; John Lennon's drug-fueled orgies with groupies from coast to coast; and what now appeared to be the biggest doozy of them all: a President, recently politically damaged from a Bay of Pigs military fiasco in Cuba, who was having an affair with a woman who appeared to be also having an affair with a mob boss.

A knock on Hoover's door disrupted his focus.

"What do you want?" Hoover barked, his fingers immediately halting from the slow rubbing they were doing up and down the images he was holding. "I'm busy."

"Sir," his aide Clyde Tolson said, "the Attorney General needs to speak with you about a developing situation in the South."

"Oh Christ," Hoover said. "I'll be right there."

Hoover put his files back in the manilla envelope and into his personal belongings. He scurried into Bobby's office, who looked agitated, and asked him what was going on.

"Mr. Hoover, I need your advice," Bobby said, nearly panicked.

"Anything, sir," Hoover responded. "I'm here for you."

"I need to know how to handle a potential crisis with Dr. King," Bobby said.

TWENTY

"It's too dangerous for you to go," the Student Nonviolent Coordinating Committee's Diane Nash said to her fellow activist, Carol Davis, a UC Berkeley student on leave who dabbled in both the budding and countercultural Free Speech and Feminism Movements, the latter of which was gaining steam with the most explosive development in science of the day: the introduction of the FDA approved oral contraceptive for women, "Enovid-10," simply known as "the pill," to regulate birth control for the first time in history.

"Why can't I go?" Carol asked stubbornly.

"Because you're a white sistah," Nash said with resignation, the beauty of her face wounded with concern.

"That doesn't matter," Carol responded. "I'm with you until the end."

"Carol, you know what they do to people like you—"

"Yes, I do," Carol interrupted, "but I don't care."

"Ok ladies," Martin Luther King's protest mastermind James Lawson said, walking into the middle of their conversation. "We've got to make a decision."

As Nash and Carol continued to talk, several civil rights groups conferred together too, forming a circle around them in their Nashville warehouse. There were members present from the Student Nonviolent Coordinating Committee, Dr. King's Southern Christian Leadership Conference, and the Congress of Racial Equality (CORE), who were trying to decide on which "Freedom Riders" they would send into the devil's den: the Jim Crow South, the old Confederacy retrofitted with a new name but clinging to the same shame.

"I'm going," Carol said. "And I want other white people to go with me."

"Carol," Stokley Carmichael said, "are you crazy?"

"No," Carol replied, "we need to integrate our rides."

"Don't you realize the one thing Jim Crow hates worse than Negroes?" Stokley asked rhetorically as he shook his head, his eyes a gallery of indignation, "is White people who support Negroes."

"I'm aware," Carol said, squaring the shoulders on her slender five foot two, hundred and five pound frame, a brittle body that belied the lioness that she was. "But if they want to get to you they're going to have to go through me."

Stokley snickered and continued to shake his head, in mocking disbelief.

"We need to let her come, Stokley," John Lewis said gently, looking at Carmichael who was standing next to Jerome "Big Duck" Smith. "Blacks and whites need to stand together in solidarity on this one."

"Alright," Carmichael said, upset that he was overruled. "But it's not her fight."

Carol got up and stood directly in front of Carmichael, put her brown hair into a ponytail, and then said defiantly, her pupils burning with passion, "it may not be my fight, but it is my ride. Let's go

TWENTY ONE

The inaugural group of Freedom Riders packed their bags in the dead of night. There were seven black Riders, and six white ones, and they walked to the Greyhound Bus Station in Washington, D.C., at 1100 New York Avenue, NW, just blocks from the White House, where they had traveled to from Nashville the night before.

John Lewis conspicuously gathered the Riders in the departure terminal, grabbing Diane Nash's hand on his left and Carol Davis's hand on his right. He asked the others to join hands as well.

"Let's pray," he said, the minister in him knowing that without divine protection their trip would be doomed to irreversible, existential failure, "and ask for God's protection."

As the group embraced each other and invoked the Almighty, a frumpled looking white bus driver with porkchop sideburns studied them closely. He looked confused, even suspicious, not knowing why an interracial group would be praying together. *Didn't they know*, he thought, *that the Lord only answers the prayers of white people and not those of black monkeys?*

Lewis, Nash, Davis and the others, including Stokley Carmichael and Jerome "Big Duck" Smith, boarded the bus together while the white bus driver seethed with resentment. But he didn't say anything to them, or say anything out loud. He, like the majority of other prejudiced Southern whites of his day, preferred a silent type of hatred, one that could be felt but not seen. He wasn't, he thought, as brave as the minority of Jim Crow whites, people like the Klan, people like the Dixiecrats, who were openly hostile to the "inferiors. "

As the Freedom Riders got situated and arranged their nondescript luggage in the overhead compartments, Stokley Carmichael sat down next to John Lewis, looking frustrated, his mind handcuffed with anger over growing strategic differences he was having with the Civil Rights Movement.

"I don't understand why Dr. King isn't coming with us," Stokley said to John Lewis, "but she is," his glare aimed straight at Carol Davis who was sitting toward the front, her hair still in a ponytail.

"Brotha, give it a rest," Lewis replied, taking out a bottle of water he had purchased from a local liquor store with the $1 minimum wage job he had saved up some money with. "She's one of us. And as for Dr. King, you know we can't risk his safety for this mission—"

"But he can risk ours?" Stokley said, glancing at the $0.15 cent McDonald's hamburger Lewis had also purchased for himself, resting in the liquor store bag along with a $0.05 cent candy bar he was planning on eating later that night.

"He risks his safety every day," Lewis rebuffed him. "Besides, he's working the Kennedy angle to make them step up and protect our ride."

"John, the politicians don't want to enforce desegregation," Stokley said flatly, "even when we win court battles that should force them to."

"The police don't want to enforce it neither," Jerome "Big Duck" Smith echoed, butting in from eavesdropping one seat over, nothing escaping his attention.

"So what makes us think Dr. King can actually get the Kennedys to do the right thing this time?" Stokley asked.

"Faith," Lewis responded with sincerity. "Just faith."

"That doesn't sound reassuring," Stokley shot back reasonably, not being as rooted in or defined by the black church as most of the Negro Freedom Riders were, or as the vast majority of the Civil Rights Movement was, it being a religious movement that happened to take on civic dimensions and not a civic movement that happened to embrace religion.

"It's all we got," Lewis said while Stokley turned to look out of the window as the bus engine began revving up.

The Greyhound pulled out of the terminal, with the ultimate destination of the Big Easy, New Orleans. It was scheduled to stop in several states along the way as well, including South Carolina and Alabama to meet up with King, in a carefully designed campaign meant to provoke the most vile reactions of the dumbest, and most powerful, of Jim Crow forces to see if the Kennedys would do the right thing on civil rights enforcement.

A few hundred miles in, the Freedom Riders began singing Negro spirituals, their usual custom—and the custom of every civil rights gathering since the beginning of the movement. They sang, as a chorus, "This Little Light of Mine," "We Are Soldiers in the Army," and, now, "We Shall Overcome."

"Hit it 'Big Duck'," Diane Nash said to Jerome Smith.

"I got you, sistah," Smith responded, starting a hum to which all the Riders began singing.

"We shall overcome one day," they sang in unison, with smiles sprinkled like musical notes all over their faces. "Oh yes we will!"

"We are not afraid today," they continued, arms in the air, feeling as entertaining as they looked. "Oh no we aren't!"

"And we shall live in peace today," they finished as they pointed their fingers at each other. "Oh yes we shall!"

As the singing faded away, the bus made good time, traveling through Virginia and North Carolina without any issues. Then it came to Rock Hill, South Carolina, where they pulled up to the local, sketchy looking Greyhound Bus Terminal. John Lewis spotted a "Whites Only" bathroom sign and said, "I'm going in."

Nash grabbed his arm and said, "be careful, John," while he nodded in agreement and replied, "I will."

The Freedom Riders watched Lewis exit the bus, before looking back at them. He gave them a thumbs up followed by a wide smile that was the crown of his contentment. He began walking toward the bathroom as several local whites stared coldly at him, offended by his presence, the narrative they had already developed about him in their minds befuddled with ignorance, imprisoned by acrimony, underwritten by a Southern fascist ideology as American as apple pie.

Lewis entered the "Whites Only" restroom, opened a stall door, and sat down, relieving himself of the food and drink he had consumed just a bit before. As he finished up and began flushing, a white male entered, quietly making the sound of a monkey.

Two more white males entered, who repeated the sound of the first white male.

Then another 15 males entered, one by one, growing in an "oo oo aa aa" chant louder and louder.

The door locked from the inside of the restroom, and the piercing sounds disappeared into silence.

"Wrong choice ni*ger," one of the white males said who ripped Lewis's stall door wide open.

TWENTY TWO

"Mr. Attorney General," J. Edgar Hoover anxiously implored, "they're trying to undermine your brother's Administration," as he placed a copy of a Washington newspaper on Bobby's desk. Bobby picked up the paper and read the headline, "Freedom Riders Injured in South Carolina as Locals Defend Themselves."

"Are the Riders okay?" Bobby asked with a look of concern as he started to read through the article.

"Oh, just some scratches. They'll be fine," Hoover said before his stubby right index finger started to point to a paragraph in the paper he had previously underlined. "The important thing is this."

Bobby looked at the section Hoover's pudgy finger was pointing to and read out loud, "it appears that Freedom Riders are recklessly trying to bait JFK into a race war by agitating law-abiding whites into physical confrontation."

"You see," Hoover said obnoxiously, "they're up to no good, just as I informed you a few days ago."

"Did the Riders do anything to provoke the attack?" Bobby asked, brushing his hair out of his eye.

"Presumably," Hoover said.

"Did they engage in any physical violence?" Bobby asked.

"That information remains to be seen sir, but presumably," Hoover also said, trying to substitute his racist opinion for actual facts, skilled in the art of turning severely warped misinformation into official government narratives, "alternative facts" as he liked to call them. "That doesn't make sense," Bobby said, standing to his feet and rolling up his sleeves. "They are Dr. King's students and they believe in peaceful nonviolence."

"Can I be frank, sir?" Hoover asked, his body language contorted to look like a concerned Boy Scout, his facial expression painted with deception disguised as serious-minded patriotism.

"Yes," Bobby said emphatically, as he admired Hoover and desired his insight; Hoover was, after all, one of the most popular and respected public figures in America who had such a positive reputation that it was bordering on legendary, like the great Sir Winston Churchill of the United Kingdom, names synonymous with courage, integrity, and fidelity.

"Can you really trust Martin Luther King?" Hoover asked rhetorically, hoping to both fish for his true thoughts about the civil rights leader as well as plant doubts about him simultaneously. "It seems that he and his people are just trying to instigate trouble."

"They are stirring the pot," Bobby said, avoiding a direct answer as he kept his true thoughts about King hidden, at least for now, even from Hoover, not wanting to potentially compromise his brother in any way.

"Exactly," Hoover replied. "And it seems they are continuing their so-called Freedom Rides into Alabama, where they will meet up with Dr. King who will be preaching."

"Really?" Bobby said.

"Yes," Hoover said, crossing his fat arms across his corpulent body. "And who knows what kind of trouble they'll try to cause down there once they link up."

"It could be bad news for the President," Bobby said before holding his chin in his hand, thoughts skipping through his mind. "The seeds of a race war."

"Well sir, I think you really only have two choices," Hoover said nonchalantly.

"What are they?" Bobby asked.

"You could call King to tell him to call off the Freedom Rides and back off of his quest for civil rights," Hoover responded, knowing Bobby would instantly reject this idea.

"I don't think he'll back down, at least on civil rights," Bobby said. "He's not a reasonable man."

"Or you could," Hoover said, hoping to get Bobby to buy into his real idea, one he had concocted after hearing about those Jim Crow bastards giving an ass whooping, "send federal troops to escort the Riders as they journey into Alabama."

"What will that accomplish?" Bobby asked, confused.

"If you send U.S. Marshals to support them on your physical jurisdiction, federal interstate highways," Hoover said, "they will feel like you are supporting them, causing them to ease off a bit from their instigation."

"But won't that agitate Southerners?" Bobby asked, again brushing his light brown hair out of his face.

"Not if the Marshalls only accompany them on federal land and then pull back as soon as the Riders get into the city limits, which is not your jurisdiction," Hoover said. "Southerners will feel like you are respecting their sovereignty, their states rights."

"So you're recommending that we split the difference?" Bobby questioned. "The Riders will feel like they're getting acknowledged by the Administration and tacitly supported and Segregationists will feel like we're not treading on their turf?"

"Precisely," Hoover said, his lips pursing upward in his trademark Machiavellian grin. "Everybody will feel like a winner."

Bobby then thought for a minute, though not deeply, again brushing his hair out of his face. He then said, "I think that will work. Maybe it will help calm things down and keep this issue out of the headlines."

"You're right, sir. Shall I notify my contacts about your plan of action?" Hoover said, in a bait-and-switch, giving credit to Bobby for his own insidious ideas.

"Absolutely."

Hoover then thanked the Attorney General, stepped outside of his office, and scurried back to his own office like a blobfish, where he closed and locked the door behind him. He pulled out his little black book and looked up the name and number of one of his top deputies in the Iron White Wall: Birmingham Police Commissioner, Bull Conner. He dialed his number.

"Bull speaking," Conner said in his twang country accent as he swiftly answered his phone, putting away what he was looking at: the KKK's official alternative calendar, known as the "Kalender," filled with alternative months like "Desperate," "Dreadful," and "Desolate," and alternative years like "Appalling," "Sorrowful," and "Frightful," a goal-system meticulously mapped out to optimize continual terror against black people.

"It's J. Edgar," Hoover said, lowering his voice slightly, ensuring nobody could hear him. "I have important information."

"What's that, boss?" Conner asked using the language of deference to inflate the nation's top cop's ego who loved to be told how in charge he was.

"The Kennedys will be deploying U.S. marshals to accompany the Freedom Riders in your part of Alabama," Hoover said.

"I knew it. Such nig*er lovers," Conner responded in disgust. "Bobby came here for a speech during the election but I knew he was just blowing hot air."

"But he's going to have the Marshalls abandon the Riders once they reach the city limits," Hoover said.

"What? Really?" Conner asked, confused.

"He doesn't exactly see it that way," Hoover responded, "but that's what he's going to do."

"What'll that accomplish?" Conner wondered, not knowing where Hoover was going with this.

"As soon as the Marshals abandon the Riders when they pull into Alabama," Hoover said, "the Klan will have 15 minutes to take care of business before your boys in blue show up with no suspects at the crime scene."

"Oh," Conner said, his slow brain starting to realize the brilliant implications of Hoover's plan. "I gotcha."

"Now just tip off the Imperial Wizard," Hoover finished, "so they can kill those bastards!"

TWENTY THREE

The Freedom Riders forged ahead, their sights set on Alabama and meeting up with Martin Luther King, who was planning on speaking about the significance of their Ride and next steps for the Civil Rights Movement. Of course, they were still shaken by the brutal thumping John Lewis took a few days earlier—who wouldn't be?—but they realized the danger they were signing up for, the hell they had previously been trained to confront head on. This was the real America in 1961, they thought, and things had once again gotten real. America might be the land of dreams and opportunities and the pursuit of happiness for white Americans, they thought, but, for them—and for Negroes everywhere—it was a land of fists and beatings and various sorts of ass whoopings they had to struggle to overcome.

"How's he doing?" Jerome "Big Duck" Smith asked, watching Carol Davis console John Lewis, whose head and hands were wrapped in bloody medical bandages, courtesy of one of the small but useful medical supplies they had been sent out with.

"I think he'll live," Carol responded, squeezing Lewis's hand lightly. "He just needs rest."

"Are we sure we want to continue this?" Stokley Carmichael questioned, trying to test the resolve of the group. "If they hurt any more of us I'm not sure I won't hurt them back."

"Stokley," John Lewis said, his beaten frame struggling to sit up. "We're better than them. Remember? We don't return insult for insult, blow for blow. What James Lawson said."

Stokley's face registered resignation, not wanting to drain his friend of energy or distract the Riders by questioning Lawson's or Dr. King's nonviolent methods in this particular moment.

Diane Nash got up from her seat in the front and walked to the back of the bus. She put her hand on Carol's shoulders and addressed the group. "We're only a few minutes out of Anniston," she said, looking out of the rear window, "and so we won't have their escort any longer."

Several of the Riders turned around to watch the small military escort Bobby had dispatched for them that trailed their bus, a couple of vehicles in all. "We don't need them anyways," Stokely shot back, more distrustful of the government when it claimed to be on his side than when it didn't.

As the Greyhound approached the city lines of Anniston, Alabama, a territory under Police Commissioner Bull Conner's control, the U.S. Marshals pulled back and disappeared into the nondescript highways as the bus exited the I-431 off-ramp.

The bus, which was going about 30 miles per hour, passed church after church, taxying its way through the city of 20,000. The beautifully designed churches, with Gothic Revival architecture that soared into the lonely country skies, seemed to be packed to the full, with white male parishioners wearing their Sunday best beginning to leave the pews in droves.

"I want to use the pay phone first when we arrive," Big Duck said, his eyes examining the parishioners. "It's Mother's Day and I want to tell my mama how much I love her."

"I deserve to use it first," Lewis joked, "in light of recent events."

"All right, all right," Big Duck responded, the edges of his mouth cracking a smile, the pain in Lewis's body and the pain in Big Duck's own heart so grand that all you could do is laugh about it to prevent them from going bat sh*t crazy.

The bus approached the Greyhound station and pulled into the terminal at 901 Noble Street, where several of the male church parishioners seemed to be heading, cheerfully reciting the message they heard in the pulpit about "Loving One's Enemies." One of the parishioners spotted Carol, smiled, and bowed his head in a courtly gentleman gesture. Carol smiled back. As the bus parked and turned off its engine, a loud noise suddenly let out like a whoosh on its left side.

"What was that?" Carol asked, before looking out of the window, trying to decipher what was going on.

Another loud whoosh let out, this time on the bus's right side.

"What the hell?" Stokley questioned, quickly jumping out of his seat as the whooshing continued, precariously tipping the bus side to side.

As Stokley looked out of the windows, he saw that its tires were being slashed by the parishioners, regular church going members who also happened to be members of Alabama's most violent KKK chapter: Eastview Klavern 13. They began to hold the door to the Greyhound closed.

The parishioners then took out crowbars, metal clubs, and chains from the trunk of a 1956 Cadillac Eldorado that had just pulled up. They began breaking the bus's windows indiscriminately.

"Look at the nig*ers," one of the sweaty parishioners said, pounding harshly on the side of the bus with a crowbar. "So scared!"

"Not as scared as the nig*er lovers!" another parishioner yelled who stared wildly at Carol. "Damn sell out!"

The Freedom Riders all moved quickly to the center of the bus to avoid the large front, back, and smaller side windows in case a brick or object was thrown in. "Duck!" Stokely said anxiously to the group, "and they won't be able to see or hit us!"

The parishioners, now suddenly numbering in the hundreds, like cockroaches multiplying in an orgy of hatred, began shaking the bus on both sides. One said, "come out, come out, wherever you are!"

"Remain quiet," Stokley whispered to his Riders. "They'll leave eventually if we don't panic—"

A loud explosion then rocked the Greyhound, violently ripping the bottom off the bus's frame, which was perilously supported by deflated tires. It erupted in fire and collapsed to the ground. Smoke began infiltrating the vehicle rapidly from the bomb that was designed to blow it up.

"Oh my God!" Diane Nash screamed, the thick fumes suffocating the inside of the Greyhound like a Nazi gas chamber. "We need to get out of here!"

The Riders, who were wheezing desperately and nearly blinded by the smoke, all made their way to the front exit of the bus and tried to push their way out of the door. But the parishioners were still holding the door shut, sealing it with an army of men hoping to fill as many body bags as they could.

"We hope you die, nig*ers!" said one of the parishioners, Thomas Blanton, who could only hear anguish and torment from the inside, causing him to tingle with the feeling of power, causing him to see his own seductive destiny as a prophet of death.

But the Riders continued to struggle, to fight, to use their collective physical and moral strength to power through. They made a second attempt to push their way out but, before they could, a second explosion battered the bus, sending shrapnel flying everywhere, like bombs dropping on a battlefield. The fire had hit a gas leak.

The parishioners panicked and decided to take cover, running as far away from the outside bus door as they could to try to stay out harm's way—and to try to keep their suits and ties from not getting dirty because, in their minds, white men were to always be presentable on the "Lord's Day."

"Let's go!" Nash said, seeing a small window of opportunity to leave the Greyhound before everyone inside suffocated to death.

The Riders scrambled outside, creating a make-shift buffer zone around John Lewis who was hobbling in the middle. They tried to run to their right and froze—they saw a group of 50 parishioners. They then tried to run to their left—where they saw an even bigger group.

"Take that!" said another parishioner, Herman Cash, as he snuck up behind Stokley and smacked him in the back with a metal pipe, knocking him unconscious upon impact, an indentation of hate tattooed on his black skull.

"Oh no!" Carol blurted out, the life in her eyes convulsing. She ran over to Stokley, jumping on top of him to try to shield his body from further beating, before being noticed by the original gentlemanly parishioner who smiled at her.

"Traitor," Blanton said, taking his metal pipe and knocking her unconscious too, blood gushing from her broken nose and dislocated jaw.

Complete chaos and carnage ensued, with the Riders being assaulted by hit after bloody hit. Eyes were gouged; teeth were knocked out; bones were broken; faces and arms were lacerated; and skulls were fractured. But the worst was to come.

"Take out the nooses," Cash said with an eerie grin on his face, "so we can hang these sons of b*tches."

Nooses were taken out of the trunk of the nearby Cadillac. But before they could be tied together in knots and placed around the Riders knecks, multiple gunshots were fired from a highway patrol officer.

"Where did he come from?" one of the parishioners asked, confused. "I thought the cops weren't supposed to be here yet?"

Red and blue sirens began approaching the scene as the parishioners got in a couple of final blows before dispersing like a mob of vermin.

Several ambulances arrived and rushed the Riders to Anniston Memorial Hospital, where they were dropped off in the emergency room. A white doctor came out to survey the damage: 13 Freedom Riders, all beaten to within an inch of their lives, who needed immediate life-saving interventions.

The doctor looked at his staff and said, "you know our policy," as the staff brought out only 6 gurneys. They put Carol on one and the other 5 white Freedom Riders on the others. Then they wheeled them back for emergency medical treatment.

"Sir," Jerome "Big Duck" Smith said, grabbing his rib cage while wincing, "are you going to bring out more gurneys to treat the rest of us?"

The doctor looked at Big Duck and said, without hesitation, "we don't treat coons here," before he turned his back on him and walked into the ER.

TWENTY FOUR

"Unacceptable!" Martin Luther King shouted as he stood in his friend Ralph Abernathy's red brick-and-mortar First Baptist Alabama church office. "Just unacceptable!"

King had just gotten word about what had happened to the Freedom Riders he was supposed to meet up with—and the medical attention the Negro Riders were refused.

"Does anyone in the South have a conscience?" King asked rhetorically, intense indignation engrossing his face. "They claim they are for law and order, they claim they are good Christians, but have they no decency!?"

Ralph Abernathy sighed.

"None at all?!" King asked, pounding the top of the dark oak desk he was standing near with fury, letting the privately guarded anger he usually concealed to the public into full view of his best friend. "Do not even the doctors who have sworn the Hippocratic Oath have any compassion for their fellow human beings?"

"You know what the scripture says, Martin," Abernathy said, starting to put on his tailored black suit jacket. "That man's heart is desperately wicked, even if he is a doctor or a churchgoer or supposedly upstanding citizen."

"Yes, Ralph," King responded, "it is. But do you want to know the worst part of it?"

"What's that, Martin?" Abernathy asked, his anger increasingly now overwhelmed by his disappointment.

"Man has convinced himself that he is good," King said, "even when he deliberately and intentionally hates his brother with his thoughts, with his words, with his fists, and with every other evil and cowardly action he has convinced himself is good."

"Hypocrisy is man's great struggle," Abernathy replied, "because he is so unaware that he even struggles with it in the first place. Look at the founders. All hypocritical slave-owners who congratulated themselves on preaching all-men-are-created-equal even while they personally kept our people shackled in chains."

"And do you know who I'm concerned about being the biggest hypocrite of them all right now," King said, his voice a temple of outrage.

"Who, Martin?"

"Bobby Kennedy!"

"What?" Abernathy asked, confused. "I don't understand."

"Bobby only sent a small military escort with the Riders to score political points," Kind intoned. "Civil rights are not about justice to him, they're not about righting wrongs to him."

"But Bobby bailed you out of jail," Abernathy responded. "And that was the right thing to do."

King didn't acknowledge the statement.

"He even had his brother appoint hundreds of blacks to the Administration," Abernathy continued. "And that was the right thing to do too."

"It was the self-serving thing," King said, with atypical cynicism and distrust building across his uneven countenance.

"Look, I understand where you're coming from Martin," Abernathy said, placing his right and left hands on his hips. "But can we really expect Bobby to be a martyr when all he's promised us is to be an ally?"

King's righteous indignation waned a bit as he absorbed his friend's statement. He thought briefly, gathered himself, and then looked up, his now bloodshot eyes pulsating redder and redder. "In the great cause of civil rights," he said in a slow and steady draw, each word spoken carefully through his large lips, "if a man is not willing to be a martyr then he was never really willing to be an ally in the first place. And never forget that

TWENTY FIVE

——

"Bobby!" screamed Joe Kennedy Senior, "we need to talk! Now!"

"Yes sir," Bobby said from the upstairs of his Hickory Hill estate, now the unofficial White House meeting headquarters where he and JFK spent most of their evenings, thinking and talking things through, to escape the translucent fishbowl known as 1600 Pennsylvania Avenue where privacy was in short supply, and outspoken political candidness in even shorter supply.

"And bring the President!" Joe Senior snapped from the bottom of the immaculate staircase.

Bobby looked over to JFK, whose face was worn with worry and the beginnings of rapid aging that only the presidency can bring on.

"Coming right down," Bobby said, brushing his hair out of his face, absorbing the emotional sign of his big brother who was coming with him.

The President and Attorney General, jackets off and ties loosened, made their way down after a minute or two from the second floor and into the dimly-lit dining room to meet their Father, who was waiting stoically. They sat down on the right and left hand side of the table, respectively, as their Father was sitting squarely at the head.

"Your Administration is turning out to be a f*cking disaster," Joe Senior barked as he held a glass of liquor in his right hand that a servant had just poured.

"First, you listen to those bastards at the CIA and try to assassinate Fidel Castro and invade the Bay of Pigs Cuba," Joe said, "and you lose multiple bomber planes and soldiers in the process."

Bobby and JFK sat silent, feeling like little boys being reprimanded.

"And you allow the United States to be humiliated by those Commies as a result," Joe Senior continued, shaking his head in disgust.

"Father," Bobby interjected, desperate to defend himself, his brother, and the Kennedy White House from what everyone in Washington, D.C. was calling one of the biggest fiasco's in foreign policy history, "the plan was drawn up in Eisenhower's Administration."

But Joe Kennedy Sr., unaffected by Bobby's deflection, continued on his tirade, changing the subject to the other object of his scorn. "And then you send U.S. Marshals to accompany a group of interracial Freedom Riders in the South?"

"That was the recommendation of Mr. Hoov—" Bobby said before being interrupted.

"I don't care whose recommendation it was!" Joe Sr. shouted. "Now the press is reporting that 'Reverse Freedom Riders' are being sent throughout the U.S. to further humiliate you and the name that I built!"

Of course, Joe Sr. was referring to the breaking news he had heard on CBS's *Walter Cronkite Tonight* that hundreds of single-black moms from Little Rock, Arkansas were being sent on "Reverse Freedom Rides." Apparently somebody, undoubtedly members of the Iron White Wall mocking the real Freedom Riders, provided these poor black women with free one-way bus tickets under the false promise of no-cost housing and high-paying jobs where none existed. And these moms were showing up in LA, Chicago, and even the Kennedy's summer vacation spot, Hyannis Port, Main, deceived that they were being given a new shot at life.

"Do you want to lose the South?" Joe snapped as his face started to boil like a New England lobster, the veins in his neck about to burst at the seams. "Do you!?"

"Father," JFK said, trying to calm the old man down, "we're doing everything we can to fix the situation."

"You two look like a couple of amateurs," Joe Sr. said, to which Bobby and JFK sighed. "You need to keep civil rights and whatever the f*ck all of these Freedom Rides and Reverse Rides are out of headlines."

"Father—"

"And you need to distance yourself from Martin Luther King!"

"I've only had minimal contact with him," Bobby replied. "I haven't even forwarded his calls to Jack."

But upon hearing this, JFK looked confused. "What do you mean, Bobby?" he asked.

"Well," Bobby said, looking like a guilty little brother caught with his hand in the cookie jar, "King has called a few times requesting to speak to you."

"And why haven't you told me?" JFK cross-examined him, slightly upset.

"Because he's not worth your time, Jack. The overwhelming majority of whites disapprove of him and even of these Freedom Rides," Bobby defended himself.

"But what does he want to talk to me about?" JFK said, ignoring the polling data to which his brother was referring that he himself was all too familiar with.

"Presumably, his Second Emancipation Proclamation you said you'd consider supporting during the campaign," Bobby responded, brushing his hair out of his face again.

"Bobby," JFK said, remembering his election promise for the first time in months, "I can handle talking with him about this. Remember, I'm the President and this is my job."

"But Jack, even the appearance of having a talk with him about this, especially with the Freedom Rides and Reverse Freedom Rides in the spotlight, could be enough to cost you not only the South, but your presidency."

"And ignite a second civil war," Joe Sr. said, pounding his fist so hard on the table that it shook the liquor in his glass, causing some of it to spill over onto the surface.

Upon hearing this, the peace-maker JFK simply said, "there's got to be some way to keep everyone happy without us losing everything."

But Joe. Kennedy Sr. and Bobby were both silent, their superstar intellects both in agreement that silence would be the best medicine to get the President to wake up and see the political danger this put him in. "Right?" JFK asked, fishing for affirmation from the two voices he trusted the most, wanting them to tell him they could figure a way out of this mess they were in. "Right?"

TWENTY SIX

The Freedom Riders, all somehow alive but looking like death crossed-over, collectively hobbled onto a new Greyhound bus one by one. They vowed, against the wishes and better judgment of their parents, to continue their ride through Klan territory despite their black and blue faces, bandaged body parts, and severe lacerations they suffered the day before, one of the ghastliest public attacks on black people the KKK had gotten away with with complete and utter impunity.

"Hey Carol," Diane Nash said as the Greyhound Bus took off and drove through the highways of Alabama, "I just wanted to say that I was really inspired by how you threw your body in front of Stokely's yesterday to shield him."

"It's nothing," Carol responded, trying to downplay what seemed like an historic first in America, especially to these Southern Negroes: a white woman actually risking personal harm to herself trying to protect a black man.

"No, really, it is," Nash reiterated. "You don't have to be here with us and risk your life. And your reputation. Yet you are."

"It's the right thing to do," Carol said, staring painfully out of the window, "even if most of my people in the North and the South don't see it that way right now."

"I just wish there were more like you," Nash said regretfully, reaching for Carol's creamy white palm, a black and white sister endowed with hearts of gold, their souls somehow not tainted by the cynicism and hopelessness of their situation, or by the cynicism and hopelessness of where America was right now, blinded by its own drunken prejudices.

"One day," Carol said referring to a vision she had for her misguided white brethren, "many will be."

As Carol uttered those words, she drew a scornful and "oh please" look from Stokley, whose blood was bleeding through the bandage wrapped around his head, looking like a black Frankenstein whose patchwork of medical gauze was a physically damning indictment of unchecked White Supremacy.

Carol turned back to Nash and, in almost a whisper, said, "Do you think Stokley will ever believe that? Believe that one day white people as a group will stand up for racial justice?"

"I'm not even sure I will ever believe that Carol," Nash responded ruefully. "But I want to."

The bus continued its trek through Alabama until it finally arrived at Ralph Abernathy's First Baptist church, where Martin Luther King would be speaking to acknowledge the Freedom Riders efforts and announce the next steps of the Civil Rights Movement he was spearheading.

"I just can't wait to see Dr. King," John Lewis said eagerly with admiration filling his voice and animating his near-broken face as the Greyhound pulled to a dead stop.

"I just hope he knows what he's doing with all of this nonviolent stuff," Stokley responded starkly, grimacing and hobbling off of the bus with the others. "Because to me, we look pathetic."

As the group exited the bus and congregated in front of the beautifully ornate two story church, Abernathy and King opened the white front doors and made their way down the long steps, looking composed and dignified, like elder-statesmen imbued with divine wisdom even though they were both only in their early 30s, like angels appearing from On High to strengthen war-weary soldiers. But these leaders' stately composure, so authentic and well-rehearsed given their prominent leadership roles, soon gave way to tears after seeing just how badly injured the Freedom Riders were.

"Thank you," King said, wiping his watery eyes filled with tears that streamed down his cheeks and onto his mustache. He then began hugging several of them tightly and reiterated, once again, "thank you."

"You truly represent the best and most courageous of us," Abernathy interjected, the same emotions overcoming him, overwhelmed not simply by the sight of their pain, but by the stunning quality of their courage and grit and audacity. "And we promise you your efforts will not be in vain."

The Freedom Riders soaked in this moment of what, to them, felt like history in the making. They also soaked in the genuine appreciation they desperately needed. After all, not only did white America disapprove of what they were doing, according to polls, but many of their parents did too, not to mention their well-meaning friends who thought they were crazy, stupid, or just plain delusional for thinking they could personally make a difference. So hearing that they were valued, by these leaders no less, was a type of validation that made their souls feel good on the inside, dousing them in a sea of reignited hope.

"Come," Abernathy said, pointing toward the front door. "We've made you some food and have set up places for you to sleep tonight. Dr. King's speech will be in a few hours and we'd love for you to join us, if you're still up for it."

"Oh yes," Lewis spoke up on behalf of the group, "of course."

The church the Freedom Riders began entering, First Baptist, was one of the largest black megachurches in the South and was the headquarters of the successful Montgomery bus boycott desegregation campaign that Rosa Parks had ignited just a few years before. And the church was, for all intents and purposes, also like King's second home. After all, he had preached for 6 years down the road at Dexter Street Baptist Church when he lived in Alabama in the 1950s and had spent countless days here with two of the greatest people he felt he could ever know: Ralph and his wife, Juanita. To King, these two were like hot chocolate on a cold rainy day, heartwarming, necessary, and completely comforting, and he could not think of more welcoming people or a more welcoming environment for the Freedom Riders to be in after their vicious ordeal.

Before they knew it, the Riders were fed and had placed their personal belongings in their sleeping quarters—sleeping bags in the church basement—as the evening drew near. About 1,500 black congregants and seasoned civil rights workers filed into the pews to hear Dr. King's speech.

The choir gave a powerful Gospel performance before the sermon got underway. They sang, once again, "We Shall Overcome" alongside "Lift Every Voice and Sing" and "People Get Ready," the song King believed was the unofficial anthem of the Civil Rights Movement.

King approached the pulpit and started to give a barn burner of a speech, documenting what the Freedom Riders had just experienced. Their pain. Their suffering. Their courage. He talked about the Civil Rights Movement keeping its eye on the prize, staying committed to nonviolence and, as importantly, refusing to quit when times got tough.

But as the congregation was in uproarious applause, a brick suddenly burst through the church window, landing on the front pew, shattering an oval shaped stained-glass window featuring the disciples of Jesus.

"What the?" Stokley asked, looking toward the broken shards on the ground.

But before he could focus on that with any level of intelligent comprehension, another brick shattered a second window.

The Congregants, as was their custom, didn't make any sudden moves. They remained cautious, just to see if they were experiencing a prank or something more.

Then, as they quieted down, there was complete silence.

Then more silence.

And finally, a loud roar.

Three thousand angry white men had formed a brigade of hatred outside of the church, shouting curses, insults, and some of the most vile words ever uttered by human beings, trying to finish what they'd started the night before with the Freedom Riders.

"Evacuate to the basement!" screamed Ralph Abernathy, peering out of one of the broken windows at the phalanx of evil he was witnessing, men held hostage by the devilish Jim Crow they were willingly serving.

One white man, slim with a tucked in gray shirt, placed a home-made bomb underneath one of the nearby parked cars and blew it up, causing shrapnel to spread everywhere.

Another white man, balding and wearing brown khakis, took out a shotgun and started firing indiscriminately into the church.

"Oh my god!" King shouted, ducking quickly on the dais before exiting the pulpit and running to the basement where the others were rushing to.

"Everybody," Abernathy yelled upon seeing the chaos, "stay calm!"

Scores of black faces, full of innocence and fear, did just as they were told. They knew a moment like this could come at any time—and it did come. If Jim Crow was anything, they knew all too well, he was persistent—and he was here to finish the job he had failed to accomplish with the Freedom Riders and especially their spiritual leader, Martin Luther King, whom they knew was egging them on.

The Congregants spread as low to the ground as they could as Abernathy told them to remember their training. To remember their courage. To remember their God.

One grandmother, almost on cue, began resolutely paraphrasing parts of the 59th Psalm: "Deliver us from our enemies, O God; protect us from those who rise up against us. Deliver us from evildoers and save us from bloodthirsty men!"

Hundreds of White Supremacist terrorists continued to throw bricks into the building, hoisting bullets through its interior, and began to lay siege as they marched their way up the steps. They began chanting and pounding on the doors like uncivilized apes.

King's heart was palpitating violently in his chest. He needed a plan. *But what?* He had faced individual would-be assassins before but never a crowd this large intent on killing anything in their path.

"Ralph!" King screamed, grabbing his friend by his shoulders, "I need to use your office to call Bobby Kennedy!"

"Just dial zero and ask the operator for the police!" Abernathy replied.

"I can't!" King said. "I believe the local police may be in the pockets of the Klan. We need the National Guard here and Bobby can authorize that."

"But I thought you didn't trust Bobby?" Abernathy asked, profoundly confused by his friend's comments. "Why would he send the National Guard?"

"I just need your phone, now!" King said, dismissing his friend's questions.

"Ok, Martin," Abernathy acquiesced.

King hurried into Abernathy's office, haphazardly shut the door, and dialed Bobby's number that he knew by heart. Surprisingly, on the first ring, Bobby, who was back in his Justice Department Office, picked up, where he was sitting at his desk underneath his giant framed picture of Snoopy and petting his dog, Freckles.

"Look, Mr. Attorney General," King said nervously, "it's Martin Luther King and I need your help! There is a white mob trying to kill thousands of Negroes here in Alabama!"

"Wait, what?" Bobby asked incredulously.

"Bobby, a white mob is trying to kill us!"

"How do you know they're trying to kill you?" Bobby said flatly, trying to gather the facts, trying to understand if King was exaggerating, completely caught off guard.

"Because they've been setting off bombs and shooting into our Church," King said. "And they're about to storm inside! Thousands of them."

"Where are you?" Bobby asked. "At First Baptist Church in Montgomery."

"Oh, at a church?"

"Yes," said King.

"Well then, since you're at a church and since you're a preacher, why don't you just say a prayer and have God save you?" Bobby asked sarcastically, his ruthless disdain for the preacher manifesting in the most mocking way it possibly could.

"What!" King screamed into the other side of the phone. "This is not a joke! I need you to send the National Guard here right now! It's a matter of life and death!"

"Quite frankly Reverend, if I hadn't bailed you out of jail during the election, you'd be dead already," Bobby shot back defiantly.

"Bobby, stop this!" King shouted. "Help me!"

Upon hearing King's urgency, Bobby immediately regretted his comments. He knew they were low-blows and, despite his growing dislike of King who he felt was a political distraction and existential threat to his brother's Administration, he knew he needed to do better than this as the Attorney General, as a Catholic, and even as a man.

"Ok, fine," Bobby snorted. "But I need to speak to the Governor and have him declare martial law before I can do anything."

"Whatever you need to do," King intoned, "do it quickly!"

Bobby hung up the phone and dialed the staunch segregationist Governor John Patterson, who had introduced him at a Presidential luncheon for JFK just a few months before. Bobby knew the Governor despised King and the Civil Rights Movement and would love nothing more than to be rid of them.

"Governor," Bobby said in a serious and no-nonsense tone, "I need you to declare martial law so I can send in the National Guard to stop a mob from killing Martin Luther King and a church full of Negroes."

"Wait? What?" the Governor asked, playing dumb, pretending like he didn't know what was going on, a common tactic of the "we know nothing" Iron White Wall during times of chaos.

"Governor," Bobby repeated again flatly, "I need you to declare martial law right now."

"For Chrissakes, Bobby," the Governor said, agitatingly, "for one church? That is too big of an ask. You or anybody should know that. I'm only one guy here."

"Listen, Governor," Bobby said with increasing sternness in his voice, "this is your jurisdiction and your call. If you don't do this, blood will be on your hands and mine. A second civil war could break out if King is killed."

But the Governor didn't respond for several moments before Bobby interjected again.

"So what do you say, Governor," Bobby stated grimly and even in a threatening way, "will you do the right thing here? If not for King, then for America?"

TWENTY SEVEN

"That damned nig*er loving Kennedy," the Imperial Wizard Roy Davis said to a small gathering of fully-robed KKK members, the Kleagles, at their Georgia church headquarters. "We had a shot at King and those Freedom Riders and Bobby thwarted it."

"And he got lots of our boys too," a 56 year-old police commissioner said regretfully, his voice full of empathy, "with tear gas from the National Guard."

"I even heard reports through our network that some of our team got arrested, finger printed, and jailed," one twangy-sounding Klansman echoed. "Poor boys."

"Why the hell did Governor Paterson give in?" quipped another, a respected emergency room physician who once, like the white doctor in Anniston, Alabama who refused to treat the black Freedom Riders, had himself refused to treat an older black woman who had suffered a heart attack—and who had died outside of his hospital as a result, pleading for help and mercy.

"I'll tell you what it is," the Imperial Wizard said, petulant rage shooting out of his eyes under his wicked mask. "It's weakness. Pure weakness."

The pointy-hatted Kleagles, whose shadows were bouncing off the crucifix in the church like a portrait of jagged madness, like some sort of deformed Picaso painting, shook their heads in self-righteous indignation, agreeing that, from their point of view, no other political or moral considerations could be more important than eliminating King. One said, when speaking of the Governor's compromise with Kennedy, "that traitorous bastard."

"Now," the police commissioner intoned, "Bobby Kennedy's trying to make our lives even harder. Apparently he is also dispatching more Justice Department lawyers to target our fine laws here in the South."

"What?" the twangy-sounding Klansman asked, completely dumbfounded as to why anyone would want to deconstruct the laws Jim Crow built to protect and embellish white privilege, white innocence, and white affirmative action that, since anyone could remember, only acknowledged and sanctified the voices of white men and not black ones.

"The last thing we need," the medical doctor piped, "is a bunch of coon loving attorneys interfering with our states' rights."

"Exactly," the twangy-sounding Klansman responded. "First they want to get rid of slavery and now, separate but equal. "What do they want to do next? Outlaw Jim Crow and run a nig*er for president?"

"Pretty soon," the medical doctor said, "we won't even have a country."

"That's right, America will cease to be great," the twangy-sounding Klansman said with co-equal fear and ignorance. "And if we ain't great, we ain't nothing."

But the police commissioner, hoping to steer the conversation in a different direction so it didn't break out into another session of endless complaining, jumped in. "Governor Paterson did inform me," he said, "that Kennedy did concede on one key issue, though," as he looked to the Kleagles who quieted their disgruntled talk.

"What's that?" one unidentified Klans member responded, curious about what ground could be given after the KKK had just unsuccessfully mounted one of its largest ever attempts at taking out the Civil Rights Movement in their 3,000 man mob attack.

"The Kennedy Administration will be cutting off federal food aid to 20,000 Negro sharecroppers in the South," the police commissioner beamed with pride. "At least that will show King and those Freedom Riders that there are consequences for their diabolical actions."

"Well, good," responded the physician, somehow satisfied. "They want to starve us out of our way of life, well, then, we will starve them out of theirs. Literally."

"Boys," the Imperial Wizard said, the rage in his beady dark eyes defaulting back to their basic, unagitated evil, a sleeplessness about them concealing the most vile of secrets. "I appreciate the conversation but now I must tell you the other reason for our meeting tonight." Of course, the KKK only met at night these days—a far cry from when, just 40 years before in the 1920s, they were held in high esteem by polite society, publicly sponsoring weddings, baseball games, 4th of July Barbe-ques and fireworks, and even father-son outings, much to the delight of most Southerners, and even the White House, which hosted some of its most revered films, in White Supremacists' most mainstream exaltation.

The Imperial Wizard continued, "the reason we're meeting is because our Contact has just informed me of some good news." The Wizards' members, who just moments before were whining about losing the America they once knew and loved, seemed suddenly full of hope, like little boys throwing a temper tantrum one minute that could be suddenly cured by the presentation of vanilla ice cream or Cracker Barrel the next. They listened with anticipation.

"He is gathering resources to pay individual gunmen to assassinate this Civil Rights Movement right between its eyes," the Imperial Wizard said. "By targeting the Kennedys and King."

As the members sat silent, thinking, musing, and desiring the possibility, the police commissioner spoke up and said, "how much per hit?" in a gleeful tone that bordered on jubilation.

"That information remains to be seen," The Imperial Wizard responded. "Our Contact just needs some time."

"How much time? the physician asked, trying to angle for more concrete details to put his constantly calculating mind at rest.

"I don't know," the Imperial Wizard replied. "A few months. Maybe a year or two."

The police commissioner sat there bristling, as did the other Klan members, their minds lighting up with all sorts of images as to what this meant—for the KKK, for the South's way of life, and for the America they believed could only be great as a whites first, preferably whites only nation. To them, this is what Manifest Destiny meant: a country of, by, and for white men, with all other persons subjected to their 'divine right' to rule, a self-evident concept that needed no explanation or justification.

"But in addition to the funds," the Imperial Wizard finished, "the other thing The Contact will need is time to prepare a bulletproof plan to pin all the responsibility on the gunmen, the ultimate fall guys, so nobody can tie any of this to us."

TWENTY EIGHT

Martin Luther King was facing immense self-doubt and crippling on-again, off-again depression, something he was trying to keep hidden from almost everybody around him. It had been about 2 years since the white terrorist mob tried to destroy him, the Freedom Riders, and the burgeoning Civil Rights Movement at First Baptist Church. And in these 2 years he wrestled over and over again with warnings from his former friend, that backstabber Richard Nixon: to be careful about "Good Bobby" and his ruthless alter ego, "Bad Bobby," who would cut your balls off and serve them to you without so much as thinking twice.

It wasn't that King wasn't mostly happy with the progress his civil rights coalition was making, especially after a failed Albany, New York segregation boycott they had launched quietly and concurrently with the Freedom Rides—because the coalition had, in more recent months, seemed to recover from this off-camera Northern setback and successfully launched Operation Breadbasket in the South to focus on job training, literacy, and voter education for blacks, all individual elements of his "Second Emancipation Proclamation."

But, despite this more recent and geographically limited success, it was that King knew that, no matter how many programs they launched for blacks, if they did not have the enforcement of the government to protect their rights—if they did not have Bobby's complete backing as the nation's chief law enforcement officer—all of their efforts would be in vain and could die, and be reversed, overnight. And this bothered King deeply, subjecting his emotions to turbulently bounce up and down like a yo-yo depending on how things were going from day-to-day and month-to-month.

As King was at his Atlanta-based Southern Christian Leadership Conference (SCLC) Headquarters sitting with his friend Ralph Abernathy, waiting to have a meeting with SCLC members and several student groups who had been organizing with them, he brought up his thoughts about Bobby again.

"Ralph," King said to Abernathy with a strong sigh, "I was right about Bobby."

But unlike before, unlike trying to defend Bobby or make excuses for him, Abernathy was more sympathetic to his friend's melancholy perspective this time. It was now the Spring of 1963 and King's words were grounded not just in hot emotion and subjective opinion, but now in reality and cold, hard facts.

"He is a man of great contradictions," King continued, shaking his head. "On the one hand, he seems to be for civil rights. But on the other hand, he is seemingly undermining us at every turn, just as my Daddy predicted."

Of course, King was referring to Bobby's Dr. Jekyll and Mr. Hyde actions that made the Kennedy Administration look like they were playing good cop, bad cop on civil rights. On the positive side of things, King thought, Bobby had recently gone into hostile Klan territory, at the University of Georgia's Law School, and publicly endorsed the *Brown vs. Board of Education* desegregation case straight to Southerner's faces; Bobby had supported racial integration by sending armed U.S. Marshals to protect a single black student, James Meredith, to enroll and attend classes at the University of Mississippi for over a year; and Bobby had done these things all while he increased convictions against organized crime by over 800% as Attorney General, and in addition to personally managing one of the most dangerous events of the 20th Century, the Cuban Missile Crisis, helping JFK avert a nuclear catastrophe with the Soviets.

But on the negative side of things, Bobby had publicly called the Freedom Rides "unpatriotic" when the Freedom Riders continued to ride for another 6 months through the South after the church mob incident; Bobby had cut a deal with Southern governors to allow them to arrest the Freedom Riders with impunity and without any prosecution from the Justice Department by not enforcing the Supreme Court's *Boynton* vs. *Virginia* decision which legalized the Freedom Rides in the first place; and Bobby had not encouraged JFK to introduce any bills, make any speeches, or commit to any major progress on civil rights in his nearly 1000 days in office.

"Martin," Abernathy said as he was compiling some notes for their impending meeting, "maybe Bobby just doesn't have a moral core. Maybe all of this is about public opinion for him," a reference to the polling that showed only a minority of whites, mostly in more progressive areas of the country like California and New York, were for racial integration and equality in the near future. "Maybe all he wanted was our votes when he needed them but nothing more. Just like Nixon."

"But Ralph," King replied, "there's got to be a moral core to this man, somewhere. A man doesn't contradict himself left and right unless there is some light in him."

"Well," Abernathy responded, searching King's face, "I know he's a devout Catholic. I hear he goes to mass 7 times a week."

"So, there's got to be something there. We just need to force it out of him," said King. "We need to find his moral compass."

"But how?" Abernathy questioned, wondering if a hard-nosed white lawyer from immense privilege like Bobby could be more than just a tepid, occasional ally.

As King was searching for an answer, the meeting that was held for the SCLC, the Student Nonviolent Coordinating Committee, and others, started to form in the outside room of SCLC's Dorchester Center office, a large red brick building with towering white columns, a Southern White House for the movement.

But before Abernathy and King could make their way there, Stokley Carmichael burst into the building and slapped a stack of newspaper clippings down in front of several top civil rights workers, including the Reverend James Lawson, Byron Rustin, Bob Moses, Diane Nash, and others.

"This is the approach we need to take," Stokley said as he looked down at the explosive clippings.

James Lawson, King's right hand man and architect of the civil rights nonviolence training, took a look. His face, normally full of peace, said it all: Stokley, the brave and intellectual savant that he was, was beginning to crack, wobble, and pop.

"Absolutely not," Watson intoned sharply to Stokley. "No chance."

"No," Rustin said echoing Watson's sentiments, giving a look as stern as his voice sounded.

"This is not what we believe in," Nash backed them up, upset that Stokley would even suggest the idea, especially before an important meeting with King.

"I think we should start to believe in it," Stokley said, unpersuaded and unconcerned with his fellow activists' reactions. "This man speaks the truth."

"The only thing he speaks," Lawson said, "is violence and hate. And we should not discuss him or his dangerous ideas one bit more."

The copious newspaper clippings, which Stokley had meticulously underlined like the Harvard-admitted scholar that he was, were of the other great emerging black civil rights leader of the era: Malcolm X. Malcolm, a tall, handsome, well spoken, and self-educated Muslim, was for everything that King wasn't. Namely, he was for civil rights by any means necessary, including revolutionary force. He believed that King was not only naive, but was humiliating himself and the black community by insisting on Gahndian non-violence when the Founding Fathers themselves hadn't even insisted on it when they made violent war for their independence in 1776 from Great Britain.

Stokley, brimming with anger and rage, said, "Why not? Huh, Reverend? Why not?" as he picked up a clipping with a headline of Malcolm accusing King of being an "Uncle Tom."

"We will not terrorize white people the way they have terrorized us," Lawson said while King and Abernathy quietly slipped into the back of the room, observing what was happening like flies on the wall, careful not to be seen or heard.

"But what has that gotten us?" Stokley asked. "I can tell you what it's gotten me. Multiple beatings. Multiple imprisonments. And for what? To allow the white man to continue to laugh at us and put his fist in our mouths knowing we won't fight back?"

"Stokley," Watson said, "that's enough—"

"No it's not," Stokley shot back. "It's the truth."

But as he said those words, King came around to the front, hoping to calm the young man down, hoping to quell the anger and fear and pain that he himself felt on the inside too—and the anger and fear and pain that nearly all black people felt whether they were for peaceful nonviolence or revolutionary force.

"Now Stokley," King uttered softly, his voice gentle like a caring grandfather's, "I know things have been hard. But our approach will win in the end." "Will it?" Stokley questioned him. "When we're all castrated and six feet under?"

King just stared at the young man but didn't say anything, his love trying to overpower Stokely's legitimate fears.

"Is that what you want?" Stokley demanded again. "Is it?"

"Look," King finally responded after he had gathered his thoughts, "I have an idea that will up the ante on the Kennedy Administration and win the hearts and minds of white Americans everywhere without us having to resort to violence."

"Well what is it?" Stokley snorted, his face contorted with pent up pain . "Because we can't continue like this, we can't continue letting the white man kick us in the head and without facing any consequences for doing so."

The various civil rights workers, about 20 in all, looked to King, wondering what potential new idea or strategy he would suggest that they hadn't already tried. It had been 8 years since the full-scale civil rights assault on the nation had begun, when King took over as a 25 year old kid in the winter of 1955, and that he had upped in intensity since JFK had become president, and they wondered: *What if anything could be done now?*

"So far," King said, "all of the white terrorism committed against us has gone unreported in the press, which is what has allowed the white politicians and white police officers to lie and say that they aren't harming us, to lie and say that we have been the agitators and the aggressors."

"Yes, Dr. King," Stokley said, continuing to snort. "That's not news."

"But if we expose them for who they truly are," King went on, "by outing them to the press, to the television media—"

"Then public opinion will turn against Jim Crow," Abernathy jumped in, seeing where his friend was going with this. "And the Kennedy Administration will have to support us. Because the American people will see their heinous acts for themselves, especially white moderates in the North."

"And how exactly do you propose we do this?" Stokley said, incredulous, despite the growing love affair America was having with television, especially shows like *Star Trek*, King's favorite, the *Dick Van Dyke Show*, *The Tonight Show* with Johnny Carson, and the news media in general.

"By launching an effort so big," King said, "bigger than the bus boycotts, bigger than the Freedom Rides, and bigger than our Breadbasket efforts, that America will know once and for all that Jim Crow is evil and can no longer be tolerated."

The whole room was silent, including Stokley.

"We will launch Project Confrontation," King continued, "and we will bring the television cameras to the heart of Jim Crow territory—Birmingham, Alabama—and bait them into doing to us what they have been doing all along: except this time, the eyes of the nation will be watching."

Stokley, taking in his thoughts, taking in the plan, looked at King, neither happy about it nor dismissive of it. He simply said. "Dr. King, I'm choosing to trust you this one last time. But if this confrontation doesn't work, I'm leaving this team and joining Malcolm X—and recommending that others come—to secure black people's rights by any means necessary."

TWENTY NINE

"Martin," Corretta Scott King said as she carefully slipped into her queen-sized bed because she was now pregnant with the couple's 4th child, "are we doing the right thing?"

"I hope so," King replied, taking one last puff of his Pall Mall cigarette before extinguishing it in the ashtray on his nightstand, the smoke forming a cloudy thickness as though it were the welcome residue emanating from a warm fireplace on a cold winter's day.

"This just seems so dangerous," Corretta continued while Martin joined her in the bed, looking completely exhausted, his body resembling the architecture of a half-coma. "Even for us."

"I don't think we have any other choice," King said. "We don't have the support I thought we were going to have."

King then paused momentarily to feel his chest, his palms pressing against the luminous cross-scar on his heart. He grimaced slightly.

"Have you gotten that checked out yet?" Corretta asked him, the worry wrinkling the brows of her beautiful, light-brown face. "I'm concerned."

"I've been so busy, honey," King said trying to find an excuse for why he hadn't seen his doctor, "that I haven't had time."

In addition to the vicious depression King was bouncing into and out of, he was also increasingly feeling chest pains. Too many chest pains. Especially for a man who was now only 33 years old. And, like any man, he didn't want to admit it— to himself, or to his wife, and he certainly didn't want to see a doctor who would force him to.

"Martin," Corretta said gently, "you need to check that out. You're under a lot of stress and your diet is so poor, I just wouldn't—"

But as she said those words, Yolanda, now 8 years old with her hair tied into two cute pigtails, bounced into the room, which seemed to be her favorite pastime, especially when her daddy was home.

"I had a nightmare again," Yolanda said, an obvious fabrication just so she could have more time to spend with her daddy. She then made her way onto her parents' bed and nestled in between them, her arms extended toward her father, her fingers still smelling like Play Doh from her Play Doh Fun Factory she had played with earlier.

"My poor baby," King said, "everything will be okay."

King held his daughter and kissed her on the head, feeling as much safety in her presence as she felt in his. In moments like this, he wondered again why he couldn't just have a normal life so he could feel this kind of love on a daily basis. He wondered why he hadn't just remained as a local pastor, or even accepted the presidency of a plush seminary school when recently offered the chance, so he could have an easy life, come home, play with his kids, and even listen to some MoTown every now and then, taking in the good things of this world, even as limited as they were in the racial apartheid that was the United States. Who knows, maybe he could even take his kids to the famous New York's World's Fair, the most spectacular and futuristic entertainment event on earth that every father wanted to take his family to, with that kind of "easy" life.

"Daddy," Yolanda said unexpectedly, as children often do when adults' minds wander elsewhere as King's clearly was, "what were you and Mommy talking about before I came in?"

Not wanting to reveal the irregular heartbeat that was increasingly troubling him, King decided to tell Yolanda about the important discussion he was having with her mom.

"Well, baby girl," King answered, "we were talking about daddy's next big project. We call it Project Confrontation to desegregate the city of Birmingham."

"How's it going?" Yoland asked, innocently, not really understanding what her daddy did for a living but still curious about it, especially because her teachers were always talking about him and calling him some sort of "prophet."

"Well," King responded, "it is more challenging than Daddy thought it would be."

"We seem to have hit a fork in the road," Corretta interjected in what, for her, was a common recurrence of uncertainty that her husband experienced despite what everyone on the outside thought: that he always "had it all together" and knew exactly what to do and say despite the countless precarious obstacles in his way. Instead, Corretta knew that he, as a flesh and blood human being subject to the same fears and worries as everyone else, often had difficult questions, but none this challenging. It seemed that he was encountering facts that refused to change no matter how hard he tried to change them. And the facts were, quite frankly, damning: despite his impassioned and frequent pleas to civil rights workers in Birmingham over the last few weeks, few wanted to participate in what King boldly predicted would be their biggest campaign yet. Black people there were not only exhausted from all of their civil rights work and backlash that had received from it, but were directly threatened with losing their employment by their white bosses as well as by potential retaliation by the KKK, a rumor the Klan was all too happy to back up.

"What's a fork in the road?" Yolanda asked, not knowing what her mom meant by the phrase.

"It's when you have two options," Corretta said, "and once you choose one option, you cannot change it or ever go back to the other option."

"Why don't you just choose the harder option?" Yolanda questioned, her parents both exchanging glances with each other, searching each other's faces for meaning from such a wise and profound question.

"Why would you say that, baby girl?" King asked, teasing out a response, trying to choose between if he should cancel the Project—and not only risk losing credibility for his Movement but credibility with die-hard activists like Stokley Carmichael who would defect to Malcolm X—and between whether he should do something that had never been done before, not even by his hero Gandhi.

"Daddy, duh," Yolanda said. "You always say there comes a time in a man's life when he shouldn't take the easy path. So just choose the harder one."

Leave it to a child, King thought, to turn his words back on him. It reminded him of a speech he had given, one of thousands he had preached by now, when he had stated:

"There comes a time when one must take a position that is neither safe, nor politic, nor popular, but he must take it because conscience tells him it is right."

But this harder path was, quite frankly, the scariest decision he has ever had to make. It was one thing to put his life on the line, and even to put adult civil rights workers' lives on the line. But this, this harder path, not only seemed downright ludicrous but also treacherous, something he had previously been vehemently against in principle.

"Well," King said, "we haven't been able to recruit very many adult protestors for our Project Confrontation—"

"So I am giving your father my blessing," Corretta butted in surprisingly, drawing an "oh wow" look from her husband, reversing her previous position, "to recruit countless children to confront Jim Crow head on, and show them that we are not backing down."

And with that, King's decision was made for him. He knew that he had to follow through on Project Confrontation in what would now have to be a children's march against segregation—because so few adults wanted to participate—even if that meant it was, despite everything screaming inside of him, a possible death march for these children.

THIRTY

I just don't see why he's being so unreasonable, Bobby wrote in his journal, an unusual occurrence for him because he found it so difficult to put his true thoughts on paper, the night before he was to have a meeting with the FBI Director, J. Edgar Hoover, who said he needed to urgently speak with him. *Martin Luther King just doesn't seem to appreciate all the things I've done for him.*

Doesn't he see that I personally saved his life twice? Doesn't he see that I risked federal Marshals to integrate the University of Mississippi and one of my Marshals died because of it? Doesn't he see that I personally challenged Southern governors on desegregation in my University of Georgia Law speech?

Bobby then took a sip of water and continued writing, furiously, from his study at Hickory Hill, with his dog Freckles sleeping at his feet.

Doesn't he see that I've had my brother appoint 50 Negroes to his administration, including judges, ambassadors, assistant cabinet members, and White House staff?

Doesn't he see that I've created a civil rights division in my Justice Department and litigated 57 cases against segregationist laws?

Doesn't he see all of these political moves I'm making for him?

Doesn't he see what I'm doing? Bobby continued to fume in the silent house, the hour nearing 2:00 am.

Yet Martin Luther King is never satisfied. He had to continue his Freedom Rides. He had to continue his protests. He had to continue angering Southerners. He had to continue to do it his way. I swear, the man doesn't know how to compromise.

And neither does my Father. The old man is one tough bulldog, Bobby wrote as he carefully avoided using any profanity as he was famously against cursing—and drinking and smoking—in large part because of his altar boy days, a role he sometimes still volunteered to do if mass didn't have enough people to fill slots.

But alas, Father has had a debilitating stroke and he can no longer speak and tell me and Jack what to do. He can no longer get his way. It's true that without him I wouldn't be Attorney General. And my brother probably wouldn't be president. But he was just so overbearing before the stroke. Though I will admit he was right about not trusting the CIA after following their advice during the Bay of Pigs disaster, which I think the CIA resents us for (and resents Jack for firing their director and proposing to cut their budget by 20%, especially given all of the crazy mind control experiments we just found out they're running).

Bobby then started to digress a bit, letting his thoughts flow freely, not caring whether he organized them in a sequential way or not.

Not that [Vice President] Lyndon Johnson, who I refer to as "Uncle Roofus," would agree with how Jack or I have approached these or other things. The way that man parades around, thinking a little too much of himself and his longtime friends throughout Washington—calling me a "snot nose kid"—really irks me. And the way he talks about my Father, calling him weak on Hitler when Father was ambassador to Britain during the Roosevelt years, boils my blood. I think I dislike Lyndon probably about as much as I dislike Martin Luther King. Not my cup of tea. I mean, the man puts his initials, "LBJ," on his cufflinks and clothes. Who does that? It's so tacky and uncouth and inappropriate.

Just like Martin Luther King's upcoming Project Confrontation in Birmingham. I mean, what is he trying to accomplish with all of this? My brother and I are doing everything we can on civil rights given our political constraints and we are making progress. Sure, I've had to compromise some with some of these Southern Dixiecrats whom I abhor, but a man in my position has to be practical. But King, he doesn't have to be practical like me. He can just go out there and continue to agitate, to make speeches, and to conduct marches to try to embarrass us, to try to make us look like we don't have a handle on our country. And the Soviets and the world are watching, seeing if they can detect any weakness they can use to exploit our country's internal armor. But I won't show them any. My brother won't show them any. Not while we're alive, not while we hold these offices.

Speaking of a man who isn't weak, I'd love to ask Mr. Hoover tomorrow about what he thinks of King's upcoming protest. Maybe he has more ideas on how we can keep the peace and balance our efforts on racial integration with King and states rights' with the South.

With those words, Bobby closed his journal and turned out the light, not knowing the trap Hoover had set for him the following morning.

THIRTY ONE

Bobby finished playing his daily round of morning tennis at Hickory Hill with his pal Robert McNamara, the Secretary of Defense, before showering, packing his lunch, and slipping off to mass at St. Joseph's Catholic Church, just a short walk from Congress and the Supreme Court.

Upon entering the stunning, multi-story brick cathedral with pointed arches and high vaunted ceilings, he listened intently as the priest read the scriptures and shared a story about one of the most venerated saints of his faith, St. Francis of Assissi.

"As we sit here today in the center of power," the Priest said, seemingly making eye contact with Bobby and the other well-to-do and powerful patrons, "let us remember that St. Francis, like many here, was a man born of great privilege and wealth."

Bobby's ears perked up a bit, a little more interested in hearing the story about a wealthy man who would one day become a saint, his life as bright and beautiful as a rainbow made of love.

"But St. Francis refused to live a life of materialism, compromise, and self-interest," the Priest continued. "He used his vast wealth to serve the poor and marginalized, to empathize with people who were hurting, and to morally stand against injustice."

Bobby closed his eyes and continued to listen, his thoughts increasingly wrestling with, and enchanted by, the heavenly skylight beaming into his consciousness.

"He started the Franciscan order, of which this parish is a participant, to help right the wrongs of this world," the priest said. "But let us remember this: when we attempt to right wrongs, our complete reward in this life is often not applause, but suffering. And we must understand this in our hearts if we are to truly heal the world."

As the priest continued to talk, Bobby opened his eyes slightly, contemplating the meaning of the message and how it could apply to him. He remembered that he suffered when his oldest brother, Joe Jr., had died tragically while being shot down by enemy fire during World War Two. He remembered how he suffered when his older sister, Kathleen, had also died tragically a few years later in a plane crash. And he remembered his continued suffering over his poor sister, Rosemary, who had had a lobotomy ordered by his Father and who had been permanently placed in a home called the "Institute for Backward Youth," cut off from her family.

Was this the suffering the priest was speaking of? Bobby thought. *The suffering you feel when a loved one or close friend is lost or hurting? Or was it something else, a different kind of suffering? A suffering meant to heal? To transform?*

"So I conclude with the words of the classical Greek poet Aeschylus," the priest said. "He who learns must suffer. And even in our sleep pain that cannot forget falls drop by drop upon the heart until, in our own despair, against our will, comes wisdom through the awful grace of God."

These words—this quote—struck Bobby very strongly. He wrote them down, proceeded to get in line to receive the eucharist, and then left the cathedral.

Bobby hopped in his Corinthian White 1961 Thunderbird convertible, which technically belonged to his brother, rubbed his dog Freckle's head, who had been patiently waiting for him in the car with a cracked window, and made the short drive to the Justice Department on Pennsylvania Avenue.

"Good morning, Mr. Kennedy," an aide said as Bobby made his way with Freckles quickly through the building. As usual, Bobby's hurried walk was imitated by many of the ambitious attorneys in the building who were hoping to gain favor by being replicas of their boss, individual echoes in the ultimate echo chamber, men who would never be accused of originality of thought or behavior or existence.

"Mr. Hoover would like to see you," the aide continued.

"Right," Bobby said eager to ask the FBI Director about his thoughts concerning Project Confrontation and discuss whatever he had summoned him to talk about. "Tell him to come to my office."

"Actually," the aide replied, "he wants to see you in his."

That was strange, Bobby thought. Mr. Hoover had always been so deferential to him these past couple of years. *Why would he insist on seeing me in his office when I'm his boss? Maybe he's come down with an injury?*

"Ok," Bobby said, part curiously. "Come with me to take notes."

"He would like to see you alone," the aide said.

This was even stranger, Bobby thought. *A meeting without a secretary?*

Bobby put down his briefcase, glanced at his oversized portrait of Snoopy on his office wall, and walked over to J. Edgar Hoover's office, leaving Freckles behind. He knocked on the door.

"Mr. Attorney General," the FBI Director said, pushing aside an uneaten cup of cream of chicken soup. "Thanks so much for seeing me in my office."

"You bet," Bobby said casually. "What's on your mind?"

"You trust me, right sir?" Hoover asked bluntly, and abruptly, the usual diplomatic niceties absent from his lips.

"Of course," Bobby shot back without thinking. "You're an American hero."

"Thank you, sir, that means a lot," Hoover responded, the left side of his mouth stretching upward, his words ready to be used as an exacting razor blade if they needed to be, practiced in the art of slicing a man's heart straight out of his chest. He told Bobby to close the door.

"Well, I'm afraid I'm going to have to ask you for a favor, Mr. Attorney General," Hoover said as he sat at his desk, his left hand placed on a small manilla envelope and his right on a much larger one.

"What do you need?" Bobby asked, brushing his hair out of his face, unsure where Hoover was going with this as he had never before requested favors from him.

"It seems that there may be some KKK chatter about potential future assassination attempts on Martin Luther King," Hoover said nonchalantly.

"Are they credible?" Bobby asked, his face dilapidated with concern, his thoughts immediately remembering the mob that tried to kill King and the Freedom Riders at First Baptist Church.

"Well, he is a troublemaker, sir," Hoover said as he deflected the question.

"But are they credible?" Bobby asked again, pointedly.

"Who knows," Hoover said. "Probably not."

"Then what is the issue, Mr. Hoover?"

"I think that, in order to keep Mr. King safe from these potential threats," Hoover said, refusing to call King by his formal "doctor" title, "we should gain some understanding of his whereabouts, his intentions."

Bobby, unsure of what Hoover was getting at, looked puzzled.

"What I mean is," Hoover continued pushing the manilla envelope on which his left hand was resting toward Bobby, "I think we should wiretap Mr. King. You know, to keep him safe."

"What?" Bobby responded, irritation banging on his chest. "He's a private citizen."

"But it will be for his safety," Hoover again said smoothly, "and the safety of the United States."

"Mr. Hoover," Bobby responded, "this country doesn't do that to its citizens."

"I already have a paid FBI informant inside of the civil rights campaign," Hoover said. "It will just help me round out my efforts to help keep him alive and to help keep the peace."

Bobby just stared at Hoover, completely appalled at his lack of concern for Martin Luther King's privacy rights.

"I'm sorry, Mr. Hoover," Bobby said. "I cannot authorize this request. It's simply not legal."

"But I think you should," Hoover shot back, his words bathed in ice. "Please open it," he said as he ushered Bobby to open the envelope he was holding marked "Confidential."

Bobby then opened it, which had the official United States wiretap authorization form. He saw the area where he would need to sign his name for the request to go through.

"Again, I'm sorry, but the answer is no," Bobby said.

"Well, then," Hoover said, "unfortunately, I will just have to show you this."

Hoover slowly pushed the other very large manilla envelope his right index finger was tapping on, which said "For Mr. Hoover's Use Only," toward Bobby.

"These are just a few items that I have to help you change your mind," Hoover said. "There are many more like this in case these don't convince you."

Bobby opened the manilla envelope. His heart suddenly dropped to the bottom of his chest, like an airplane falling out of the sky.

He started to go through page after page, fear increasingly animating his face. The documents were detailed reports of the President, who had been bugged for what looked like years now, and who was shown to be having multiple extramarital affairs.

"I have the names of the women, Bobby," Hoover said as he got up from his chair and walked toward Bobby, hovering over him in a position of complete domination.

"Actress Anita Ekberg," Hoover said as he pointed to the official FBI records. "Communist call girl Ellen Rometsch. Mafia darling Judith Campell Exner. White House intern Mimi Alford. CIA spouse Mary Pinchot Meyer."

Bobby was stunned, one-upped by the man whom he thought had complete integrity in Washington DC—and by the man who was the most trusted public official in America.

"Not to mention that slut Marilyn Monroe," Hoover said matter of factly, the reality of the deadness of his soul now transparent to Bobby. "Shall I go on?"

Bobby continued to sit there, searching for words, searching for some kind of response, searching for some kind of counter-defense. But all he could utter was, "Mr. Hoover, please."

Hoover, who had returned to his desk, placed squarely between two American flags, looked completely smug and satisfied.

"So Bobby, make this easy on yourself," Hoover continued, "I'll keep your brother's sexual escapades our little secret in exchange for you authorizing a wiretap on Martin Luther King."

He then said, without a hint of irony or shame in his voice knowing that he was attempting to blackmail the Attorney General of the United States—in the Justice Department Building no less—"do we have a deal?"

THIRTY TWO

Martin Luther King kissed Coretta goodbye before leaving his home in the dark hours of the morning. Suitcase in tow, he was not wearing his typical 3-piece fedora suit, French cuffs, and black oxford shoes, a look he deliberately cultivated to give off a stylish air of seriousness and sophistication as the de facto moral spokesman of black people. Instead, he decided he was going to wear blue jeans and a denim shirt—a style associated with the black poor and working class.

After closing his bedroom door and creeping lightly through the upstairs hallway, he went into each of his 4 children's rooms and kissed them on the foreheads, including Martin Luther King III who was sleeping with his teddy bear "Love," and Yolanda, who was half-asleep but nevertheless realizing that her daddy was leaving on yet another trip and whispered, "I love you."

"I love you too, buttercup," King responded to her, more hopeful than he felt, feeling regretful he was leaving his baby girl again. He then walked out of the front door, locked it, and made his way to the yellow taxi waiting to take him to the Atlanta airport. He was scheduled to board Eastern Airlines, one of the "Big 4" airlines along with United, American, and TWA, and be at his destination within a couple of hours. This new age of travel with commercial airplanes, combined with the recently built federal interstate highway system connecting American states and cities to each other from coast to coast for the first time, made travel throughout the continental U.S. more manageable than at any time in history.

After boarding the plane, he was met with the typical reception whites normally treated him with: complete disdain. One brown-hair white woman, sitting next to him, gave him the side eye; two white businessmen who appeared to be in their late 40s or early 50s, sitting a row over, put on the meanest and most intimidating stares they were taught by culture to manufacture; and several white stewardesses, mostly slim and fairly attractive, whispered pejoratives about him in each other's ears. But King didn't flinch; not only was he not going to let this bother him but he was going to retaliate by doing the best thing he could think of: heap hot coals on their heads by being exceedingly kind and polite to them.

"It's nice to see you," King said, smiling, to one of the young stewardesses who walked by, the slogan of the airline ironically embroidered on her Eastern Airlines lapel pin: "We want everyone to fly."

"Nig*er," she responded under her breath, not acknowledging him or his statement. "Damn, nig*er."

King just stared straight ahead, pretending like he didn't hear the statement, knowing that Jim Crow's little sister—the Jazebellian women who unofficially made up "Jane Crow"—could be just as prejudiced toward blacks and, at times, more so than their brethren. He remembered an innocent young black boy, Emmit Till, who was tortured and lynched a few years before because a Jane Crow woman, Carolyn Bryant, had accused him of whistling at her.

The plane then took off and flew its short route into Birmingham with only light turbulence along the way.

The Reverend Fred Shuttlesworth, King's friend and ally and the local on-the-ground leader of the Civil Rights Movement there, picked him up after the plane landed.

"My old friend," Shuttlesworth said after he had hugged him, "You ready for fireworks?" referring to what would no doubt be a circus: their impending campaign to desegregate Birmingham, a city known for its theatrical and, at times, buffoonish version of racism—a city they needed to display this foolishness if they were going to show the world on live television just how abhorrent White Supremacy truly was.

King laughed and said, "if it goes the way I think it's going to go, it's going to be more like the 4th of July."

Of course, both men, who always said they weren't civil rights leaders who just happened to be pastors but were, instead, pastors who just happened to be civil rights leaders, were religious to their core, but still didn't take themselves too seriously. They knew that if God was for them, nobody could be against them—and this gave them relief and allowed them to joke about things that would make most men weep. On the other hand, though, they also believed that if God didn't show up, their work, and their lives, would be over in an instant.

"How many death threats did you get this week?" King asked Shuttlesworth as the car engine revved up, fishing to see just how much opposition Birmingham, led by Police Commissioner Bull Connor, may have been stirring up.

"Three," Shuttlesworth said matter of factly. "You?"

"I stopped counting," King half- joked. "I'd die of a broken heart if I kept track."

"Martin," Shuttlesworth suddenly asked in a little more serious tone, "I know I'm not supposed to ask this because we're both ministers and all. But are you afraid to die?"

King, who was initially enjoying the light banter, didn't respond immediately. He rolled down the side window and began puffing on a Pall Mall cigarette as they made their way into the city.

He observed "Whites Only" signs posted above drinking foundations.

He observed "Whites Only" signs posted above stores of all kinds.

And he observed that white churches, which had recently started their own private schools to protest and mock *Brown vs. Board of Education,* had put up signs that read "for white students only."

He finished puffing on his cigarette before answering his friend's question.

"You know, Fred," King finally intoned, "polls show that I'm the most despised man in America right now. Sooner or later..." he said without finishing his sentence, his voice trailing off.

"It's okay, Martin," Shuttlesworth responded, "we shouldn't be thinking or talking like this anyway."

The two rode quietly on, continuing to pass the institutionalized racism that white men and women ensconced in their community, thinking about all they were enduring mentally, emotionally, and physically, thinking about how the pharaoh of racism was determined to never let black people go.

"How are our most recent recruitment efforts here?" King asked, not only trying to change the subject but also trying to see if there would be any chance they wouldn't have to recruit, and deploy, children for this boycott. King had informed him by phone a few days earlier that this was about the only choice they had left, barring a miracle or intervention by Bobby Kennedy. The last thing he wanted to do was to subject children to potential harassment, or worse, if he could somehow prevent it.

"To be honest," Shuttlesworth said, "about the same. People are tired. People are scared."

"I understand," King replied, hiding the disappointment he was feeling. Yet, he understood why everyday civil rights workers —why everyday people with children and families and jobs— didn't want to participate this time given all they had been up against, and all that they would be up against. But it still disheartened him.

"But the Freedom Riders are here," Shuttlesworth said. "Ralph Abernathy, James Lawson, Diane Nash are here too."

"Have they all been informed of the plan?" King asked.

"Yes," Shuttlesworth said, "tomorrow we will hit the Negro schools throughout the community to recruit the children to join our efforts."

"Good," King said. "I think they're our only hope to bring Jim Crow to his bloody knees."

THIRTY THREE

Bobby, his head still spinning from Hoover's blindside kick in the balls a few days before, had been on continuous phone calls this past week with Martin Luther King, monitoring what was happening in real-time. He was desperately trying to do everything in his power to have King call off Project Confrontation, which King was telling him was "the biggest campaign the Civil Rights Movement has ever launched," much to Bobby's chagrin.

Even several white ministers in Birmingham, who considered themselves "moderate" on race relations, tried to persuade King to call it off. Their rationale, in an open letter published by newspaper for the entire community to see, was that King was an "outsider" and that he should halt his efforts, and efforts on behalf of black people, because they would cause too much trouble and disturbance for their "peace-loving, law-abiding" white community. They told King that he needed to "wait" for justice to one day come to him and his people, even if that wait took much longer than he expected. It was, they reasoned, King's duty to protect the rights and interests of white citizens even if most of these same citizens didn't give a damn about protecting the rights and interests of black ones.

"This is a nightmare," Bobby remarked in frustration to his top civil rights deputy at the Justice Department, the Yale-educated Burke Marshall, as he paced back and forth in his office, his black tie brushing to and fro across a short-sleeved dress shirt, his standard work outfit. "An absolute nightmare."

"Maybe we can negotiate with him?" Marshall asked, his eyes looking intently through his round black glasses, accentuating his dark black hair and virile jawbone, a man who looked like a straight-laced WASP if ever there was one.

"Unlikely," Bobby responded.

"Is he really recruiting children to march?" Marshall questioned, sighing, himself a father of 3, not understanding how King would be okay with potentially putting children in harm's way. "Or is he just using the threat of children as leverage to get what he wants?"

"He said he was recruiting them," Bobby said flatly. "High school football stars and cheerleaders."

"Ah," Marshall said. "Popular teenage kids."

"And apparently these popular kids have recruited hundreds of their classmates to march," Bobby said as he continued to pace, his arms crossed tensely.

"Wow," Marshall responded, in slight disbelief.

"They've been training them in local churches, teaching them to be nonviolent."

"But these are kids?" Marshall asked. "You know how they can be if provoked," referring to the idea that young people of all ages or races might be impulsively prone to lash out. "Remember how you were when you were young?"

"I know," Bobby said, briefly recalling his well-known reputation as a pugnacious youth and tough guy who was unafraid to back down from a fight, including the time he had busted a glass bottle over a guy's head during an altercation. "But King has assured me that his movement has never before used violent means and that he even personally searches his protestors for weapons and firearms."

"But what if the Klan responds to these kids, like they did with the Freedom Riders?" Marshall said, fearfully, "and tries to hurt them?"

"That's what I'm afraid of," Bobby responded, concern clouding his face.

"Do you think the Klan would openly attack children?" Marshall asked. "Or do you think the children will act as a kind of deterrent to the Klan?"

"Like with the Freedom Rides," Bobby said, "these kids are probably daring them to attack, I think. But unlike those rides, and unlike when the mob attacked them and King at the church, apparently they will be on live TV if they are."

"What!?" Marshall said, incredulously, immediately realizing not only the political fallout this could cause but also the very real potential of this sparking something worse. "We can't allow this. We have to stop this—"

"I've already called the three television networks," Bobby said as he cut him off. "CBS, NBC, and ABC. They said they were running it. They said after the reports of what's been going on in the South it was too big of a story to pass on."

"Dammit," Marshall said.

"I know."

"How long will this go on?" Marshall pressed. "Hours? Days? Weeks?"

"King won't tell me," Bobby replied. "He's playing his cards close. He says he wants complete desegregation in Birmingham."

"Complete desegregation?" Marshall asked, skeptical because he knew first hand how hard Jim Crow fought since he was the man Bobby appointed to oversee the 50+ desegregation lawsuits the Administration launched against it. "They don't even want to desegregate the bus terminals which we got a Supreme Court victory on."

"That's right," Bobby said. "But King says they must desegregate water fountains, lunch counters, department stores, schools, the works."

"But they still fly the Confederate Flag there," Marshall protested, beginning to wonder if King might be a little naive for thinking he could successfully desegregate such a place in a wholesale and not retail way, a gutsy all-or-nothing move. "Their Confederate Constitution even said that all black people would forever be slaves to them. They're not going to accept this."

"I think that's what King wants to prove," Bobby said, brushing his messy hair out of his face as it had been bouncing back and forth during all of his pacing.

"You mean, for everybody to see how absurdly the South treats blacks and refuses to abide by the rule of law which they proclaim to love?" Marshall asked.

"Exactly," Bobby said.

"Even if it is only their twisted version of the rule of law," Marshall responded, pushing his glasses upward on his slender nose. "One that justifies everything they want and condemns everything Negroes want."

Bobby, who had had hundreds of these conversations with Marshall before, just shook his head in agreement. He knew how much Marshall hated segregation, but he also knew how much he needed to keep this protest from embarrassing the Administration and sparking a potential second civil war if it got out of hand.

"Should we send in U.S. Marshalls?" Marshall asked.

"No, not yet," Bobby replied. "I'm going to go over and see the President and get his direction."

Bobby then put on his coat, leashed Freckles, and hurried out of the building. He hopped into his Thunderbird and drove over to 1600 Pennsylvania Avenue with his radio on, listening to WAMA 88.5, Washington's brand new talk station. So far, there was no talk of Birmingham, where King had started protesting a few hours earlier, which he thought was a good thing. After all, he concluded, no news is good news.

He parked his vehicle, told Freckles to wait for him as he cracked the windows slightly, and proceeded to enter the West Wing before making his way past the Cabinet Room, where JFK met with his 10 cabinet officials, and the Roosevelt Room, where his brother's brainy, Ivy League staff often met. He then approached the Oval Office, where an exceptionally attractive female aide wearing a Yves Saint Laurent yellow miniskirt and Prada Milano pumps told him that the President would see him now.

"Bobby," JFK said as he looked up from his 1,300 pound, 19th century oak Resolute desk that the great President Franklin Delano Roosevelt once used, "Have you heard the latest about King?"

He came inside, first spotting his nearly 3 year-old nephew, JFK Jr., playing under the desk with a Moon Landing Set. He then approached his brother.

"No, Jack," Bobby answered. "Please tell me he's alive."

"Well, the good news is that he is alive," JFK said. "They have arrested him, along with 54 other adult civil rights workers, including his Freedom Riders, and are thinking of putting King in solitary confinement."

"What?" Bobby said incredulously. "If that's the good news, then what in the world is the bad news?"

"I got a call from the Governor of Alabama," JFK continued, "who told me that the Birmingham police will be prepared to take any action, including lethal action, to stop a group of school aged children they just spotted marching if they do not immediately cease and desist."

"Lethal action against teens?" Bobby questioned, appalled and furious.

"No," JFK responded. "Against children. Some as young as 5 years old."

THIRTY FOUR

A group of black children, who had originally gathered at the 16th St Baptist Church on 6th Avenue for their training and deployment by King's nonviolent protest mastermind James Lawson, were beginning to make their way conspicuously through the streets of Birmingham, despite the television press nowhere to be seen.

The children, about 50 in total, were singing "We Shall Overcome," led by their 5 year old "lead singer," who was wearing pink bows in her hair and a dress with a sunflower print that her mom had personally sewn for her.

"We are not afraid, we are not afraid, we are not afraid today," the young leader with golden brown eyes said, her peers joining in with her. "Oh, deep in my heart, I do believe we shall overcome some day."

As the children marched northward, their signs came into display. One was holding a poster that read, "Can a man love God and hate his brother?" Another had a sign that said, "D-Day is Coming." A third child had made a sign that stated, "I am a foot soldier."

A white barber with a portly belly, about 58 years old and sporting a white slab of thinning hair, stepped on the outside of his shop as he saw the children march by. "What are these little coons up to?" he said to himself, never before seeing such a sight in his life, his country bumpkin mind caught off guard, before spitting the tobacco he was chewing on out of his mouth.

One child, overhearing him, gave him a defiant wink.

The children had ditched school today without so much as telling their parents what they were up to. They knew that even though segregation was wrong, even though separate but equal was wrong, that their parents would oppose their efforts for fear of their safety. So they said nothing to them, keeping their plans a complete secret.

"Only a few more blocks until we reach the Mayor's office," one child said, smiling, as the children were hoping to, in their spirited naivete, negotiate desegregation with him themselves, reasoning that they could since all of the adult leaders like King had been brutally arrested and jailed just hours prior. But as they started to make a right turn on 7th Avenue to approach City Hall, they ran into the exact people they were hoping to avoid: the most racist and hate-filled police in the country, led by their balding, double-chinned Commissioner of "Public Safety," Bull Conner, who, to them, appeared to be an American Psycho, just like the Alfred Hitchkock movie of the same name that had been released three years earlier.

"Where do you think you're going?" Conner asked in a mocking thick country twang, flanked by dozens of white officers to his left and his right, who looked as stone faced and angry as the children have ever seen any human beings look. Who looked like they were dragons sent from hell itself.

"Uh oh," the 5 year old leader said, terror assaulting her like a wicked taskmaster, just as it was all of the children.

"I said, where do you think you're going?" Conner again asked, as he stepped forward, slowly, in a power waddle shifting left and right.

The children just stood there. Their pulses racing. Their hearts pounding. Their lips full of silence. Their souls full of fear.

"You think you can just skip school and march illegally in my streets without consequences?" Conner screamed as his officers drew their guns and pointed them straight at the children. "Do you!?"

THIRTY FIVE

Martin Luther King, still wearing his denim shirt and pants, was enraged while sitting in the squalid cell to which the Birmingham Police had confined him—on Good Friday of all days—completely cut off from what was happening on the ground "out there." But he wasn't incensed simply because he was thrown in jail yet again, this being the umteenth time. He was incensed because something else had gotten under his skin, something that was spreading like a ticking-time bomb.

I can't believe these people, he thought to himself. And they call themselves ministers? They call themselves Christians?

King was reading for the first time the open letter the "moderate" white ministers from Birmingham had written to him, who said they were for racial integration but who had called him an "outsider," who told him to end his trouble-making Civil Rights Movement, who told him that the police should be praised for keeping "law and order" in the face of his defiance of the South. The letter was printed in the one newspaper that Bull Conner had sarcastically let him have earlier in the day, hoping to get this exact reaction from King.

I can't believe it, he thought as he continued to read. Are they really serious? Is this really what the moderate, "non-racist" white church, across the South and throughout America, which has refused to ever let me speak in their pulpits not even a single time, thinks is right: people who say they are for civil rights in theory, who say they are for equality in theory, but who oppose it when they see it in action? So that they can see themselves as good people without having to get their hands dirty, so that they can see themselves as morally innocent without having to advocate for changing the status quo, so that they can see themselves as privately righteous so that they can justify their embrace of public cowardice?

King then saw a young red-headed guard walk by and called out to him.

"Sir, I need a pen," he said matter-of-factly, his stately and diplomatic tone belying the anger pulsating in his bones.

"For what?" the red-headed guard asked, squinting his distrusting eyes, unsure of King's motives.

"For a letter I need to write right now," King quipped, sounding urgent.

The guard reached in his pocket and surprisingly gave King a pen, as his outrage began to grow into righteous anger, over what the moderate white ministers had said. He thought, if these were "friends" of integration—accusing him of inciting violence, praising racists like Bull Conner, and telling him and black people they need to wait for justice to magically come—who needs enemies?

King took the newspaper, *The Birmingham News*, and began scribbling in its margins. He wrote, "Seldom do I pause to answer criticism of my work and ideas…" as he initially attempted to strike a calm and diplomatic tone. But then his growing anger took over, the anger he personally felt being dismissed and denigrated as a black man, and the anger he felt for the centuries of black people who had experienced the same, who were all told to wait their turn in a line of hope that never seemed to move, a bankrupt concept that white "allies" told them to believe in using a sprinkled web of useless words and logic.

In this moment, he remembered the millions of blacks from Africa sent on death marches to board slave ships for America. He remembered the chains and the shackles and dehumanization of the plantation system. He remembered the projects built in the ghettos blacks were forced into; the G.I. Bill blacks who fought in wars were legally denied access to; and the humiliation and soul-crushing mindwarp White Supremacists tried to psychologically impose into the very DNA of his people, as if the supposed divine fiat of White Supremacy mandated the legal and social inevitability of these things, and as if these things were or would be overcome by blacks waiting "their turn," believing that whites would somehow find it in the goodness of their hearts to change their minds, and their actions, from hatred to love or, at the least, acceptance and equality when it came to blacks.

"We have waited for more than 340 years for our constitutional and God given rights," he continued to write, his letters shrunken to their smallest size to fit into the paper's negative space.

"The nations of Asia and Africa are moving with jetlike speed toward gaining political independence, but we still creep at horse and buggy pace toward gaining a cup of coffee at a lunch counter."

"Perhaps it is easy for those who have never felt the stinging darts of segregation to say, "Wait."

"But when you have seen vicious mobs lynch your mothers and fathers at will and drown your sisters and brothers at whim; when you have seen hate filled policemen curse, kick and even kill your black brothers and sisters; when you see the vast majority of your twenty million Negro brothers smothering in an airtight cage of poverty in the midst of an affluent society;

"When you suddenly find your tongue twisted and your speech stammering as you seek to explain to your six year old daughter why she can't go to the public amusement park that has just been advertised on television, and see tears welling up in her eyes when she is told that Funtown is closed to colored children, and see ominous clouds of inferiority beginning to form in her little mental sky, and see her beginning to distort her personality by developing an unconscious bitterness toward white people; when you have to concoct an answer for a five year old son who is asking: "Daddy, why do white people treat colored people so mean?"

"When you take a cross country drive and find it necessary to sleep night after night in the uncomfortable corners of your automobile because no motel will accept you…"

"When you are humiliated day in and day out by nagging signs reading "white" and "colored"; when your first name becomes "nig*er," your middle name becomes "boy" (however old you are) and your last name becomes "John," and your wife and mother are never given the respected title "Mrs."; when you are harried by day and haunted by night by the fact that you are a Negro, living constantly at tiptoe stance, never quite knowing what to expect next, and are plagued with inner fears and outer resentments; when you are forever fighting a degenerating sense of "nobodiness"--then you will understand why we find it difficult to wait. There comes a time when the cup of endurance runs over, and men are no longer willing to be plunged into the abyss of despair.

But with this sentence, he stopped, his hands shaking, his brow perspiring, feeling the weight of the world in his chest. He placed his hand over his cross-scarred heart and felt an irregular palpation, a palpitation that wanted to make his insides explode. Tears began to well up in his eyes as he pleaded, "Dear God, please help us."

THIRTY SIX

Bull Conner stood there, a smirk embracing his smug face, feeling like a tough guy, his officers' guns still pointed straight at the heads of the innocent black children.

"Looks like these little bastards want to stop," he quipped to his officers, who all looked equally smug and satisfied.

One of the children, who was about 11, started to hyperventilate. Another had soiled her pants, the left side of her jeans stained with a runny urine which dripped onto her white shoes, dying them yellow.

"Scared nig*ers!" one dough-faced officer said, eliciting laughter from the others.

One of them responded back to him, "scaredy cats, scaredy cats," like he was a child himself, educated in one of the Dixiecrat South's most prized possessions: insult and mockery.

As the officers continued to laugh, something happened. In between their chuckles of hate, they heard something faint in the distance.

"What's that?" one of the officers asked the others, sounding confused.

Several of the police then looked beyond the 50 children right in front of them, who were still standing frozen.

"You've got to be kidding me," one said exasperated, his eyes growing as wide as his oversized waistline. "This is bullsh*t."

Hundreds more black children were marching their way toward the standoff, in fact more children than the eye could reasonably count or estimate. And they were singing. And they were chanting. And they were being trailed by television cameras documenting their every move, NBC, ABC, and CBS making good on their promise to cover the protest.

"Sh*t," one police officer said out loud as his look, and the other officers' looks, turned from smugness to fear. The childrens' numbers were simply overwhelming; they were a brigade of young black crusaders, an army of grace, like little angels flying low to the ground.

"Boss," an officer said to Conner, "what do we do?"

"Drop your weapons, boys!" Conner screamed, knowing the negative image this would project, knowing that guns pointed at the heads of black children would call his tactics into question. "And arrest these monkeys at once!"

"But sir," one said, "we don't have cuffs that small," making an outline of a small circle with his hands to show that many of the kids' wrists were too tiny to fit adult handcuffs.

"Then find some kind of tie to cuff them and throw their asses in jail," Conner barked, trying to start the arrests before the media could see them.

The Birmingham Police did exactly as their master told them. Dozens of officers approached the children, who had remembered their nonviolent training and didn't resist, and tied them up. The officers decided to deliberately tighten the knots to not only leave indentations in the kids' wrists, but to cut off as much blood circulation as possible, seeing if they could get any to pass out or, in their hideous best case scenario, die from lack of oxygen.

"Ouch," one black child who had just been arrested said, "that's hurting me."

"Shut up, criminal!" shouted the white police officer who then threatened to backhand him, raising his large right palm in the air.

The hundreds of black children who were marching spotted what was going on, pointing several hundred yards in front of them.

"Oh no," one of them said. "We need to hurry up."

The marchers started to increase their pace, still singing, still chanting, still maintaining military-like discipline that would have amazed even George Washington himself, a unified, and outmatched, battalion seeking only one thing: complete victory.

"Stupid nig*ers," Conner said watching them approach, "arrest them too!"

As hundreds of children showed up, the police called for more backup who brought squad cars and paddy wagons, arresting as many children as they could lay their hands on.

One young white reporter, from CBS in New York, who looked skeptical and increasingly disgusted at what she was seeing, approached Conner. She asked him pointedly, "Excuse me, what is going on here?"

"Disorderly conduct," Conner said as sweetly as he could, changing his persona to project the propaganda the Iron White Wall believed about itself: that they were innocent, good people just trying to do their jobs. "I have orders from the Mayor stating that there are to be no protests this week. These people, these men and women, are breaking the law."

"Sir, these are children and the First Amendment affords them the freedom of assembly," the reporter shot back.

"Oh, I quite understand what you're saying," Conner said with deceptive, slithery charm. "Unfortunately these people don't have a permit to be out here and so they're engaging in criminal activity."

But before the disgusted reporter could ask any more questions, Conner excused himself, telling her he needed to get back to keeping law and order so no violence could break out. He said, after all, anything could happen when you have this many suspicious men and women in one spot, violating the law.

Conner walked away and hopped into a squad car. He helped to transport the first few hundred children to jail while he rode shotgun in the lead vehicle, including escorting their 5 year old black leader. Once he got inside, he started barking orders again to his unquestioning, obedient staff. He told an administrator, referring to the 5 year old leader, to "fingerprint" her and lock her up," as well as the rest of them. The line to the jail started to wrap multiple blocks around the building after scores of police cars and paddy wagons dropped more and more black children off.

With lightning speed and efficiency, their version of a White Supremacist blitzkrieg, the police stuffed the children inside of the dark holding cells like sardines, jamming them into all four corners to maximize every square inch.

"Now I know how they must've fit all those slaves in those ships," joked one booking officer who forcibly arranged the children into their cages.

"That's funny," responded another, impressed by what he perceived as his colleague's quick wit.

The jail was full. But the line outside of it, the countless arrested children tied up and humiliated because they dared to believe in their own worth, because they dared to exercise their constitutional rights, kept getting longer and longer.

"We have no more room," Conner said, quite proud of himself.

But before he could bask anymore in his own hubris, one of his staff members cut him off.

"Boss," one officer said to him, "I just got a call from an officer saying there's reports of thousands more boy and girl Negroes who just showed up to march."

Conner looked at him, irritation increasingly hardening his face, wondering what he needed to do to extinguish this rising black fire.

"What should we do?" lamented the officer.

Conner thought for a moment and then said angrily, "These little bastards want to keep messing with me. Well then, I'll really give them somebody to mess with. Ready our fire hoses and attack dogs."

THIRTY SEVEN

King wiped the tears out of his eyes as the pain in his chest subsided. These tears, like so many he had shed before this, were not tears of self-pity. They were tears scarred with the reality he felt that, despite his best efforts and the efforts of so many others, white people—white moderates in particular, people like these white ministers and like Bobby Kennedy—didn't seem to want to search deep within themselves. They didn't seem to want to search for some measure of empathy, for some wellspring of compassion, for some perspective beyond their own self interest to try to understand the suffering of black people.

He thought to himself, *Get it together Martin. You need to keep writing. You need to really tell them how you feel. You need to tell them the truth. People raised in a culture to only look out for themselves will never understand unless you tell them the truth. Even if they initially deny or dismiss this truth, even if they hide from this truth, even if this truth finally stings them enough to force them to do something about it. Even if this truth destroys the myths and identity they've built their lives on—and even if it destroys the lies they've built their society on. You need to tell them this truth.*

He picked up his pen from the bottom of his jail cell, stared at it like it was a weapon of psychological and social liberation, and began to write again in the margins of his paper.

"I must confess that over the past few years I have been gravely disappointed with the white moderate. I have almost reached the regrettable conclusion that the Negroes' great stumbling block is not… the Ku Klux Klanner, but the white moderate, who is more devoted to "order" than to justice; who prefers a negative peace which is the absence of tension to a positive peace which is the presence of justice; who constantly says: 'I agree with you in the goal you seek, but I cannot agree with your methods of direct action.'"

As he continued writing, he ran out of room on the page. He flipped to the inside of the newspaper, finding its narrow margins after quickly scanning the headlines the Birmingham's press corps had written as the most important stories the community seemed to care about: sports scores and a review of the city's favorite television show, *The Beverly Hillbillies*.

King readied his pen, which seemed to be taking on the same supernatural eloquence with which his tongue also spoke. He continued to express his disappointment with the white moderate, who he saw not just as the white clergy who wrote him the letter, and Bobby Kennedy, but also the white church write large, "who paternalistically believes he can set the timetable for another man's freedom; who lives by a mythical concept of time and who constantly advises the Negro to wait for a more "convenient season."

King then stopped and thought for a moment. He felt he needed to be even more blunt, that he needed to strike at the heart of the white moderate's image of itself as pure and blameless on civil rights.

"Shallow understanding from people of good will," he wrote, "is more frustrating than absolute misunderstanding from people of ill will. Lukewarm acceptance is much more bewildering than outright rejection."

There. He said it. He said what he had been wanting to say all of these years but never had the chance to before this: that the white moderate was simple in his thinking, naive in his actions, and counterproductive in his support of black people, which he thought of as a charity case, not of as a true American brother who was deserving of not only as much respect as the white moderate, but even more respect because of everything he had to endure in the face of the long-standing terrorism committed against him.

But before he could write any further, the red headed guard came to his cell.

"On your feet, coon," the guard said as he opened the jail door with a long silver key. "You're being transferred to solitary confinement."

King sighed and rolled his eyes in genuine exasperation. Now this, he thought, as the guard cuffed him and led him out.

King was then paraded from out of his cell and marched through the corridors of the jail. But as he started to look to his left and his right, he was hit with a sudden jolt of torment, like that of a plantation worker being struck with a harsh, cold, leather whip: he now saw countless cells, filled with innocent black children, who stared back at him as if they had seen a ghost, as if they knew their collective nightmare was about to get worse.

THIRTY EIGHT

Despite the jail overflowing with hundreds of black children, now totalling nearly 1,000 who had been put behind bars, more children kept showing up to protest. Kept showing up to march. Kept showing up as a wave of young black justice.

"Where are all of these kids coming from?" one young black girl asked herself aloud, holding up a handmade sign that read, "Desegregation Now! Desegregation Tomorrow! Desegregation Forever!" in a quip attacking the "Segregation Now! Segregation Tomorrow! Segregation Forever!" attitude that permeated throughout most of the city's white population.

A black boy, marching nearby, heard her and responded, wearing a bright smile on his face. "I don't know where they are coming from, but I know we can't be stopped!"

One group of children, numbering in the hundreds, made their way toward City Hall and stood outside chanting. Another group of children, also in the hundreds, started doing kneel-ins inside of libraries and segregated white churches. Yet another group of children went inside of department stores and lunch counters and began their sit-ins.

Local residents and workers were horrified at what they were seeing, feeling like an alien takeover had overtaken them. There were thousands of children now, marching for their destinies.

Inside of one of the Birmingham sit-ins, at a famous Woolworth restaurant, America's top diner and department store in the 1960s, one overweight middle aged white woman who appears to have just gotten a perm, looked at the two black boys next to her at the lunch counter, one on her left and one on her right. Appalled, she protested to the waiter, demanding that they "get these damn coons out of here!"

The waiter, realizing that his entire lunch counter, and restaurant, was now filled with black children, became apoplectic. He said, "Shoo!" as if the kids were racoons, dirty and rabies-infected pests who always seemed to be looking for trouble.

The little black boy, sitting next to the overweight portly woman, looked at the waiter but didn't flinch after the stupid remark. He politely said in his Negro Southern drawl, "Sir, I'd like to order a lemonade." He then reached in his pocket and pulled out a nickel, the posted price for the drink, and the posted price for most of the other food in Woolworths, a five-and-dime store.

The waiter said, "We don't serve nig*ers here!" He then spit in the child's face, letting his disgust and make-believe racial superiority assert itself, a fairytale mindset that even the most lowly and downtrodden Dixiecrat white men were trained to believe: that no matter what, no matter how poor, or how powerless, or how uneducated, at least you're not a nig*er.

The boy held his anger inside and wiped the green spit off his cheek. The black boy sitting next to him, and the other black children at the counter, looked tense, their stomachs doing hula hoop twists. But they maintained their peace and didn't flinch. One. Bit.

The waiter again said, after seeing the recalcitrance of the children, "Shoo!" this time also wildly gesturing with his arms like one of *The Three Stooges.*

Nevertheless, the children still didn't move.

The overweight woman, who was sitting in front of her half eaten toasted ham and cheese sandwich, Woolworth's signature food item, looked dumbfounded. She let out a loud gasp of disapproval and left the store. Upon exiting, she spotted a few tough looking white men and spoke something to them, as she pointed at the black children through the window.

"Ma'am," the waiter said to her apologetically as he ran outside after Her Portliness. "I'm so sorry. I'll take care of this."

He then re-entered the restaurant, walked over to the piping pot of hot coffee he was brewing, picked it up, and revealed a scowl of invisible swastikas all over his face.

On the outside of Woolworths, just a block away, things were getting more tense there too. Bull Conner had left the station, along with a legion of officers, and had made their way back to the city center, responding to the call they heard about the growing protests.

As Conner looked into a sea of nameless, young black faces, as he looked past the media cameras which were recording live, he took out his bullhorn. "Listen up," he said to the children, "you are breaking the law. You must vacate immediately or we will be forced to vacate you."

One black child, who had earlier seen his sister get dragged off to jail, shouted back at him. "You can't make us do nuttin!"

"I don't make empty threats boy!" Conner screamed, letting the charm he normally turned on in front of reporters and cameras completely vanish, the hate-filled caricature he had increasingly become revealing itself publicly for the first time.

The black child, not missing a beat, responded back, "Sir, neither do I!"

Conner, looking as stoned faced as the Moai statues on Easter Island, nodded to a couple of white officers who were holding a large hose and standing next to a fire hydrant. The officers turned it on, its pressure vibrating throughout their hands and body, ready to roar.

Back inside of Woolworth's, the waiter picked up the coffee pot, which was completely full. It was brewing at 200 degrees fahrenheit. "When I say, 'Shoo,' dammit you shoo!" the waiter said as he violently threw the blisteringly hot pot into the face of the black boy, scalding him, disfiguring him, letting him know that the tangible heat of hell was now activated against him. The child began shrieking in agony as his bloody skin started to blister and peel away.

The other black boys at the counter rushed to console their fellow marcher. But as they did, the white men who had been watching from outside entered the restaurant and jumped the children from behind. After assaulting them in the heads with blow after vicious blow, the boys fell to the ground with tears, screams, and blood gushing everywhere. The white men, who were just regular members of the community and not even Klan members, started to brutally kick the boys for good measure.

"Take that, nig*er!" one of them said as he put his size 11 shoe straight into the mouth of one of the boys, shattering his jawbone, laughing in delight at the human misery he believed blacks deserved for their very existence.

Meanwhile, back outside in Bull Conner territory, Conner decided to give one last warning to the children who were gathered, including the little boy who was defying him in front of his police force and in front of the cameras, and all of America, to see.

"I'm giving you to the count of 3 to vacate, *boy*," he said, his pupils bulging with ferocity.

He then began to count. "One. Two. Three…"

As the countdown finished, the police officers with the fire hose aimed it straight at the head of the little black boy Conner was confronting. The force of the water, pulsating with rage, burst out like a battering ram, hitting the child with such force that it knocked him over, and knocked him out. He lay there, unconscious, traumatized by the brutality of an instrument of mercy that had been instantaneously transformed into an instrument of hate. He lay motionless with a puddle of blood gathering around his small head.

The two officers, still holding the fire hose, then began to point it at other children, knocking them over one by one, like human dominoes during target practice, their bodies crushed by the ferocious power of liquid bile, their blood running down the street like a river stream.

Conner ordered additional fire hoses throughout the area, his version of a waterpark of death, a dastardly imitation of the FunTown theme park he liked to take his grandchildren to.

But as he stood there, his soul possessed by unmitigated power, something was off, even for him: he wasn't smiling. He wasn't smiling at all.

As he took in the carnage, he couldn't believe what he was seeing: the children had decided to fight back. They began locking their arms together, a brotherhood and sisterhood of love, of survival, united to withstand the weaponized water coming their way, so close and so connected with each other they no longer could be swept away by the flooding currents of his Iron White Wall.

Conner began walking quickly throughout the scene, making scattering movements like a cockroach, and made his way toward one of his armored paddy wagons. He whispered something into an officer's ear, who nodded in agreement. The officer then went into the back of his paddy wagon and let out his best friend: a vicious, hyperventilating german shepard, trained to protect, trained to kill.

The officer released the dog, which started to push speeds upward of 30 miles an hour, straight toward a little black girl it had spotted. It opened its mouth with its sharpened fangs, and, in an instant, did something never before seen on camera.

THIRTY NINE

"Oh my God!" JFK screamed to Bobby, as they both sat transfixed, jaws forced agape by bestial horror, like millions of other white and black Americans, who had unwanted front row seats to view hell on earth. "What are they doing to these poor children?"

In real time, the President and his Attorney General were watching the fury Bull Conner had released upon the innocent black child crusaders in front of the 19-inch RCA black-and-white television located in JFK's private study on the second floor of The White House.

They saw a large, professionally-trained German shepherd sink its deep fangs into a little black girl, savagely piercing her delicate skin, ripping apart her flesh as though she was captured prey, gnawing on her exposed bone and tissue like a rabid, merciless vulture, intent on sawing her in half as nonchalantly as eating a light afternoon snack.

They saw a police officer beating a child with a billy club, striking the child in the face over and over again, knocking his teeth out, causing the saliva and blood in his mouth to spew together in an unholy union of White Supremacist matrimony.

And they saw the hoses—those damn fire hoses—beating fiercely against the bodies of little child brigades, everyday kids trying to stand up for their rights even while their local Dixiecrat government was demanding that they stand down.

"Bobby, we have to stop this," JFK uttered, urgency piercing his voice, his unique Boston-Irish accent pulsating with moral and existential concern, disturbed by the true-crime American horror story he was witnessing.

"I can't believe these people," Bobby responded, completely disgusted, his eyes wide like he had seen a ghost, the white in his pupils being overtaken by spontaneous little red veins. "I really can't believe them."

Despite his reputation for ruthlessness, Bobby did have a heart for kids, no matter their color. And it was genuine. After all, he was the happy father of eight kids now, with his ninth child on the way within weeks, and if there was one thing he could not stand, if there was one thing he could not tolerate, it was kids being abused. What decent person could?

"What are we going to do, Jack?" Bobby asked, fuming, restraining himself from recommending U.S. Marshals go to the scene of the crime and beat the sh*t out of Bull Conner and the Birmingham Police, showing them there would not be impunity for their actions, that they would be held accountable by a force more powerful than themselves.

Thinking for a moment as he paced, JFK quickly decided on a course of action. "I'm going to federalize the Alabama National Guard," he said, "and stop this evil immediately."

"Jack," Bobby replied, weighing the political calculations and possibility that such an act might instigate a potential second Civil War, "I don't think you should do that, as much as you and I want to, at least not yet. Just call the Mayor, tell him to order his police force to cease and desist, and for God's sake, do your best to have him sit down for desegregation negotiations with Martin Luther King."

"That sounds like a wise course of action," JFK said, certain that his little brother almost always had the right answer at the right time, understanding that even when you do the right thing—and especially when you do the right thing—there are still consequences, damning and negative as they might be. "But do you think they'll actually negotiate with King?"

"I don't think they have any choice," Bobby said, brushing his hair out of his face.

"Why?" JFK questioned, confused, wondering where his little brother was going with this.

"Because those Jim Crow bastards have just caused the entirety of the American public to turn against them."

FORTY

Birmingham looked like a portrait straight out of the Civil War with its creative venom and iniquitous carnage spread everywhere. Except this time the scene wasn't North versus South or even Union versus Confederacy. It was child versus racist—and the racist ideology that kept Jim Crow whites and the systemically prejudiced institutions they ran entrapped in a poisonous, delusional prison of their own making.

In other words, in Birmingham it was little black children publicly exposing for America, and the world, to see the impoverished idea of weaponized White Supremacy that kept generation after generation of Southern whites spellbound, deceived, and trapped in a racial straightjacket that would be sure to render many of them villains of history—and be sure to cause future generations of Southern whites to deny that their forebears' hatred of blacks wasn't as bad as it really was. After all, if they did this whitewashing after the Civil War, if they tried to insist that "The War of Northern Aggression" was really about states' rights and not slavery, as so many in Birmingham and elsewhere throughout the Jim Crow South did in a hideous mythology campaign to continue to deceive their own people, they would surely try to erase their culpability for this black ass whooping too. In other words, with the blood of innocent black children on their hands, they would be sure to insist that this was not really that big of a deal, a minor footnote of history to be quickly blotted out of the record once the dust settled and the people forgot.

But in the midst of all this, in the center of this tortuous tension, was still the elephant in the room: whether or not Birmingham would be utterly and completely desegregated. And Martin Luther King, along with his adult aides who had been released from jail after JFK placed a call to the Mayor of the city, knew this. So did the obstinate City officials, who told King and his crew to meet them at the Gaston Motel for negotiations. The Motel, located at 1510 Fifth Avenue, just blocks from City Hall, was a faded brick two story building adjoined by a Z-shaped motel sign, birdbath, and courtyard patio. It was one of the few places that remained intact after the chaos, and seemed like the perfect place for discussions, particularly without the black children who had also been freed from jail.

As hour after hour went by without so much as a single citing of any City officials, one of the Mayor's Dixecrat aide's finally knocked on King's motel room door. The aide blurted out loudly, making sure his voice was heard through the thin partition separating them, "Mr. King, the Mayor will see you now."

"It's about time," King responded to himself, extinguishing his Pall Mall cigarette that was calming his rocky nerves, motioning to several aides to stand, frustrated that, even after pressure from the President of the United States and ubiquitous news coverage, Birmingham officials were still engaging in gamesmanship, unable to understand the seriousness of the moment, or to show any respect or deference to King or his team for their time, or even any remorse for their actions toward the child marchers.

King left Room 15, along with Fred Shuttlesworth, Ralph Abernathy, and a few others and entered the Mayor's makeshift negotiating quarters a few doors down that smelled like mischief. The Mayor, Albert Boutwell, who was about 60 years old and who wore round glasses and an "aw, shucks" country demeanor, was a typical son of the South. Both his mother's father and his father's father were Confederate soldiers, and White Supremacy raged in his blood like a genetic aphrodisiac.

"Mr. King," the Mayor said, surrounded by his suspicious-looking and sycophantic country aides, "take a seat."

Ralph Abernathy interjected, defensively, "it's Dr. King to you, not Mr. King."

But the Mayor didn't take kindly to the remark. He turned his head and gave an icy stare to King's best friend, thinking to himself, *You better watch it boy.*

"Mr. Mayor," King said deliberately, picking up Abernathy's cue and subtly jabbing back at the Dixiecrat politician who did not have the educational credentials King did, "we must negotiate a settlement of justice."

"What are your terms?" The Mayor said flatly, no emotion in his face, no humanity in his heart, no desire to even be at the meeting in the first place, forced only by the media and political pressure knocking him around like the empty straw man that he was.

"I've outlined our terms in my letter," King responded, gently pushing the newspaper that had printed what was being called *The Letter From A Birmingham Jail* which he had written in the margins of the newspaper while he was incarcerated. "Have you read it?"

"The whole damn country has read it by now," the Mayor barked back, upset by the publicity it was getting for King—and the negative publicity it was bringing to his city, its infested underbelly revealed for all to see, disclosing that the heaven it tried to project on the outside was ruled by the hell it truly was on the inside.

"Then you will understand that my terms are complete desegregation," King responded. "Immediate desegregation."

"That's not possible."

"And why not?" King asked, accustomed to the standard ploys the Iron White Wall pulled: resist even if you're in the wrong, resist even if you know you're going to lose, resist even if it costs you everything so that, if all else fails, at least you can protect your master race fairytale, your greatest source of pride and identity.

"It just isn't," the Mayor said, his circular reasoning showcasing that even he understood the baselessness of Jim Crow, the tragedy of its totalitarian logic crumbling when put under even the faintest of microscopes.

"We want complete desegregation," King reiterated, stoically, while Abernathy, Shuttlesworth, and the others likewise remained stoic.

"I don't see how we can do it," the Mayor replied, sitting back in his chair, trying to play a poker-faced tough guy. "I really just don't see how."

"I will grant you that, Mr. Mayor," King said, "I would never accuse you or the South of having the insight or know how to do anything other than maintaining the status quo; I would never accuse you or the South of having the insight or know how to do anything other than maintaining your own selfish and self-righteous interests; and I would never accuse you or the South of having the insight or know how to do anything that would cause you to give up power over people you love to oppress."

"That's unfair," the Mayor shot back red-faced and angered, staring coldly at The Reverend, looking like he wanted to slug him in his big black auburn lips and slit his throat with his jagged eyes.

King, still stoic, put his right hand on his face, resting his chin between his fingers, employing the awkward discomfort of silence, one that he ironically learned from Richard Nixon, letting his statement sink in more and more, like a surgical punch ripping through the politician's' dirty insides.

After a few moments had passed, the Mayor finally piped up. "Look, what you're asking is a lot," he said. "My residents would never go for it."

"Let me ask you a question then, Mr. Mayor," King retorted, taking his hand off of his face and leaning forward, his posture as stern as a strict military commander's or school headmaster, his backbone sculpted by years of war.

"Okay," the Mayor said, hesitantly, not sure if he should allow himself to be cross-examined by a man he didn't want to admit was his intellectual superior, a man with a doctorate of philosophy and theology, a man who was a moral lawyer if ever there was one.

"Do you believe Birmingham is a part of the United States or not?" King questioned, his voice even.

"Of course it's a part of the United States, what kind of absurd question is that?"

"Very good," King responded, laying his trap. "Do you also believe that Birmingham should abide by law and order?"

"Absolutely, that's what makes America great."

"Well said," King replied. "Then shouldn't Birmingham abide by the laws and orders of the United States government too?"

"Only the laws that are right and that we find just," the Mayor quipped, a phrase states' rights politicians belched like parrots when trying to hide the insidiousness of their racism, of their justification of ethnic inequality, of trying to pull a fast one on people they viewed as intellectually inferior.

"Didn't we fight a civil war about this?" King asked as he cocked his head indignantly. "About states rights' as your people call them? About you just not being able to cherry pick and choose which laws you follow and which ones you don't?"

But the Mayor didn't respond.

"And didn't your side lose?" Abernathy jumped in. "And lose big?"

"This is ridiculous," the Mayor said, his scoff plastered all over his face as well as the faces of his now infuriated aides. "I don't need to put up with this."

"The facts hurt, don't they?" Abernathy said in what was a statement more than it was a question, as the Mayor again met him with an icy stare.

"Look," the Mayor responded, frustrated and finally acknowledging some semblance of defeat, "I can agree to desegregate the schools but that's it."

"That's not a concession," King fired back. "The Supreme Court decided that you had to do that almost a decade ago in *Brown vs. Board of Education*."

"And all you've been doing is breaking the law since then," Abernathy said. "Willfully depriving another Negro generation of equality and opportunity."

The Mayor sat there, defiant in his heart but seeing the slippery slope he was standing on, especially with the nation watching what his City would do, watching how it would try to make atonement for the single most vile act ever publicly committed by police officers against children. "What I will agree to desegregate is—"

But as the Mayor said this, the windows in the building suddenly shattered. Shrapnel flew everywhere, glass torpedoing to and fro as though it were employed as a merchant of death, narrowly missing the pugnacious Mayor but striking one of King's aides.

The brick foundation, which held up the walls, started to collapse. And not a sound could be heard in the room as smoke filled its remnants, an eerie ghost factory of a place that had been filled with people.

An improvised explosive device had been set off, a lethal execution mission unleashed by The Contact and his paid-off KKK mercenaries to murder Martin Luther King yet again.

Ralph Abernathy, with a horrific silent ringing in his ears, looked over at King, and asked,"Martin, are you okay?" to which he got no response. So he again asked, even more urgently, while shaking his friend's body, "Martin, are you okay!?" to which he also got no response.

FORTY ONE

"Dammit!" The Imperial Wizard barked in the dark of night to his pointy-hatted Kleagles at their Georgia church headquarters, their wet carpet soggy and musty from a recent water valve break, its mildew scent permeating throughout the pews like bile floating through a hot sewer. "You had Martin Luther King in your crosshairs like a sitting duck and you screwed it up!"

"Our bomb guys did their best," one Klansman replied, a police officer with thick black eyebrows who had consulted by phone with the Birmingham Klan member who set off the bomb at the Gaston Motel. "This nig*er just doesn't seem to want to die."

"Clearly," the Imperial Wizard said, his face hardened with contempt, his eyes a ravine of boiling bitterness. "But now The Contact is pissed."

"It wasn't our fault," the police officer responded, positive that he had walked the Birmingham KKK through how to correctly design and denote a homemade explosive device. "We tried boss."

"We're lucky The Contact isn't asking for his money back," the Imperial Wizard shouted as he put his hands on his hips, starting to pace back and forth, his mind racing with the kinds of thoughts only the head of the KKK could have. The kinds of thoughts only a mind devoid of conscience could harbor.

"Is there a new pot for another hit on him?" a local judge asked who could only think and talk about money these days, greed and corruption having completely overtaken him now that he was two-timing his wife with a big breasted blonde secretary half his age he had been lavishing gifts on, including a recently approved FDA breast implant procedure, enhancing her cup size to DD, trying to make her look like a real life Barbie doll, his Aryan fantasy trophy that earned him respect among the other Klansmen who fetishized this type of woman for themselves, their idea of females being socially conditioned by the superficial images put out by Hollywood and New York's Madison Avenue. "I think we can get him next time."

"Another pot is the least of our worries right now," the Imperial Wizard shot back. "After the bombing, the Mayor agreed to complete desegregation like a pussy and, even worse, that damn Kennedy just went on television and gave a speech about civil rights, about how he's going to introduce legislation in Washington to support these coons."

"What faggots," the local judge said, referring both to JFK and the Birmingham Mayor, whom the Klan had had no problem treating as potential collateral damage in the bombing.

"Kennedy's entire speech sounded like it was lifted straight from King's *Letter from a Birmingham Jail*," The Imperial Wizard responded. "He condemned our way of life, he condemned our divine right to rule."

"Sell out," the police officer said. "His little brother Bobby came down here begging for votes during the election a few years ago and this is the way they return the favor? By aligning themselves with colored scum?"

"Well, even if whatever bill he is proposing passes we can just ignore it, like always," said one Klansman, a state senator, sure that their typical deflection tactics against implementing laws they disagreed with would be successful, as they had always been.

"Not anymore," barked the Imperial Wizard. "He has federalized the Alabama National Guard and could do the same to other Southern states' national guards to enforce their bills, to enforce their Supreme Court decisions."

"He can't do that!" shouted a potbellied member in the back, ignorant of both America's Constitution as well as its longstanding 1807

Insurrection Act, which granted the President broad and express authority to do so, to override local police forces. "It's unconstitutional!"

"I agree," the state senator echoed, equally as ignorant. "But how do we fight back against this persecution of our way of life?"

"Well, we continue targeting the Kennedys and King to snuff them out once we get a clean shot," the Imperial Wizard said. "But in the meantime, we can do something that will put the brakes on this entire bill, to show them there are consequences for their actions, to show them that we can stop their momentum dead in its tracks."

The Kleagles looked on with anticipation, always excited about what type of plans their innovative master wizard would cook up, even on the spot.

Peering back and forth across his unholy congregation The Imperial Wizard said, "Let's take out those little nig*ers in Birmingham who caused us all of this hassle."

"You mean those ones from 16th Street Baptist Church the media has been talking about?" the police officer asked, referring to the thousands of children who had marched in the children's crusade, and somehow miraculously survived both jailing and bestial attacks from Bull Connor's boys in blue.

"Yes," the Imperial Wizard stated coldly. "And let's take them out while they are attending Sunday School."

FORTY TWO

While the dust was still settling from the chaos of Birmingham, Bobby had traveled to his brother's Big Apple penthouse apartment, 24 Central Park South, the same place he had first met Martin Luther King during the Presidential contest. He was in New York City for some official business but decided he also wanted to unofficially hear from some prominent blacks about their thoughts on everything the Administration was doing on behalf of civil rights, especially after the trauma of a few days ago during which time they bailed King and the children crusaders out of jail, and especially after JFK's recent civil rights speech, their first public pronouncement on the issue since he became president.

The penthouse bell rang around 7 pm, and Bobby, whose dark three-button Oscar de La Renta jacket and skinny tie made him look like the *James Bond* character mesmerizing America, looked over at the door. After a few moments, he got up, walked to the entrance, and engineered a genuine smile as he reached for the knob.

"My old friend," Bobby gushed, opening the door, greeting the handsome and dapper actor-singer Harry Belafonte who, like usual, had a tight shirt on showcasing his swoon-worthy muscular build. "It's good to see you."

"It's nice to see you too," Belafonte responded, embracing Bobby with a warm bear hug—two old confidantes exchanging the joy of reuniting, the joy of being satisfied in each other's presence—before gesturing over to the small group with him. "I'm sure you know James and my friends."

Of course, the world-famous Belafonte was referring to the Afro-chic distinguished group of black people flanking his left and right, including the most famous black writer of the day, the magnificently intellectual James Baldwin, as well as the brilliant Broadway creator Lorraine Hansberry, the stunningly beautiful artist Lena Horne, an NAACP and Urban League official, and the Freedom Rider Jerome "Big Duck" Smith, who, unlike the luminaries walking in, was a virtual unknown to both Bobby and the group.

"Please, please," Bobby said as the prominent black group filed in and began making themselves comfortable, "let's have a toast."

A couple of Bobby's house servants dressed in black suits and ties and white gloves served champagne to all present, except Bobby who, even on occasions like this where he was playing the host, refused to consume alcohol himself.

Bobby lifted his glass filled with sparkling water and toasted, "Here's to civil rights progress."

Everyone in the group, except Jerome "Big Duck" Smith, raised their Sasaki Crystal Aperitif glasses and clanked the stemware together, an echo of hope spreading throughout the luxurious living room like a fresh lilac flower, a light scent perfect for the occasion.

"As you all are aware," Bobby bragged, optimistic he would receive affirmation and adulation for his statements, "My brother and I have done more on civil rights than any Administration in the history of our country."

"Here, here," Belafonte said.

"And now we're proposing a new bill to prohibit discrimination on the basis of race once and for all," Bobby continued, "to strengthen our work on civil rights, as we have already litigated dozens of cases against Jim Crow and appointed hundreds of blacks to the Justice Department and federal government."

"Amen," the NAACP official said, as other group members could be seen uttering the same word.

"I think, given our work, that even in 40 years time we could have a Negro President," Bobby said. "And I say this because my people, the Irish, have been discriminated against just like you all, but after just 2 generations, after the poverty and hell we escaped, we have a president. And your turn will come soon too if you keep pulling yourselves up by your bootstraps."

"Mr. Attorney General," James Baldwin said, a look of bewilderment outlined on his face, "with all due respect, but my people have been here 350 years and have nothing to show for it. And you think we are just going to pull ourselves up by the bootstraps when every boot we work to put on, to pull ourselves up with, is stolen from us?"

Bobby smiled nervously, not expecting Baldwin to contradict him so publicly, so truthfully, so abruptly, especially during what Bobby considered a celebratory social engagement if not a moment of self-congratulation, especially after the successful Birmingham desegregation agreement and incredibly well received speech JFK had just given on civil rights. Bobby replied, "Well, that's why I wanted to meet with you all today. To see, from your perspective, how we can make more political progress for your people."

"If you want to see progress," James Baldwin said bluntly, "you need to have the President personally escort black students into white schools to enforce desegregation in Birmingham. That'll be real progress."

"Whoa now, James," Bobby responded, his smile increasingly diminishing, stunned by such a bold and controversial idea. "That would spark a potential civil wa—"

But Bobby cut himself off, not wanting to plant any ideas, not wanting to stoke any fears, not wanting to foment the seeds of civil war he knew Jim Crow would happily fight again if the people in this room provoked it—and, make no mistake, they had the power and celebrity to provoke it if they wanted to. "I mean," Bobby continued, "the best political course of action would be to see how we can support the civil rights movement behind the scenes, as we have been doing, and not with political stunts and pageantry like the President escorting black students to class."

But the room was silent, with an air of hostility brewing, as the looks on people's faces transformed from pleasant to determined, from one of social propriety to one of missionary activism. Bobby, assessing the sudden change in the room's temperature, started to think to himself, *Didn't they just see what Bull Conner did to those kids who pulled the stunt of standing up for themselves? Didn't they see the kind of demonic lengths to which White Supremacists go when they are directly confronted on their home turf? Didn't they see that it was better to wage war through laws, through courts, and through softer means that wouldn't involve bloodshed—or worse?*

"You know," Jerome "Big Duck" Smith said, speaking up for the first time, his tall frame emerging from the back Northwest corner of the penthouse, "that's the problem with you."

"I'm sorry," Bobby shot back, confused, offended, wondering why some nameless person would say such a thing to him. "But who are you?"

"I'm a Freedom Rider," the 24-year old Big Duck said, chest out, chin raised, stepping closer to the Attorney General, whom he physically towered over. "And I've been arrested, bombed, bludgeoned, and beaten to within an inch of my life countless times."

The rest of the group, who also didn't know the Freedom Rider until now—or how he had even gotten an invitation in the first place—stared at him. But it wasn't a stare of disrespect or rejection. It was the exact opposite. Their faces started to glow with admiration, their eyes growing bigger and bigger from the type of respect they were instantly bequeathing upon the young man that fame, fortune, or power can't buy you. The type of respect that says, *damn, so you're one of those courageous kids risking your life to set Negroes free.*

But all Bobby could say in response to the Freedom Rider, whose Freedom Rides he originally opposed and opposed very publicly was, "Oh."

"Furthermore, the problem with you and the President," Big Duck continued, "is that you see civil rights as a political issue and not a moral one."

"It is a political issue," Bobby responded, flatly, as he searched the room for support, looking first at Harry Belafonte, who diverted his eyes, and then at Lorraine Hansberry.

"Don't look to us for support," Hansbery said. "He's the one you need to be listening to."

Bobby opened his mouth to speak again, but "Big Duck" cut him off.

"You don't think the people in this room can't see through you, Bobby," Big Duck retorted, looking brave and scared at the same time. "You don't think that we can't see that you're two-faced."

"I beg your pardon," Bobby responded, his face flush with irritation, like a clear glass that has just been filled with fruit punch, like Good Bobby was being slugged by Bad Bobby.

"You brag about how no administration has ever done more for colored people," Big Duck continued, "while at the same time you appoint segregationist judges to enforce Jim Crow in the South, cut aid to black sharecroppers, and allow racist police forces to arrest Freedom Riders. You think we're too stupid to see that?"

Bobby's eyes got wider while he took a big gulp before responding in a tone-deaf way, "sometimes in politics, you have to make compromises."

"Don't you see Mr. Attorney General, that white politicians have compromised us for centuries?" Big Duck asked rhetorically. "Just to accommodate their fellow white man's prejudices who they are too cowardly to take on."

"Look," Bobby responded flatly, putting his hands on his hips defensively, "I'm not your enemy."

"But are you colored people's friends?" Big Duck asked. "I mean, you didn't even invite Martin Luther King to be here to get his advice about how to move forward on civil rights and he's our leader!"

Bobby again searched the room, and again received no validation, no understanding, no benefit of the doubt from any of his guests, who were now not only seeing the wisdom and truth in the young Freedom Rider's statements, but also that Bobby had deliberately not included Martin Luther King at this meeting.

"If I could snap my fingers and make civil rights happen overnight," Bobby said angrily, "I would. But I have legal constraints. I have political constraints, something you really need to consider."

"It seems to me, Mr. Attorney General," James Baldwin jumped in and said, "your greatest constraint is neither legal nor political, it is moral."

"Why are you attacking me?" Bobby barked, his palms pointing upward in confusion, his body language even more defensive. "I'm here to help you."

"We're attacking you because you're supposedly the best white America has to offer," Big Duck said, "and without you changing your civil rights stance from one of caution and trepidation to one of genuine and aggressive courage, you will continue to engage in moral treason against the colored people who believe in you the most, who voted to put your brother into office. You will force us to turn on you, to turn on America."

"Wait, what?" Bobby said incredulously and accusingly. "You sound like a radical, like one of Malcolm X's people who want to take up arms against white people, who want to burn everything to the ground. I just don't understand how you or any Negro would want to turn on America, especially right now, in light of all of our victories?"

"If you don't come out for civil rights with more conviction, me and my people just might turn into the dangerous radicals you don't want to see, that America don't want to see," Big Duck continued. "Because right now you don't realize that we follow Dr. King, we follow the way of nonviolence. But I don't know how much longer I can, or how much longer my people can; I don't know how much longer we can take getting our asses beaten and humiliated by the cruelty of the white man while you call this political victory."

"But," Bobby responded, unsure of what to say back, "it makes no sense to me how anyone could go from being nonviolent to violent. Either you are or you aren't."

"It's not that simple, Mr. Attorney General," Big Duck said without thinking. "You push a man far enough, you rape his women long enough, you steal his wages often enough, you deny his freedom strongly enough, he will turn on you…and he will do it in a bloody revolution."

Bobby, now starting to see what Big Duck was saying, starting to see the point he was making, asked him a question. "Do most of your people really feel this way?"

But Big Duck didn't answer. The expression on his face and on the faces of the group said it all: *Yes, hell yes, one thousand times yes.*

Bobby was speechless.

The group sat there staring back at him, the tension thick, the resolve full, the prophetic witness knocking on his heart, taking a small moral, and not just political, foothold in his innermost being.

After a few more moments had passed, Lorraine Hansberry looked around and said, "come on everybody, let's go. Nothing more to talk about here."

"But," Bobby said, his words still escaping him, his loquacious well run dry. "But."

"It's too late," Hansberry continued as the group got up and started filing out one by one.

But before Big Duck closed the door, as the last one out, he said to the Attorney General, "And this is why we can't put the brakes on civil rights. Until you and moderate white allies start to see things from our perspective and not just from your own, we will never have true equality in America."

"But we have a new bill," Bobby responded weakly, in one last ditch effort to try to connect to the young Freedom Rider, in one last attempt to try to salvage the meeting from being the complete and utter failure that it was. Just as it had been, in this exact location no less, with Martin Luther King almost three years ago.

Big Duck just looked at him and said, "That's great, Mr. Attorney General. But while you may have a bill, we still have a battle. And that's why Dr. King has announced his next move: a March on Washington, to shame you and your brother into doing the right thing, not just legally but morally, just as we shamed Birmingham officials, to take justice into our hands even if this justice runs you all over like a mighty freight train, even if this justice breaks out in bloody revolution. We are that serious

FORTY THREE

Bobby was not only dumbfounded at the outcome of his meeting at 24 Central Park West but, more and more, he was furious. Even though he was starting to see, in the faintest of ways, the moral and emotional realities of the suffering of black people, he was upset that his and his brother's efforts weren't more appreciated by civil rights leaders; he was upset that, instead of receiving the applause he had expected, he had instead received criticism he thought he didn't deserve; and he was upset that, despite JFK putting forth a civil rights bill for which Martin Luther King should have been happy, he was instead going to be protesting the Administration through his newly announced March on Washington, which officials were estimating could attract over 100,000 people—far greater than the few thousand in Birmingham—and wall-to-wall live television coverage.

Bobby, now back at his home at Hickory Hill for several days, tip-toed throughout his mansion at 1 am, past his statues of Mary and various crucifixes, and went into his private study. His pal Freckles followed him in and lay at his feet, their shadows bouncing off of the room's glowing white walls.

He reached for his leather journal and pen, next to his legacy 1952 phonograph record player his brother had given him as a gift when he won a seat in the U.S. Senate a decade ago, and began writing, liberating his feelings at will.

It seems that no matter what I do, Martin Luther King is determined to say it falls short. I recommended that Jack give his speech on civil rights right after Birmingham—and King, through his actions, said it fell short. I recommended that we put forth a civil rights bill for nationwide desegregation, on one of the very tenets of his Second Emancipation Proclamation, and King's workers see it as purely symbolic. I ask King to call off his March on Washington, even after I met with him personally at the White House recently, to prevent a potential outbreak of violence here in Washington and civil war throughout the nation, and he brushes off my concerns. It seems like he never wants to compromise because everything I ever do is never good enough for him.

Yes, he has shown a little bit of bravery for risking his life by taking on those Jim Crow idiots. But he's no hero, far from it. And him risking those poor children's lives to march? I can say unequivocally I would never allow my children to do that. What parent would? Heroes don't do that, they don't risk the innocent to fulfill their agenda, they don't risk the next generation to support their own.

But now the Soviets, and the world, are watching because of King's provocations and Jim Crow's responses, peering into America's dirty laundry, seeing that our children are on the opposite side of fire hoses and billy clubs, and they will exploit it to take down our country. They've fooled many black leaders into becoming Communists, like W.E.B. Du Bois, and I suspect they may be trying to get to more, especially people like James Baldwin that put out influential literary pieces. Speaking of, I didn't like how he spoke to me in my brother's home, how he disrespected me like that, or how that young Freedom Rider disrespected me like that. I'm going to ask that bastard J. Edgar Hoover to wiretap Baldwin's phones. Just as I begrudgingly agreed—was manipulated into agreeing, really—to have him wiretap Martin Luther King's. If these civil rights leaders are genuine, and say they are sincerely doing their work on behalf of Negroes and not Communists, then their actions will exonerate them. Besides, in King's case, I couldn't risk Hoover releasing his files on my brother. I love Jack too much to let anyone harm him or anything to threaten what he's building at the White House.

I have to confess, however, that civil rights is a hard issue, harder than I ever thought it would be. There's no managing Negroes, you just can't do it. I'm starting to see that their pain is just too great. But they still need to realize that they have to filter this pain through politics, through patience, through the long-game, if they ever want true freedom and equality. I don't think I'm being paternalistic by believing this. After all, I am their ally and they should not be indicting me or my brother for all that we are doing for them; we're allies!

But Bobby started to stare at the last sentence, his gaze transfixed on the last word, his thoughts obsessing over the term "allies." He then picked up his pen again and wrote, *Or can we—or should we—try to be something more than allies? And if so, what?*

FORTY FOUR

Martin Luther King, now fully physically but not psychologically recovered from the existentially wicked bombing attack a couple of months ago at the Gaston Motel in Birmingham, was busy at work with his team preparing for the March on Washington. One of his top aides organizing the event, Bayard Rustin who had been previously arrested on anti-gay sodomy laws in California, was performing miracles by synchronizing a vast collection of civil rights groups that were making plans to bus in hundreds of thousands of mostly black people from all across the country, something that had never been done before in history.

But with a crowd this size Rustin wanted to make sure that every security effort was being made to prevent violent outbreak. After all, although he knew Birmingham made all of the national headlines given Bull Conner's vicious brutality, there were still countless other communities that had had their own violent confrontations with and ass whoopings of civil rights marchers this year that had gone unreported in the national news—in Goldsboro, North Carolina, Somerville, Tennessee, St. Augustine Florida, Pine Bluff, Arkansas, and more—and he wanted to, with any power vested in him, keep this from happening in the District of Columbia, not just for PR purposes but because he deeply loved black people and didn't want to see any more get hurt or humiliated.

At the makeshift SCLC headquarters in Washington, DC, King spotted Rustin in the hall, who was walking at his usual frantic pace. His cropped mini afro, square black glasses, and well groomed mustache coupled with his African Dashiki wardrobe made him hard to miss.

"Bayard," King said as he chased down the slender, well-dressed organizer, "how are things looking on the ground?"

"Pretty good, except I need the Kennedy's to make sure they not only provide federal security but also lots of trash cans," Rustin responded, serious, resolute, reassuring, a man nearly 20 years King's senior that King deeply looked up to for his administrative and moral brilliance.

But King, who was a mesmerizing speaker and symbol for the movement but not a hands-on, logistical type of leader who dealt with practical things like this, simply asked, "Why do trash cans matter to Bayard?"

"Because the world will be watching, Martin, and I don't want there to be even one piece of litter on the ground," Rustin replied. "We will not allow Jim Crow or racist whites to accuse us of being savages, of defacing property, of being unclean. We want the nation to see that Negroes are respectable people who will leave a place as nice, or nicer, than we found it."

"That's smart," King said, happy that Rustin, who had previously organized other marches on Washington, including a much smaller march on Washington in 1957 that King had spoken, was at the helm. Somebody who could think of all of the details like trash cans. Somebody who was always thinking about how to show that blacks are dignified, moral people, not brutal savages intent on creating chaos, anarchy, or defacing an environment, as blacks were all too often depicted as by a society that didn't respect them. By a society that didn't trust them. By a society that didn't really know them, or try to know them—the real them—at all.

"We just need to make sure Ralph Lawson is able to train all of our people," Rustin said, shifting the conversation a bit, "to be nonviolent if provoked. You know how split our people are on this, just as you once were, and if Jim Crow or the KKK tries to provoke us things could get out of hand right away for those in our community who don't believe in nonviolence when attacked."

"Right," King responded, believing Rustin always had great instincts about where the pulse of the Freedom Movement was at any given time, and great instincts on what approaches to take—and which ones not to take. It was, after all, Rustin who had personally convinced King to become nonviolent, to personally follow and embody the teachings of Christ and the practices of Gandhi, who showed King he no longer had to carry a gun to defend himself or his family, which King had done before meeting Rustin.

But before any more conversation could be had, a 28 year old young male aide, who was wearing a gray suit and slightly shined shoes, approached the two leaders.

"Dr. King," the aide said, looking sheepish as he didn't want to disturb him in the middle of his conversation, "a Senator is on the phone and urgently wants to speak to you about the march."

King thanked the aide for letting him know, patted Rustin on the shoulder, and excused himself, making his way to the War Room where the phone was located next to a psychedelic-looking purple and orange 1963 Astro Silver Lava Lamp one of the youthful civil rights workers must have brought in to decorate the office with. King picked up the phone.

"This is Dr. Martin Luther King," he announced, invitingly. "Whom do I have the pleasure of speaking with?"

"This is Senator Strom Thurmond," the Senator gruffed, who was a decorated lieutenant colonel during World War Two's D-Day, a Dixiecrat, and a fierce opponent of civil rights.

"Oh, yes, from South Carolina?" King asked, trying to be amicable even with feisty foolish foes like Thurmond who were known as slick seducers of men's hatred.

"That's right," the Senator responded matter-of-factly before getting straight to the point. "Listen, if you do not stop this so-called March on Washington and stop that faggot Bayard Rustin from organizing it, then I'm going to have to stop you."

"Senator," King said calmly, gently, but firmly, "I'm afraid I'm going to have to disappoint you. America needs this march and so it will go on despite your disapproval of it."

"It really shouldn't," the Senator retorted, not wanting to accept the answer, like every Jim Crower who didn't get his way, denial and refusal being his typical artillery.

"It really should go on," King said back, the conviction in his baritone voice solid, unwavering, unintimidated even by powerful senators in love with their own prejudices and false ideas that black people are all "yes men" who are too cowardly, stupid, or self-interested to ever tell a white man "No."

"Well, then," the Senator replied, "I'm going to have to go to the Senate floor and let America know that your March on Washington organizer, Mr. Rustin, is a Communist, a draft-dodger, and a homosexual."

Whoa. Where did that come from? King thought.

"Senator—"

"And I will also reveal to the world a photo I have from the FBI showing you taking a bath while Mr. Rustin is pleasurably watching you in the bathroom," the Senator said.

Huh?

"Senator," King replied, confused, struggling to stay on topic, "I will not stop working with Mr. Rustin or call off this march."

But before he could say anymore, the Senator simply called him a "f*cking homosexual," and hung up the phone abruptly.

King stood there with the corded phone in his right hand, listening to the dial-tone, absorbing yet another verbal attack from a member of the Iron White Wall, his nerves suddenly high-strung and mind flashing back to the bombing and various attacks he had been the target of throughout the years.

After too long, Rustin wandered into the War Room and saw King just standing there, looking morose, even comatose, staring blankly.

"Everything okay, Martin?" Rustin asked, concerned.

"I think so," King responded after an awkwardly long silence, still not sure what to make of the exchange with the Senator, or why the Senator would bring up him taking a bath in a hotel room with Rustin speaking through the crack of the door without so much as looking at King—or how the Senator would know about it in the first place. Or have an FBI photo?

"Well, good," Rustin said, not thinking too much of why King initially seemed too emotional to respond, too busy dealing with logistics to contemplate further, something King appreciated about Rustin's forward-looking mindset. "We have our musical performers set, a plane picking up celebrities in Hollywood, and all of our speakers finalized."

King smiled faintly, nodded approval, but still seemed like he was somewhere else.

"And speaking of speakers, have you prepared your speech yet?" Rustin asked, trying to get King focused, "Any idea what you're going to say to America?"

FORTY FIVE

Tension suffocated the 80 degree humid air in Washington, D.C., on August 28th, 1963. It was march day, theatrically staged in the dog days of summer, a profound pronouncement of black solidarity within the corridors of the most powerful city in the world.

Hundreds of thousands of black people were set to descend upon the Capitol to support the child crusaders of Birmingham and to demand their rights. But despite the brutality that was showcased on television weeks earlier, not everybody was for the march, as John Lewis was seeing.

The once-bloodied Freedom Rider, now 23 years old, was wearing a dark suit, pin striped tie, and a look of courage permanently etched into his young face as he stood in a hotel lobby. He was reviewing a collection of newspaper clippings he'd been gathering up and said to himself, "What do we have here?"

One clipping from the *Washington Post*, revealed that, despite white Americans' initial horrific reaction to the beatdown of the Children's March, nearly 60% were opposed to this protest, citing their concerns for more potential violence and their desire for a more non-confrontational approach to be taken by King and the Civil Rights Movement.

Another clipping, from the *New York Times*, highlighted that Malcolm X and other more militant black leaders were condemning the event, calling it "the Farce on Washington," believing it to be nothing more than a publicity stunt, a picnic in the park for Happy Negroes, a delusional cake walk for nonviolent colored people who were too afraid to confront their oppressors by any means necessary.

A third, and final clipping he was reviewing, outlined how the Kennedys had flip-flopped on their stance on the event. While they initially publicly opposed it, the piece said, they begrudgingly came to cautiously support it, tepidly lending minimal effort to prevent potential bloodshed but stopping short of endorsing it, stopping short of making any speeches or appearances there, despite invitations to do so. The paper claimed the Kennedys were afraid of being stoned by the more militant blacks who might be there, so they had declined their bully pulpit, and declined to give the presidential imprimatur, the official stamp of approval from the federal government. If anything, the paper said, the Kennedys would be watching warily politically calculating their next steps depending on the outcome of the march.

"Put those down," Martin Luther King demanded as he approached John Lewis in the lobby of the Willard Intercontinental Hotel, one of only seven hotels where black people were allowed to stay in all of Washington, D.C., with throngs of well dressed black allies by his side. "Justice always overrides politics in the long run. Justice always renders public opinion in its favor eventually."

"Yes sir, it does," Lewis responded, who took one last glance at the clippings before dumping them in a nearby trash can.

"You look good," King said, eying the polished Lewis up and down like a proud father would do to a son on his wedding day. "You ready?"

Of course, King was referring to the fact that Lewis, as a beloved Freedom Rider, was representing young blacks all over America as one of the speakers of today's protest—officially called the "March on Washington for Jobs and Freedom"—only one of 10 orators to be given the podium on this day.

"I am," Lewis responded determinedly. "I'm ready to give them nonviolent hell." He then took out his speech, which was heavily redacted, showcasing the crossed-out more aggressive parts of his remarks, and showed it to the Reverend.

King nodded his approval. "Let's go," he said as he extended his hand forward, making an ushering gesture, "and meet with Congress."

The plan, for King, Lewis, and the other primary leaders, was to meet with Congress in the morning while scores of blacks were simultaneously arriving by bus. They were then to join with the people after their Congressional briefing and begin marching in the afternoon for 1 mile between the Washington Monument and Lincoln Memorial, which would culminate in performances by the likes of Bob Dylan and Mahalia Jackson and their speeches, of which King was scheduled for roughly 4 minutes in length.

As the group made their way in several black Cadillacs to the Capitol, buses from as far as the eye could see started showing up, entering from the north, south, east, and west, a new one arriving every 2 minutes.

"Whoa," one 60 year old black woman aboard a Greyhound said, her mouth ajar, as she and the others descended into the neo-classically designed city modeled after ancient Roman architecture meant to inspire and intimidate friend and foe alike. "I've never seen this before," she continued, taking in building after building, their Corinthian columns, triangular pediments, ornamental porticos, and geometrically symmetrical domes seeming as old as democracy itself. "It's stunning."

But the beauty of Washington, America's most significant community, belied its deepest secret, its greatest contradiction, its most depressing lie: the slaves who built it, the capital dedicated to freedom and equality throughout the world. This woman knew, and so did the others with her, that not only were the fabled White House, Congress, and Georgetown University structures built with enslaved Negro hands, but so were the personal residences of George Washington at Mount Vernon, Thomas Jefferson at Monticello, and James Madison at Montpelier. And with this knowledge—and this newfound experience, seeing it up close and personal—a strange kind of resentment and hope filled this woman, her heart aching with pain because of the ironic tragedy of it all but also stirring with optimism because of the pride she could take in the skillful craftsmanship of her people who were never given credit for the beauty they had created.

They drove past the Lincoln Memorial and parked in one of four zones Bayard Rustin had designated for them. As the woman left her seat and stepped into the hot, muggy, swampy atmosphere, she looked around and saw more black people than she had ever seen in her life, more black people in the nation's capital than had ever previously been there at a single point in history.

She also saw activist celebrities like Charlton Heston, Sidney Pointier, Marlon Brando, Paul Newman, and of course, Harry Belafonte, who were not demanding special treatment, but who were instead one with the people, holding signs and participating in the struggle just like everyone else.

Before long, the march got underway, with over 250,000 blacks strong, with scores of progressive Whites, Jews, Asians, and Latinos joining, including Carol Davis and the other Freedom Riders. Countless signs read "Praise the Lord," "Carry it Forward, We Are With You," and "Before We'll be a Slave We'll be Buried in Our Grave." It was a sight to behold, every dark and light hue of God's colorful rainbow represented en mass, civil rights workers and hippies and feminists and environmentalists and rockers among them, many with bell bottom jeans, flower patched clothing, and psychedelic tie-dye garments.

Marchers made their way down two parallel streets, Independence and Constitution Avenues, gathering along the 2,000 foot long Reflecting Pool, and filled in all the way up to the Lincoln Memorial, where the Great Emancipator looked down like a stoic judge, waiting for them to present their case to history, challenging their generation to rise to their best, trying to discern if they would make this moment *their moment.*

As King and his entourage arrived for the speeches, they were in disbelief: the number of people who had come out in solidarity, despite the negative poll numbers of white Americans, and despite the threats of violence by racist whites, was simply overwhelming, an answer to prayer if ever there was one. But right as the first speaker started delivering his remarks, standing proudly as a witness for black humanity, somebody sabotaged the speaker system, and his voice immediately went silent.

FORTY SIX

The crowd looked confused, just like the speakers on stage. They gave each other an anxious glance.

"Sh*t," Bayard Rustin said, before rushing offstage to find a mic technician, somebody who could help get this moment back on the air. The world was watching, he thought, and civil rights leaders were starting to look like amateurs, people who couldn't afford or figure out how to get the loudspeaker system to work, people who weren't ready for primetime, people who would let this moment slip away—or be taken away, just as so many others had been by somebody hoping to thwart the efforts of black people.

"You," Rustin said, his voice filled with worry as he pointed, "Come here." The Army Corps of Engineer personnel, blonde haired and wide eyed, saw not Rustin, but instead history, provoking him to fulfill his minor role, telling him he needed to put all of his training and technical know-how into action.

Rustin and the technician rushed to the stage, where the anxious crowd quieted, starting to wonder if all of their efforts to get here— most by bus but some by train, cars, and even roller skates—were worth it. The civil rights leaders thought the same thing, knowing television cameras were rolling live and that the broadcast networks could cut away at any minute.

The technician worked away, trying to find which wires to the speaker system had been tampered with, trying to see if there was some way to re-connect them by tying them together—or even taping them together.

King, who always looked dignified even under pressure, said to Rustin, "tell him to hurry up," just as the engineer got everything back up online.

Activists returned their attention to the stage after they heard a "testing, testing, 1,2 3," hopeful that the centerpiece of the marches—the musical performances and speeches—could get underway.

John Lewis was the day's first speaker and delivered an impassioned plea, to great applause. Other speakers soon followed, abbreviated only by performances by singers like Mahilia Jackson, King's favorite Gospel Singer, and Bob Dylan, the great white iconoclast and countercultural Rock n' Roller.

The Rabbi Joachim Prinz, the President of the American Jewish Congress representing the countless Jewish people who strongly supported black people, and lead Rabbi in Berlin when the tyrant of terror Hitler was tormenting the world, spoke next, right before King.

The Rabbi waxed eloquent, comparing the suffering of black people to that of the Jews and why the Jewish people had a historic mandate to eradicate this suffering. Of course, he was referring to the many Jews who co-founded or helped finance the most prominent black civil rights organizations in American history, including the NAACP, King's Southern Christian Leadership Conference, the Student Nonviolent Coordinating Committee, and others. He then emphatically stated, comparing indifference in Nazi Germany to white indifference in the United States, "A great people who had created a great civilization had become a nation of silent onlookers. They remained silent in the face of hate, in the face of brutality and in the face of mass murder."

The crowd's attention was rapt, hanging on this spiritual leader's every word, listening to him finishing up his remarks. "America must not become a nation of onlookers. America must not remain silent."

As the Rabbi finished, King thought his speech was deeply profound, that it was deeply heartfelt, that it was everything he was trying to say in his *Letter from a Birmingham Jail,* so brilliantly summed up: combatting the white moderate's indifference to other people's suffering.

King then took a big gulp, his heart racing, and started to make his way toward the microphone. Despite his oratorical prowess and experience speechifying, he was still nervous—who wouldn't be? He had never spoken live to a group this large before, throngs of black and multiracial supporters packed into every last circumference in the tiny space of the Lincoln Memorial and Reflecting Pool. He had also never spoken directly to the American people before. Sure, he was a national figure who was becoming increasingly prominent given his *Letter* and various marches, but the public had never heard him speak. They had never heard his voice, his conviction, his sincerity, his hope, his desire. They had never heard from the man before. They had only heard about the man, his ideas and actions filtered through an often hostile or indifferent press corps and political system. But now it was their turn to hear him.

He stepped up to the podium, surrounded by countless other speakers and organizers, and looked into a sea of love, soaking in the affection of hearts united in a grand philharmonic of racial unanimity. Wearing a black suit with a black tie, he grabbed both sides of the lectern.

His heart was pounding even harder than before. He had been up until 4 a.m. writing and rewriting his speech, trying to fit the essence of the struggle for equality into only a few minutes, crossing out lines and phrases here and there, scribbling so much on the legal paper that his speech was indecipherable to anybody but him. He then opened his mouth.

"I am happy to be with you today in what will go down in history as the greatest demonstration of freedom in the history of our nation," he said.

"Five score years ago," he continued, "a great American, in whose symbolic shadow we stand today, signed the Emancipation Proclamation."

He followed up and said, "We have come to our Nation's Capitol to cash a check. When the architects of our great republic wrote the magnificent words of the Constitution and the Declaration of Independence, they were signing a promissory note to which every American was to fall heir. This note was a promise that all men, yes, black men as well as white men, would be guaranteed the inalienable rights of life, liberty, and the pursuit of happiness. It is obvious today that America has defaulted on this promissory note."

But as King continued, and then finished up his prepared speech word-for-word, he was receiving only lukewarm responses, cool claps from civil rights activists who had heard him deliver much better addresses than that which he was delivering here. They wondered what was up, whether his nerves had gotten to him, whether the amount of eyeballs on him in person—and the millions of eyeballs watching on every screen in America—were too much.

Mahalia Jackson, who was standing right behind King and who had remembered that he had given an electrifying speech previously in Detroit and Chicago, piped up and said, "Martin, tell them about your dream!"

King's mind raced, visualizing the words he had delivered time and time again, almost as though they were painted as a giant picture in his mind's eye, almost as though they were being held up on cue cards by the angels themselves.

Without missing a beat, King started improvising, transforming from a packaged presenter of rehearsed oratory into the Baptist preacher that he was, letting his baritone voice whose words could dance like a melody, escape for the first time.

He roared, his belly on fire, his tongue graced with stultifying power, his lips thundering like Zeus, "I have a dream!"

The polite but somewhat tepid crowd, fanning themselves with the program, took quick notice, looking like they had been caught off guard by a thief breaking into their homes in the middle of the night, looking like their very beings were being arrested with something magnificent, something beautiful, something lovely, something true.

"I have a dream one day that this nation will rise up and live out the true meaning of its creed. We hold these truths to be self-evident that all men are created equal," he said, righteous indignation filling his lungs, heavenly power anointing his words, each letter and vowel carrying the weight of struggle.

"I have a dream that one day out in the red hills of Georgia the sons of former slaves and the sons of former slaveowners will be able to sit down together at the table of brotherhood," he said, the crowd transfixed in awe of the spectacle they were witnessing, transfixed by a black genius representing the best of black tradition: the ability to electrify, testify, and call on people to resoundingly shout amen.

"I have a dream that one day even the state of Mississippi, a state sweltering with the heat of oppression, will be transformed into an oasis of freedom and justice," he said, as tears and cheers ricocheted in waves like a hurricane ripping through water, its flood filling the audience with depths of life, with depths of awakening.

"I have a dream that my four little children will one day live in a nation where they will not be judged by the color of their skin but by their character," he said, punctuating what for most was a spellbinding experience, a personal and collective salvation, a moment of historic witness unrivaled in the history of the world.

King went on and on, his reputation and stature and legacy rising with each second, increasing with every sentence, amplifying as his speech spontaneously turned into something more than a speech, something more than a sermon, something more than had ever been seen before in the United States: he went on and on not as a man, but as a transfigured symbol, carrying an immortal message designed to pierce hearts, designed to make the greatest country in the world believe in the ideals its founders said it stood for, designed to cash in on the long overdue promissory note.

As King exited the stage, he was no longer just a man, no longer just a minister, and no longer just a civil rights leader. Instead, he had, within minutes, become a spiritual and political icon of the first order, the spirit of his dream being released into the soul of America like a battering ram, simultaneously uplifting her spirit, challenging her conscience, and forever convicting her of her most chronic and pressing sin: the rationalized and self-justified apathy that says black people's problems are not my problem.

FORTY SEVEN

"Damn," JFK uttered almost incomprehensibly, a look of stunned awe haunting his face, his blue-green eyes twinkling like they had just seen a shooting star boomerang across the sky, his heart bewitched with growing wonder, his mind and body frozen in a jaw-dropping astonishment that was sure to be sweeping throughout America. "Just damn."

"He's quite good," Bobby said somewhat reluctantly from a distance, spotting the President upon entering the White House after monitoring the March from the Command Center at the Justice Department, his face rivaling that of his brother, equally impressed at the Reverend he didn't seem to hate as much, at the rival whose arguments seemed to be making more and more sense to him. *Was he starting to like King?* He thought. *Or was he simply overcome by the emotion of the moment, by the most powerful speech he had ever heard?*

"We need to invite Dr. King to the Oval Office at once," JFK said, "and his associates too."

"Okay," Bobby replied, realizing that, despite his now incapacitated Father's wishes for them not to be seen publicly with the controversial civil rights leader, not to be seen publicly with black people in general, this moment demanded it.

"Oh, and Bobby," JFK continued while the Attorney General started to head toward JFK's adjacent private office to telegraph aides he had on the ground at the March to summon King, "tell the Vice President to come too."

Ugh, Bobby thought. Not Lyndon Johnson, aka Uncle Roofus, the crass, smooth talking former Senate Majority leader who Bad Bobby had managed to successfully marginalize the last 3 years, keeping him on the sidelines while he served as the President's closest adviser. *He's the last guy I want to be around*, he thought.

But all Bobby could say in response was, "Right," understanding that, unlike him and his brother, Johnson could ram legislation through Congress by the sheer force of his personality, and he would be needed if they were to get JFK's new civil rights bill through. JFK could maybe sell the bill to the public, he thought, but only Johnson could sell it to crusty politicians, unmoved by his brother's good looks and larger-than-life persona, which many D.C. legislators privately cursed and jealousy dismissed, Washington being firstly a cesspool of toxic envy and lethal self-seeking cleverly operating under the banner of "public service."

Before long, JFK, Johnson, and Bobby stepped just outside of the entrance of the West Wing, right near Pebble Beach from which the Press Corps typically broadcasted, and waited for King's Cadillac entourage to arrive from its short drive from the Lincoln Memorial.

"Dr. King," JFK said, watching the Reverend and his aides step out of their recently parked vehicles, "welcome to the White House."

King immediately felt the same charm JFK flashed back at his Central Park apartment in New York right before the 1960 election. He saw the big smile, the grinning teeth sparkling from ear to ear, each tooth so white it appeared bleached. He sensed his easy-going nature. And he remembered just how much he personally liked JFK, the man he had reluctantly voted for against his then-friend and betrayer, Richard Nixon, who he hadn't spoken to since his narrow defeat.

"It's nice to see you, Mr. President," King responded as he shook the Commander-in-Chief's hand vigorously. He then turned his head leftward, glanced at Bobby, nodded hesitantly, and acknowledged him from afar by saying, coldly, "Bobby."

"I'm sure you know the Vice President," JFK said trying to make the moment less awkward, introducing the 6'4 Texan to the 5'7 King, both of whom uneasily embraced, not sure what to make of each other, not sure if these two sons of the South could be on the same page.

"The Vice President and I will meet you inside the Oval Office shortly," Bobby said to King, "while the President talks to you privately beforehand. The rest of your aides can come with Lyndon and me."

With that, King had his first private audience with JFK, who escorted him for the first time through the house that slaves built, making their way through the West Wing and into the East Wing, where they passed the ceremonial Red Room, Blue Room, and China Room, which Jackie Kennedy had just redecorated, giving these spaces accented 60s charm befitting her personal stylishness and desire to modernize what she felt should be the country's most glamorous residence.

JFK then led King outside to the newly remodeled 125 foot long Rose Garden, based on the symmetrical French floral design of the garden of the Palace of Versailles, which was brimming with grandiflora roses, tea roses, shrub roses, and bright seasonal flowers, making its color pop like a kaleidoscope, its tulips and daffodils and fritillaries chicly singing, blossoming into a pregnant sensation of enchanting beauty, along the West Colonnade.

"Dr. King," JFK said as he and the Reverend came to a natural stop, now being far away from everyone, including the Secret Service, "I need to tell you something."

"What's that, Mr. President?"

"Well, two things," JFK continued, while King curiously monitored the President's face, the person Bobby had prevented him from getting a meeting with for nearly 1,000 days. "First, that was one hell of a speech," JFK said, his head bobbing up and down in strong approval, in deference to the man whose greatness he had just realized, in appreciation of the once-in-a-lifetime display of oratorical fireworks that had painted a dazzling imprint on his psyche. "Congratulations, really."

"Thank you, sir," King responded modestly, sincerely, not letting the ecstasy he was filled with turn into a display of hubris or excessive self-congratulations. Not only was that not like him, he thought, but it would be unbecoming too.

"The second thing is," JFK continued, his eyes starting to dart back and forth, his face marked with the slightest of uncertainties, his personal discomfort growing by the millisecond, "is that you're under FBI surveillance."

King's face, suddenly crestfallen, was in disbelief, a knot forming in his stomach as big as a Dixiecrat noose. He now knew why the Senator from South Carolina had called him a homosexual, had said he had pictures of him taking a bath with Bayard Rustin nearby, and had said he would try to destroy him.

"And I'm only telling you this so that you can be careful and protect yourself," JFK said, as he regained his composure, "because we're allies now and I want to see to it that the civil rights bill is pushed through congress without distraction, I want to see to it that your Movement is successful."

Wow, was the only thing King could think. How could this be happening? Especially at a time like this, just after he had experienced his greatest professional moment and perhaps one of the greatest moments in American history. He knew those Jim Crow idiots could be capable of something like this, but the federal government too? Right now? As his mind raced, he continued to think: *What was the basis for this? What was the rationale for his life to be put under a legal microscope like he was some sort of predatory criminal, like he was some kind of Soviet spy or mafia don or Benedict Arnold?*

He struggled to respond, his loquaciousness denied to him, his words jumbled together in his mind, a confused, dyslexic array of fogginess. He remained silent, his thoughts still bouncing all around like a pinball machine, for what seemed like an eternity but was really only a few seconds. He finally then pieced something together and uttered, abashedly, "did you authorize this, sir?"

JFK just looked at him and, in a moment of unadulterated honesty, said, regretfully, sadly, "no, Bobby did."

"I see," King replied, outwardly calm but seeds of rage building within him, an animosity toward Bad Bobby emotionally soaring as high within him as the speech he just gave.

"But don't let that worry you," JFK responded, trying to be reassuring, trying to act like it was no big deal, trying to let the Reverend know he was truly on his side. "I know you probably have nothing to hide."

The President then told them they could head back inside. They entered the Oval Office, where just years before President Dwight Eisenhower, despite passing the 1957 Civil Right Act with Richard Nixon's help, refused to meet with King, stating that if he met with the Reverend he would have to meet with the KKK, you know, to give both sides equal opportunity, personally believing the Civil Rights Movement was tantamount to white terrorist groups like the Klan in one of the more stupid things an American president believed, though not the stupidest by a long shot.

The Vice President, right on cue, made some niceties as King settled into his seat next to his aides who were already assembled, and spoke of all of the power he had accumulated over three decades on Capitol Hill; spoke of the strategy he was formulating for the new legislation to outlaw public and private segregation; and spoke of how he was going to crack the whip on Republicans and Democrats alike through his famous "Johnson Treatment," ensuring the passage of this bill, ensuring that the first element of Second Emancipation Proclamation King so desperately wanted—the three-pronged approach providing legal desegregation, voting rights, and economic revitalization—would be kicked into high gear.

But while Johnson went on and on about the nuances of tactics, about which congressmen he could sway, about the mechanics of making sausage on Capitol Kill as bill-making is called, King was still seething inside, wondering how JFK could be so nonchalant about the FBI watching him, wondering how Bobby could so callously abuse his power, wondering why he could be so naive about politicians doing political things for supposedly political reasons.

King looked over at Bobby and saw, for the first time, the Attorney General giving him something of a slight smile, behaving as though he was increasingly Good Bobby, behaving like the past 3 years of rivalry could be morally skirted over, pretending like he had not put his white legal foot straight up his black ass. King wanted to puke and, even more than that, he wanted to temporarily give up his commitment to nonviolence in this moment to personally show Bobby how he really felt, wanting to slug him in his beautiful Bostonian face. King's anger, to put it simply, was apoplectic.

"Well," Bobby said after Johnson concluded his remarks, "that settles it, we're a team now so let's march forward to victory." He then stuck his hand out for King to shake it in allegiance, a plea to unite the civil rights Movement with the most powerful men on earth, and anxiously waited for King's response, who just stared at him blankly, the vibes the Reverend was manifesting as frigid as Antarctica itself, like a cold avalanche he now wanted to bury Bobby under.

FORTY EIGHT

"Quick everybody," Corretta Scott King said excitedly to her 4 children, "fall in line! Daddy just got home!"

Little Yolanda and Martin Luther King III ran like rugrats, positioning themselves in their makeshift choir, as their 2 year old toddler brother, Dexter, and recently born sister, Bernice, watched from a nearby mid century crib with the recently released *Green Eggs and Ham* book by Dr. Seuss inside of it, their eyes wide with wonder about what was going on.

Corretta, hair recently permed and looking beautiful in an elegant green Ann Lowe designed dress, made her way to the old piano next to them, which was in the living room directly across from the H.T. Cushman couch, placed right underneath her numerous college degrees, and even under her high school diploma, which displayed that she was valedictorian of her class, just like her husband was of his, who had graduated from secondary school when he was only 15.

"Okay," Corretta said, "when he opens the door we start, just like we practiced."

The kids could hardly contain themselves, for they hadn't seen their daddy in weeks, who was averaging only about 10 hours a month at home prior to his March on Washington.

The door slowly opened and, in a split second, Martin Luther King was assaulted with wave after wave of love, hearing the sound of affection that only family could provide, observing his musically brilliant wife serve as the pianist, and watching his children sing, in unison, in celebration of his speech.

"For he's a jolly good fellow, for he's a jolly good fellow, for he's a jolly good fellow, which nobody can deny," they sang, laughter and enthusiasm and giggles accompanying their beat, a special moment they didn't want to end.

King, who until now had been ruminating with anger his entire trip home from Bobby's actions, broke into a smile as wide as the large watermelon he liked to eat. His heart melted like butter as he looked into the beaming faces of his family, his wife glowing with pride, his kids proud as any kids would be, little Martin Luther King III holding his teddy bear "Love" tightly with one arm and his father tightly with the other.

Yolanda then ran and jumped in King's arms, squeezed his frame tightly, and giggled, "Daddy, I have a dream too!"

"Oh do you now?" King retorted, his smile still ample, his soul so full, swinging his daughter around in a circle, and planting kisses all over her red, embarrassed cheeks.

"I do!" Yolanda exclaimed. "One day all of God's children will have this dream!"

Corretta then made her way to her husband and gave him "the look." You know: *that look*, the one when your spouse does something so impressive it makes you quiver with carnal passion on the inside. He quickly returned the gaze to his wife.

King put Yolanda down and embraced his wife, kissing her on her sumptuous lips, concupiscence emanating from his bosom, comfort and relief resting in his heart.

Corretta put her head on his shoulder and remembered all they had experienced together, 10 years this year since he proposed to her on Valentine's Day. She remembered their wedding day with his sexy white tux and black bow tie. She remembered their honeymoon, taken in the backroom of a funeral parlor, because Honeymoon suites were denied to blacks who married in the South. She remembered the time when they briefly moved to India to study the Gandhian ways of non-violence together. She remembered buying their first home together in Alabama and their second home, right here in Vine City Atlanta, too. And she remembered the moment she decided to give up her promising music career, to stand by his side, to be his anchor, to help him see his Movement through, which she was now seeing was all worth it. She knew, deep down and out loud, that her husband was now not only the prophet who spoke just for black America, but who would be, in time, be the prophet speaking for all of America too.

As she continued to rest her head on his shoulders, the phone rang. Yolanda ran to grab it in the kitchen.

"Baby, no," King said, gently trying to enforce his no phone policy given the number of threats made against his life that he wanted to shield her from, to protect her innocence, to protect her childhood, to protect her dignity.

But Yolanda ignored him and picked up the phone anyway, answering in her sweet 7 year old voice, "herro?"

The other end had brief silence before a scream abruptly belted out, "tell that nig*er King that we're going to kill him and all those little kid nig*ers who thought they could get away with ruining America." The phone then clicked, leaving a screeching dial tone in its wake.

Yolanda hung up the phone and, after about a moment, started to cry, tears streaming violently down her face.

"Baby, what's wrong?" King asked, quickly making his way over to comfort her, fearing the worst. "What did they say?"

But all Yolanda could do was keep crying. King then stooped down to her level and wiped her tears away, trying to reassure her that everything was okay. But all she could say was, over and over again, "Daddy, don't die. Please don't die. I don't want you to die."

FORTY NINE

Birmingham still reeked with tension, a cesspool of hot sh*t and vomit mixed together. The mayor had reluctantly followed through on his deal with Martin Luther King to desegregate the city and his white residents were mad as hell because of it, their racist fury more damning in defeat than in victory, their anger unabated by all of the national criticism they were receiving, their collective psychological defense mechanism and reactionary political nature telling them they were really just victims in all of this, scapegoats of a conspiracy of liberal, and probably Communist, oppression.

Two freckle-faced tween white boys wearing country overalls from a remote part of town, one steering a green Coast to Coast branded bicycle and the other, his brother with bright red hair, riding on his handlebars, and packing a loaded Astra 680 Revolver, were on their way to an "Anti-Integration Rally" to add their voice to the chorus of Jim Crow grievers: racist white men and women who saw any progress for blacks as a profound loss for themselves, a zero-sum mindset that their white Southern forebears had cultivated for hundreds of years in an all-or-nothing "us vs. them" battle royale of the races propaganda campaign. They rode past the 16th Street Baptist Church, the launching site of what was now being called "The Children's Crusade," and sneered at it until they noticed four white men breaking into its basement, wondering what they were up to, hoping they were doing what *they thought they were doing.*

"That-a-boy," said one of the pinched-faced white men, Thomas Edwin Blanton, Jr., a local Walmart employee and KKK member with matted black hair, to Bobby Frank Cherry, a fellow Klansman, just outside of the church. "Way to get in der."

Cherry, who had just picked open the lock on the door, slowly opened it. He, Blanton and two others, Herman Cash and Robert Chambliss, also Klansmen, entered one by one, noticing nobody present, it being 6:45 a.m.

"What a disgrace," Blanton remarked disgustedly, looking around the immaculately kept church, assessing the layout of the multistory facility, trying to take in the lay of the land of the place. "They call this the house of God?"

Cash quipped, "Ever'body knows God hates nig*ers," generating hyena-like laughter.

The group continued to look around, searching for spaces, anticipating finding an area that could really make their surreptitious efforts worth it. They spotted the girls' restroom. "Here," Blanton said, jerking his head rightward, "this is perfect."

Chambliss, who was carrying a large duffle bag, set it down and unzipped it, revealing 15 dynamite sticks, their wicks and blasting caps freshly made, affixed to a timing device.

"Let's put them just right here," Blanton continued, "and get out of here."

They camouflaged the appearance of the dynamite, hiding it under hand-made Nativity props and angel images designed by the Sunday School children, and then made their way back outside.

"They fiddin' to get what they deserve," Cash said, a rush of adrenaline wallopping out of his throat, "for all this trouble they brought to our God-fearing community."

The men then hopped in their red Studebaker truck and made their way to the "Anti-Integration" rally a few blocks away, one of many that was going on in recent days, spurred on by the Governor's admonition for White Supremacists to keep fighting, to never surrender, even if local politicians did, even if Washington D.C. did, and even if, heaven forbid, all of America, did too, convinced by the "white is right" and "white will always overcome might" narrative circulating around town.

At the demonstration, hatred paraded itself out in the open air like a Macy's Thanksgiving Day Parade float, Confederate flags flying high, swastikas dancing in the air, belief in the inevitability of the triumph of their unholy will, certainty that they were doing God a favor in stopping the intermingling of the races—and the advancement of black people.

Police were on hand to monitor the occurrences too, happily waving Confederate flags in their hands, clinging to the fantasy ideology they had been brainwashed to believe by people who, themselves, were brainwashed to believe, in their revisionist "Lost Cause" narrative, the rare case where the history of race in America, at least in the Land of Dixie, was written by the losers, not the winners, casting themselves in the best possible light by falsely claiming that "The War of Northern Aggression" was a preemptive attack against Southerners to take away their states' rights, a war that was a virtual impossibility for the Confederacy to win given the North's superior firepower.

A local Dixiecrat politician made his way to the stage propped up on some hay—right next to a Confederate Memorial Statue, one of over 1,700 the South had erected in their Lost Cause mythology since the the end of the Civil War, usually on the steps of local courthouses or state legislatures, a symbolic "FU" to Northern Whites and to Southern Blacks if ever there was one—and gave a demagogic speech, verbally shredding the 3 schools that had recently integrated under the proverbial bayonet of the federalized national guard, and lambasted what he called "the assault on states' rights," the most important legal doctrine in all of America, which was greater, he said, "than the Constitution itself."

"But if you remember nothing from today," the Dixiecrat continued, "remember this: that nig*er King and those nig*er-worshiping Kennedys will one day get what's coming to them, so be not afraid of the future, for it is ours!"

The crowd cheered before the Dixiecrat shouted, "White Power!" which they eagerly and forcefully shouted back at him.

As the rally ended, the two white boys with the loaded revolver jumped back on their bike, rode past 16th Street Baptist Church, and saw that thousands of blacks were making their way into its pews. They then saw a young black boy, William Jackson, who was wearing a three-piece gray suit and who looked about 12, grab his stomach as if to indicate he had a tummy ache, before what they thought was his mother mouthing for him to walk home.

William left and walked a few blocks alone. The white boys started to follow him, riding slowly behind him from a few meters away, pretending to mind their business everytime he looked back, stalking this little boy—this little nobody, they thought, this little slave, they thought—like prey.

Finally, turning around, the little black boy said, "Hey, are you following me?"

"Shut up, coon!" one of the white boys said, pulling out the Revolver and quickly firing it, as William's small, innocent body collapsed to the ground, meeting the same violent and anonymous fate as so many of his ancestors did in this very spot: the devil's den of racial hatred.

The shots could be heard back at the 16th Street Baptist Church. But arriving members shook off the sound, thinking it was probably fireworks or gunshots from one of the many gun shows, this being a fanatical Second Amendment community, and kept on with their business.

Inside the church, upstairs, the Reverend, John Cross, Jr., was preparing to preach a sermon entitled, "A Rock That Will Not Roll," to a congregation of thousands who were excited to continue celebrating King's speech and all of the success many of their young church members were having to desegregate the city. Downstairs, in the basement, 4 little girls—4 little marchers from the Children's Crusade—were preparing to sing in the choir, the best in all of Birmingham, along with a handful of others.

One of the girls, Addie Collins, was trying to put on a colorful sash of another little girl, Carol Denise McNair, while the other two, Cynthia Wesley and Carole Robertson, were putting on their choir robes, which they had just gotten after selling enough lemonade at their lemonade stand to buy.

"Come upstairs," the head of the choir, Carolyn Maul, said, from halfway up the brown staircase, "We need to start soon girls."

"We're coming," Addie Mae responded, still playing the sash, "just give us a minute."

But as the little girls were making their final wardrobe adjustments, they didn't get the chance to go upstairs. The 15 sticks of dynamite planted next to Jesus and Mary and the Wise Men in the Nativity, enough destructive power to bring down a 747 airplane, went off right where they were standing.

FIFTY

"This is Walter Cronkite of the CBS Evening News and, ladies and gentlemen, I have some unfortunate news to report," the veteran anchor announced, his voice choked with sadness, as The Freedom Riders watched from a television screen at the Student Nonviolent Coordinating Committee's headquarters in Atlanta.

"Earlier today, at about 10:22 a.m., a bomb explosion was set off at the 16th Street Baptist Church in Birmingham, Alabama," Cronkite said. "And four little Negro girls were killed."

Stokley Carmichael, James "Big Duck" Lawson, Carol Davis, Diane Nash, and others were taking in the carnage, their expressions wrecked with agony, their minds full of vehement disbelief that the very place the Civil Rights Movement had just secured one of its biggest moral victories had just become the setting of one of its greatest emotional defeats.

"The little girls, Addie Mae Collins, Carol Denise McNair, Cynthia Dionne Wesley and Carole Robertson were found, in its basement, stacked on top of each other," Cronkite continued, before struggling to squeak out, "with one body decapitated."

"Oh Dear God!" Nash screamed, falling to the ground, weeping and wailing. "No! No! No!"

"They were just children," Carol Davis said, eyes full of tears, her body writhing with sorrow. "How could they!"

Emotional devastation had overtaken the Riders as they continued to listen to the broadcast, its graphic details getting more horrifying by the second, its psychological impact growing more disturbing, its terror being made manifestly real by the uncontrollable physical pain they too were experiencing vicariously in this—a pain, they felt, that was even greater than the bombings and beatings they previously had personally endured in their own marches, sit-ins, and Freedom Rides.

"This is bullsh*t!" Stokley Carmichael screamed, his eyes blood red, his face a repository of rage, his veins pulsating in his neck and arms, frantically pounding against his dark skin, wanting to break free, wanting to enact revenge. "No more!"

Big Duck just looked at him, tears violently pouring out of him, devastation strangling his ability to breath, his ability to speak, his ability to navigate this moment.

"We need to fight back," Stokley said, "but not with any of this nonviolent sh*t."

Diane Nash, who was also crying hysterically, looked up with shock, and asked him, "Stokley, what do you mean?"

"I mean we need to fight back by any means necessary!"

"But," Nash said, her voice more hushed but still quaking, "that's not our way, that's not Dr. King's way. Not even in this tragedy."

"His way doesn't work," Stokley coldly declared about Martin Luther King, "and I will no longer follow it—or follow him."

"What?" Nash asked confusedly. "I don't understand."

"Then let me be real clear with you," Stokley said slowly, enunciating each word with lawyerly precision. "I am going to start fighting these crackers, with more than just meaningless words, unrequited love, and all this kumbaya sh*t."

He then pulled out a gun from the breast pocket of his black leather jacket—a Glock 17—and loaded a bullet into it, to the horror of the other Freedom Riders.

"Stokley?" Nash said, bewilderingly, "no!"

Stokley then smacked the weapon against his head. "Don't tell me no!" he said, "when Negro children are dying, helplessly, unable to defend themselves, all because we're too afraid to defend them! Too afraid to take the fight straight to whitey's ass!"

"That's not the solution," Carol jumped in saying, her head shaking disapprovingly back and forth, left to right, her hands wiping tears from her chin and cheeks.

"Shut up, b*tch," Stokley said indifferently, "you ain't even one of us."

Big Duck looked over and, after gathering himself, spoke up, "Stokley, brotha, she's just trying to help."

"I don't need her help or the white man's help," Stokley said angrily. "They never did nothin' for me!"

"But we have a bill," Nash said, "from the Kennedys. We're going to get our rights soon."

"Oh, a bill huh?" Stokley said condescendingly. "What is their little bill gonna do? Get passed through the Congress so these Dixiecrat crackers can just ignore it like they've been ignoring all of these Supreme Court decisions and bills and Constitutional Amendments?"

"It's a step in the right direction," Nash replied, mildly defensive.

"No, this is," Stokley said, cocking the gun. "This is how we take our rights back, through force, through revolution."

"We will lose our moral witness if we do that," Nash replied, shaking her head.

"The only moral witness we need is to put a bullet through whitey's head," Stokley said defiantly. "That's how we'll gain our rights. That's how we'll gain our respect."

The Freedom Riders shot each other a look, unable to comprehend what their fellow Rider was saying, hoping he wasn't serious, fearing that his personal pain was just too much to bear.

"Brotha," Big Duck said, trying to show some empathy, trying to speak rationally to him in a strategic and calculating way he could understand. "I feel exactly the way you do."

Stokley, chest puffed up, smiled, and looked validated at the reassurance.

"But…I agree with Diane," Big Duck continued in reversing his sentiment after some reflection, "we can't fight fire with fire, we simply don't have the numbers. Whites would outnumber and overwhelm us with their firepower, their police, their military."

"I don't care about any of that sh*t," Stokley responded dismissively. "I want to do to them the same thing they did to these little girls, the same thing they've been doing to our people for centuries!"

"So you're going to go shoot some white people to make yourself feel better," Nash said. "Then what?"

"Then I'll go shoot some more," Stokley responded.

Nash shook her head in disapproval.

"For the last few years," Stokley said, "I've let you talk me into all of this nonviolent stuff, all of this Christian and Gandian turn the other cheek bullsh*t. But no more."

Stokley then reached into his pocket, pulled out a business card, and held it up for all to see.

"What's that?" Big Duck asked, curious why Stokley would seemingly change the subject so abruptly to talk business of all things.

"It's our future," Stokley replied. "Some guys from Oakland have recruited me to be the Chairman of a new black power group they're starting, one that follows the teachings of Malcolm X, one that is not afraid to use force, unlike all of you sissies."

"And you're going to leave us, just like that?" Nash questioned, exasperation piercing her voice, "and accept this chairmanship just so you can use force?"

"Yes."

Big Duck shook his head, chagrined, along with the others. A beat passed before he asked, "Stokely, what's the group called?"

"The Black Panthers," Stokley responded daringly, right as he put the card back in his pocket and walked out on them before turning around and saying, finally, "and they will bring us the revolution Dr. King never could, and that you all never could either."

FIFTY ONE

"I'm glad you're finally going to see the doctor," Corretta Scott King said to her anxious-looking husband in their Vine Street Home. "You've been needing to for years."

"I really don't want to," King responded, his face full of reluctance, his eyes wandering, his body recalcitrant at the thought of getting a medical check up.

"And after this appointment," Corretta said compassionately, "you need to see a psychiatrist."

Those dreaded words, King thought. P.S.Y.C.H.I.A.T.R.I.S.T. Words no black man of his generation wanted to hear, especially him. He wasn't crazy, he thought, nor did he want to be airing his increasingly dark thoughts, even if those thoughts were causing him to crack and sizzle like bacon on a skillet when nobody but his wife was watching.

King put on his black suit coat, kissed Corretta on the cheek, and exited the front door. He hopped into his Chevy Impala with a V8 engine and began driving—and thinking.

Two months had passed since the heinous 16th Street Baptist Church bombing, he remembered, and two months had passed since he preached at those precious little girls' funerals. But he couldn't help but wonder: *Am I to blame for this? Am I the reason they died? Should I have permitted children to march in the first place? Am I the real monster because I allowed this?*

He made a left turn and stopped at the light, which was affixed on a string just above it. His pupils glared into its bright red circle, its rays sucking him further into the abyss of nightmarish ruminations, further into feelings of gloom and insecurity, further into the damning thoughts he couldn't help but be thinking: *Am I good enough to lead this movement? Am I good enough to be Corretta's husband? Am I good enough to even be a father, considering I will likely lose my life sooner or later, and cause my children to grow up without the daddy they love?*

His mind raced forward like a psychedelic zigzag before he heard a honk behind him. He had been staring at the light too long, well after it turned green, a victim of his own devastating meditations, an increasingly daily occurrence, especially after his daughter Yolanda begged him not to die in the midst of the death threat she had just overheard fresh off of his "I Have a Dream Speech."

He drove forward while chest pain surged through him as though it were an out-of-control electric volt.

When the car finally came to its destination, he parked in a nondescript rural office park, and made his way into the medical building in the black part of town, a rare propserous Negro community in America, a privilege afforded to him by Corretta's singing around the country here and there to pay the bills.

King entered through the front door and every eye, despite their assorted illnesses, stared at him—and then erupted in applause, his celebrity now a veritable phenomenon. He wore a polite appearance and pretended that everything was okay as well-wishers gave him intense adulation and congratulations.

But a middle aged black woman wearing a popular 1960s weave said, perceptive as she read his sad eyes, "Dr. King, everything okay?"

"Oh, yes," King, who was 34 years old, responded, lying. "Just getting a regular checkup."

But the woman didn't believe him—you couldn't get anything past her or, for that matter, past most black women, their B.S. detectors being legendary. Nevertheless, she stayed quiet and played along out of profound respect for him and what he was doing for the Negro community.

After filling out some basic paperwork, a nurse escorted him to the back where he saw the physician waiting.

"Dr. King," the older, distinguished and regal looking black Physician said, extending his large right hand, "thank you for your work."

King just smiled as he shook it.

"Now," the Physician continued, "what can I help you with today?"

King, who was notoriously guarded except for with his wife and one or two close confidants like Ralph Abernathy, wanted to tell him everything in what felt like an on-again, off-again mental health breakdown he was having. He wanted to tell him that he felt responsible for those little girls in Birmingham who died; that he felt increasingly inadequate, as a husband, father, and leader; that he was having nightmares of the civil rights movement spiraling out of control to an inevitable defeat because of its many fractions like Malcolm X's and now Stokley Carmichael's defection; about how all of the death threats he was receiving were beginning to make him increasingly loopy and disconnected from reality; about how all of this pressure, the weight of the suffering of the millions of black martyred and enslaved and oppressed souls he represented, felt like an iron albatross placed around his neck; and about how he thought about ending his life, just like he attempted to do twice as a child, in a self-justified act of escape to make an early entrance into Heaven.

But all King could muster was, "I've been having some light chest pains."

"Oh, I see," the Physician replied. "I'm surprised it's only that."

"What do you mean, Doctor?" King asked, trying to fish for more, wondering if the doctor had some sort of special insight into his condition even though King didn't tell him what his condition really was.

"Well, there's this new psychological concept I've been reading about in the medical journals," the Physician said, "called Post-Traumatic Stress Disorder, or PTSD."

King cocked his head, intrigued about the name.

"Apparently, the soldiers who have been coming back from the growing war in Vietnam," the physician continued, "have been needing psychiatric treatments given the trauma of war they've experienced, having suicidal ideations, feelings of despair, mood swings, and general hopelessness and depression. I just assumed it would be the same for you, given all that you've been leading our people through, all of the trauma you've experienced with bombings and assassination attempts and what not."

"That's an interesting theory, this PTSD idea," King said, pretending not to lend any personal credibility to it, though it sounded spot on to him. "But I'm fine, my thoughts are quite stable," he lied, believing that, if he said anything, he would have to give in to Corretta and see a psychiatrist, the last thing he felt he could afford to do. It could be weaponized against him by opponents of civil rights, he thought, and, even in his fragile and emotionally distraught state, he couldn't risk it—not for himself and not for the Movement.

"Well that's good to hear," the Physician responded, before telling King he needed to give him an electrocardiogram and related heart tests, to see how his heart was doing and what seemed to be causing him chest pain.

King took off his shirt and laid down on the doctor's table. The Physician then placed 12 electrode sensors on his sternum, right across his cross scar, followed by other medical equipment, and, after a little while, began to frown heavily, showing displeasure at what he was seeing on King's ECG readings.

Fearing the worst, King asked, "What's up, doctor?"

"I'm afraid to say this," the Physician said, more closely examining the graphs on the charts, "but the reason you've been having these chest pains—"

"Is it a heart attack?" King interrupted him, not letting the physician finish which was uncharacteristic of him given his excessively polite manners.

"No," the Doctor replied somberly.

"Cardiac arrest?"

"Worse than that."

"Then what?"

"Dr. King," the Physician continued, "according to your charts, your heart is around 60 years old."

But King tried to make a joke about the statement. "My wife says I have an old soul you know."

"But not just that," the Physician hesitated to say, "you have an old body too."

Staring briefly before finally saying something, King asked, "what does that mean?" while his face distorted with worry.

"It means that if you don't cut back on your stressful work with the Civil Rights Movement causing your heart to accelerate in age rapidly," the Physician said, noting black men in America had only around a 60 year life span, "you could drop dead at any moment."

King's eyes bulged, his body language flabbergasted. *How could this be*, he thought. *Wasn't he a young man? Didn't he have so much more to give of himself? Of his ideas? Of his energy? Could he truly drop dead at any moment, dying from a decaying and broken heart?*

He then shook his head ruefully, remembering the damned if you do, damned if you don't position he was in. He thought, if he cut back or quit the civil rights movement, he would be called a coward. But if he didn't, he would likely be killed by some random Jim Crow assassin— or, worse yet, killed by his very own heart, the one thing he thought was different about him, special about him; the one thing that gave him his kindness, that gave him his empathy; the one thing that kept him going in spite of his, and his people's, hopeless despair.

FIFTY TWO

Bobby couldn't sleep. It was the eve of two momentous events in his life, his 39th birthday and a contentious Congressional committee vote on JFK's civil rights bill to ban legal segregation throughout America just like it had been banned in Birmingham, both happening on November 20th, 1963, and he was tossing and turning in bed, unable to get his body to come to a state of rest in his gray cotton seersucker pajamas.

But Bobby's restlessness, hyperactive though it typically was, wasn't only because of his anticipation for all that was going to happen this week; it was also anxious restlessness because of Martin Luther King, who now, two months after Bobby extended his hand to him at the White House after the March on Washington, refused to return his calls—or, as King's people said, would call him back once The Reverend returned from "vacation." But all Bobby could think was now that King was working with Johnson on the civil rights bill, *Why would he need me? Now that King knew we had wiretapped him, why would he want anything to do with me, the man who was spying on him? Why would he ever call me back, especially after a so-called vacation in November? Who does that*, he thought, *take a vacation in November? Why did he seem to care so much?*

He got up, without waking his wife, and made his way to his upstairs study down the hall, turning on the light at his desk. Glancing down, he noticed the quote he had written down from the priest at St. Joseph's Catholic Church near Capitol Hill on the day J. Edgar Hoover blackmailed him, the quote from the Greek poet Aeschylus, and read it. *He who learns must suffer. And even in our sleep pain that cannot forget falls drop by drop upon the heart until, in our own despair, against our will, comes wisdom through the awful grace of God.*

Even at this late hour, this quote still struck him powerfully. But he wondered: *Why would I be seeing it now, after all these months of it being nowhere in sight?* Not that he was superstitious, but he did believe that everything has a meaning, and he wanted to know the meaning behind this. *Is it simply a coincidence, an awful quote appearing during what could be one of the best weeks of my life? Or is providence trying to tell me something, warn me about something, open my eyes to something that I desperately need to see?*

Since the Children's Crusade, the bombing of the 16th Street Baptist Church, and the March on Washington, he had been doing a lot of soul searching—and a lot of reading, particularly about black people in America, and he had been questioning himself, interrogating himself really, more than he had ever done in his life. He thought, *Are civil rights really not only a political issue, but also a moral one? Is this quote trying to tell me I need to truly listen to King, to truly listen to black people, to truly try to feel the awful Grace of God in their lives? Or is this quote just a reminder of the transformation he had been undergoing in his own heart, the incredible discomfort he was feeling about his political assumptions about and relations to black people being radically challenged, being profoundly upended, being possibly overturned?*

He had, in recent days, not only been deeply reflecting on the message behind King's "I Have a Dream Speech" and what the young Freedom Rider Jerome "Big Duck" Smith had confronted him about at his brother's New York apartment, but he had also been reading black authors for the first time in his life—and reading about black people more generally too—and, the more he took in their collective essence, took in their electric soul, the more he realized that he was never truly taught the truth about them in all of its glorious beauty. Instead, he realized that nearly everything he knew about blacks was almost always distorted, omitted, or filtered through white people of his generation who were at best, usually uninformed or indifferent to blacks, and at worst, woefully vicious in their systematic campaign to dehumanize them. And this made him sad—and angry. His eyes were starting to open to the fact that he didn't really understand the black condition; that he didn't really understand the black intellectual and artistic tradition; and that he didn't really understand, on more than just an abstract and intellectual level, the black oppression and suffering that King was marching for, that the Freedom Riders were marching for, that those little murdered girls from Birmingham were marching for.

But now he felt like he was starting to see, almost as though blinders had been partially ripped off of his eyes all of a sudden, almost as though he was having a come-to-Jesus moment, almost as though he was permitted to see only through the perspective of "Good Bobby," the righteous moral man, and not Bad Bobby, the ruthless politically calculating opportunist. In these last several months, he had been pouring through countless literary texts of the black greats like Frederick Douglass, W.E.B. Du Bois, Booker T. Washington, Sojourner Truth, Ralph Ellison, and, yes, even James Baldwin, despite the showdown in his brother's New York apartment a few months before; he had been pouring through the records and the albums of great black musicians like Ray Charles, Louis Armstrong, James Brown, Aretha Franklin, and Ella Fitzgerald; and he had been pouring through the great black artists from the Harlem Renaissance like Augusta Savage, Horace Pippen, and Elizabeth Catlett. And, while he was doing all of this, his heart was becoming bigger, softer, and more understanding with each work he took in, his mind starting to see things almost exclusively from black people's perspectives and not his own, his heart unwrapping the fact that the measurement of black pain should not be through the privileged lens of the many, as most white moderates, himself included, had measured it, but rather through the afflicted lens of the few, as most blacks, like Martin Luther King, had experienced it.

Bobby had also, in this time, emotionally contrasted what he was learning about the richness and vibrancy of black history and culture with the crude works of racism and bigotry so often exercised against blacks. He was emotionally contrasting this with the fact that Abraham Lincoln had offered official federal reparations to millions of blacks through his 40 Acres and a Mule program, only to have his policy reversed and the land stolen back from blacks by his Presidential successor;

He was emotionally contrasting this with the fact that the eugenics movement, active for over 100 years, was advocated for by the best white scholars at Ivy League institutions, including professors who taught him at Harvard, to provide a scientific basis for their belief in black racial inferiority, falsely claiming blacks had smaller brains, and taught this false belief to hundreds of millions of white students over the years as "scientific fact" in K-12 schools and higher-ed institutions;

He was emotionally contrasting this with the fact that whites had produced hundreds of thousands of academic papers and popular press books—and now Broadway shows and Hollywood movies—depicting blacks as savages, idiots, and subhuman buffoons without so much as batting an eyelash while, at the same time, black people never did any of this to white people;

He was emotionally contrasting this with the fact that blacks were falsely portrayed in society as predators toward white women when, in reality, statistics showed these white women were 200% more likely to be raped or murdered by white men and not black ones, a statistic members of the Iron White Wall worked overtime to conceal from whites and blacks alike;

He was emotionally contrasting this with the fact that many of the Southern congressmen and senators who were voting on the civil rights bill had participated in "confederate balls" back in their college fraternity days, glorifying white men's mythical superiority over blacks in their obsession to resurrect the Confederacy in spirit if not in reality;

He was emotionally contrasting this with the fact that, even for moderate whites like himself and his brother, they mistakenly thought all of the hatred practiced by racist whites over hundreds of years and thousands of discriminatory laws and social structures—even the rampant discrimination and disrespect against countless blacks who fought alongside George Washington during the Revolutionary War, for Abraham Lincoln during the Civil War, and for America during World Wars One and Two—could be overcome by blacks if they just simply pulled themselves up by their bootstraps, magically, one by one, like Horatio Alger, when the whole system was designed to exploit them and denigrate them even when they did everything they were told to do;

And he was emotionally contrasting this with the fact that, if you were a black person in America today, you could not even marginally succeed without relying on, interacting with, or being subservient to white people but if you were a white person in America today you could wildly succeed without so much as having to think about black people, much less have any association with them.

But as Bobby was ruminating, caught up in his emotions, a faint knock was heard on his study door; it was his wife, Ethel.

"Dear," Ethel said gently, her eyes squinting from the light protruding through the crack of the door, her brown hair glowing with a light blonde hue at this angle, "are you going to come back to bed?"

"I'll be in soon, sweetheart," Bobby responded. "I've just had a lot on my mind and couldn't sleep."

Ethel came closer, re-tying the turquoise blue robe she was wearing over a babydoll negligee nightgown a little more tightly, pulling up a stool next to his chair, and sitting on it. "Anything you want to share?"

"Well, Bobby said," hesitatingly. "I need to confess something."

Ethel looked at him, curiously.

"I think I've been wrong, Ethel," Bobby continued. "Dead wrong, about black people, about my approach to civil rights."

Ethel squeezed his thigh tight and said, as sweetly as she could, sounding like a white civil rights radical and activist, "I know you have."

"What?" Bobby shot back, dumbfounded by his wife's response, not expecting her to so quickly or readily agree with him—not prepared for his wife, who he always said was his better half, to tell it as she saw it.

"I know that you've been wrong dear," Ethel said, peering into his eyes, looking deep down into his soul which seemed to be coming fully alive, which she had been quietly observing in recent weeks.

Bobby's conscience looked back at her and, in a gentle whisper, asked, "How did you know?"

"You're a man who believes strongly in right and wrong, Bobby," she responded, briefly looking at the crucifix on his desk, "but you're also a man who doesn't see what he doesn't want to see."

"Meaning?" Bobby said, softly.

"Meaning that you didn't see the pain of colored people," she continued, "because you weren't seeing them as people. You weren't seeing their humanity, their individuality."

"Right..." Bobby said, regret in his voice, his words trailing off into silence.

"You were seeing them as a political issue and even as a charity case," she said. "And not as God's children, like both of us, like all of white people, who have individual hopes and dreams, specific and unique aspirations for themselves and their families to do the best they can in life, without other people trying to keep them down because of all of this made up racial superiority nonsense."

Sympathetically, Bobby nodded his head in agreement.

"But," Bobby said, again softly, "I still don't know how you knew I was coming to this realization."

Ethel smiled and, darting her eyes from left to right and then from right to left, said, "look around."

Bobby's office had become a treasure trove of all things black and, caught up in all of his study and thought—not to mention his responsibility as Attorney General of the United States and chief aide to his brother—he had overlooked this. To top this off, he had even been studying the speeches and writings of Martin Luther King, which he furiously underlined, highlighting quotes of King's that struck his heart like "the ultimate measure of a man is not where he stands in moments of convenience and comfort, but where he stands at times of challenge and controversy"; "there comes a time when one must take a position that is neither safe, nor politic, nor popular, but he must take it because conscience tells him it is right"; and "life's most persistent and urgent question is, What are you doing for others?"

"A man who wants to see the truth," Ethel said, wisdom flowing from her lips, "is sooner or later going to come by it."

"Why didn't you say anything to me sooner," Bobby asked, "especially considering how I've behaved toward Martin Luther King, and how tepid and cautious Jack and I have been on civil rights until recently?"

"Because when you're acting like Bad Bobby," Ethel joked, a playful devilishness sparkling in her eyes, "there's no way I can get you to act like Good Bobby."

"Hey," Bobby said, a smirk cracking around the edges of his lips.

"It's true," Ethel said. "You could have only convinced yourself of this, convinced yourself of this truth. Nobody else could have. Not

Martin Luther King. Not the Freedom Riders. Not those little Birmingham girls. Not white radical civil rights activists. And not me. Only you."

Bobby leaned over to hug her and squeezed her tight; she reciprocated and gave him a soft kiss with her delicate, cherry-red lips, sending desire through his body.

"But the question is," Ethel said, pulling back a little with her right hand cupping the left side of his face, "what are you going to do about it now? You have responsibility not just for finding the truth, but for doing everything in your power to act on it, to right wrongs, to be a genuine white champion for Negro rights. So now all you have to ask yourself is, whether you will or whether you won't?"

Bobby got up and paced back and forth, gathering his thoughts for a few moments, which were seemingly less concerned about political calculation and gamesmanship, less concerned about strategizing, and less concerned about seeing how he could win and score points to get his brother ahead on civil rights by being selectively opportunistic. He said, "I'm going to try to get into Martin Luther King's good graces… and, then, I'm going to tell Jack that we need to make civil rights the moral centerpiece of our Administration, and for all of the right reasons, not just the political ones. We need to actually try to right wrongs, using the bully pulpit we have set before us."

"Good," Ethel said, proud and approving of her husband. "When can you tell both of them this, about your truth and your plans and your bully pulpit?"

"For King, I don't know given that he won't return my calls," Bobby said regretfully, "But for Jack, I'll do it soon. He's heading to Dallas with Jackie and the Vice President for a parade in his convertible, and I'll tell him the minute he gets back."

FIFTY THREE

J. Edgar Hoover was furious. The dough-faced Director of the FBI had been informed that JFK's civil rights bill, which was being vehemently debated in the House Judiciary Committee, had just passed by a narrow margin—and was being sent to the full floor of the House, where it was expected to pass by a hair.

In his office at the Department of Justice, as American flags peered over his left and right shoulders, two of Hoover's chubby digits reached for the rotary phone on his desk and dialed a number.

"This is Hoover," he said, as Howard W. Smith, a staunch segregationist congressman from Virginia who had campaigned against *Brown vs. Board of Education* and who was the powerful chairman of the House Rules Committee, answered. "Any chance you can stop this disgrace of a civil rights bill from reaching the entire House of Representatives for a vote?"

Of course, Hoover was referring to the fact that Smith, as head of the inimitably obscure but all-powerful Rules Committee, could potentially stop the legislation from proceeding to have all 435 elected members vote on it, by loading it down in deceptive, archaic, and highly questionable legal procedures, making it dead on arrival.

"Well," Smith responded, anger in his voice over what was happening to his country, to the America he knew and loved, "I've tried every tactic known on God's green earth to stop this thing."

"And?" Hoover asked, his chest leaning into his desk, hovering over his cream of chicken soup, wanting to hear good news, hoping he would receive the answer he had heard countless times before when he wielded his influence to make his will happen however he wished, even in Congress.

"I don't think so," Smith replied, irritably. "I've tried everything."

"Damn!" Hoover barked. "Damn Kennedy!"

"I feel the same way, sir," Smith said. "He's gonna destroy our country with all of this nig*er sh*t, gonna make us the United States of nig*er lovers."

But Hoover wasn't interested in talking about what the Kennedys were trying to do or airing polemics, as much as these were some of his favorite pastimes he got off to; he was only interested in placing more calls now, in engaging in more action, in imposing the status quo so that he could prevent this bill from seeing the light of day.

"I've got to go," Hoover said, abruptly. "We'll be in touch."

"Okay, bye," Smith continued, as he hung up, recognizing the urgency the FBI Director was under, confident that he too would do everything he could to freeze this bill in its tracks.

But then an aide with a large stack of manilla folders marked "urgent" inconspicuously walked into Hoover's office and saw a look of venomous rage on his face, his features distorted by fury. Hoover, who had been flipping quickly through his rolodex and writing down numbers, noticed him.

"Damn it!" he screamed, "I thought I told you to always knock before you enter, you little pansy ass! Get out of here!"

Hoover then took his bowl of cream of chicken soup and hurled it at him, smacking him in the upper right shoulder, cream spewing everywhere, its white contents heavily contrasted with the aide's black suit jacket, its chicken making a mess all over the floor.

"Now clean it up!" Hoover barked. "Now!"

The aide ran out of the room, dejected and humiliated, to fetch some cleaning supplies before returning and mopping everything up. As he cleaned the spill, Hoover's blood shot eyes were murdering the young agent with luminous intensity, his animosity toward Kennedy and blacks being projected onto this helpless young person.

After the aide left, Hoover locked the door, closed the blinds, and started making calls furiously. He phoned various members of the Iron White Wall: lawyers who could potentially sue to block the implementation of the civil rights bill; judges who could potentially rule it unconstitutional; politicians in the South who could potentially stop it from being enforced; several members of the KKK and CIA; and, curiously, a handful of others, whose numbers were not listed in his rolodex, whose numbers he knew by heart.

Moments later, Hoover received another knock on his door; it was the aide again, looking sheepish and frightened, holding the same manilla folders he originally brought in.

"What do you want now?" Hoover snapped, before noticing the folders. "What do you want me to review?"

"Threat assessments," the aide replied, sheepishly, "against the President."

"Can't this wait?" Hoover questioned, chilly and harsh indifference piercing his voice.

"Well, sir," the aide said, "that's why I came earlier. Our agents in the field and our analysts here in the office thought you should see them. They're marked urgent."

"Ugh…Fine," Hoover responded, ushering the aide to approach his desk, rudely snatching the folders out of his hands.

Hoover's sweaty fingers started following the words in the report from left to right, taking in page after page of data, page after page of on-the-ground reports agents were hearing, page after page of specific threats against JFK's trip to Dallas, which he was en route to on Air Force One right now, and page after page of actionable intelligence the FBI had collected about it.

The aide stood in the corner watching his boss, hoping not to draw attention to himself but also hoping to get an answer for the request within it as soon as possible.

"Sir," the aide said uncomfortably, "are you going to approve the request?"

"From my professional judgment," Hoover said, closing the files, smugness painted across his face, "I can't recommend this."

He then handed the folders back to the aide who looked completely bewildered—shocked even.

"So you don't recommend the FBI station more agents in Dallas to protect the President of the United States?" the aide asked.

"No."

"And you don't recommend our agents inform the Secret Service of the threats against the President to encourage them not to put the roof down in his Presidential convertible as he is scheduled to do during his parade in Dallas?" the aide questioned, incredulity in his voice.

"No," Hoover said, stoically. He then paused for a beat and said, with a wry smile on his face, "the President's life is not in any danger."

FIFTY FOUR

Walking with a loaded rifle in his hand, Stokley Carmichael cocked his head, then his weapon, and said, "the revolution has begun."

"That's right, brotha," Bobby Seale echoed, agreeing with Stokley as both he and Huey Newton, the Air Force veteran and law school student that they respectively were, cocked their rifles too.

The Black Panther Party, as they were calling themselves, had just been born with Stokley's arrival in Oakland, and it was about to take on its first street mission.

Wearing slick matching leather black jackets, black berets, black sunglasses, a panther button, and afros, they had made enough money selling copies of Mao Zedong's "Little Red Book" of Communism to purchase their firearms, which they were openly carrying given a loophole Newtown had found in a California law that the National Rifle Association had been exploiting for years.

"I finally feel what whitey has felt all of these years," the handsome and light-skinned Newton said, holding a Pistol Mitraliera assault rifle, rubbing his strong fingers across the body of this AK-47-like contraption, "and that's power."

The group hopped into their black Buick Riviera and began driving, passing by the Acorn housing Project that blacks had been forced into after the white city council had kicked the city's black residents out of their single-family homes to build a subway for white citizens, a gentrifying phenomenon that was happening all over America, and began its patrol.

"King is an Uncle Tom," Seale said, "who would never do what we're about to do."

"Exactly," Stokley said, shaking his head in judgment at his former leader—and mentor. "He's too soft, too passive, not what Negroes need right now."

"He had his chance," Seal agreed, "now it's our turn. We're going to give Negroes jobs, healthcare, and dignity."

"And don't forget," Newtown, their newly appointed "Minister of Defense," said,"protection."

Of course, they were expressing the sentiment that a growing number of blacks embraced, especially blacks who were starting to listen more and more to Malcolm X's messages, even blacks who had once followed King's nonviolent path: to meet violence with violence and not with peace, to meet ass whoopings and bombings and death with the same in kind, to inflict pain and terror on those who would inflict pain and terror on them.

Spotting a police car, one of many new ones given the recent massive increase to its operating budget designed to "militarize" local law enforcement, the Panthers started to follow it. Intense passion animated their faces as well as bitter memories, not only of racist cops like Birmingham's Bull Conner, but also of white cops in their own neighborhoods, who had just shot and killed an unarmed black boy, with impunity, an event that was happening as frequently in the West and North as it was in the Jim Crow South as all of the statistics were showing.

"I hate crackers," Newton said, their vehicle trailing behind by about a hundred meters, "damn pigs."

"Scum," Seale replied, spitting out of his rolled down window, wiping his lips in disgust.

The police car turned the corner, making its way to a decrepit park where a group of black boys and teenagers were playing basketball.

The Panther's stopped their vehicle at a distance, carefully watching the interaction, curious how their inaugural "copwatching" session was going to turn out, curious if they were going to have to use lethal force to provide the physical protection from the police that blacks had long said terrorized them, almost always to vehement white disagreement, skepticism, or indifference, almost always to some white person somewhere saying black people were making stories of police brutality up or were exaggerating them or were, worse yet, mostly deserving of the brutality, even when seeing people like Bull Conner and the Birmingham Police Force terrorize innocent blacks on camera.

An overweight, middle-aged white cop, Jim Miller, stepped out of the left side of the vehicle. Then a younger, 20-something year old white cop, Allen Harris, stepped out of the right.

"Do we go now?" Stokley asked, rifle pointing prostate in the air, heart palpitating at a million miles an hour.

"Not yet," Newtown responded, staring straight ahead, a fierce frown on his face. "Just wait."

The cops approached the black basketball players, stepping onto the court in the middle of the game.

"Lookie what we have here," the older cop said, grabbing the ball from one of the players, "an awfully fun game of basketball."

The players looked at them, quizzically, as the older cop tossed the ball to the younger cop.

"It does look awfully fun," the younger cop echoed, who started to dribble and make mocking circles around the boys.

"Um," one of the players said, "can I have the ball back please?"

The younger cop came to a halt, started laughing, and stepped up closer to the boy, bending over to his height, his arrogant eyes making contact with him, and said, "you sure can," as he continued to refuse to hand over the ball, his hand holding the ball above the boys head in a taunt.

"Okay?" the boy asked rhetorically in response.

"I'll give it to you," the young cop said, "if you admit that you and your little friends robbed the liquor store last night."

"What?" one of the teenage boys stepped in and said. "We was here minding our business, playing basketball like we do everynight."

"Store owner said a group of kids came to his store and stole some candy," the younger cop responded.

"No, that's crazy? We don't even hang out together outside of hooping," the teenager said, referring to playing basketball.

"You seem to match the description," the young cop said.

"What? How?" the teenager asked.

"You match the description because you're coons," the young cop said, forcefully.

"Man," the teenager said back, "f*ck you."

"What'd you say to me boy?" the young cop replied, quickly moving closer to him, slapping him so hard in the face that he drew blood in his mouth. "You never disrespect a cop!"

The old, fat cop smiled, satisfied by the vastly unequal power white cops exercised over innocent blacks not only in his generation, but of every generation leading up to this one.

But then he noticed the players starting to move toward the teenager, trying to form a hedge of protection around him like they saw the kids do in Birmingham, trying to prevent him from being struck again, trying to stand up for themselves, trying to say "no more."

"Freeze," the old cop said, drawing his gun, stopping the boys in the tracks. His partner then drew his gun too.

But then they heard a voice say, "freeze or else what?"

But the cops didn't know where the voice was coming from.

"Freeze or else what?" the voice asked again.

The cops then turned around and saw the Black Panthers pointing three rifles directly in their faces, close enough to be in their nostrils, black men full of fury, ready to defend those who couldn't defend themselves, ready to inflict pain upon those who for so long had inflicted pain on them. Stokley then said again, as he cocked the gun, shoving it more into the face of one of the cops, "freeze or else what?"

FIFTY FIVE

The first shot came barreling out of the rifle, hitting its target right near the jugular, making its way in a clean trajectory straight through the neck.

The second shot immediately followed, narrowly missing its mark, ricocheting off of a nearby object.

But then a third shot, the bullseye shot, the shot that could never be forgotten, raced forward with tragic fury and struck his skull, cracking it wide open like a cantaloupe.

Screams erupted into chaos as the President's dead body slumped over in Dallas at a parade, on November 22nd, 1963.

The Presidential convertible carrying the First Lady, who was wearing a pink dress and hat, sped forward, trailed by a second limo holding the Secret Service, and a motorcade of vehicles, with the Vice President, members of the CIA, and others, which all quickly disappeared into a dark tunnel.

Jackie Kennedy was screaming hysterically, JFK's thick blood all over her face, dripping down off of her clothing, both arms wrapped tightly around the man she loved. "No! No! No! No! No!" she yelled over and over and over again, each "No" louder and more haunting than the one before it. "They killed my husband!" she cried. "They killed my husband!"

Secret Service's high-powered guns were drawn but it was too late: they had already left the scene of the crime, Dealey Plaza, from which the shots were fired, and now their new mission, which had changed in a split second, was to get Jackie to safety and the President's body to a nearby hospital.

The motorcade made its way to Parkland Hospital and abruptly stopped at its entrance. An EMT with a gurney, wide eyed, couldn't believe what he was seeing; he rushed over to the limo where JFK lay, and helped place the President on it. Jackie was still screaming and wouldn't let him go. She kept saying, "They killed my husband! They killed my husband!"

The gurney made its way through the hospital, hordes of aides and Presidential detail following it, all the way to the autopsy room, where Jackie was forced to wait outside. But her tears continued like an avalanche, cascading down her face, as she sat down in a chair hyperventilating and sobbing uncontrollably.

The Vice President stared at her, unsure of what to say or do, frozen in shock, as the rest of America was about to be once they heard the news. Jackie briefly glanced up, her eyes full of water and mascara completely destroyed, and saw him looking at her. She said, after trying to compose herself somewhat, "Lyndon, I need a phone."

"Right," the Vice President responded sympathetically, "let me see where I can find you one."

Before long, he returned with a hospital worker who said she would escort the First Lady to a telephone she could use.

Jackie made her way a few doors down with her and stumbled alone into an empty room, where she spotted a phone. She started dialing Bobby's number, getting it wrong several times, unable to recall it from heart as she had so many times before. But, finally, she was able to remember it and got him after a few rings. When he picked up all she could manage to say was, "Robert," calling him by his formal name, before her voice started trailing off in heavy tears.

"What's wrong?" Bobby asked, worried, never having heard his sister-in-law like this before.

"Robert!" she screamed, suddenly.

"Are you okay?"

"Robert!" she screamed again.

Now Bobby was scared, not understanding what was going on.

"Robert!"

FIFTY SIX

Bobby collapsed, his 155 pounds falling to the ground, smacking the wooden floor with a vicious thud. All the air had been sucked out of his lungs and, in total and complete disbelief, he began wailing, his eyes a torrent of tears, his body shrunken in contorted heartbreak.

"Why God, why!?" is all he could say. "Why did you let this happen!?"

Ethel ran into her husband's study from the bedroom down the hall, which still had leftover decorations from his birthday party two days before, to see what was going on.

"Bobby?" she said anxiously, before she spotted him in a fetal position crying, rushing over to his fallen frame, holding his disfigured body in her arms, brushing her hands through his hair. "What's wrong?"

"Why God!?" he screamed again, unable to answer his wife's question, "why!?"

The kids also heard the commotion from downstairs and ran up to the study. Bobby, whose face was crimson red, looked over at them when he heard their little steps assemble at the door.

"Kids," Bobby struggled to say, seeing that not only were his kids there but Jack's kids too, since they were having a sleepover given their parents' trip to Dallas.

JFK Jr., who was about to turn 3 in a couple of days, asked, "Uncle Bobby, are you okay?"

Bobby, unable to control himself, began wailing even more, emotion belting out of him in a way none of the children had seen, and in a way Ethel had never seen.

The children looked at each other, concerned, and then afraid. Caroline, JFK's first born, ran over to him, her 5 year old arms beginning to hug him, and said gently, "It's okay, Uncle Bobby, it's okay."

But Caroline didn't know what had just happened. Neither did the other children—or even Ethel.

"Why God, why?" Bobby started screaming again—and then again and again—as all of the children now rushed over to him too, one by one, circling around him, forming a cocoon of love and safety and protection.

Bobby continued to wail but, eventually, after a few minutes of feeling the childrens' tender embrace, was able to sit up just a bit, tears still powerful in his eyes. He reached for JFK Jr. and Caroline, grabbing them by the arms, squeezing their little bodies tightly, trying to be their protector just like he was their dads.

"Kids," he said, his nose runny, his voice quaking, "I need to tell you something."

They both looked at him, unprepared for what he was going to say.

"Your dad…" he said, struggling to say the words, struggling to say what no human being ever wants to say to any child, much less to two of their own kin, "your dad, won't be coming back."

"What do you mean, Uncle Bobby?" Caroline said, her face full of innocence. "He told me he was coming home later tonight and that we would play the Mouse Trap game he gave me."

Wiping a tear from his right eye, Bobby said, "what I mean to say hunny is that, something very bad has just happened to your dad, and he won't ever be coming home."

But no words came out of her mouth in response. And no words came out of the other childrens' mouths either. Their eyes began to swell, their little bodies began to writhe in pain and, collectively, they began weeping. They now knew, and it was more than they could bear.

"I'm so sorry," Bobby said, weeping along with them, torment filling their souls, anguish echoing out of Hickory Hills. "I'm so sorry."

"What happens now, Uncle Bobby?" Caroline asked, tears flowing down her rosy cheeks, fear and confusion animating her entire essence.

But what could he say to that? Their dad was gone, their uncle was gone, and the man he loved more than any other man in the world, the man he worshiped and adored more than anyone else in the world, the brother who was his identity and literal reason for being, the brother he protected at all costs, the brother he believed would one day change humanity, was gone. What, honestly, could he say to that?

Bobby squeezed Caroline and then looked into her little brown eyes, their typical twinkle completely dimmed out. He said, his voice still choppy, "We're going to pay honor to your dad by laying him to rest and making sure the world never forgets who he was."

But Bobby also meant something more than this, something he didn't want to say, not to them, not to anyone, especially in this moment of anguish. He also meant, "Not only are we going to honor my brother, but I'm going to find out who killed him and come after them worse than hell itself."

FIFTY SEVEN

It was the middle of the night and Bobby heard a scream. He ran down the hall, opened the door to one of the spare bedrooms, and entered.

"Jackie, Jackie," Bobby said, quickly approaching his sister-in-law who was looking distraught, curiously wearing mascara to bed that was dripping down her face, "it's alright."

He hugged her, placing her head over his shoulder, and gently stroked her back, like a father would do to a child. "Shhh," he whispered, "it's alright."

Since the tragedy of a few months before, Bobby had moved Jackie into his home, along with his niece and nephew, to whom he became their surrogate father, and watched over them. Not only was Jackie having recurring nightmares—living the scenes of Dallas over and over again—but she was blaming herself for her husband's loss, drinking heavily, and making suicidal comments on a regular basis. She was in no position to be on her own, and Bobby saw to it that she wouldn't be.

After a few moments, Jackie looked up at him and said, "Thank you. I'm sorry to keep doing this to you."

"Don't worry," Bobby reassured her, "that's what family is for."

But the truth is, Bobby felt the same way Jackie did: completely devastated, bleeding from the inside out, hardly able to contain his grief, his thoughts darkened by the inhumanity of the world, his doubts about the future more pronounced than ever. In the intervening months, he had laid his hero to rest; wrestled with whether to become Vice President of the United States for the crass machine politician he hated, Lyndon Johnson, who was sworn in on the plane that brought his dead brother's body home; and went on a secret search for JFK's assassin, vowing to himself to find the truth and to bring whomever really killed him to justice, his or the public's.

Putting Jackie back to bed, Bobby walked down the hall, entered his study once again, with Freckles joining him, and walked over to his desk. This had been his sanctuary, or solitary confinement really, since the tragedy, as night after night he couldn't sleep, couldn't eat—in fact, he had lost so much weight he looked like a bag of bones—and couldn't function like normal, cutting himself off from the world as much as possible, refusing to leave this room more often than not.

He spotted one of Jack's tweed blazers and put it on, something that had become a recurring habit, and, spotting Aeschylus's quote once again, which he had now knew by heart, read it:

He who learns must suffer. And even in our sleep pain that cannot forget falls drop by drop upon the heart until, in our own despair, against our will, comes wisdom through the awful grace of God.

Bobby had meditated on these words so frequently by now they had become a part of him, absorbed into his very soul, trapped in his psyche and subconscious, forbidden from ever leaving his life again. He had felt the awful grace of God and he didn't know what it all meant. He made a sign of the cross, which he was doing multiple times a day now, and picking up a pen, wrote another journal entry.

Father God, I don't know who I am right now or what to do. Please give me wisdom and guidance, and please take the pain away, please take the suffering away, please take the agony away, for I don't know if my heart can go on. It feels like my chest is going to explode. Jack meant everything to me and, to see him go just like that, has stripped my life of all meaning. It's done the same thing to poor Jackie. She could try to overdose at any time, so please protect her Father, for she thinks she will be reunited with Jack the moment she does. But she doesn't realize the pain that it would bring Caroline and John Jr., not to mention that for me, Edith, and our family, it would be unbearable. I understand how she feels, but please give her the strength not to act in haste, the strength to overcome her nightmares, and the strength to overcome the alcoholism that seems to have bewitched her.

I feel like I'm at a crossroads and my mind is going in so many directions, so much confusion that I can't think straight, and I hope I'm doing the right things. I can't in good conscience become Lyndon's Vice President, I just don't trust him and his escalation of our involvement in Vietnam, and I can't testify before the Commission he has set up to investigate Jack's death because it's just too painful. The government is trying to push a lone gunman narrative, trying to say Lee Harvey Oswald did it on his own, trying to keep the public calm and not whip up mass hysteria, but I'm not convinced they're right. Even worse, I wonder if I'm the one who is wrong here, I wonder if I'm to blame for what happened to Jack?

I have my reasons they're wrong about Lee Harvey Oswald: J. Edgar Hoover called me right after Jack was shot and had no emotion in his voice, no compassion, and I know how much he hated Jack and wanted to see civil rights stopped. I also know how much the CIA hated Jack, too, after we cut them off after the failed Bay of Pigs fiasco they led and after we attempted to cut their budget by 20%. They never forgave Jack for that, or forgave us for calling into question their chemically-induced mind-control activities, MK-ULTRA, which sickens me. Castro also never forgave us for trying to assassinate him, nor did the Dixiecrats, after we put an end to our alliance of convenience and came out fully in support of civil rights. I can't prove it, but I wonder if any one of them had anything to do with it? They all had a motive—Hoover because civil rights just passed the House judiciary committee; the CIA because, well, they're pissed and that's what they regularly do, topple leaders and governments; Castro because he was trying to get even, trying to shift the balance-of-power in favor of his puppet masters, the Soviets; and the Dixiecrat KKK because their way of life, the way of White Supremacy, is being slowly overturned, as it should be, though I now believe it should be radically overturned, as quickly as possible.

But I wonder, Father, if somebody or something else could've killed Jack and this worries me the most. I've gone after the Mafia with a vengeance, launched hundreds of raids against them, prosecuted countless mobsters, increased convictions by 800%, and even deported some of them whom I couldn't get enough evidence on to lock up. But truth be told, Jack got involved with one of their wives in a moment of weakness, while I was doing all of this, and this probably pissed them off even more. Could they have placed a hit out on him because of what I've done as Attorney General with his behavior only making the issue worse? They certainly had a motive to do it, even though I thought the motive would have always been to put the hit out on me. They should have killed me, Father, they should have killed me!

I've tried to track down as much evidence as I can for all these potential suspects and, if I find somebody or the somebodies who may have done this, I'm going to release armageddon on them; the feeling of revenge is just too strong to escape right now.

But do you want to know what else is too strong to escape? Honoring Jack's legacy by pushing forward his civil rights bill, which is being filibustered in the Senate after passing the House, and trying to earn Martin Luther King's respect and support. He called Jackie after the funeral to offer his condolences, but he didn't speak to me, and still hasn't returned any of my earlier calls. Still, I don't blame him. But I want to speak with him. No, I need to speak with him. I need to work with him. But I don't know how. The suffering of Negro people—and my own suffering—has shown me that this is what I need to dedicate the rest of my life to now that Jack is gone: speaking up for those who suffer most and becoming true allies with those who speak for them. With all of this power and money and fame that I have, I have the responsibility to do so. I know I need to, like my priest said years ago, follow the example that St. Francis of Assissi set, by looking out for the widows like Jackie, the fatherless like my niece and nephew, the poor, the immigrant, and the downtrodden, not as an afterthought, not as political opportunism, but as my greatest ambition, my ultimate priority. But, Father God, what direction do I take to try to do this? My life up until now has been about getting my brother ahead, advancing my career, not about being a moral crusader, not about speaking to the concerns the affluent throughout America and the people in Washington regularly ignore and typically hold in contempt. With Jack no longer with us and me thinking about quitting Lyndon's Administration soon, I really have no idea how to do this. I feel like a man who doesn't know what to do to move forward with what I feel you calling me to do.

FIFTY EIGHT

"So, what's it been like being one of the only white girls in the Civil Rights Movement?" a slim, white, wide-eyed UCLA girl wearing colorful bell bottoms asked.

Carol Davis, the courageous white Freedom Rider that she was, didn't hesitate to answer. "Empowering…but I would also add, I'm not the only white sistah involved in this thing."

Looking around a makeshift Mississippi civil rights headquarters, Carol was surrounded by thousands upon thousands of mission-driven, tie-dye wearing white youth, college students who were organizing what they were calling "Freedom Summer." These students, hailing from Harvard, Yale, UCLA, UC Berkeley, Stanford, and from all across the country, were not only inspired by the little black kids they saw marching in Birmingham standing up to fire hoses and police dogs and standing for Martin Luther King's Dream, but also outraged at what had happened to the little girls at the 16th Street Baptist Church bombing and to President Kennedy. As they said over and over again, they knew exactly where they were when they heard about his assassination, as it had forever marked them, scarred them, and made them realize that the America that had provided them so many privileges was also an America that had viciously denied these privileges to others, an America that they loved too much not to stand up to, and to stand against, when it was mercilessly hurting its own people, and even barbarically killing its own President when he dared to do the right thing for blacks.

To these white youth, many of whom were forbidden by their parents of getting involved in civil rights in the first place, the events of recent times made them reach one emphatic, overwhelming conclusion: that white people now only had three options when it came to blacks, and two of those options were self-delusional cop outs. One option was to be a "white racist" and support Jim Crow, segregation, and White Supremacy in all of its inglorious bankruptcy. The second option was to be a "white moderate" that Martin Luther King eloquently described in his *Letter From a Birmingham Jail*, which might have been the majority of the country, who claimed they were for "equal rights" for blacks in theory but not personally willing to do anything about making those equal rights a reality in practice. To them, moderate whites claiming they were for black rights without actually helping blacks was like a grown grandchild saying they were for helping their hospitalized grandma get the help she needs even though they know grandma is sick and dying from cancer, has no visitors or callers, and can't afford any of her medical bills, but claiming they want the best for grandma when they live right around the corner, haven't one time come to comfort her, or lifted a finger to help pay for her care even when they have the money to do it, preferring to spend it on themselves and ignoring her calls when she has been reaching out to them because they are too uncaring or selfish or self-interested or distracted, getting on with their lives without having to think about anybody else in a worse position than them in life. In other words, the white moderate was the ultimate hypocrite to these students, claiming to believe one thing but doing something else entirely when their beliefs were put under the crucible of testing. The third option, and only option that was legitimate in their minds, was to be a "white radical," somebody willing to say, "Even if I didn't cause slavery or Jim Crow or racism, and even if I don't personally benefit from helping blacks, I'm going to use my social witness as a white person to do something my forebears should have done a long time ago: demand justice and equality for a powerless, humiliated, and colonized people who are crying out for help."

"You're right," the slim UCLA student responded, righteous fire blazing in her eyes, in response to Carol. "You're not the only white sistah or white person here anymore."

Of course, all of these radical white students had recently mobilized because the Civil Rights Bill JFK originally proposed the previous year in 1963 had been filibustered for months on end in the Senate after it passed in the House, despite the opposition from the J. Edgar Hoover-backed House Rules Committee Chairman, and despite a major push from the new President, Lyndon Johnson, the former cunning Senate Majority leader whose ultimate joy was found in power, whose ultimate peace was found in exercising it, and who couldn't get it through Congress on his own as he once bragged he could. So instead of continuing going at it alone, Johnson called on Martin Luther King's support, who had been maintaining a low profile in recent days—who had been hiding his true mental and physical health from everyone except his wife—and, who, in turn, called on the Freedom Riders, Student Nonviolent Coordinating Committee, and others' help to come together to get more black people registered to vote. Around 2% of blacks were registered in the South thanks to Jim Crow but if more registered and voted, with the promised protection of President Johnson, they could throw out Dixiecrats who were blocking the bill during the upcoming 1964 election and get it enacted.

Walking frantically in the makeshift headquarters, which was full of mounds of donated food from a local NAACP chapter for the activists, Carol said, "You and you," her brown hair in her typical ponytail, looking like a Civil Rights General, pointing at two students, "take these voting forms and go with him," shuffling the volunteers over to another volunteer, putting addresses and maps in all of their hands. "You there, take these," she said to a fourth volunteer, pointing them to go register voters with the group she had given instructions to.

"Thank you for this opportunity," the white bell bottoms wearing UCLA student sincerely said to Carol, after coming up to her, recently having arrived from a mid-to-upper class area of the country, a similar social status she shared with many other Freedom Summer volunteers, 90% of whom were white and many of whom were Jewish. "This means the world to me, to see what's going on with my own eyes."

"Yes," another white female sophomore from Harvard said to Carol too, "thank you for all that you've been doing all of these years while we've been on the sidelines."

But Carol didn't smile or say you're welcome to them. Instead, she told them they should be thanking black people like her Freedom Rider friends Diane Nash, John Lewis, and James "Big Duck" Lawson, fellow college students who were also there, for their lifelong courage and commitment, and for having to still put up with racism and harassment when all of the white student radicals got to pack up and go back home to ideal lives and circumstances once Freedom Summer was over. She told them how hard the work was, how dangerous it was, and how racists in the South would react to people like them once they went out in the field in a few minutes.

"Oh," the UCLA student said, surprised, understandably a little naive, never having been exposed to the ideology of White Supremacy weaponized against radical white anti-racists, "you mean they hate white people who support civil rights more than they hate colored people who do?"

"Yes," Carol said, pulling up the right sleeve on her shirt, revealing several nasty scars she had received during her time as a Freedom Rider, from when her bus was blown up and when she was beaten to within an inch of her life. "We're worse in their eyes. They see us as traitors."

The UCLA sophomore stared at Carol's scar, then into her eyes, and back at the scar again.

"But don't pity me," Carol said, deep sounding conviction in her voice. "We need to do the work our white parents and grandparents should have done generations ago, support colored people the way they should have but never did."

The UCLA student said, "Absolutely. And if that's what it takes to bring freedom and dignity to our colored brothers and sisters," she continued, no longer looking at Carol's scar, "then that's what it's going to take."

The Harvard sophomore nodded in agreement, fearlessness in her eyes, ironically juxtaposed next to the tie die in her shirt, emblematic of the growing peace and hippie movement recently hitting college campuses, and sweet demeanor she possessed, her face looking like a young cherub, with extra rosy cheeks slightly brushed by long straight blonde hair.

"Let's go ladies," Carol said, grabbing voter registration rolls and beginning to walk briskly out the door of their makeshift headquarters before the two students could blink.

Catching up with Carol, all three of them made their way onto a dirt road, taking in the conditions that Jim Crow had kept black people oppressed in for so long, taking in not only the extant reality of separate but equal but also the incredible unreported poverty levels and starvation this left most blacks in, especially black children. As they continued their brief walking tour, Carol explained the history of voting rights to them, explained how blacks had to pay money to vote in so-called poll taxes, how they had to pass literacy tests even though they were denied the right to read and an education from the government, and how the Dixiecrats even set up "white primaries," banning all black people from voting despite the enactment of the 13th, 14th, and 15th Amendments, just so that they could economically, socially, and politically enslave blacks over and over again.

The girls spotted a long dirt road with a house at the end of it that matched their records. They walked over to it, up its steps, and knocked on its door.

"Can I help you?" a voice said, sounding like an old black woman, probably a sharecropper, distant, scared.

"Yes," Carol responded, "we're here on behalf of Martin Luther King's organization, "And we'd like to register you to vote."

"Why?" the voice asked, suspicious.

"Well," Carol struggled, "so you can…vote for politicians who can help change things for the better around here."

"Why would you care anything about that?"

"Because," Carol replied, "change should have come here a long time ago."

"White people don't want change, not for people like me."

"We do," the Harvard student blurted out, her sincerity echoing in her voice.

"How can I trust you?"

"Like we said, we're with Dr. King's group," Carol said.

"You better be careful, sayin' that around here."

"We're taking all proper precautions," Carol said reassuringly. "We're safe going out in groups and not alone."

"That's not what I hear, you claimin' to be safe."

"What do you mean?" the UCLA girl asked.

"Just heard on the radio 'bout 3 of your volunteers down here."

"What about them?" Carol asked, curious.

"I heard that police just found two white boys and a colored boy down here tryin' to register Negroes to vote, dead, buried near the lake."

Carol's heart skipped a beat, as did those of the girls with her, who shrank away, terror striking them, in a moment that had just gotten real. One of them reflexively put her hand over her mouth and said, "Oh my God," as the old black lady told them the deceased names, revealing that they were indeed fellow sojourners they knew, who had just arrived the night before, just boys to the world but now instantly mighty men of valor to them.

The old black woman looked at them through the screen door, absorbed their pain, and compassion overcame her. She stepped outside and said, "I know what it's like to lose people for no reason," reaching for their fingers, lovingly grabbing two of the girls' hands. "They lynched my husband and my brother and just know that their deaths, the deaths of these young boys, and the work you're doing will not be in vain. You have to believe it in your soul, more than you believe in reality itself, because that is the only thing that will give you hope: simple belief, against all knowledge and logic and facts. Just belief. It's the only thing that has sustained colored people for this long, for all that we've come up against: belief."

Wiping tears from her eyes, the UCLA girl, her hand still holding the old black lady's, squeezing it more tightly, said, "I believe," before looking over at her two activist sistahs who also said, in solidarity, "We believe too."

FIFTY NINE

Freedom Summer was proving to be one of the deadliest and most dangerous civil rights campaigns to date. Not only had 3 boys been murdered in cold blood, but nearly 100 white students were brutally and mercilessly beaten along with dozens of churches and homes being firebombed and burned to the ground in a relentless fury. To the racists who committed these atrocities, the local KKK and White Citizens Councils among them, absolutely nothing justified seeing young, educated, well-to-do white students come to their turf to support the impoverished and powerless blacks Jim Crow had been keeping down for so long. To them, this was the equivalent of a capital crime, an unholy shot in a civil war that was heating up, and all trespassers had to pay the ultimate penalty, just like JFK had, who went a little too far in supporting Negroes when he proposed his civil rights legislation.

But what these racists didn't understand is that, like with the cartoonish Bull Conner and the Birmingham Police, their hellish overreaction was designed to be used against them, in an act of strategy and gamesmanship by the Civil Rights Movement, activists who were thinking 10 steps ahead of them, like chess players, patiently working toward a checkmate, willing to sacrifice their lives in a cause whose time had come, willing to do whatever it took to overcome, and be overcomers.

And today was the day they were hoping to take one step forward in overcoming, in reaching this checkmate, in out-gaming the racists who felt, through violence and intimidation, that they had outgamed them. Because of their actions, the Freedom Summer volunteers had garnered enough attention and support to put pressure on white western and northern Senators—the ones who had held out by being noncommittal, enabling the filibuster to go on endlessly—to come out in favor of the Civil Rights Act of 1964. This meant that now only one vote was needed to overcome this filibuster, and President Lyndon Johnson felt he had it. So he invited Bobby, Martin Luther King, and scores of civil rights workers to the White House to celebrate and sign the legislation should the bill pass early this afternoon, which he was expecting it to, far earlier than this fall's Presidential election.

Bobby, who had gotten the invitation from Johnson earlier in the week and who was still reeling from his brother's death, put on one of Jack's tweed blazers, shoved a rosary in his trousers for protection and note in his breast pocket, and hopped into his Thunderbird to make the short ten mile drive from his Hickory Hill home at 1147 Chain Bridge Road, in McClean Virginia, to 1600 Pennsylvania Avenue. He turned on the radio, WAMA 88.5, which was broadcasting the action on the floor of the U.S. Senate.

The radio journalist, who sounded a bit like an old school East Coast WASP mixed with a play-by-play baseball announcer, said, "All eyes are on what is about to happen next. After an epic filibuster by Senator Robert Bryd of Virginia on the Civil Rights Bill, and after Republican Presidential Nominee Barry Goldwater supported him on it, it appears that the legislation will live or die based on the vote of Democratic California Senator Clair Engel, who is terminally ill, suffering from brain cancer, and who has not maintained any of his congressional duties in recent months."

Bobby continued in his car, driving over the Arlington Memorial Bridge, next to the cemetery where he had laid Jack to rest, which he glanced at in the rearview mirror, and turned up the radio.

"But now, being dramatically wheeled into the Senate in a wheelchair, Senator Engel has arrived. He appears unable to speak," the journalist said, "but it looks like he is pointing to the patch he has over his eye, to indicate an "aye," vote, in favor of the bill, meaning, ladies and gentleman, JFK has posthumously gotten his wish, a major piece of Civil Rights Legislation passing through Congress, ending all legal segregation and discrimination in public and private institutions, perhaps the greatest legislation in the last 100 years of this nation."

Upon hearing this, Bobby started honking his horn, over and over again, as tears welled up in his eyes. Passersby couldn't believe what they were seeing: the Attorney General of the United States, who had barely been seen in public for months, celebrating wildly, his thick light brown hair flying freely in the wind, his typical stoic public image abandoned in emotional and cathartic ecstasy.

Bobby drove faster, making turn after turn on E Street and 17th Street, and finally made his way to the front entrance of the White House. Secret Service immediately recognized him, opened the gates, and let him drive in, past Pebble Beach, and park his car right next to several waxed black Cadillacs, Martin Luther King's preferred travel car.

Bobby went in through the West Wing doors, the usual entrance when his brother was President, more gleeful than he had been in months.

"Mr. Kennedy," a female aide said, a beaming smile from ear to ear, "right this way." She escorted him straight to the Oval Office.

He peered inside before stepping in and saw that the room was completely packed. There were lobbyists and congressmen and civil rights activists and, of course, his nemesis too: the President of the United States, with whom his relationship had grown even more sour, especially after Bobby had turned down the Vice Presidency—he knew it was only politics, that Johnson was only trying to capitalize on the popularity of a slain president by trying to include his little brother as his number two—with Johnson now privately complaining to his aides that all Bobby wanted to obsessively talk about was his dead brother and an obscure Greek quote in their few meetings together since the tragedy.

But Bobby also spotted somebody else, somebody he hadn't seen in years, the man who wasn't returning his calls.

The President, who had gotten rid of all of Jack's items, and didn't even keep a picture up of him or his family—like millions of Amercicans had started to do—made his way to Bobby. He said, "We did it," shaking his hand, smiling for the cameras, pretending that Bobby was his friend, pretending that he even liked Bobby in the first place, being the Nixonian-like political chameleon that he was.

"Stand here," the President said, guiding Bobby behind the desk, which had the freshly passed Bill on it, along with countless Presidential pens, and further guiding him right behind Martin Luther King, who didn't turn around or acknowledge Bobby at all.

After Johnson ceremonially signed the bill and gave the attendees their Presidential pens as mementos, Bobby saw an opening to talk to King, who had moved about 15 feet away, mingling with others. He walked over.

"Dr. King," he said, extending his hand, not knowing what to say, "it's nice to see you."

But King just nodded slightly and quickly put his hand in his pocket.

"Listen," Bobby said, still somewhat taken aback at King's reluctance to speak to him, and refusal to shake his hand once again, "I've been meaning to tell you something."

"Yes?"

"It's just that," Bobby said, gliding his hand through his hair again to brush it back, "I've been thinking a lot and—"

"Excuse me," King said, sounding slightly emotional, "but I have to go. I have more work to do. I'm sure I'll see you around."

Bobby felt defeated. What he wanted to tell him was that he was sorry for how he treated him when Jack was alive, that he believed in what King was saying, that he now felt America needed not only the 1964 Civil Rights Act, but also the Second Emancipation Proclamation, including voting rights, fair housing, and economic opportunities for blacks, which today's bill did not cover, just as King had been pushing for all along. But he also wanted to tell him that he had a resignation note in his breast pocket he planned to give Johnson at the end of this function and, in lieu of being the Attorney General, that he was planning to make the Second Emancipation Proclamation the purpose of his life, alongside King, by declaring his immediate candidacy to become an elected Senator just like his big brother once was and, more importantly, to become a white moral champion of civil rights to complete the work he felt Jack never got the chance to do. He felt this is what all of his reflection and prayer and pain had led to and he wanted King to know it.

But instead of saying all of these things to King that he had been aching to get out, Bobby walked up to the President, handed him his resignation note, and left the building—a man with a Herculean chip on his shoulder without an ally by his side.

SIXTY

"I'm such a hypocrite," Martin Luther King said, puffing on a Pall Mall cigarette, looking over at his Father, Daddy King, who he had not spoken to for some time in any meaningful way, since before he had defied him by voting for Kennedy in the 1960 election against his wishes.

"You're not a hypocrite," Daddy King replied, who was wearing a pristine gray tailored suit, hot off of preaching a jaw-dropping sermon at Ebenezer Baptist Church, as he took a sip of lemonade that Corretta had just set on the table of their Georgia home, along with some homemade chocolate chip cookies. "There's no need to say that you are."

"But you don't understand, Daddy," King sighed, shame outlining his face, flicking ash into the ashtray next to his right hand, "I did it twice."

"So?" Daddy King responded, picking up a cookie, a few small crumbs falling here and there on his lapel.

"But you raised me better than that," King said.

"I don't see why you have to shake a man's hand who sold you out," Daddy King replied, "just because his brother's dead."

"But Daddy," King said as he picked up an opened letter, which was on top of a *National Geographic* magazine announcing the recent discovery of homo erectus in Tanzania, Africa—the birthplace of humanity—as well as a concealed medical report from his doctor, "this just came in the mail."

Daddy King reached for the envelope, took out the letter, and scanned the words, which began to glow excitedly in his pupils, each sentence becoming more luminous than the one before it.

"They're giving you the Nobel Peace Prize?" Daddy King asked, joy in his voice.

"Yes," King said, ambivalent.

"My son is getting the Nobel Peace Prize!" Daddy King shouted. "Praise the Lord!"

"But it's for trying to establish peace between people," King said, his voice still uncertain, "and I can't even shake a man's hand who's trying to establish peace with me."

"He only wants to make peace with you because the world now sees your value, which makes you a hot commodity, the youngest Nobel Peace Prize recipient in history," Daddy King said, holding the letter triumphantly above his head. "Plus it will help him with the large Negro population in Brooklyn for his Senate race in New York."

"I'm not so sure that's the reason," King said, resigned. "I'm really not."

"So let me get this straight," Daddy King responded, lowering the letter, his reasonable and lawyer-like mind kicking into action. "The man who refused to return your calls, refused to allow you to meet with the President, refused to take any moral stand on civil rights for years, and who put you under FBI surveillance has suddenly wanted to reconcile with you, just as he's up for an election and you become a bonafide superstar, and you feel like a hypocrite because you won't shake his hand?"

Corretta, who had been walking in and out of the room throughout the conversation, watched her husband closely from just outside of the doorway, to see what he would say in response, as she had been extra watchful over his stress levels since he had told her about his failing heart, since he had been on a wife-mandated sabbatical at home, which he used to write a book about the Civil Rights Movement.

"Yes, I feel like that makes me a hypocrite. Besides, what if he's genuine, Daddy?" King asked.

"What politician ever is?" Daddy King shot back. "Remember I told you not to trust the Kennedys? I was right, they didn't do anything for you."

"They did just pass the 1964 Civil Rights Bill," King said.

"They had no other choice," Daddy King barked, "you put too much pressure on them with Birmingham and your speech in Washington. They had to do something, and in the end it was Johnson who got the job done, not them."

"Maybe," King said. "But years ago I asked Ralph Abernathy if I could find Bobby's moral center. But what if, instead of me finding it, Bobby's found it for himself?"

"Bullsh*t."

"Negroes can't accomplish our work alone," King continued, caught between the reasonable belief that Bobby hadn't changed and, perhaps, just perhaps, the unreasonable belief that he had. "We need allies."

"What about the Black Panthers, they'd be good allies?"

"They don't believe in nonviolence," King said sharply, "we could never work with the—"

"But look at all the good they're doing," Daddy King said, playing devil's advocate, impressed, like millions of other black people, at all the progress they'd been making. "They've created free feeding programs for children, community health clinics, and provided free clothing and transportation for our community."

"And one of their founders is wanted for killing a police officer," King replied, again sharply.

"Officer probably deserved it," Daddy King said, dismissive, picking up another Betty Crocker cookie to shove into his mouth.

"Daddy, a Negro killing a cop is just as bad as a cop killing a Negro."

"Let's agree to disagree," Daddy King responded, feeling cops had put way more innocent Negroes in body bags than the other way around, which was statistically very true, and that they deserved what was coming to them, which was a hotly debated and divisive topic in the black community.

King agreed to disagree with his father.

"But let's not disagree on this," Daddy King said, sounding like the wise preacher that he typically was, "before you go and shake Bobby's hand, before you agree to do anything for or with him, watch him, study him, see if he's real, and make sure you don't put yourself in a position for him to sell you out again."

"Understood, Daddy."

"He has to earn your trust," Daddy King finished, before ending somewhat morbidly with, "even if it's with his blood, like his brother."

SIXTY ONE

Like a cockroach, J. Edgar Hoover moved fast, breathed quickly, and had the ability to keep surviving despite his head being cut off, his clandestine efforts to thwart the 1964 Civil Rights Act defeated decisively, and his ability to manipulate the Attorney General of the United States no more, with Bobby's seemingly abrupt resignation.

His fat body scurried into the Justice Department, his steps heavy and recognizable, as he made his way into his office, his cream of chicken soup piping hot, awaiting his arrival. Like always, he closed the windows and blinds upon entering his abode, and sat at his desk.

He then picked up the phone and dialed 202-456-1111.

Without missing a beat, a female switchboard operator answered, matter-of-factly, and said, "This is the White House, how may I direct your call?"

With his customary deceptive charm, Hoover responded, cocking his oval-shaped head to the side, his chin becoming one with the blubber on his neck, "Hi honey, I like the sound of your voice."

"Well thank you, you're sweet," the switchboard operator answered, friendliness and even some mutual flirtation in her tone recognizing the popular and powerful voice that was on the other end of the line. "I'll patch you through to President Johnson."

"Thanks baby," Hoover slithered, as the line temporarily went silent, giving him time to think of what he might say, of what he needed most, of whether he would need to do any strong-arming. Then, before long, the most powerful man in the world picked up.

"Edgar, my old friend, how the hell are you?" Johnson asked, happy to be speaking with the man who had been one of his closest allies in Washington, D.C. the last thirty years, the man who had been sharing dirt with him for just as long, including smutty information about Johnson's former Presidential boss, and scores of others.

"I'm doing just fine, Lyndon," Hoover said, completely comfortable in not feeling compelled to formally call Johnson by his title "President." "Listen, I ordered my agents not to do any investigations into Jack Ruby," referring to the man who had murdered JFK's supposed assassin, Lee Harvard Oswald, the day after JFK had been killed, per Johnson's request to crush any official inquiries into the matter.

"Good," Johnson replied, relieved, "no need to go down that rabbit hole."

"So I'm going to need you to do me a favor in exchange," Hoover declared.

Somewhat nervously, Johnson replied, "Anything for you, my old friend."

Of course, Hoover detested that Johnson had pushed through civil rights, against his hush-hush efforts, but he wasn't going to bring this up even though every racist bone in his body ached to; if anything, he strategically concluded, he wanted to keep secret just how much he hated blacks, with totalitarian passion, and how he directed the FBI to do the same, from anyone who didn't need to know, as he knew the President wouldn't budge on the issue, especially because of the historic nature of the recent desegregation legislation that would perhaps cement the President's legacy forever—unless he screwed it up by doing something else, like mismanaging the Vietnam War he was hellishly escalating. So instead, he felt he needed something else, something that Johnson could easily do, something that would allow him to regroup in the eyes of his "yes men" at the FBI after his recent defeat—and to regroup after Bobby's recent exodus—so that he could double down on his fury against Martin Luther King, and somehow add a new target to to his hit list, Bobby Kennedy, should he need to play additional hardball with him in the future if he won his New York Senate seat, something he knew the President wouldn't mind since the Commander-in-Chief had recently privately called Bobby a "co*ksucker."

"Well, Lyndon," Hoover said, trained in the art of diplomacy, trained in the art of manipulative ass-kissing, trained in the art of the bait-and-switch ask, "if it wouldn't be too much to ask, I'd like for you to send a bill to Congress to make me FBI Director for life, so I can grow my work to root out these damn Communists, and make sure they don't undermine the great work you're doing in Vietnam, especially the mandatory draft you're empowering young men to enter to protect our country."

Being the skilled powerbroker that he was, also trained in how to listen-between-the-lines, Johnson knew Hoover was full of sh*t. But he also knew that this rationale would be enough political cover to explain this Stalin-like request, an Un-American power coup if there ever was one, to his aides and congressional allies, and, more importantly, enough political cover to keep Hoover from potentially unleashing his wrath Johnson's way should that be what Hoover might threaten him with next if the President denied his request, revealing the long list of past and present skeletons somebody who had a lifelong career in Washington like the President had. So all Johnson could say in response was, "Edgar, this will be one hell of an honor for me to do and I will have legislation drafted and sent to Capitol Hill by next week."

"Thank you, Lyndon," Hoover responded, feigning appreciation. "Well," he continued abruptly, "I know you're a busy man, so I won't keep you, but I'm sure we'll be in touch soon."

The President gave his farewells and hung up the phone. Hoover just sat there, a big smile on his face, impressed with himself by the persuasion he exercised with the eighth consecutive Commander-in-Chief he'd served under—or perhaps over.

His chubby right hand then lowered the phone, hung it up in celebration, and picked up his silver spoon, dunking it in his soup, which had cooled a bit, and took a few bites. He then set the bowl and silverware to the side and began digging into some ultra thick files from the Confidential stack, next to new ones he was now keeping on the NAACP, the Black Panthers, which he was encouraging the FBI to spread rumors about, provoke violence within, and to infiltrate undercover, and even

Thurgood Marshall, the black lawyer who had successfully argued the *Brown vs. Board of Education* case, who was being talked about as becoming the first colored Supreme Court Justice of the United States.

"Let's see what new information they've gathered for me," he said to himself, "on this nig*er Martin Luther King."

As he flipped through the files, Hoover reviewed the information that had been gathered on the Reverend over the last few years, officially a part of his COINTELPRO or counter-intelligence program he had blackmailed Bobby into authorizing, including King's potential associations with Jewish financiers with connections to American communists, whom he knew were clearly not the Soviet kind, and King's gay adviser, Byron Rustin, who he was trying to use to suggest to sympathetic Senators like Strom Thurmond of South Carolina that King was a homosexual, which he incontrovertibly knew was not the case.

But as he continued to flip through the files, he saw something new, something more salacious, something that put an even larger smile on his face, something that came in heavily edited as suspect-looking memos and audiotapes, for which he had multiple copies. "Well, well, well," he said, as he pressed play on one of the tapes, hearing loud and muffled sexual moans, "this is interesting."

The memos accompanying the audio tapes, written by ambitious FBI agents trying to get on Hoover's good side to advance more quickly in their careers, with odd comments hand-scribbled next to their type-written words, were damning, as much for their downplaying of King's genuine selflessness—they overheard him saying how much he hated fame and how he would donate all $54,000 of his Nobel Peace Prize money to the Civil Rights Movement, not keeping even a penny for himself—as they were for their recommendations to "neutralize" him by producing "desired results without embarrassing the FBI," including finding King in sometimes compromising situations that were outside of the scope of Bobby's wiretap, and of civil rights in the first place, which the FBI had labeled as the most dangerous terrorist threat facing the United States on the same level as undercover Soviet Spies trying to destabilize the government.

"Degenerate," Hoover said in response to the tapes, twistedly amused, rewinding and playing the tapes again and again and again, trying to memorize their rhythm, intensity, and play-by-play action, hypnotically transfixed by the voices and sounds he was hearing, ones, given his lifelong professed virginity, he only ever came across in times like this.

He then took out a stationary letterhead, put it into his typewriter, and began tapping the keys in a memo to send out to the whole of the FBI, whose subject line read, "Martin Luther King: Discredit, Disrupt, and Destroy."

Hoover then took out a second stationary letterhead and wrote this one by hand, writing, with words he had long been wanting to say to King, *You are a colossal fraud and an evil, vicious one at that. The American public will know you for what you are—an evil, abnormal beast, worse than Satan himself. And so you know, you only have one thing left to do: kill yourself before your fraudulent soul is bared to the nation.*

Hoover then placed the letter into a large brown box followed by a copy of the audio tapes, before barking at an aide to come into the office.

"Yes, Sir," one of the aides who quickly came in, said, the same aide who spilled the cream of chicken soup all over Hoover's shiny floor over a year ago.

"I need you to take this box and mail it," Hoover said, a wry smile on his face.

"And to whom would you like me to mail this, Sir?" the aide asked, pensively.

"Martin Luther King's wife."

SIXTY TWO

"Carpetbagger!" screamed the junior United States Senator from New York, a Republican from upstate named Kenneth Keating, his face boiling crimson with rage. "Bobby doesn't even live in the state!"

"From what my colleagues are telling me," said the *New York Times* Reporter with sandy blonde hair interviewing the incumbent politician in his midtown Manhattan office, "an exception has been made for that."

"What do you mean an exception has been made?" intoned Keating, apoplectic, the veins in his neck thrashing up against his skin, erupting on the inside of him, trying to break out and strangle America's now former Attorney General, a man romancing the political world saying things like "A revolution is coming."

"Apparently, the Democratic party bosses were able to pull some strings," replied the *New York Times* Reporter. "Now that he's in the race, do you think that you can beat him?"

"I shouldn't have to beat him," Keating said, still incredulous, "he's not even registered to vote here!"

"Do you want to put that on the record?" questioned the Reporter.

But Keating, being a smart politician, knew that he shouldn't put that on the record; JFK's assassination was still too fresh in voters' minds, and the Kennedy name was taking on greater meaning, greater impact, and greater currency in the President's death than it ever had in his short life, youth and potential being forever exalted and eternalized in a life taken too soon, too tragically, too unexpectedly, and Bobby was certain to benefit from this, the Senator reasoned. Nevertheless, Keating acted against his better judgment, against his political instincts, and in concert with labeling his famous opponent, whose family was swiftly taking on mythological overtones, as an "outsider" in a strategy that would probably be sure to fail, outrage overcoming him. Instead, he simply said, "Yes."

"Alright," the Reporter said. "So your argument is that because he doesn't live here, as the former Attorney General of the United States who represented all of the United States, including New York, and who advised his brother on all domestic and international matters concerning the country, is not qualified to serve here?"

"Yes," Keating answered, unsure, unable to come up with an argument to respond to his weak carpetbagging claim. "He knows nothing about New York."

"But he used to live here for 15 years as a youth," the Reporter said, challenging the Senator, trying to incite more controversy for the piece he was writing.

"That was a long time ago," Keating responded, before quickly trying to change the subject. "Besides, I've done a fine job in the Senate."

"Thanks for your time," the Reporter said, abruptly putting his yellow notepad into his red leather briefcase.

"That's the whole interview?" Keating replied, slightly offended, protest evident throughout his expression, wanting more time to get his two cents in.

"Yes, sorry," the Reporter apologized. "I've got to go try to find Kennedy for a quote, his first campaign event is in a few minutes and I'm hoping to catch him."

The Reporter then excused himself, stepped outside, made the short walk to Penn Station, and boarded the "A" train, for Brooklyn, an overwhelmingly black borough, with some official counts putting the Negro population at well over 80%, a fitting place for Bobby to campaign, especially because it has the second highest concentration of Negroes anywhere in the country, an ironic place given that Bobby's

Father, Joe Sr., warned his brother and him of being photographed with black people just four short years ago.

Upon exiting the subway, the Reporter's jaw literally dropped. He had never seen a crowd this size before. Not only was it larger than any campaign event he'd ever seen, including Presidential campaigns, including JFK's, but it was a larger crowd than even the Beatles were getting, their British invasion into America reaching feverish heights, a rock band whose celebrity bordered on madness at best and lunacy at worst.

"Excuse me," said the Reporter to one of the tens of thousands of people he walked over to in what looked like a mob scene, "but you're not here to see Bobby Kennedy are you?"

"As a matter of fact, I am," said the man, who appeared to be a black construction worker with a hard hat on, trying to peer over the heads of the people in front of him to see if he could catch a glimpse of Bobby.

"These people too?" the Reporter asked, looking around at the throngs of individuals doing the same thing as the man with the hard hat.

"I think so."

As the Reporter took out his notepad to write down descriptions of the crowd, observing their anticipation, observing their excitement, observing their hope, he noticed that, despite the heavy black population of Brooklyn, there were lots of other ethnic groups here in large numbers too: Puerto Ricans, Hassidic Jews, Dominicans, West Indians, Chinese, and others. Taking note of this, the Reporter wrote, "Are these people, traditionally discriminated against and excluded by the white majority, hoping Bobby will do for them what he and his brother appeared to do for blacks, with the 1964 Civil Rights Act, hoping to get a chance at inclusion too?"

But before he could write anymore, a small motorcade pulled up, just outside of the large housing project across the street, holding New York's new Democratic senatorial candidate, riding in a 1964 Ford Galaxie 500, with the top down.

"We love you," yelled one woman, startling Bobby with her enthusiasm, his head turning toward her, as he stood in his seat, reciprocating with the Kennedy smile his brother had made famous.

"Yes we do," yelled another woman, in what then set off an echo of similar statements and declarations from thousands of people, all piercing affections wrapped in hope, ensconced in belief, cloaked in an optimism that belied their beleaguered, ghettoed circumstances.

Bobby turned to the Mayor of New York, who was riding with him, and said, his eyes somewhat sad, and his constitution marked with guilt, "This should be for Jack."

"What?" the Mayor asked, a Democrat who had helped get him on the ballot in the state along with an Irish party boss from the Bronx, both fellow Catholics.

"I mean," said Bobby ruefully, "all of this love, it's for my brother, not for me. He's their hero."

"Don't think that way," the Mayor responded. "They came for you."

The Reporter watched carefully everything that was going on and still couldn't believe his eyes, which he thought were lying to him. He observed, among other things, that it took approximately 30 cops to help Bobby get out of his vehicle and through the crowd, to the makeshift podium which was only 30 feet away. 30 cops!

As Bobby stepped up to the podium, his hair and suit disheveled from people grabbing at it and at him, trying to psychically absorb the growing Kennedy mystic, he looked a bit disoriented from the amount of attention he was getting. He felt, ever so faintly, that he didn't deserve it but, at the same time, that this was where he was supposed to be; that this was an answer to the prayers he had been praying, searching for guidance on what to do with his life; and that this was how he could extend his brother's legacy and help blacks—and, from how it appeared to him right now—help so many others too, people nobody was talking about, or seemed to care about, in modern America. But Bobby was also looking disoriented, too, because he had always been a behind-the-scenes guy, even as Attorney General, second to his brother, and, despite his personal name and political stature, was not really known to the public or acquainted with the reality of now being a national and global celebrity, not just another mostly-obscure political type, a noteworthy individual like most U.S. Senators who had never actually done anything of substance to actually be notable.

Again wearing one of JFK's tweed jackets, Bobby began speaking, continuously brushing his light brown hair out of his left eye. And, the more and more he spoke, the more he sounded like his older brother, quoting the exact same lines and luminaries JFK used to, and, the more and more he spoke, the more he looked like his brother, mimicking how he would put his left hand in his pocket during a speech while his right made a forward chopping motion. It appeared to everybody watching, including the Reporter, that Bobby was JFK reincarnate, not just a symbol or metaphor of the slain President, but the very personification of him, a second-coming of the Kennedy era, a new opportunity, a fresh hope, ignited after the former flame was violently extinguished so many months before.

But what everyone noticed too, as Bobby continued to speak on and on, was that he also started to sound unlike his deceased brother and, for those who at least somewhat knew his public persona from his Attorney General days, like the Reporter, started to sound unlike his typical self. Instead of the cool and easy charm, the middle-ground rhetoric, and tip toeing around big issues like civil rights his brother almost always did, and that he almost always displayed publicly too, Bobby jettisoned the careful language and took the biggest, and most taboo, issues head on, sounding more like a religious leader than politician, channeling a little more MLK—Martin Luther King—than JFK, framing the rights of blacks in moral terms, to unexpectedly strong applause, and challenging the whites in the audience to wake up to the obligation they had to stand against injustice their fellow Americans were experiencing, in a speech which represented perhaps the greatest political aboutface in history, of a man who seemed like he was not selling out to money or politics but who seemed to be, increasingly, selling out to conviction.

As Bobby finished and stepped away from the microphone, the Reporter squeezed through the massive crowd, and somehow made his way to him, good reporters having a knack for getting to the right place at the right time.

"Bobby," the Reporter asked, "your opponent says you're a carpet-bagger, what do you say to that?"

"If this election is about who's lived in New York the longest," Bobby answered, his reply well-thought out in advance of the question, "then I'm not the right guy. But if it's about who will be the best Senator, I think I am."

"What will you focus on if elected?" the Reporter followed up, trying to get as much newsworthy information as possible for his editors back in the news bureau about the political phenomenon that he was witnessing.

"Racial harmony, youth, education, and good jobs and homes for blacks and all disenfranchised people everywhere," Bobby responded, genuine.

"What does that look like?" the Reporter asked, pushing for more, intrigued at a politician sounding like an altruist, like a living help-the-least-of-these Bible verse. "Any specifics?"

Bobby then stopped, looked at the man, and thought briefly, ideas swirling back and forth in his mind, bouncing off of his beautiful head of light brown hair. Ever since his intense study of the words and works of great blacks, as well as his growing appreciation for the necessity of King's Second Emancipation Proclamation, which included, among other things, economic empowerment for Negroes, he had thought about what he would specifically do, and how he would do it. But given the tension in the country, and chance of a potential second civil war, he didn't think he could come out and say that—use the word "Emancipation" in any context—his political antennas still being attuned to the sensitivity of language and its ability to spark further, and unnecessary, conflict, and bloodshed. So instead he said, "I have an idea for an economic revitalization development, right here in Brooklyn, one that could be a model for America and turn around the plight of black citizens for good, and I'll be releasing it soon."

"That sounds very ambitious," the Reporter shot back. "Will you be working on this with the recent recipient of the Nobel Peace Prize, Martin Luther King? It sounds similar to what he's trying to do for Negroes?"

But Bobby, continuing to stand there, frozen in place, couldn't tell him that not only would King probably not work with him, but that he wouldn't even talk to him; he couldn't tell him about the shame he felt for how he had treated King behind the scenes, for years, that he never got called out on; and he couldn't tell him that he felt more could have been done on civil rights if only he had pushed his brother to do more while he was alive, instead of trying to play politics, instead of trying to manage perceptions and appearances, and instead of trying to appease, for the sake of winning the 1960 election, the Dixiecrats. So Bobby just stood there, an even keeled expression on his face, but feeling dumbfounded shame in his heart, evidence of Catholic guilt if there ever was any, Bad Bobby being severely convicted on trial by Good Bobby.

"Well," said the Reporter, "are you going to work with King on this?"

But Bobby had no response.

SIXTY THREE

The Ku Klux Klan was meeting in the dark of night, members' shadows juxtaposed harshly against each other, casting what appeared to be an image of countless human vermin conspiring together for some sort of feast.

But this was no ordinary gastronomical get-together; it was a ceremony, a special "Klonvocation," held at the birthplace of the modern KKK itself: Stone Mountain Georgia, near where the Imperial Wizard typically met in his pedestrian Georgia church headquarters, celebrating the completion of what they were describing as the greatest monument ever built, decades in the making, greater than the Pyramids of Egypt, the Taj Mahal of India, and the Arc de Triomphe of France, in their eyes.

Originally designed by Klan member Gutzon Borglum, who was also the architect behind Mount Rushmore in Keystone, South Dakota, the new Southern structure towered into the heavens, reaching nearly twice the height of the Washington Monument, and it roared across the earth, stretching to two-times the length of the Reflecting Pool in front of the Lincoln Memorial, where Martin Luther King had given his now-famous speech a year and a half ago, and depicted the Confederate South's three most beloved heroes, all of whom were riding horses and holding hats high above their heads, the conferral of gentlemanliness that was more true in myth than in fact: Robert E. Lee, who's Southern army kidnapped free blacks in the North and sold them into slavery in the South, was on the memorial's westernmost front; Stonewall Jackson, who led the military charge to preserve slavery and White Supremacy, was square in the center; and Jefferson Davis, who, as president of the Confederacy during the Civil War, was accused of, but never prosecuted for, treason against the United States, flanked its eastern edge.

"This is the greatest day of my life," one new 25 year old KKK member said, a truck driver, his white robe illuminating a bright yellow, like piss, reflecting the ray of heat the 30-foot burning cross blazing in the center of their ritual was emanating.

"Forget the greatest day of your life," another new KKK member, around 40 years old and a corporate lawyer, said, holding the official White Supremacist bible known as the "Kloran" that outlined their beliefs, titles, and rituals in detail, "this is the greatest day in the history of America."

Both men, surrounded by thousands of robed others, were there not only to celebrate their monument of might, but also there for an initiation of brand new Klan members and to hold a national strategy meeting for how to stop the growing threat of Bobby Kennedy, who had just won his Senate bid days before—just as they stopped his brother—or, at least, "somebody" had stopped his brother, there being rumors up and down the ranks that the now-deceased assassin, Lee Harvey Oswald, had had contact not only with their group right before the murder, but also with the Soviets, American mobsters, and multiple others.

Roy Davis, the Imperial Wizard, who Klansman always said was emperor of the invisible empire, was overseeing the assembly and was paying close attention to following protocol, being the stickler for strict order that he was, ironic given his chaotic criminal past and con man present. "Now," he said, looking around at the three thousand or so new members they were indoctrinating into their conspiracy of existential carnality, standing right in front of more senior members, "it is time for our official 'Ku Klux Klan Kreed'."

The new members, including the two who were in awe of White Supremacy's grandest memorial before them, repeated the Kreed along with the others, their voices echoing off the mountains all around them, in their pledge of allegiance:

"We avow that the distinction between the races of mankind has been decreed by the Creator, and we shall ever be true in the faithful maintenance of White Supremacy."

The new members then screamed "White Power!" and started popping open cans of thick, bitter beer and eating cheap hamburgers and hotdogs, generously underwritten by one of the green-robbed Grand Dragons and his "exalted Cyclops" buddy, and shared their stories of why they had come to join the Klan: some were infuriated at the passage of the 1964 Civil Rights Act; others wanted to be part of a "brotherhood of believers," trying to protect their country before they lost it forever to the blacks and now the liberals and commies and Jews and Catholics and foreigners, a growing list of enemies in what, and more specifically who, was wrong with America; still others were bent on hell and destruction, wanting to harass blacks, like nearly all of them did, including skinning, torturing, and raping them, among other things, if they were female, or creatively executing them if they were male, their bag of sadistic tricks in unlimited supply, malevolent magicians of mayhem that they were.

The 25 year old Klansman, who had taken a bite of a hotdog under his white hat and gotten relish on his country beard, said to the 40 year old, looking at the Imperial Wizard, "so what do you think our leadership is gonna do with Bobby Kennedy now that he's in the Senate trying to push economic equality for nig*ers?"

"Kill him," the 40 year old lawyer Klansman responded, laughing, raising his beer and clicking it in solidarity with the younger tow truck driver, hatred being the most common unifier of men the world had ever seen, expressing humanity's heretofore unofficial gospel.

"The good Lord couldn't have spoken truer words," the younger Klansman replied, the smile under his pointy hat as wide as Stone Mountain Georgia itself.

"But we need to stop Kennedy before it's too late," the older Klansman said, worried, frustrated, "before he can do any real damage."

"Right. But if we can't get a shot at him soon," the younger Klansman said, "given all of his security and Secret Service protection, what else can we try to do to slow him down?"

"Well," the older Klansman said, "for starters, every Dixiecrat in the South has rapidly re-registered as a Republican, millions of us altogether like a blitzkrieg, forever leaving behind the unforgivable Democrats, and so our Party will stand as one against Bobby and his Party, the Party of coons and coon lovers."

"That's a good start."

"Exactly," intoned the older Klansman, "even though Barry Goldwater lost the Presidential Election to Lyndon Johnson, at least we made Jackie Robinson and other coons so uncomfortable we forced them to leave our Party this year. At least now we can be unified in our opposition against these kumbaya faggot loving white nig*ers and the black nig*ers they defend."

The younger Klansman then raised his beer in a second toast, clanking it with the other, the vibration of the tin making a faint sound, their conversation being a microcosm of the conversations happening all around them, the twisted thoughts and twisted words somehow seeming coherent to them, in their reinforced and uncritical group-think, their potent elixir.

"Now, what do we do about Martin Luther King, since so far he's evaded all of our hit attempts and hasn't been seen much publicly lately?"

"That's about to change."

"Really?"

"According to what I've been hearing," the older member said looking over at the Imperial Wizard, "the big guy knows some high level people who are tracking his whereabouts and what he's about to do."

"The Contact, you mean?"

"Maybe."

"Who do you think it is?"

"Don't know. Maybe an FBI Boss. CIA Boss. Somebody else high up."

"I heard it might be a Mafia member with eyes everywhere who hates coons as much as we do."

"Is the same guy tracking King's whereabouts the one offering rewards for if we kill him?"

"Good question. I don't know that either."

"Well, what have you heard about what King is gonna do?"

"He's planning another big march like he had in Montgomery last year with the children."

"Ugh."

"What I heard is that he's going to march 50 miles on foot like some Gandhi sh*t from Selma, Alabama across a bridge, all the way to Montgomery to demand national voting rights for nig*ers."

"First they get 'quote un quote' desegregation before the law and now they want voting rights? For chrissake monkeys can't vote. Everybody knows that."

"Exactly."

"How do we avoid getting embarrassed by him this time? The media was so unfair to us during his last march and made us look like a bunch of crazed know-nothing fools when it is we, the enlightened and civilized ones, who are doing America a favor by keeping these low-class coons in their place."

"I think one of our members may have just the answer," the older Klansman lawyer said, his head turning to the right, his eyes peering into the pupils of another tribesman who he knew was a powerful judge, as the green of his pupils turned orange, glowing with Homeric flames of rage.

SIXTY FOUR

Once again, Bobby couldn't sleep in his Hickory Hill abode; between Jackie's sleep terrors down the hall and his recurring nightmares and continued grief, this past year had been a miserable experience whenever he had hoped to shut his eyes.

Tonight or rather, today, at the 3:45 am hour that it was, was especially tough for him, it being the official one-year anniversary of his best friend's death. Despite winning his election a few weeks ago by a decisive margin, and despite the gargantuan crowds he was getting wherever he went, all he could think about was his brother, what he could have done if he was still alive, what he could have done if he was still standing by his side, helping to guide the young President into his heroic destiny; all of the history and all of the fun and all of the memories they could have created together. In this moment, and in the 365 moments and days before it, all he could do was think deeply and hurt relentlessly, his flesh still continuing to scream, his blood still continuing to cry, his hope still aching for the past to return, for his brother to somehow come back to life.

"Ethel," Bobby whispered, sitting up in his bed in the master bedroom, trying to adjust the inflection in his voice to sound normal so as not to frighten her with his profound agony, "I'm going to go see Jack."

"Okay," she said, her gentle voice reciprocating his whisper, wanting to be strong, and being strong, for her man. "Be strong, my love."

Bobby then kissed her on the cheek, walked slowly to the bathroom, shaved and took a shower, got dressed, again put on one of Jack's tweed blazers, and walked downstairs, trying to make as little noise as possible, so as not to wake anyone. But Freckles chased after him, whom he reached down to pet quietly, and as he did, he looked to his left, and saw a shadow standing alone in the room next to the front door. It was Jackie. And she was smoking a cigarette, which wasn't unusual given her lifelong habit of consuming two packs a day, and had an empty drink on the rocks in her hands.

"Bobby?"

"Yes."

"Are you going to see Jack?" she whispered.

"I am," he replied before offering, hesitatingly, "Would…you like to come with me to see him?"

"Yes. I mean no. I mean, I don't know," she responded, anxious and conflicted, coming further out of the shadow she was standing in and into the light, revealing to her brother-in-law that she had been up all night crying, makeup smudged in a befuddled cacophony of affliction, the kind of pain that only a widow knows.

"I'm so sorry," Bobby said, moving toward her, grabbing her in a heartfelt hug, tears swelling in his eyes, overwhelming his eyelids, and running hard down both sides of his face.

"I miss him so much," Jackie said. "It's too hard."

"I miss him terribly too," Bobby responded, stroking her back, trying not to let his tears wet her hair that was pressed against his cheek. "But he would want us to be strong for him."

Jackie sniffled loudly and then pulled away from Bobby, struggling to place her empty glass in her right hand with the cigarette in it to reach into her nightgown pocket for a used tissue, which she found; its creases and wetness and mucus were full of agony as she blew into it.

"Is it okay if I go to see him?" Bobby asked gently, wanting her permission. "I want to go before any press or crowds get there, to be alone with him."

"You should go, Bobby," Jackie acquiesced. "It's important that you see him."

"Thank you," Bobby said, softly.

"But can you promise me one thing?" Jackie asked.

"Anything."

"Can you tell Jack how much I still love him?"

Looking at her, he said, "I will, with all my heart."

Jackie then hugged Bobby again and gave him a kiss on the cheek before he exited the front door with Freckles, and hopped into his Thunderbird.

On the drive over, Bobby's thoughts were a jumbled contradiction. At times, he remembered his childhood with his brother, remembered when Jack came home with a Purple Heart from World War Two, and remembered all of the travels they had done overseas and good times they had had together, away from politics. But at other times, the only thing he could think of was Jack's funeral, how Jackie had to arrange it quickly, of having to choose to follow the same burial protocol of another assassinated president who helped blacks, Abraham Lincoln, and of his little nephew, John Jr., and how he had saluted his father's casket as it was lowered, draped in an American flag, into the ground.

Within minutes, Bobby was at Arlington National Cemetery, the site of Jack's grave, and hundreds of thousands of other graves, and it was closed. But that didn't matter to him, the aggrieved maverick that he was. He simply scaled the eight foot tall fence and began making the 15 minute walk to his brother's resting place, the tombstone a half mile from the entrance of the 624 acre plot of land.

As he spotted the grave, he began to weep, his heart palpitating in asphyxiated emotions, drowning him in overwhelming pain, and he fell to his knees.

"I'm so sorry, Jack," he wailed. "I'm so, so sorry."

He then pulled out a three-leaf clover he had in his pocket, next to his now customary rosary, and placed it upon the engraving of JFK's tomb, a stand-in for the holy trinity, that was immediately beneath the eternal flame that was lit for his brother, symbolizing everlasting life. He told Jack how much he loved him, how much Jackie loved him, about his recent Senate victory, and about how he was following in his footsteps. He told him that he hoped he was half as proud of him as he was of his big brother. And, most importantly, he told him that he was watching after his kids, Caroline and John Jr., as if they were his own.

"Jack," he continued, "I'm going to do my best to do what you would have done if you were still alive. I'm going to give my all to our Negro brothers and sisters, and my all to Americans of all stripes."

Bobby then got off of his knees, dusted them off, and turned around, slowly walking away from the gravesite. But then he paused and did a slight about-face and said, "And, Jack, one last thing: I know my all might require that I give my life, just like you did. And if it does, it would be my honor to do so, so that one day, I can lay in rest right by your side, where I truly belong."

SIXTY FIVE

"Excuse me, Sir," a young FBI aide said, knocking on his boss's door, "but I have something for you."

"What is it?" barked J. Edgar Hoover, who didn't bother to look up from his desk, fidgeting with a newspaper he was reading that quoted Martin Luther King's recent comments about the Bureau.

"It's about the package you had me deliver to Mrs. King."

As soon as he heard those words, Hoover looked up excitedly, breaking out of the hypnotic trance under which he typically fell at work, especially when he was focused on King. Iniquitous hunger began to appear on his face, the edges of his mouth progressively twitching with glee, and said, "please tell me what she said."

"She didn't say anything."

"What?" Hoover responded, his smug countenance quickly inverting into a frown, looking like a child who was expecting a favorite toy in their Christmas stocking but instead received a big fat lump of black coal in its place.

"She didn't say anything, Sir," the aide repeated.

"I heard you the first time, you twat," Hoover snarled, before picking up his file on Martin Luther King, which was conveniently handy on top of other files on his desk, and wildly flipping through the pages, eventually stopping on page 2,657 of the secret documentation he had on the Preacher. "Did you send the package to the right address, 234 Sunset Avenue, Atlanta, Georgia?"

"Yes," the aide said, reluctantly, looking at the return address from the package in his hand.

"And that nig*er b*tch didn't say anything when she got it?"

"No sir, nothing."

"How do you know?"

"We had an undercover agent watch her from a distance as she received it."

"Did she listen to the tapes, read the note?"

"No. She sent it back to us, to have us analyze it as a 'quote' hate crime."

"Hate crime? What the hell is a hate crime?"

"Although there's no federal law on the books for it, apparently it's when people make threats against a person based on their race or—"

"Shut up! Just shut up! That's a bunch of liberal Communist bull-sh*t!"

Hoover got up from his desk and started pacing back and forth, crossing multiple times in front of the two American flags that stood immediately behind him. His aide, dumbfounded and frozen in fear, watched his boss's corpulent body waddle silently, waiting for instructions, as Hoover's lawyerly mind searched for ideas and for ways to weaponize the Iron White Wall.

"I have three thoughts," Hoover finally said, stopping in place, his reading glasses falling to the brim of his nose, making him look nearly as arrogant and condescending as he actually was. "The first is that you need to put Mrs. King under FBI surveillance."

"Do we have an order for that from the new Attorney General?" the aide asked, innocently.

"My words are the order," Hoover barked, offended that he could possibly be questioned by anyone, much less some young aide who he thought barely knew how to wipe his own ass.

"I will put in the surveillance order right away," the aide said, quickly getting the memo not to question an order from Hoover, the FBI not being a place where free discussions or inquiry is accepted, much less tolerated.

"The second thing is," Hoover continued, matter-of-factly, "is that I need you to convene a press conference downstairs with the lady reporters immediately."

"Right now?" the aide responded, curious why his press-shy superior would abruptly want to chat with reporters. "Why Sir?" he blurted out.

"Because I said so!" Hoover exclaimed, his voice increasingly truculent, extremely irritated at what he felt was becoming a cross-examination; to him, being asked the "why" behind his actions was like a toddler asking an adult why the sky is blue, why the grass is green, or why racist white men think it is their biological right is to run the world.

"Yes, right," the aide replied, not wanting to further cross the line, not wanting the nation's top cop to fire him at best, or make his life a living hell at worst, knowing that Hoover could do either, on a whim, without so much as a second thought. He then asked, "and what's the third thing, Sir?"

"I'll tell you after the press conference."

"Right," the aide said, feeling like a lap boy, as most agents felt, emasculated men trapped under the weight of an overlord whose quixotic lust for power had transformed him into the most insufferable of characters, bent on ruling with an iron fist of irrefutable venom.

The aide then left Hoover's office to gather the female reporters who were stationed by their various news bureaus in the Department of Justice. They apparently had been requesting to interview Hoover this morning in response to Martin Luther King's recent criticism of the FBI, his first such public comments, over its recent handling of a few cases in the South. As soon as the aide returned, about 15 minutes later, he let Hoover know the reporters were ready for him.

Hoover, who had prepared a statement in the meantime, made his way downstairs, each heavy step reminiscent of a self-assured fuhrer, and turned on his "insta-charm" upon entering the makeshift press room.

"Ladies," Hoover lied, his face genteel, feigning innocence, "you're just the people I wanted to see."

One female reporter, about 33, with sandy blonde hair, light blue eyes, and a voluptuous shape, even apparent despite her conservative wardrobe, said, "Mr. Hoover, thank you for meeting with us. What is this, the first time you've ever spoken to the press?"

"Second," Hoover smiled, winking flirtatiously at the reporter, staring her up and down, conspicuously meditating on her very large breasts, thinking the thoughts of a dirty old man.

"So," the sandy blonde reporter said, ignoring his blatant sexism and sexual harassment, common among powerful men in these times, and all times, a universal right of passage for those with enough 'leverage' to know it buys them immunity from social and legal prosecution, "I'm assuming you've heard about the Nobel Peace Prize winner Martin Luther King criticizing the FBI's handling of certain cases in the South with regard to American Negroes?"

"Before I respond to Dr. King," Hoover said cooly, charm still in his voice, "let me tell you about all of the great work the FBI is doing to keep Americans like you safe." Hoover then rattled off an impressive-sounding array of facts, myths, half-truths, and political spin, all part of the devastatingly successful propaganda campaign he had been using for over 40 years as Director of the FBI to maintain his popularity with the mainstream public. After he finished, which seemed like eons later, he began speaking about King.

"When it comes to Martin Luther King, however," Hoover said, his voice transitioning from calm and collected to angry and agitated, "all I have to say is this: he is a complete and utter fraud and the truth will come out about him soon enough. Mark my words."

Surprised, the sandy blonde reporter, along with the other reporters, didn't know how to take this statement, especially because King's reputation and stature were rising among not only Washington and East Coast reporters, but among moderate whites throughout the country as well.

"That is all, thanks ladies," Hoover said, taking one last glance at the sandy blonde reporter's substantial bust, abruptly ending the meeting before they could dig into any details, and before he could have time to shoot himself in the foot for revealing too much information—or revealing the secret programs he was running against King and other blacks, which would have ruined everything, exposing the carefully laid web of deceit he had woven all of these years, and causing backlash against his pristine public persona.

After he left the room, his young aide hurried after him and complimented him profusely on his eloquence and composure during the press conference in the long walk up the stairs. Hoover, being the sucker for flattery that he was, ate it up, and encouraged him to say more about his "masterful" performance, which the aide did, offering descriptive adulation. As they got to the floor on which Hoover's office was, and walked over to it, they stopped.

"Oh, and sir," the aide said, remembering Hoover had had three thoughts on his mind but had only mentioned two of them, "what was the third thing you wanted to tell me when we were alone just a bit ago, that you told me to ask you after the press conference?"

Without missing a beat, Hoover said, "I've gotten some intelligence that Martin Luther King's life may be in danger."

"Oh?" the aide responded, this being the first time he'd ever heard his boss mention the numerous death threats that had been hidden or downplayed about King at the Bureau.

"So," Hoover continued, "I need us to embed some undercover agents to travel with him on his flight, and trip, for his upcoming march in Selma, Alabama."

"To protect him, Sir?"

"Yes," Hoover said, "Of course. To protect him."

SIXTY SIX

"You're on in 3, 2, 1…," the white CBS producer counted down, his hands mimicking his words, from behind the 16mm television camera, a large black Eclare NPR device, the most advanced media contraption of the 1960s, allowing sound to seamlessly sync with vividly crisp images.

"Ladies and gentlemen, this is Walter Cronkite," the legendary broadcast host said, his words sturdy, like his trademark dark mustache and sincere expression, a unifying voice of clarity and reason to an increasingly polarized country, split over whether whites should be supportive of black rights, how to handle a war in Vietnam that President Johnson was feverishly escalating, and now on a spate of domestic programs the Commander-in-Chief had just launched at home called 'The Great Society.' "And, once again, I have some bad news to report to you about the Civil Rights Movement coming out of the South."

The producer stared at his anchor, then to his teleprompter, which had recently replaced the cue cards from which the newsman had used to read, and back to the newsman, crestfallen by the seemingly endless brutal events in the Land of Dixie, a cesspool of negative nadirs for Negroes if ever there was one.

"After a white police officer shot and killed an unarmed Negro American," Cronkite said, "civil rights activists have started to demand justice in Selma, Alabama; justice against the white police officer, who local political and judicial officials are refusing to bring charges against; and justice for Negroes, who are saying that white officials are denying them the right to vote so that they can bring in new elected leaders who will take their concerns seriously—including the killing of their young men by police officers."

Shaking his head in the affirmative, the producer—a radical white Berkely grad, who was a secret fan of both Martin Luther King and now Bobby Kennedy, though he couldn't say this to betray his impartiality—second-guessed himself on whether he should have written a news script for Cronkite that provided more context and background information for this situation for viewers. In particular, he was concerned that whites wouldn't understand that, despite the success of the interracial Freedom Summer last year, which helped pass the 1964 Civil Rights Act, and despite voter registration efforts all across the South, Dixecrats—almost all of whom were now Republicans—had kept around 99% of blacks from voting in elections in countless areas, including in Selma, and were still in open defiance of many federal laws and Supreme Court rulings, making progress difficult to impossible to enforce on the ground.

"Today," Cronkite continued, "these demands from civil rights workers, made real in a series of marches that have taken activists on foot over fifty miles from Selma to Montgomery, have resulted in what is being called 'Bloody Sunday,' a day, like in Birmingham Alabama years before, that saw local law enforcement viciously beat, maim, and crush countless Negro Americans."

Footage started rolling of the beatdown: of thousands of police officers and state troopers launching tear gas against nonviolent protesters; of billy clubs being smashed into faces, bodies, and genitalia; and of Freedom Rider John Lewis, having his skull bashed in to the point of near-death, alongside fellow Freedom Rider Carol Davis and other Freedom Summer volunteers, who were also ransacked and savaged, on the Edmund Pettus Bridge, where they encountered the Iron White Wall like never before, making Birmingham's Bull Conner's earlier police evil look like a whitewashed Disney fairytale. Cameras even managed to get into local jails, which had locked up thousands of activists, to show the officers beating blacks in their cells too, revealing a near-demonic infusion of enmity, the sardonic nature of White Supremacy actualized at the behest of the cop who murdered the unarmed black man, claiming this would be a deterrent against negroes who put cops' lives in "danger" and threatened the royal throne of white law and order.

"Sources tell me that the Reverend Martin Luther King, who was not present today, is on his way from Atlanta to lead thousands more Negroes to protest this incident," Cronkite said, his eyes stern, his gaze resolute, his patience over the whole ordeal thinning. "But a local judge has just issued an injunction against civil rights workers making it illegal for more than 3 of them to congregate together or protest if they gather at the Edmund Pettus Bridge. The judge says that if Dr. King defies this order he cannot guarantee the Reverend's safety or the safety of any of the Negroes with him."

Just as Cronkite finished, the producer was writing something large, on cue cards, unable to help his radical instincts, and got his anchor's attention.

"And one final thing before we break for a commercial," Cronkite intoned, rapidly reading the producer's words scribbled in large letters before uttering them aloud. "The federal government, led by President Johnson, is refusing to provide any type of armed protection for this protest, despite civil rights workers' requests to have federal law enforcement sent in to protect them and their constitutional right of assembly."

SIXTY SEVEN

Martin Luther King had fully exited his wife-ordered sabbatical. During that time he had made few public appearances besides accepting his Nobel Peace Prize in Sweden, his depression and irregular heartbeat still volleying back and forth like a volcano that starts and stops from erupting in fury, as he was still tired as all hell, having preached more than 7,000 sermons at churches in the last few years and traveled more than 4.5 million miles on the road in less than a decade that he had been the face of the Civil Rights Movement.

Just before he got into Selma late last night, along with Corretta who insisted on coming with him after she got her brother-in-law to watch the kids, he had phoned and telegramed every religious minister he knew, of all faith and racial backgrounds, and implored them to join him, to put their bodies and careers and reputations on the line, to live out the justice that God required them to live, to take on, what was now clear to everybody, the type of vicious cruelty blacks were up against, hidden from society no more, and hidden from white moral conscience no more. Several ministers, white moderates mostly, who agreed with King's crusade privately, were nevertheless too afraid to enlist, thinking he was sounding too much like a dark messiah, like a man who was signing not only himself up for a death wish, but of all of his disciples too, without having any armed security or protection from the feds.

But not everybody reacted like these "preachers of righteousness."

"My brother," the Rabbi Abraham Joshua Heschel said, his white beard appearing architecturally perfect, his smile twinkling brighter than the purest Hanukkah menorah, "I am with you to the end."

"Thank you," King responded, hugging and embracing the most significant Jewish intellectual and spiritual leader of the 20th Century, who had, along with hundreds of other black, white, and radical inter-faith leaders, answered the call to stand with oppressed blacks on their "re-do" march in Selma, at King's behest.

"It's good to see you, Rabbi," echoed the Reverend Ralph Abernathy along with countless other SCLC ministers, who repeated the same, and who were out in force, alongside hundreds of other black and white religious leaders, and thousands of interracial supporters, who could not believe what they witnessed on television, including Bobby Kennedy's former white Deputy, Burke Marshall, whom King wasn't sure if he was there on his own recognizance or on Bobby's. Was Bobby still trying to talk with him, he wondered, and should he, especially after hearing Bobby's public rhetoric about blacks change so much for the better, and especially after he was still feeling guilty for not shaking Bobby's hand and so harshly and uncharacteristically giving him the cold shoulder, twice?

As the ministers and marchers prepared to set out, posters were handed to various activists that read: "We march together: Catholics, Jews, & Protestants. For dignity and brotherhood of all men under God Now!"

Walking arm in arm, they stepped out onto the humid streets of Selma with their posters—and with numerous American flags in tow—to walk down the same path activists had paved hours before, and had been viciously beaten on hours before, on the Edmund Pettus Bridge, unaware they were being watched, and joined, by J. Edgar Hoover's undercover FBI agents. They were, however, all too aware of the other dangers that surrounded them: hostile local whites who believed deeply to their core that blacks were an inferior subspecies disgracing God's green earth; plain-clothed KKK members looking for an opening to strike should the television cameras, which were out in force, not be rolling; and the impenetrable police presence, which waited for them on the Bridge, and dared the marchers to take them on, looking forward to giving a second beat down in so many days, feeling invincible with the absolute certainty that no local or state prosecutor would ever bring a case against them for maiming, or killing, a black person, or a person who supported a black person, even on camera.

King and his wife, Heschel, Abernathy, and the others marched ahead, followed by John Lewis, Carol Davis—who despite seeing King in person once before was still awe-struck at his sight—and countless of the other original Freedom Riders and last year's Freedom Summer Volunteers. They began singing various songs, their voices rippling through the antiquated streets of the city, the spirit of harmony quelling their anger, especially King's, and transforming it into love; not the sentimental kind, but the fierce kind, hearts that choose to treat racist whites with respect that racist whites would never give to them.

Some of the marchers, when they weren't singing, told King how they, as teachers or students, had taught "literacy" and "citizenship" tests to blacks that the old Dixiecrats forced blacks to take in attempts to ensure black success, to try to help blacks to vote despite the barriers set up against them; others told him about all of the hard work they were putting in to keep blacks from falling into despair over the plight they were experiencing; and still others told him how tired they were—so, so tired, just like King was—of doing the right thing and receiving the wrong thing in return from the Iron White Wall, namely ass whoopings or various types of insults, economic degradation, and the inability to help themselves or their kids get ahead which they said, in some cases, even their moderate white friends, the few who would bother to associate with them, denied, claiming they could make it "if they just worked hard enough," even in the South.

"Damn nig*ers," one state patrol office said, from a distance, as the nonviolent marchers continued to forge ahead, coming into crystal clear view, and as the thousands of law enforcement officials stood firmly by, chests barrelled out, chins raised, and creamy fingers on alert with firearms, billy clubs, and tear-gas, all in abundant supply.

"When do we open fire?" asked another officer, an eager undercover KKK member, spotting King, who he hated as much as he hated the white Rabbi he was standing next to, the Jews being the second-most despised people in a White Supremacist's world.

"Wait, Finn, just wait," the first patrol officer replied.

"Alright," Finn muttered in return, his country drawal strong.

But King just kept singing, along with the others despite seeing thousands of officers in front of them, approaching the Edmund Pettus Bridge, now just over one thousand feet away, at rapid speed.

"If you come on this bridge," the state trooper screamed, using a bullhorn, holding up a copy of the Judge's injunction, "we will open fire!"

But the civil rights marchers didn't stop, their behavior and path unaltered.

"I repeat: if you come any closer," continued the state trooper, "we will open fire!"

But again, the marchers kept coming closer, ignoring the demand, seeming completely oblivious to his statements.

The officers looked around at each other, confused, and, one after another, put their hands on their gun holsters, or on their billy clubs, salivating for an encore performance from Bloody Sunday.

But finally King, and his marchers, started walking more slowly, and made their way all the way to the edge of the Bridge, stopping before putting a single foot on it. The officers stared at them coldly and the marchers stared right back at them, a showdown of self-righteousness versus true righteousness, furious power versus moral power, condescension versus humility, in full display.

"Do not cross this Bridge," the officer repeated at the top of his lungs, "or there will be consequences!"

King's eyes met the officer's, but his voice did not. He simply started to kneel, putting both knees on the ground. Corretta followed his movements, and then the others did, all falling to their knees with the grace of angels, including the slick undercover FBI agents with them.

"Let us pray," King said, as his ministers and activists broke out in spontaneous interfaith intercession. "Heavenly Father," he continued, "please forgive these men, and the generations of white men and women before and after them who think like them, for they know not what they do."

But the officers, scowls and dumbfounded expressions on their faces, glanced down at the prayer warriors and up at the television cameras all around them, and truly did not know what to do.

SIXTY EIGHT

"Cowardly Uncle Tom mother f*cker—"

But before Huey Newton, the Minister of Defense for the Black Panthers who took pride in making white police officers sh*t in their pants—like he had two years ago on the basketball court in Oakland when he murdered one of them—could finish his sentence, the Black Panther Chairman and ex-King nonviolent disciple Stokley Carmichael switched off the television, not wanting to watch any more of Walter Cronkite's CBS coverage of the Selma march.

"He's a traitor to his people," Stokley declared with flared nostrils, after watching King and the interracial ministers and activists pray, get up, and turn around, avoiding violating the Judge's injunction—the same Judge who was an undercover KKK member, who had been present at the Stone Mountain, Georgia Klan orgy—by not crossing the Edmund Pettus Bridge, and avoiding getting iced by the litany of police officers standing in their path. "And besides," Stokely continued, "we have bigger fish to fry."

Of course, Stokely was referring to yet another police officer killing of an unarmed black man, one of over 65 that had happened in the last two years alone. Like in Selma, only this time in Watts, a territory the Panthers were becoming more active in. But what was different in Watts, and different in many of the 65 shootings besides Selma, which were coming from white officers increasingly in the North and West and not just the Jim Crow South, were that angry blacks, unlike their Southern civil rights counterparts, were starting to fight back, and not in the way white moderates liked, or in the way that racial integrationists Martin Luther King or Bobby Kennedy liked either, throwing fuel on the fire of a potential second civil war that Jim Crow wanted to start. It seemed like they were falling into the great prophet Frederick Douglass's prediction: "If black men have no rights in the eyes of white men, of course the whites can have none in the eyes of blacks. The result is a war of races, and the annihilation of all proper human relations."

Looking left to right, Bobby Seale asked, "Do they have everything they need?" before glancing at Newton, who picked up his checklist that showed shipments of weapons and supplies the Panthers had sent to unidentified local affiliates, including the Watts neighborhood of Los Angeles.

"They do," Newton replied confidently.

"Okay then," Seale said, looking in the mirror, brushing his freshly groomed afro a bit, "so now we wait."

Stokely walked from the right side of the Oakland apartment they were staying in and sat on the velvet couch next to Newton. He picked up the checklist, which Newton had put down, and which was placed on top of a newspaper clipping of Malcolm X's recent assassination. The speeches he listened to on vinyl tape had molded Stokely's thinking, especially by getting him to believe the white man is "a blue-eyed devil" who encouraged blacks not to intermingle with whites, and wanted them to match fire for literal fire, like he had convinced the Black Panthers to believe too.

Before too long, a phone rang and Seale picked it up. "Yeah," he said. "Alright. Okay. Mmm hmm," he continued, hanging up after the 10 minute briefing.

"I'm hearing that police are calling the response in Los Angeles the 'Watts Riots,'" Seale said. "The LA police commissioner called Negroes 'monkeys in a zoo,' and got the approval to send in over 14,000 national guardsman to try to stop our people's protests."

"So they sent in the National Guard," Stokley opined, "for a few blacks with some guns but do nothing when civil rights marchers like John Lewis when they got their heads bashed in by local white police officers during Bloody Sunday?"

"Yep," Newton responded. "Damn crackers."

"They didn't just send them in because of the weapons," Seale interjected. "They sent them in because Negroes have stormed buildings, barricaded off street blocks, and most importantly started to force white people out of their cars."

"Oh really?" Stokley asked, intrigued.

"Yeah, any whites just so happening to drive on the freeway through the area are getting stopped, pulled out of their vehicles, and getting they asses beat."

"Serves them right," Stokley said, with a smile. "For all those years staying silent about the plight of Negroes and refusing to let us buy or rent property anywhere outside of the ghetto, especially in places like LA City and Beverly Hills and Santa Monica—the most racist and exclusionary places—legally banning us from living in these places for decades."

"Any deaths?" Newton asked, more interested in the body count than in housing laws local California whites made, including blocking blacks' ability to move into most communities, granting whites a huge edge in real estate and school funding based on that real estate's property taxes, a decades in the making 'white affirmative action' meant to keep most whites rich or middle class, most blacks poor, and all but the most successful of "token" minorities out, a practice happening throughout the United States, just as huge housing projects and crime-ridden ghettos had been set up to move blacks into as a matter of deliberate public policy.

"Yes," Seale shook his head. "More on our side than theirs. Thirty four blacks have been murdered."

"How many whites?" Newtown inquired, concerned. "Two dead," Seale responded. "And both are cops."

"Damn," Newton said, redness overcoming his handsome light black face. "We need to mobilize so that that number reverses next time. Whitey needs to get his."

"Yes. But do you want to know what else we need to do?" Stokley asked, an answer already formulated in his mind.

"What?" asked Seale.

"We need to invite Bobby Kennedy to a face-to-face meeting with us to tell him our plan for this country, and how we will light it on fire if it doesn't change soon," Stokley said, pointing to the official Black Panther "10 Point Plan." "He's running around America acting like blacks are the new whites and we need to have him put his money where his mouth is if he wants to keep this nation intact."

"And that is a lot of money," Newton joked.

"But do you really think he would ever visit a group like ours, though?" Seale asked, genuinely curious. "He seems to like happy Negroes like King, not radical ones like us."

"Oh, he'll come," Stokley responded, "if he wants to stop this growing outbreak of violence…and if he doesn't want to show himself to be a coward like King."

SIXTY NINE

1968

Two and a half years had passed since the Black Panthers demanded to meet with Bobby and he was still swiveling in and out of grief, mourning the ghost of his larger-than-life brother. But it had gotten better in fits and starts for him, especially considering the whirlwind of activity he had been engaging in as an energetic Senator who people were now calling on to run for President, which he was strongly leaning toward doing so he could be just like Jack. Because Bobby loved and hated hard, his emotions were as black and white as an African zebra's coat, and he could never stop feeling strongly for his brother no matter how hard he tried, and no matter how much time had passed. He could never stop searching for answers either.

Unbeknownst to almost everybody around him, outside of his time in the spotlight giving speeches, passing bills, and crisscrossing the country, he had secretly hunted for Jack's "true killer" as he called him, increasingly unconvinced that Lee Harvey Oswald had done it. He had come across a lot of fragmented information during this time, like a 25,000 piece puzzle with hundreds of missing pieces, leading him in all kinds of directions, which caused him to strongly lean into his belief that the FBI, CIA, KKK, Mafia, or some other group or individual, was the real culprit behind it, or somehow in cahoots together as multiple culprits, in some type of "conspiracy theory," a term the CIA recently invented to describe schools of thought, or people, they wanted to discredit.

It was 2:00 am and, like usual, Bobby was up, thinking, strategizing, and unable to sleep. He once again turned to his journal, his new source of emotional exorcism, after brushing his hair out of his face.

Bobby began writing another journal entry under a dimly lit desk light, which had become more common these days, not only with the house being "scream-free" now that Jackie and her night-terrors had moved out of Hickory Hill into a new place in Georgetown, but because Bobby was more reflective than ever before, trying to make sense of his thoughts and life and all that was going on in America in this tumultuous time known as the 1960s, especially early 1968, as it now was.

Well, here goes, he wrote. *You and me again. You know, I used to find it challenging to write in this thing, not only because of time constraints, but because it was frightening to examine myself. To look into my motives. To uncover my assumptions. To seek out my dark side. But I don't find it difficult anymore. I've realized that, after all of this rumination, this is the best thing I can do to gain clarity about myself, to see who I truly am, what I truly want, and where I need to go. And nowhere have I gained more clarity recently in my thinking than about why people gave me that awful nickname "Bad Bobby." When they called me "Bad Bobby" to describe my earlier ruthless days, truth be told, they might have had a point. I was no holds barred; I took no prisoners; and I didn't care about crushing people because, well, that's just who I was, and people could take it or leave it. So when they called me that name I just ignored it because, as I've come to believe, men of action are rarely ever men of insight, especially if they traffic in politics like me, and their beliefs about themselves and dogmas toward the world are held as an uncritical religion, for better or worse.*

But what I've come to understand these last couple of years is that "Bad Bobby" never went away, and "Good Bobby" never replaced him. Instead, I feel as though these two have become one, with my ruthless ambition to get Jack, or myself, ahead, replaced by my ruthless desire to right the wrongs of this country, to be bold and uncompromising in the face of political and existential pressure, and to not back down against the people that want to keep discrimination alive and keep blacks, and other impoverished groups, proverbially dead.

When I went to visit Mississippi in particular, not long ago, I realized that the suffering of blacks was not confined to just the material and spiritual legacy of slavery, separate but unequal, lynchings, and denial of the right to vote, as damning as these are, but extended into the economic and living conditions of blacks too. If white people could have seen that malnourished little Negro boy with a distended tummy that I saw, the roaches and filth and degradation he lived in, they would have been shocked—and appalled. We would have never allowed that kind of poverty, that kind of literal hunger and food insecurity, to come upon our children; yet not only have we allowed it to happen to black children, but we have legally sanctioned it and, for those in the North, have turned a blind eye to it. It's just not right. Almost every Negro child lives in poverty in America. None of them have a good place to live because we force them into squalid, tiny hell boxes and applaud ourselves, at least the white moderates among us, for giving them "affordable housing." And none of them have decent schooling, because whites still won't let them integrate with their children—even white televangelists have set up their own "Whites Only" schools and these are supposed to be the people of God who serve the downtrodden. The same is true for Chicanos; I went and saw the horrible conditions their people are in in California, especially their farmworkers that Cesar Chavez is organizing on behalf of, and the way we treat minorities in this country is not only appalling, it is criminal. Truly. We should be ashamed of ourselves not because we are morally repugnant people like the old Dixiecrats but because we hold all the financial and political power to do something about this and we aren't. Our hearts have been morally ambivalent, and our souls have been spiritually indifferent, and we need to wake up to this privation. It is not enough for us to privately agree with eradicating destitution so we can feel good about ourselves; if we believe this in private but still do and say nothing about it in public, and do not march on the streets or commit our own resources to it, we are worse than hypocrites—we are enablers of a system that we rationalize by saying we cannot change it on our own so we give ourselves excuses to do nothing, and thereby perpetuate the poverty we claim we want to see minorities overcome. And, by my count, this is absolutely disgusting.

But even though that mad man Lyndon Johnson has launched his Great Society program and supposed "War on Poverty" to tackle some of this, this is just not the right solution. He's trying to force upon black people, and other minorities, Washington-mandated policies that just aren't working, that are keeping people in a cycle of inescapable poverty. What we need is my program that I've launched in Brooklyn, "Bedford Stuyvesant," or "Bed-Stuy" as people have come to call it, that is inviting big businesses like IBM and Ford in, creating quality education and job training programs and decent housing led by local residents, and reversing the tide of dysfunction that whites have damned blacks into since they brought them here in chains over 300 years ago. I'd like to expand this successful program nationwide, but I feel like progress on civil rights has come to a complete halt, with very little to show for the last couple of years.

For one, Martin Luther King took his efforts to Chicago after I helped pass the Voting Rights Act of 1965, but King was incredibly unsuccessful there, just as he was a few years before when he unsuccessfully took his civil rights campaign to Albany, New York, and was forced to abandon his efforts and head back to the South. But what I'm concerned about with not only this, but also with him, is all of the coldness I'm now once again suddenly feeling off and on toward him—that bastard J. Edgar Hoover sent me a supposed tape of King making unkind remarks about Jack years ago, which has made me question why I was trying to earn King's respect in the first place, which he has not been giving to me at all these past few years. I need to earn Negroes respect, yes, but do I need to keep trying to earn King's respect? It's so hard because of the love I have for my brother, Jack, and the love I should have but don't for King. If I'm being honest I did say and do some regrettable things to King years ago, and did stop Jack from doing more on civil rights, so maybe I need to get over the fact that King may still feel put off toward me, but I'm no longer as sure about asking for his forgiveness as I once was when I was trying to reach out to him. What I am sure of, however, is that what the man has done to awaken my conscience to civil rights, and my deep love of Negroes, is a debt I will always owe him, and that's how I need to think about him— with gratitude—even if I have to force myself to.

And what he has done as a nonviolent protestor is truly remarkable and something I'm also grateful for, truly. Given the death threats he is under daily, which I myself am now under constantly too because of my work on civil rights, is nothing short of heroic. Never before in history, except for Gandhi 20 years ago in India, has anyone led a peaceful movement to successfully convince their over-lording government to change. And King has done it, something our white Founding Fathers were never able to do, and something no European people has ever been able to do in the history of this country or any country: resolve conflict without resorting to bloodshed, and without violent war, to enact necessary change. As an aside, can you imagine if King led a violent rebellion against whites, what that would have looked like? Can you imagine what it would have looked like if blacks had then committed even one-tenth of the atrocities toward whites that whites committed toward them? If blacks had enslaved whites, whipped whites, impoverished whites, and told whites they were only three-fifths of a person? Do you think a white person would have led a peaceful, "nonviolent" movement on behalf of downtrodden whites against powerful blacks? This would have never happened, not on this side of the universe. Never. Because man is inherently a brutal, violent creature. And white people certainly fall into this category. And because King didn't do this to whites, and because blacks didn't create their own version of the KKK or do the things Jim Crow constantly accuses them of doing to whites, whites owe their deep gratitude to blacks, for showing us what it means to be loving, when we haven't even attempted to be loving in return, and for showing us how not to return violence for violence.

But what concerns me, despite what King has accomplished in his Civil Rights Movement, and what I'm trying to do, is that there is a more militant Negro community out there, a smaller but more dangerous "Black Power" agitator, who wants nothing to do with King, integration, or figuring out non-confontational approaches to solve our racial crisis, splitting the Civil Rights Movement effectively in half, or into multiple factions. But can I really blame these militant people for agitating and doing this? Perhaps I'd demand change with the barrel of a gun if my people, the Irish and the Catholics, were terrorized the way blacks have been for so long.

Some of it is just too much, though. The shootouts the Black Panthers have had with the police all over the country; their armed takeover of the California legislature, ironically causing even the NRA to advocate against open-carry gun laws; and the general menace their image projects could undermine all of the progress of civil rights this past decade, defeating themselves in the process too. Besides, they need to respect law and order; not every cop or police department is racist, though many are, especially but not exclusively in the Jim Crow South. But they need to demand justice the right way.

So far, I've avoided meeting with these agitators. I just didn't want a repeat of the meeting that happened to me in Jack's New York apartment years ago, when I felt insulated by that young Freedom Rider and was forced to defend my civil rights record. But you know what, I've grown a lot since then, and I'm going to meet with the Black Panthers and see what they have to say. I think it's time; I think it's time that I be even more ruthless about helping blacks, even if that means talking with the Panthers and getting their view of things. I've read their 10 Point Plan and I agree with them that, among other things, we need economic empowerment for blacks in the country. And I'm going to meet with them on their turf without any security; they need to see that I mean them no harm and that I mean serious business about progress for Negroes.

I also need to put this icy feeling I've been having toward Martin Luther King behind me and invite him to testify before my poverty committee in Congress, to jump-start civil rights again and see if we can get Bed-Stuy into every Negro community in America. King's been saying some good things about black economic empowerment too, and empowerment for poor people of all types. I think Bed-Stuy's financial and housing approach may be right up his alley, as a key and final pillar of his Second Emancipation Proclamation, after desegregation and voting rights. I think it's certainly up black peoples' alley too, based on all of the personal feedback I've been hearing from them in my travels across the country. But the question is, is King ready to bury the hatchet between us? Am I? For the sake of Negroes? For the sake of America?

SEVENTY

"I'm torn, Bobby," Jackie Kennedy said. She was visiting Hickory Hill for the first time since her move to her flat in Georgetown, and she, Bobby, and Ethel sat on the back porch, drinking vintage Bigelow Tea a few mornings after Bobby's latest journal entry, and watched all of the children on a Sunday afternoon run around in the backyard playing hide-and-seek. There were 13 little ones in the family now—2 of Jackie's and, given Bobby's deep Catholic beliefs about procreation, 11 of his own—and they were just starting to re-adjust to life with Jack gone.

"I'm torn too," Ethel said, uneasiness wrinkled across her forehead, concern accentuating the creases on both sides of her mouth, her lipstick slightly smudged by her teacup.

"I mean," Jackie continued, "it's a lot to take in."

Of course, both Jackie and Ethel were speaking the same language, the sentiments of reason and restraint, after hearing Bobby's plans. Not only did he inform them that he had invited King to testify soon at his Senate committee meeting about his Bed-Stuy project, an invitation King surprisingly accepted, and which irked the family, especially Jackie, who was extraordinarily sensitive to the criticism Bobby had told her King made about her husband in FBI wire-tapped tapes; but he further informed them that he had also set up a meeting, alone, to visit the Black Panthers—and, if that wasn't enough, he had also decided to announce his run for President of the United States after just a couple of years in the Senate, against a sitting incumbent President no less, one who just so happened to be Jack's successor, and the source of Bobby's increasingly public and rhetorical disdain.

"I understand your concerns," Bobby replied, the intonation in his voice a fait accompli. "But after lots of prayer and reflection I feel strongly I need to do these things."

"But it's so dangerous," Jackie said, her eyes wrecked, instinctively reaching for Bobby's hand and squeezing it, drawing a sharp glance from Ethel.

"I know," Bobby responded, platonically squeezing her hand in return, their friendship now iron-clad, developed from their trauma-bond, and one which they both had come to enjoy for mutual comfort.

Ethel, cocked her head a bit and stared at the two, before they let go of each other's fingers.

"Honey," Bobby said to his wife, putting his hand on her knee, "it's not like tha—"

"I know," Ethel lied. "It's just that I know how much you look to Jackie for advice, and to me too, and we both agree that you should not run for President."

"Exactly," Jackie said.

"But why?" Bobby asked, incredulous, brushing his hair out of his eyes that the wind had blown through in a swift gust.

"Because they will kill you!" Jackie blurted out, her bluntness being no accident, her words designed to underscore her vehement disapproval and weaponize her opinion against Bobby, and to help her and Ethel keep him alive, in case the worst might happen to him, a fear she had had since Bobby decided to enter public life as an elected politician.

Before he could say anything in return, John Jr. ran up to the porch and quickly assessed the seriousness on everyone's faces. "Uncle Bobby," he said, "why are mommy and Auntie Ethel staring at you like that?"

But Bobby couldn't tell him the truth; not now, for even though his nephew had turned seven years old a few months ago, he felt placing a cloud of death-talk on the shoulders of any young child, especially one so intimately acquainted with tragedy, was a betrayal of innocence, something no adult should shower upon a child's conscience. Instead, Bobby simply said, "oh, we're just having a little grown-up political talk and we're just thinking about some things."

"Are you sure?"

"Absolutely."

"Just political talk?"

"Yes, and nothing more."

"Okay," John Jr. said, satisfied with his uncle's reassuring manner before being summoned back to the game of hide-and-seek with the other children and Freckles, who was jumping and frolicking around with them on the grass, between the trees, and in the deep recesses of the grounds of the estate.

Ethel and Jackie, still stone-faced, continued to look at Bobby, who didn't respond directly to Jackie's earlier admonition. So she pressed in.

"You know that's what they'll do to you, right?" Jackie said, making a statement more than a question. "Like they did to Jack!"

"She's right," Ethel echoed, her voice choking, her words difficult to utter.

"Look," Bobby said, trying to exercise grace and patience, "running for President is just another way to help push forward civil rights, to lift up the poor, and to end this war in Vietnam that Lyndon has recklessly escalated."

"But you can advance civil rights and help the poor in the Senate," Ethel said emphatically. "Even Martin Luther King is going to be there soon to testify, at your request, about your Bed-Stuy project. Who knows, maybe it can be used as a model for the entire country, to make things right economically for Negroes once and for all."

"And," Jackie said, reinforcing the thoughts of her sister-in-law, "you can advocate to put this damn war to an end as an outsider, not an insider."

"Besides," Ethel said, "you know how treacherous Lyndon can be, and nobody has ever defeated an incumbent President in a primary, particularly not one as vicious as him."

"I know. But it's just something I feel I really need to do," Bobby shot back, single-mindedly, like a young boy who didn't know about the penalty he might face for trying to play hero, or perhaps who knew and didn't care. "To right wrongs."

"Do you have a death wish?" Jackie again pushed, genuine tears starting to stream down her cheeks. "You don't have to do this! You don't have to be a martyr like my husband!"

Bobby's head dropped, sinking below his shoulders, knowing he had no response for this, feeling the weight of her expression as a piercing anvil in his soul. He then reached into his pocket, next to his rosary, and pulled out a paper with the quote from Aeschylus about the awful grace of God he had started carrying around in his pocket of late. He opened his mouth.

"Don't," Ethel immediately stopped him, waving her hands in the air. "I've heard this before."

Shocked at her dramatic response, he folded the paper in half and put it back in his pocket. He then thought briefly, and then some more, and said, "Sometimes, we don't get to choose our fate but our fate gets to choose us."

"Robert, don't talk like that!" Jackie cried, calling him by his formal name, angry. "This has been hard on all of us. I want to be with Jack again too, but this is not the way to do it."

"But," Bobby said, repeating himself, "I have to do this. If, as a rich and powerful white man, I don't stand up for blacks and the downtrodden of all types, and stand against this needless war, who will?"

"Not you," Jackie snuffed quickly. "Just not you."

SEVENTY ONE

Bobby took no pleasure in defying his family; he decided to run for President. After listening carefully to them, he was unpersuaded by their existential reasoning to stay in the Senate and fight for reforms from that institution, a place where professional debutantes go to unleash their windbags upon issues they know little about, and release their windpipes into skirts they would really like to, he concluded. But the question that kept lingering in his mind was whether he was expressing genuine altruism, or even moral courage, by running for President? Or if was he being reckless, not caring if somebody made good on all of the death threats against him, not caring if he left his wife without a husband and his children without a father, risking his life just like King had done all of these years? Was he being Good Bobby or Bad Bobby, or a little bit of both, with this decision? Were his motivations as black and white as he typically saw the world? Or, he also thought, was he just trying to be like his brother, the hero of Camelot?

Since announcing his run, from the same location in the chambers of the Senate as Jack had, while wearing one of Jack's black blazers, with a rosary in his right pocket and the quote from Aeschylus in his left, Bobby had barnstormed the country, laying out his agenda for America, including education and economic empowerment for blacks and the poor of all types, getting out of Vietnam, gun control, and ending tax loopholes for the rich. And his message, combined with his "no spin" aggressive and blunt style, attracted audiences even bigger than his Senate race had three years before in New York. Not only were tens of thousands of people waiting for him at every stop, but, on at least one occasion, there was a caravan of cars over two hundred miles long waiting to hear him speak. Two hundred miles! Not only was he now definitively bigger and more popular than the Beatles and emergent Jackson 5 and Rolling Stones, but he was also more intimidating, forcing even his nemesis, President Johnson, to recently drop out of the Presidential race during the primaries, something no president had ever done in history.

But despite all of this activity, and success, as well as winning several primaries by heavily and almost exclusively campaigning in black areas of the country, Bobby was more razor focused than ever, and focused on two things besides becoming the most powerful man in the world: getting King to testify at his Senate committee, and potentially reconciling with him after all these years, and talking to the Black Panthers, who were reminding him of their invitation to talk and calling him a "coward" if he didn't show up, saying he couldn't blame his absence on being "too busy."

However, tonight was the night, finally, to make good on his promise to meet with these agitators and see what they had to say. On his flight to Oakland, one of his white travel aide's turned to him and asked, "Senator, are still sure you want to meet in the dead of night with the Black Panthers?"

"Yes."

"Really?" the aide responded, dumbfounded and nervous not only for Bobby's safety but also his own.

"Absolutely."

"But you know how dangerous they are, right?" the aide asked, fear exploding in his Ivy-League educated brain.

"I'm familiar with their record."

"But don't you think that it is ironic that a law and order former Attorney General is meeting with a bunch of cop killers?" the aide pleaded.

"They're not all cop killers."

"But some of them are."

"And for those who are, they should be prosecuted."

"Senator, one of their founders is on the run, wanted for murdering a cop," the aide nervously interjected.

"I don't believe he will be at the meeting."

"But you're not worried about optics, how this will make you look Sir?"

"Listen, you know I don't consult public opinion polls or have focus groups conducted, so why would I be concerned with people finding out if I have met with some agitators? Besides, they may have some good points to make."

"But Sir, they could also try to take you hostage to try to prove their point, or even kill you."

"So what if they do?" Bobby shot back, running his hand through his hair, brushing it out of his left eye.

With those words, the aide decided to remain quiet for the rest of the flight, as the plane continued on and eventually made its descent into the Oakland International Airport. He also decided to stay quiet in the car ride over to the undisclosed apartment that was holding what J. Edgar Hoover was calling a "domestic terrorist group." But despite his silence, he kept thinking to himself: "Is my boss fearless, hopelessly crazy, or even kind of suicidal?"

The black Lincoln Continental they were riding in pulled up around 1:02 am California time, to the projects Stokely Carmichael and Bobby Seale were occupying, along with several others. Bobby and his aide stepped out of the vehicle and made their way to the third floor.

"Knock, knock," Bobby said, speaking the verbal password the Panthers and his team agreed to use prior to the meeting, letting everyone know it was the Senator who would agree to come without his Secret Service protection or security detail. After a few silent and tense moments, the door opened.

"So this is it, huh?" Bobby asked, looking around at the dimly lit room which had a poster of the deceased Malcolm X on one of its walls and even a poster of one of their co-founders, Huey Newton, who was absent and on the run from law enforcement for murdering a police officer. There were also about a dozen male Panthers there, all in their leather black jackets, sporting afros and AK-47s, an assortment of handguns, and munitions strapped to their bodies like sashes. Sitting between two Panthers, on a velvet couch, were a couple of female Panthers, an ultra sexy black woman originally from Queens and a startling skinny white woman, clearly an ex-hippie whose once-striking beauty was slightly fading with whatever drugs she was on, and whom the Panthers appeared to share for sexual fulfillment given her femme-fatale mystique and promiscuous dress.

"Please sit, Senator," Stokely Carmichael said, his poker face stronger than even Richard Nixon's, who was now running against Bobby for President on the Republican ticket in a would-be rematch of 1960: Kennedy vs. Nixon.

"Okay," Bobby responded, making his way over to a chair immediately across from the velvet couch, as Stokely and Bobby Seale made their way to it too, excusing the male and female Panthers who had been previously occupying it.

As Stokley pulled out a piece of paper, a Panther with an AK-47 walked over to the door, locked it, and stood guard. The other Panthers then took out their weapons too.

"So," Stokely said, leaning back nonchalantly, "tell me how it feels to be a blue-eyed white devil?"

SEVENTY TWO

Looking into his Willard Intercontinental Hotel bathroom mirror and staring at the cross-shaped scar on his chest and then back up again at his face, Martin Luther King couldn't stop thinking about his meeting later today in Washington, D.C. at Bobby Kennedy's Senate Committee hearing. Though it was a little after 4 a.m. D.C.-time, he had had difficulty sleeping that night; difficulty figuring out what he would say in the Capitol about Bobby's Bed-Stuy project; and even more difficulty what he might say to Bobby should he want to talk further afterward, a hunch King had, given Bobby's desire to speak multiple times years before that he rebuffed and his concern that Bobby, especially if he was reverting to Bad Bobby, might ask him for his endorsement for President, trying to use him to sway the election like he had eight years before for his brother.

King placed his right hand over his scar and gently outlined its outer edges, rubbing his index finger from its southern tip to its northern, then horizontally from its easternmost edge to its westernmost. He then re-buttoned his pajama shirt and went back to his bed, sat down, and reached for the King James Bible on his nightstand, which was next to the remarks he prepared to give to the Senate Committee, the same Bible he carried with him everywhere he went. It had been with him through all of his important meetings, marches, speeches, and assassination attempts, and he looked to it for wisdom in moments of incredible uncertainty, like right now, to figure out what to do.

He put on his reading glasses and opened it to the New Testament, to the Book of St. Matthew, the same book he had read in the Reidsville State Prison so many years before, when Bobby had self-servingly bailed him out of jail. But instead of his eyes immediately focusing on the 5th chapter like it had in the jail, the chapter that talked about how to handle being persecuted, his tired pupils honed in on the 6th chapter, its 14th verse, and dialed-in. Reading it aloud, he said, "For if ye forgive men their trespasses, your heavenly Father will also forgive you: but if ye forgive not men their trespasses, neither will your Father forgive your trespasses."

King immediately shut the book, the all-too-familiar pain wrenching in his chest again, his heart palpitating with uncertainty. He thought to himself, why was it so easy to forgive racist cops, KKK members, Jim Crow acolytes, and even people who tried to kill him, but so damn hard to forgive Bobby? It just didn't make any sense. He thought, why was it easier to forgive an enemy who you knew hated you than to forgive a "friend" who supposedly didn't? After all, Bobby did bail him out of jail, did launch those lawsuits against Southern segregationists, did help pass the 1964 and 1965 Civil Rights Acts, and, over the last 3.5-4 years, seemed to be a genuine champion of Negroes. But still, why was King resisting forgiveness? Resisting reconciliation? Resisting acting like the Nobel Peace Prize winner that he was? Why had he been so political, so indifferent to Bobby these past few years, in the same way Bobby had been with him all those early years before? Was it some sort of subconscious revenge, especially after being wiretapped all of these years? Or something completely different? Like hypocrisy gnawing at his heart? Was Bobby, who seemed to be his own mirror in some ways, revealing his own inner and flawed contradictions, revealing perhaps a Good Martin and Bad Martin in his own right?

But before he could think any further, or ponder any more of his emotional incertitudes, he felt some kind of nudge, the same kind he would get from time to time as a Baptist minister, to pray. So he just sat there and said, "Father God, I don't know what's going on with me and Bobby, or why it's so hard to forgive him, but I just ask you to be with him and to protect him, wherever he might be right now and whatever he might be doing right now, so that we can meet later today and ensure that Your will can be done in our relationship, Your will can be done for Negroes, and Your will can be done for all of America. Heal me, and heal us, if that is Your will."

SEVENTY THREE

"I beg your pardon," Bobby said, glancing over at the red IBM Standard Issue clock on the wall, which read 1:10 am California time.

"You heard me the first time," Stokely Carmichael responded. "But in case you're hard of hearing—"

"Which it clearly seems like you are," Bobby Seale interjected, his nostrils flaring in a back-and-forth contraction.

"Then let me repeat myself," Stokely continued, harsh intonations in his voice. "I said, how does it feel to be a blue-eyed white devil?"

Hearing this question—this insult really—everything inside of Bobby wanted to respond in kind, wanted to give the Panthers a piece of his mind, wanted to remind them of all that he had done for blacks, and, as importantly, wanted to let them know he was nothing like those abominable Dixiecrats or Jim Crowers, the furthest thing from a blue-eyed white devil as there could possibly be. But instead of defending himself, Bobby simply dropped his guard, not wanting a repeat incident of what he had experienced years before when the Freedom Rider, James "Big Duck" Lawson, chewed him out in his brother's Park Avenue apartment.

"You call me a blue-eyed white devil, like the late Malcolm X called white people," Bobby said. "Is this because you think I am, or because you think all white people are?"

"Please," Stokely responded. "What kind of question is that?"

"I'm asking seriously," Bobby said, his eager expression appearing comical to a couple of the more cynical, hardened Panthers who thought this blue blood was out of his league.

"Of course all white people are," Stokely stated flatly.

"And why do you think all white people are devils?" Bobby asked. "And not just some or even many?"

"Because the white man oppresses Negroes," Stokely said, "and other whites cheer them on for doing it. This is the history of the Negro in America."

"This is a true statement," Bobby replied, "which I cannot refute."

"And," Stokley said, somewhat taken aback at Bobby's honesty and agreement, "they can't be trusted to do the right thing."

"This is also a true statement," Bobby said. "Right now, I don't think many white people can be trusted because they haven't proven themselves to be trustworthy toward the rights and needs of blacks."

"Not many white people," Stokely replied. "All white people."

"So," Bobby said, disregarding this overstatement, "what's your plan to change this, to change how whites have historically acted toward blacks?"

looked at Bobby Seale and then at several of the other Panthers.

"Man," Stokely said, shoving a piece of paper carelessly toward Bobby that had the Black Panthers 10 Point Plan on it, which fell to the ground. "We got a plan."

Reaching down to pick up the paper, Bobby began briefly reviewing it again. "Thank you for sharing," he said. "I've read this previously, several times, and I agree with much of it."

"You do?" Stokely said, dumbfounded, wondering if Bobby was trying to trick him.

"Yes, really I do," Bobby said. "With all my heart."

"Are you sh*tting us?" Bobby Seale blurted out, not wanting to hear this. "You're just a white devil lying to us, like all them other lying white devils. All you want is our votes because you're running for President."

Other Panthers started to nod no to each other, shaking their heads "that's right."

"Otherwise," Bobby Seale continued, "why else would you be here?"

"To learn," Bobby replied with earnestness and humility. "To understand where you're coming from, to try to understand the pain you feel."

"Man," Bobby Seale said, "that's bullsh*t."

"I'm here aren't I?" Bobby said.

"You're just a rich pretty boy who has never felt a day of pain in his life," Bobby Seale said.

"That's right," an unidentified Panther echoed. "White people don't feel pain even when they family gets kilt. You all heartless devils."

Sensing his Irish blood boiling, Bobby's emotions started having a tantrum on the inside. He gave a side eye to his aide, who looked simultaneously angry and fearful.

"I understand how your personal history, and the history of your people, would cause you to feel this way," Bobby said, as he turned back to face Stokely and Seale, and ignored the provocation, remembering all the reflection work he had done in his journal about Jack's death, and the raw scab he didn't want to be picked wide open about it, despite the pain and rage it made him feel. Instead he simply followed up by saying, "what else would you like to get off your chest?"

"Well," Stokely said, at a bit of a loss for words, looking around the room, not expecting the Mafia-prosecuting ex-Attorney General to be so calm, so placid even, at least on the outside, and to invite him to further lay out their grievances against him, and against all white people. But before he could say more, Panther after Panther began speaking, and hurling, additional insult after insult, like missiles designed to destroy their target, testing Bobby with every type of accusation under the sun, trying to get his white face to turn red so they could pop him like a red helium balloon, so they could expose his fakeness, his naivete, which they thought every well-meaning white person had. But still, Bobby seemed, at least on the outside, unmoved by the words and even by the weapons they were waving wildly back and forth, half pointing at him.

"Are you finished?" Bobby finally asked, after around 45 or 50 minutes of non-stop verbal assault, like a gang beating mercilessly on a victim, except that the victim in this case was actually calling for it.

"We're done for now," Stokely said, his confidence balanced with caution, his mind exploding with cognitive dissonance because of Bobby's non-reaction.

"Okay, thanks," Bobby responded. "But now I have a question for you."

"Oh, so now you want to cross examine us?" Bobby Seale asked, disgustedly. "I knew it. This is all just a game to you."

"No, no game," Bobby said sincerely but toughly. "Just a genuine question."

Stokley gestured with his hands, giving Bobby permission to speak, with every ear in the room listening intently.

"Suppose I become President," Bobby said, "and I back the aspect of your 10 Point Plan to provide economic empowerment for Negroes. How much money would the black community need to finally make things right?"

"Are you talking about reparations?" Stokely asked, his Harvard-admitted mind swirling with thoughts.

"What I'm talking about," Bobby continued, "is not simply cash handouts. I'm asking how much money is needed for education, housing, job training, and business creation to bring true economic equality between blacks and whites?"

"You know how much," Stokely said, testing Bobby again.

"Actually I don't and so I'm asking you," Bobby replied.

"Billions," Bobby Seale said, speaking the first vague number that came to his mind.

"How many billions?" Bobby pushed him further, as silence filled the environment.

Looking around at the calculating faces, Bobby's aide then raised his hand like a student waiting to be called on in class, to everyone's surprise.

"Yes?" Stokely said.

"Well, I have an MBA from Harvard and wrote a paper about this," the aide said, "and I think I have a number."

"You do?" Bobby asked. "Well, what is it?"

"Um," the aide continued, nervously, "well, the wealth gap is about 1,000 percent between blacks and whites in 1968 dollars, and with the economy being about one trillion dollars, I think we would need to spend at least $2-3 trillion bucks to even things out with the races in terms of pay equity."

Of course, the aide didn't mention the fact that he had also researched while at Harvard that, during slavery, whites had stolen more than $30 trillion in monies from their slaves in unpaid wages—not to mention that much in unpaid wages during Jim Crow, nearly doubling the theft to $60 trillion they had taken from blacks—and used it to buy millions of homes that they would pass onto their children, which was the number one source of wealth generation and accumulation in America; that they used this stolen money to build thousands of schools and universities to educate their children in the best facilities, with the newest textbooks and equipment, while simultaneously denying monies to educate black children; and that they used this stolen money to start businesses, create chambers of commerces and charity groups, launch little leagues, begin suburbs, and countless other things that exclusively benefitted not only slave owning families, but white communities in general because of the taxes they provided to create a comfortable way of life for millions of whites. And the aide didn't mention this because he was afraid that his boss, his radical white boss, just might want to propose something dramatic to make up for this if he knew the extent of the white theft, so he said nothing, believing the country would not be ready in this moment in time for such a thing.

"Two to three trillion?" Stokely asked in response to the aide, eyebrows starkly raised.

"That's right," the aide said. "I calculated the numbers myself. That's just to get Negroes caught up in today's pay."

"Does that number sound good to you gentleman?" Bobby asked, his eyes dancing back and forth among the faces of the various Black Panthers, searching out their reactions.

"Hell yeah," said the Black Panther standing guard at the door.

"Okay then," Bobby said, getting up from his chair. "I'll see what I can do."

"Wait, what? Are you really going to get Negroes trillions of dollars?" Stokely asked.

"If I can get that money into setting up multiple Bed Stuys throughout the country, a successful economic and educational project for blacks I launched in New York, I think we can make a lot of progress on this," Bobby said, walking over to the door. "But it's going to be a fight."

"Man," Bobby Seale said, "that's just a useless campaign promise. Just like your brother promised all of these things for Negroes and didn't deliver."

"Well," Bobby responded, "I certainly hope it's not an empty promise. I'm going to ask Martin Luther King later today at a Senate Committee meeting to see if he agrees with this so I can try to do this even as a Senator, right now. Does that seem like a good plan to you all?"

But they didn't say anything back. They couldn't say anything back because, for the first time, their well-deserved cynicism toward politicians, and their ass-beating experiences in the streets, which was impervious to bullsh*t, actually turned into cautious hope, an emotion they had never felt before about their country.

SEVENTY FOUR

"Gentlemen," the Contact uttered as he spoke in a deliberately muffled voice on an early morning conference call with the KKK's Imperial Wizard and a few unidentified individuals from various lines of business, "let the games begin."

"Do you finally have the money, Sir?" the Imperial Wizard asked, impatience and joy mixed in his voice, strangling it with unfettered anticipation.

"I will address that issue in a moment," the Contact said calmly.

"Alright," the Imperial Wizard retorted, as several top Klan members huddled around him in their Georgia church headquarters, trying to see if they could hear the low-pitched voice on the other end of the line to not only hear his plan, but to try to decipher who he might be.

"It is clear to me," the Contact continued, "that, like his dumb ass brother John Kennedy, Bobby Kennedy thinks he can try to be some sort of white savior for coons."

"Damn nig*er lover," one unidentified voice responded.

"As a consequence," the Contact said further, "he will now meet the same fate as his dumb ass brother."

"But Boss," a second unidentified voice interjected, "Numerous people have been trying to get a hit on him and even on Martin Luther King for the last few years."

"That's irrelevant," the Contact hit back dismissively. "My network is bigger than ever before and, with Bobby announcing where he'll be days in advance because of his Presidential Campaign, and with my information on King's whereabouts razor tight, both of their days are numbered."

"So you have the money, Sir?" the Imperial Wizard again asked.

"The biggest bounty I've ever offered," the Contact uttered with understated pride.

"Excellent," the Imperial Wizard replied.

"But as importantly," the first unidentified voice interrupted, "how do we make sure their deaths don't get pinned on any of us?"

"The same way we did with John Kennedy," the Contact said, reassuringly.

"But don't you think that people will start to talk?" the first unidentified voice said. "Doesn't the idea that there would be multiple low-level 'individual' gunmen involved in the murders of three famous people, all individually acting alone to take them out, seem a little far-fetched? I mean, the Soviets and Castro, who are working with organized high-level assassins in America, can't even seem to get a shot at these guys."

"How do you know they are not involved in our efforts?" the Contact shot back. "Just mind your business."

"Okay," the first unidentified voice said, knowing not to cross whomever he was talking to that held such sway, fearing that too much questioning could jeopardize himself or his family, whom he worried the Contact may have already identified.

"We will get away with it," the Contact stated further, "by making our assassination prize money only available for previously convicted felons or immigrants, thereby making it easier to blame the hits on the individuals or even on foreign governments."

"That's brilliant," the Imperial Wizard said. "And what happens if…I mean when, they're caught. Do we have them killed just like we had John Kennedy's assassin killed?"

"Sure," the Contact said nonchalantly. "But even if they're not killed, no dumb ass jury in America would find them not guilty."

"And," the Imperial Wizard said, liking where this was heading, "no government official will want to keep these cases open. Look at how quickly they closed the Warren Commission after supposedly investigating JFK's murder."

"It was a sham," the second unidentified voice said with glee. "President Johnson made sure of it."

"Exactly," the Contact responded. "So we have nothing to worry about."

"Do any of us get the money," asked the first unidentified voice, "if one of our guys gets referred and takes them out?"

"No," the Contact replied sharply.

"Why not?" protested the first unidentified voice.

"Because there can be no trace back to you, or to me," the Contact said.

"So where do we go from here?" the Imperial Wizard asked, knowing that when the Contact said he had money in the bank, there really was money in the bank.

"Send your fall guys to me," the Contact continued, with a smile on his face, "and I will make sure they accomplish their work quickly."

SEVENTY FIVE

Palms sweaty, heart palpitating, and with an uneasy look on his face, Martin Luther King made his way through the picturesque rotunda of the U.S. Capitol building, just after he had smoked a couple of Pall Mall cigarettes outside. He walked through National Statuary Hall, in the middle of the edifice "of, for, and by the people," which contained numerous statues of confederate leaders, including the President of the Confederacy Jefferson Davis, and his right-hand military enforcer, Robert E. Lee, among others, in a tribute to White Supremacists that the old Dixiecrats in the U.S. Congress made sure to keep conspicuously displayed.

"This is unacceptable," King thought to himself, as the powerful and predatory-seeming eyes of the statues glared down at him. Although he was a celebrity, and although his words and moral authority were used to help pass major civil rights reforms just a few years earlier, his standing in Congress, and with the American public, had plummeted again, in the see-saw of superficial public opinion, to historic lows even for him. He was simply speaking out too much against not only White Supremacy, but also against the Vietnam War, which was a "no-no" for this blood-thirsty group of Congressional leaders watching him who personally stopped at nothing, including willfully lying to the public to turn even those who were at one point for King against him, to impose their fury halfway around the world. These political leaders thought, in a moment of collective absurdity even more stupid than the logic they typically used to think about things, what is this Negro, who is supposed to stick to his narrow lane and talk only about civil rights, doing talking about ending wars, especially a proxy jungle war we need to win to show how much better than the Soviets we are? Why should a Nobel Peace Prize winner actually want to call for establishing peace? It simply makes no sense.

As he made his way to the Senate side of the building, entering an adjacent chamber containing the Committee meeting at which he was to testify, his "public face" kicked in, dignity and poise and grace overcoming him. He walked in, step by slow step, and spotted the row of United States Senators, sitting on the dais, with their stark white hair matching the bright and cracked hue of their skin. Then he spotted Bobby. Their eyes locked and, in what appeared to be a psychic dance transmitting some sort of profound connection—Was it love? Was it Hate?—they acknowledged each other.

King sat at the table as a young Congressional assistant brought a glass of water to him. After gulping half of the liquid down, he took the oath to tell the whole truth and nothing but the truth, and was asked to share his prepared remarks. Upon finishing, he was grilled by member after member about his thoughts of poverty among Negroes, and among all people, and asked why Negroes couldn't just pull themselves up by their own bootstraps and not ask for government handouts to buy homes or get jobs like "all other decent hard working Americans." Knocking these questions down like a bowler knocking down all the pins in a strike, King easily pulverized their tortured logic before Bobby set his gaze on him.

"Dr. King," Bobby said respectfully, calling him by his formal title for the first time ever, and not appearing jet-lagged or like he had been in California with radicals just hours before, "thank you for your excellent remarks."

"I appreciate the invitation to be here, Senator," King responded, surprising even himself at how genuine the comment came out, and how genuine he felt about them.

"As you know," Bobby continued, "I'm deeply invested in making sure Negroes in America get quality education, housing, and job training and placement, and I think the results of my Bedford Stuyvesant project in New York demonstrate that we can expand this program on a national scale."

"It is a national model, Senator," King said, wanting to make his thoughts about Bed-Stuy very clear. He had visited and studied carefully the last couple of years—seeing that Bobby had, against all odds and overwhelming opposition, convinced the U.S. government to invest billions of dollars on behalf of blacks. "I would say, it is the most successful educational, financial, and housing development program for Negroes in history."

"Thank you," Bobby said. "So based on this project, and based on information that I've gathered from a recent meeting…" but Bobby failed to say who it was with, as even King, not to mention everyone else in the room, would be shocked that Bobby had met with the Black Panthers to get their opinion on things. "How much money do you think we will need to bring true equality between blacks and whites in this country?"

"That's a great question, Sir," King responded. "I've never been asked, nor have I ever thought about, a specific number."

"That's alright," Bobby said. "Do you think two or three trillion dollars, in the form of investing this money in launching numerous Bed-Stuy projects throughout the country, will be enough to catch Negroes up with whites?"

King's mind, like the Black Panthers' minds hours before, swirled with shock and surprise. "Well, I was no math major, but that certainly does sound about right."

"Thank you," Bobby said again. "That's all I have."

The Committee made some formal announcements before adjourning. But Bobby, who was still sitting there in his chair, ushered over to King who was packing his things in his briefcase, and mouthed, "Can we talk?"

Bobby then came off the dais quickly and, for the first time in 5 years, shook King's hand enthusiastically, his emotions even more positive about King not only after King's Bed-Stuy project support, but because he saw him in the flesh and all sorts of thoughts, and feelings, came over him, the kind of thoughts and feelings that only proximity could bring. The kind of behavior that only a supernatural answer to a prayer about healing, forgiveness, and reconciliation could somehow bring.

"Thank you, Doctor," Bobby said. "You know, your idea of a Second Emancipation Proclamation, with the end of legal segregation, establishment of voting rights, and furtherance of housing and good jobs for Negroes, gave me the idea for Bed-Stuy."

"Please, call me Martin," King responded, as the two made their way out of the Committee room and back through the Capitol building. "I'm so glad it helped, truly."

Countless people watched, including Senators who had run against Bobby for President on the Democratic ticket such as Eugene McCarthy and George McGovern, and made up all kinds of scenarios as to why they might be talking. One ex- Dixiecrat Congressman, talking to a fellow Southern House member, remarked, "You don't think Kennedy is going to ask that nig*er King to be his Vice Presidential running mate, do you?"

The ex-Dixiecrat House member responded, "Not a chance in hell. I'd personally call for civil war if he did. These two have already ruined this country enough as it is, and I couldn't allow them to do it any more harm."

Bobby finally came with King to his office and Bobby dismissed his staff for privacy, escorting King to inside his private office, where they both took seats at a round oak table.

"Martin," Bobby said, before blurting out suddenly, matter-of-factly, and straight to the point, "it's been a long road and I just want to say I'm—"

"Sorry," King said.

"Jinks," Bobby replied, his lips curling into a smile, along with King's, a genuine moment of connection, instant relief filling the air, the years of ruminating on dark feelings toward each other vanished, like it had never happened, men embracing their own maturity and the importance of the moment, men acting like men and leaders and the heroes that they both were.

"You know, Bobby," King said, before correcting himself. "I can call you Bobby, right?"

"Of course."

"Thank you," King said. "You know, I've been thinking over and over again why I didn't shake your hand after the March on Washington and at Lyndon's 1964 Civil Rights Act signing. And it eats at me inside. And I'm so, so sorry. That behavior was beneath me."

"I understand why you didn't," Bobby shot back. "And I'm so sorry for what I did to you. I didn't have to prevent you from seeing Jack or even wiretap you, but I did. And I was wrong."

"Yes," King said, his levity dissipating just a bit. "But I do want to know, if you'll permit me to ask, why did you do it? Did you know it was wrong at the time? Did you feel it was the only choice you had at the time? Did you do it out of malice?"

Bobby's eyes darted back and forth, uncomfortable not because he was being questioned, but because he knew that if he told King it was to protect Jack's sordid affairs from coming out, he would be betraying his brother who he was equally protective of in his death as he was in life. Instead Bobby said, "I did it for political self-preservation. I was selfish and, at least in one area of my life, I'm probably still pretty selfish."

"I see," King responded, disappointed, his head drooping between his shoulders.

"Martin," Bobby said, trying to make King feel better without revealing any secrets, "there are things about my family that you would never believe. That America would never believe. And I felt I had to protect them. But it doesn't make it right and I'm ashamed of myself for it. I feel guilt about it everyday."

"I feel guilt too," King said, not only in trying to sound sympathetic toward Bobby, but to seemingly get something off of his chest too. Perhaps to share with Bobby something he strangely felt he couldn't share with anyone else. "But my shame is toward things I know you and Mr. Hoover know I've done to my wife that I will never be able to live down. I'm not always the person she needs me to be, or the person I want to be, or the person everyone sees me as."

"Martin," Bobby said. "May I ask you a personal question?"

"Yes."

"From one Catholic to one Christian, or really from one Christian to one Christian," Bobby continued, knowing exactly what King was talking about given his former access to King's FBI tapes and files, "have you asked for her forgiveness?"

"I begged for it," King replied right away, a solemn look triggered on his face, a man looking truly repentant and sorrowful for his actions. "She is my everything and she didn't deserve what I did to her."

"Did she, I mean, forgive you?" Bobby asked, somewhat awkwardly and uncomfortably.

"She's a better person than I am," King said. "She did."

Bobby replied with a heartfelt nod. "That's good."

"But now may I ask you a question, Bobby?" King responded.

"Yes, Martin, of course," Bobby said, brushing his hair out of his face, leaning in a bit more.

"I don't know how to say this without being offensive, and not to change the subject, but are you here to ask for my endorsement of your Presidential run?" King asked. "Like you and your brother asked me for his?"

Bobby chuckled and said, "I'm a very different man than I was eight years ago when we met."

"That's right, you're blacker," King joked, drawing laughter from the Senator, praising him without explicitly offering complimentary words for his deep conversion from a politically cautious opportunist to a transformational freedom rider, putting blacks at the center of not only his political agenda, but as a major part of his life's identity and calling.

"Not just blacker, but also perhaps more enlightened?" Bobby poked back at him, his quick wit always ready to engage.

"Maybe," King said, chuckling.

"Let me just say this Martin, without any doubt," Bobby said. "I am not here to ask for your endorsement in any way, shape, or form."

"Good, because I don't endorse politicians," King said, a devilish smile on his face; it had been a practical reality and lifelong policy he made sure to stick to, of not publicly using the word "endorse" to back particular candidates or parties, even if some seemed better than others at times. "But I will do everything in my power, starting tomorrow, to get you elected as President of the United States."

But all the comment produced was silence.

And more silence.

And even more silence.

Until finally, Bobby said, while looking genuinely humble, "Wow." And, after thinking for a moment, asking, "Does this make us friends now?"

"No," King said, also sincerely and rather matter-of-factly, to Bobby's surprise.

"Allies?"

"Not that either."

"Then what?" Bobby wondered, a little let down.

"Bobby," King said. "We're too different to be friends or allies. You're white, I'm black; you're Catholic, I'm Christian; you're rich, I'm poor; you're from the North, I'm from the South. We are from two different worlds."

Bobby sunk further into his chair, hanging his head low.

"But, what I can say is that we are more than friends," King said somberly, "and more than allies."

"Really?" Bobby looked up with hope.

"Yes," King said. "We are brothers. United in our fight for equality for blacks; our belief in the dignity of well-meaning whites; and in making sure our country works out its hypocrisies, just as we, as individuals, we, as men, have had to work out our own crooked hypocrisies, so that we can help America live up to its greatness, live up to the democratic ideals it loves on paper but struggles to practice off paper."

"We bleed the same blood," Bobby said. "And there's nothing that can bond us more than that."

"Exactly. Blood forged by mutual respect," King responded, "which is the greatest force on earth." He then looked down at his watch and, apologetically, indicated he had to catch a flight.

"So…" Bobby said, as King was exiting the door, "are you really going to try to help me become President?"

"You can count on it," King said. "If I can manage to keep myself alive."

SEVENTY SIX

April 3, 1968

After flying back briefly to his home in Atlanta, King set out for Memphis, Tennessee on April 3rd, 1968, with eerie dread haunting every aspect of this trip. Before arriving on Eastern Airline Flight 381, the plane was significantly delayed, with the flight attendants saying that there had been a death threat reported by the FBI against King, and as a result everyone's bags were checked for explosives in what may have been a violent attempt to blow up the plane. On top of that, when King finally did get into Memphis—to preach at the Mason Temple—the weather was acting up and acting out, a vicious storm brutally thumping the city, screaming "It's not safe for you here Martin! Leave immediately!"

But despite King's delayed flight, and despite the horrific, hurricane-like rain, a capacity crowd had gathered outside of the Temple, waiting for hours to see the Preacher, determined to brave the weather no matter the cost, to see the man who had made it his life's purpose to set them free. However King's friends, including Ralph Abernathy, who were there to pick him up from the nearly-flooded airport and take him to his destination, felt a little deflated by the gloomy mood he was in.

"What's wrong, Martin?" Abernathy asked, once again sensing the despondency that King had been slipping into and out of all of these years, concerned about the uneasy expression he had been wearing, appearing hollowed out like a ghost, more so than usual.

"I don't know," King replied, staring wearily out of the window of the white 1968 Cadillac Eldorado they were riding in, "something just doesn't feel right. Something in my gut is telling me I shouldn't be here."

"Here," Abernathy said, "take one of these," as he slipped King a cigarette and lighter, to help calm his nerves. "Maybe it's just anxiety."

"No, Ralph," King said, "it's something else."

King lit up, filling the Eldorado with smoke because he didn't want to roll the window down, and took puff after puff, his hands shaking uncharacteristically with fear and despondency.

They made their way through the bleak city, dropped off their bags at the Lorraine Motel, and set out for the Mason Temple, a three story brick cathedral which seated about 5,000. As they pulled up and before they got out, Abernathy asked, "are you sure you want to speak tonight, Martin? You don't need to do this. You don't need to be here, you have more than earned your right to rest."

"To be honest, I don't want to speak," King replied, "I don't have the energy or the focus. But Ralph, something tells me I need to speak. I really do. It's urgent."

The doors of the Cadillac opened and they made their way inside and up to the dais, where King took a seat, and Abernathy introduced him to thunderous applause. Standing upright, and making his way to the lectern, King's eyes darted back and forth, searching the room like an anxious detective, his suspicion palpable, causing quite a few people to whisper to each other about what he was doing. A loud rumble then smacked the stained-glass windows and pounded harshly against the ceiling, making a bomb-like shattering sound, and King ducked quickly, causing even more people in the audience to comment about the strange behavior they were witnessing from the Preacher. Abernathy, who by now had sat down behind him, wondered if he should try to intervene and get his friend out of there; this looked like it was headed for disaster and the last thing he wanted was for his friend to have a panic attack, or worse, a nervous breakdown or heart attack.

Standing up again, King continued to look around the room at a mass of worried but supportive faces and began speaking. He started slowly but, after a little while, found his bearings about himself and picked up some momentum; and the more he spoke, the more he began to sound like himself, like the man this audience saw him as: Black Moses, their liberator who had guided them through the desert and now to the outskirts of their Promised Land.

King spoke not only of why he was there, but what had brought him to this moment in the first place, nostalgia suddenly sweeping through his mind and words, his remarks being completely spontaneous and off the cuff, just like they had been in the last part of his speech during the March on Washington. He spoke about how he had been stabbed many years before and, if he had sneezed while the knife was still in his body, he would have lost his life, and told of a young girl who sent him a letter who said that she was sure glad that he didn't. He then said if he had actually sneezed, he would have missed history: all of the student sit-ins; all of the protests; all of the courageous Freedom Rides; the Birmingham Campaign and Children's Crusade; "I Have a Dream"; the Selma marches; all of the new Civil Rights Acts; and the outpouring of love and hope he was now feeling in his heart, overcome by the energy and belief from the audience who was lifting him up with their powerful spirit just as he had, for so many years, lifted them up with his.

But as King went on, another loud thud rocked the building, and his focus began to change again, and revert, to the ominous mood he came in with. His voice sounding more urgent and fever-pitched than ever, he told them, almost like he was giving his own eulogy, that he wanted to be remembered as somebody who tried to give his life serving others as a drum major for justice. He then finished his speech by saying, as his countenance shone with a prophetic authority and vision only God could have given him:

"Well, I don't know what will happen now; we've got some difficult days ahead.

But it really doesn't matter with me now, because I've been to the mountaintop. And I don't mind.

Like anybody, I would like to live a long life—longevity has its place.

But I'm not concerned about that now. I just want to do God's will.

And He's allowed me to go up to the mountain. And I've looked over, and I've seen the Promised Land.

I may not get there with you. But I want you to know tonight, that we, as a people, will get to the Promised Land.

And so I'm happy tonight; I'm not worried about anything; I'm not fearing any man. Mine eyes have seen the glory of the coming of the Lord!"

Tears welled up in his eyes and, stumbling back to his seat as if he was drunk, he collapsed, as the crowd poured out overwhelming emotion for the most powerful speech they had ever heard him give, or heard anyone give. They then began rushing the stage, shaking and hugging King, telling him how much they appreciated him, the difference that he made in their own lives, and that there was no black man as inspiring as him in all of history.

All of this came together in a blur until, waking up the next morning on April 4th, King began to again get his bearings. As he woke up and got started with the day, a peace started to anchor his soul, and he even began jumping up and down on his bed in the Lorraine Motel, having a pillow fight with Abernathy and some of the other ministers staying with him. After laughing hard and basking in this moment of levity, he decided to call his family, wanting to hear their beautiful voices, and to tell them about his speech.

"Hello?" Corretta said, picking up her end of the phone, her lovely voice exciting her husband.

"Hi sweet love, it's Martin," he said upbeat, "and I'm calling to say I love you."

"I love you too," Corretta responded in sincerity, grateful to hear his voice after the terrible weather report she had heard on the radio about Memphis the night before. But before she could say any more, little Yolanda, his precious daughter, snatched the phone from her mom.

"Daddy!" Yolanda said, standing next to her two siblings, including little Martin Luther King who was holding his teddy bear named "Love." "Is that you?"

"It is buttercup," King responded.

"How did your speech go?" Yolanda asked.

"Oh just fine," King said, warmth and joy in his voice. "And how is your science project going?"

"It's good," Yolanda blurted out with some giggles. "So are you coming home soon?"

"Buttercup," King said reassuringly, "daddy is coming home sooner than you think."

The phone then went blank. King tried to dial it again but there was no ring tone. After trying a few more times, he resigned to try again a little later.

He then got up from his chair, opened the door, and stepped outside, giving well wishes to some on-lookers as he stood on the balcony. But as he was speaking with them, something came over him, and he began looking around suspiciously like he had the night before. He looked to his left and saw nothing. Then to his right. Still nothing. He looked down from the second floor. Again, still nothing. He then took a deep breath and started to tell himself everything would be okay and that he was probably overreacting. But after a short few moments of positive self-talk and relief, he decided to look straight ahead to check one more time, just in case. But this time, this last time, it was different; it was something.

SEVENTY SEVEN

"Senator Kennedy," the Indianapolis Police Chief pleaded bitterly, "it is not safe for you to be here!"

"I don't care," Bobby responded, panting as he walked quickly to his motorcade on the tarmac at the airport, his hair flipping and flopping in the wind generated by the gush of the airplane's jet engines.

"But Senator," the Police Chief intoned again, now running after him, shouting against the roar of the engines, "we can't guarantee your safety!"

Bobby ignored the statement and closed the door of the black Lincoln Continental he had slipped into, one of several in his army of Presidential support vehicles provided for what was supposed to be a routine campaign stop, as two aides went around to the other side and hopped in too.

"On the plane flight over," one aide said as the motorcade began creeping its way into the city, "we prepared some remarks for you to give to your local campaign team as well as to your black supporters." He then tried to hand the scribbled notes to Bobby.

"I'm not going to visit our local campaign team," Bobby replied, "and I'm not going to give your speech."

"Excuse me, sir?" The aide said, respectful but surprised, watching Bobby pull out some sort of note with a quote on it from his pocket, one he knew the Presidential candidate always carried with him but also never showed him, nor any of his other aides, either.

"I need to speak to them from my heart," Bobby said, tears in his eyes. "As broken as it is."

Before long, the bevy of vehicles pulled up to 17th and Broadway, the blackest part of Indianapolis, in what could only be described as a ghetto of ghettos. Bobby, wiping his eyes and taking a deep breath, got out.

"Senator," a local white politician and supporter said to him as Bobby made his way from his vehicle with his typically fast stride, "it's not safe for you to be here. There could be people gunning for you too."

"Where's the podium?" Bobby responded, again ignoring people telling him he needed to look out for his own safety, telling him not to be so reckless, or ballsy, with his own body, and with his own mortality, like Martin Luther King had been, like his brother had been, misunderstanding the calling that some men had to be faithful to more than life itself.

"There is no podium," the local politician said. "We took it down to stop you from—"

"Is there a microphone?" Bobby asked angrily, spotting a nearby truck in his line of sight, and beginning to make his way over to it.

"Yes," the local politician said, obsequiousness in his voice, fearing Bobby as much as he loved him, and not wanting to upset him further given the grief and sensitivity of the moment.

"Then put it up," Bobby said with a military-like order, his demeanor all business, reminiscent of his days serving in World War 2, covering up the agony that was exploding inside, a fiery volcano of trauma ready to blow.

After the local politician set up the microphone, Bobby jumped onto the flatbed of the truck. Thousands of supporters, who hadn't yet heard *the news*, cheered and hooted and hollered for him, waving "Bobby Kennedy for President" signs enthusiastically in the air. One little black boy even had a poster that said, "Black and White Together Forever."

"Could you lower those signs, please?" Bobby said, addressing the crowd with palpable grief in his voice, realizing that he needed to tell them the worst of what everyone feared would one day happen, but still somehow would not be able to believe it when it did. "I have some very sad news for all of you," he started.

The little black boy, who was still holding the sign that he just lowered, looked up at his mom and dad, who both looked confused and frozen even.

Bobby continued, almost unable to say what had to be said, "Martin Luther King was shot and was killed today in Memphis, Tennessee."

Everyone's hearts immediately sank, and their jaws immediately dropped in a collective wailing that no words could adequately describe. Tragedy, catastrophe, and ruin combined not only to consume them, but to become them, a spiritual holocaust that ripped their hearts and souls straight from their bodies, and replaced their sense of normalcy, as difficult and damning as it typically was, with a new kind of hell, one that seemed inescapable with no kindred leader to guide them through.

"Martin Luther King dedicated his life to love and to justice between fellow human beings," Bobby went on gently, struggling to get the sentence out. "He died in the cause of that effort."

Tears began streaming down the little boy's face, unable to comprehend how his hero, the man that had a dream who was going to make things right once and for all between the races, could no longer be with them, unable to understand how, or why, anyone would do such a thing to a man who was so loving, so peaceful, and only trying to help people, black and white alike, be the best of themselves, and only trying to help his country, become the best of itself too.

"In this difficult time in the United States," Bobby said further, emotion choking his voice, "It's perhaps good to ask what kind of a nation we are and what direction we want to move in?"

Bobby then paused briefly and tried, wrestling with the apocalypse percolating within him, not to break down and start weeping with the mourners, not to let his herculean emotions undo the leader he felt he had to be in this moment, not to allow the kind of agape love he now had for King, a love that could only be born by blood and respect, overwhelm what he needed to say right now, so that he wouldn't sabotage the emotional consolation he needed to provide for everyone's hearts, including his own.

"For those of you who are black," Bobby continued crestfallen and bereaved, "considering the evidence that there were white people who were responsible, you can be filled with bitterness and with hatred and a desire for revenge. We can move in that direction as a country, in greater polarization, black people amongst blacks, and white amongst whites, filled with hatred toward one another."

The little boys' parents, whose eyes were bloodshot from tears and who looked filled with the exact understandable resentment toward racist whites Bobby was talking about, took in the statement, letting it hit not only their minds, but absorb, ever so painfully and unevenly, into their shattered souls, sensing where Bobby was about to take them.

"Or we can make an effort, as Martin Luther King did, to understand, and to comprehend, and replace that violence, that stain of bloodshed that is spread across our land, with an effort to understand compassion and love."

Transfixed by what Bobby was saying, by who he now perceived as his White Moses if ever there was one, the little black boy clutched for both of his parents' weary hands, his left reaching for his mother's shaking palm, and his right for his father's overworked and blistered one, and held onto them with every ounce of the non-existent strength he had, believing in every scarring word that was pronounced.

"For those of you who are black and are tempted to be filled with hatred and mistrust of the injustice of such an act against all white people," Bobby continued, "I would only say that I can also feel in my own heart the same kind of feeling. I had a member of my family killed, but he was killed by a white man," as faces stared upsettingly back at him, remembering the equal heartbreak they had felt when another of their hero's was killed too, not even 5 full years before this.

Bobby, looking into the eyes of the people he loved, of the people's whose cause became his cause and who, throughout the country, the people who collectively and unanimously united together to make him the frontrunner to be the next President of the United States of America, then thought of the quote that was on the paper he was holding, the same quote he saw right before his brother was murdered, the same one he had on his desk when he transformed himself into a civil rights crusader by studying and dedicating his life to black America, and the same one he used to rely on making his decision to run for President.

"My favorite poem was by a poet named Aeschluys," Bobby went on, the quote from the poem not only committed to his memory but also etched in his soul, "he once wrote, 'even in our sleep, pain which cannot forget, falls drop by drop upon the heart, until in our own despair, against our will, comes wisdom through the awful grace of God."

Upon uttering these words, Bobby knew his time was short. He then told the audience that what is needed in the United States is not division, not hatred, not violence, not lawlessness, but love, kindness, and compassion toward one another, and feelings of justice for those who still suffer in America. He told them that the vast majority of white people, and the vast majority of black people, want to live together, want to improve their quality of life, and want justice for all human beings. He then ended by saying, as he looked sincerely at the little black boy with the sign and pleaded for the Almighty's help, "Let us say a prayer for our country and for our people."

Hands started clapping as Bobby finished up and jumped off the flatbed truck, leaving the audience who was still shaken, before making his way back to the motorcade, which was to take him to his hotel. Inside the car, in what felt like an endlessly long and awkward ride, one of the aides examined Bobby carefully, who was completely silent, a blank sadness wrapped across his face, a shell of the man who had just spoken to thousands to give them hope.

Bobby then got to the hotel, said good night as he exited the vehicle with calmness and composure, and went into his room alone. After about a second, he fell to his knees and started weeping, the tornado of feeling bursting out of him, destroying any sense of emotional restraint he had left. And all he could say was, over and over again, "Why, God, why? They killed my brother! Both of my brothers! They should have killed me instead! Why didn't they kill me instead?"

He began violently wailing about the room, asking *why, why, why*, a man completely shattered and undone by anguish.

But before Bobby could continue going on, before he could continue questioning what had just happened, before he could sit in his pain any longer, he heard a knock on the door, which he wanted to ignore. But then he heard the knock again and again, before finally deciding that he needed to open it, his face red from the torment of tears and agony which defined him, to see one of his aides standing there. "Yes?" he said, feeling crushed.

"Senator, I'm so sorry to bother you," the aide responded, completely taken aback at the state of his boss and regretful that he had to come to his hotel room right now. "But you need to know something."

"What's that?" Bobby asked, his right hand wiping away unstoppable water flowing down his cheeks.

"Riots have broken out from black Americans all across the country because of Martin Luther King's murder and, if they're not stopped, we could be in another civil war at any moment."

SEVENTY EIGHT

At the announcement of Martin Luther King's death, more than 100 riots had broken out by blacks throughout America, in nearly every major city except Indianapolis, where Bobby had urged peace and unity between the races the night before. Places like Chicago, New York, Boston, Detroit, and Oakland were up in flames, and over 70,000 federal and state troops were deployed to try to quell them, especially to try to prevent any more killings because over three dozen murders and 2,500 maimings had just taken place in the ensuing 24 hours by a frustrated and angry people who felt there was no other option than to take revenge on the society, on the system, that killed their nonviolent icon. And Bobby, the presidential frontrunner that he was, needed to figure out a way to stop this, especially stopping this from erupting into an all-out war between blacks and whites, a fight that the Iron White Wall would most certainly welcome, but one that could bring America existentially to its knees, like it had been brought to 100 years before in its last major Civil War.

On his plane ride back to Washington, D.C., Bobby was still reeling deeply from King's assassination, a pain that was so profoundly personal, like Jack's death had been, in part because it was so abrupt, in part because of all of the great work they could have accomplished together, and in part because it was done by people who were truly evil, whose ideology was truly evil, and whose people not only had murderous intent toward him, but also genocidal intent toward blacks, a hatred so strong that every Negro would be annihilated from the face of the earth if these people could get away with it, and Bobby was emotionally overwhelmed by this.

"Senator," one of Bobby's aides said to him on their third flight together in three days, accompanying him to see the Black Panthers in California, announce King's death in Indianapolis, and now back to Washington, D.C., where the rioting was the worst by a long shot, "I hate to even ask, but are you sure you want to march with the black protestors?"

Looking out of the window as the plane was descending into the recently opened Dulles International Airport, Bobby didn't respond, his eyes glowing with the red embers of the flames he was observing in the distance, depression haunting his face.

"Sir?" the aide said, again trying to "talk some sense" into his boss but also trying to ensure his safety, as well as his own.

"It's worse than I thought," Bobby said back to him, face fixed out of the window, looking hopeless. "Until now, blacks haven't really held America accountable with force."

"Accountable with force?" the aide asked, confused.

"Yes," Bobby said, "with force."

"What are you saying, Sir?"

"This is why Martin Luther King was so important. Because he inspired an oppressed people not to do back to us what we did to them."

"By using force?" the aide asked, even more confused than he had been.

Bobby then stopped looking out of the window and started to look back at his well-meaning, brown-haired assistant. "Don't you see?" Bobby said, "that, even right now, they are only doing a tiny fraction to whites of what we've done to them?"

"I don't understand, Sir," the aide replied. "Are you justifying the violence?"

"You don't get it," Bobby said, shaking his head slightly. "He was not only their leader, but he was their symbol, their hope. And they feel like their hope has been extinguished."

"You're their hope now," the aide responded, trying to encourage his energetic and inspiring boss who he had never seen despondent like this. "You're their leader."

Ignoring the comment, which he thought was inappropriate not just given the moment but because he was also a white man, Bobby said, "He did everything in his short 39 years to make this country live up to the ideals it cherishes on paper but doesn't operate by in practice. And in return, he got a bullet just like Jack."

"But Sir," the aide continued, downplaying the ominous idea he thought Bobby might be implying would happen to him too, "you're young, only 42 years old yourself. As President you can do what both of them were trying to do. Carry on their legacy."

But Bobby didn't respond to this either. Instead, as the plane landed, looking chagrined, he said, "I'm going to stand with blacks with all my heart and all my resources and all my power for as many more days as God may grant me. As few as those days might be."

The aide, like Jackie Kennedy and Bobby's wife Ethel several months before, started to get concerned. *Was Bobby hoping for death? Was he prophesying it, overwhelmed by all the death threats against his life? Or was he simply being a realist, what with his best friend Jack and his new brother King both being assassinated for advancing civil rights? Was he simply too distraught to go on?*

As the plane door opened, like in Indianapolis, Bobby walked quickly across the tarmac and hopped in the makeshift motorcade prepared for him, along with the traveling aides from the flight. Looking through the rearview mirror, the specially trained Secret Service driver, who had once served his brother and who was sitting next to a heavily armed Secret Service agent wearing glasses, said, "Heading home, Sir?"

"Not yet," Bobby replied. "Take me to the middle of the rioting. I need to be there."

"I can't do that," the Driver said. "Buildings are on fire, police are in riot gear, tear gas may be deployed. You could be killed."

"This is not a discussion," Bobby responded sharply. "This is an order. Take me there now."

The driver looked up at Bobby but said nothing, stepping slowly on the pedal, knowing he had no power to override the Senator from New York. He, along with the other Lincoln Continentals and assortment of vehicles in the fleet, began making their way to ground zero. He turned on the radio, WAMA 88.5, which announced that J. Edgar Hoover had just dispatched over 3,000 FBI agents to search for King's murderer, in a manhunt that identified escaped convict, and would be porn-director, James Earl Ray as suspect number one, last seen in his white 1966 Mustang heading South. Bobby wondered to himself, *Was this manhunt, described as the largest ever in history, a genuine effort by Hoover to find King's killer? Or was it an overcompensating PR stunt to make Hoover look good and placate angry blacks? Or was it something else, something far worse and more sinister, something disguised to conceal dirty hands that the FBI might be trying to cover up, just as they had been trying to cover up their concerted campaign to destroy King for an entire decade, something he had learned after he had left his role at the Justice Department four years ago?*

Eventually, the motorcade made its way to 7th and U streets, straight in the heart of downtown, in the middle of many of the important buildings, which looked like a war zone, with millions of dollars of damage clearly done. As the motorcade stopped, Bobby started to get out.

"Stay in the vehicles," Bobby said, looking back at his shocked aides and security detail. "You are not to come with me."

Walking through the debris all by himself, Bobby went deeper into the 22 block territory where the rioting was still going on. As he took everything in, the Attorney General in him, his law and order instincts, hated seeing the damage and destruction; on the other hand, the civil rights crusader in him, with his heart for blacks and equality for all, understood exactly where they were coming from. And he felt deeply conflicted inside.

"Get out of here, whitey," one young black rioter said, not recognizing the Presidential frontrunner in the middle of the night with all of the fumes from the fires bellowing around him.

"Actually," Bobby said with his characteristic Boston Irish accent, "I'm here to join you, to peacefully protest the murder of Martin Luther King."

When the young black rioter got closer, he saw who was saying this to him. "Oh, sorry," he said, looking incredibly nervous, realizing it was the man that he, and most of the people he knew, had voted for in the Washington D.C. Presidential primary recently.

"That's alright," Bobby replied, grabbing the youngster by his shoulder and squeezing him in a fatherly way. "Do you have any friends here?"

"Is that a trick question?" the youngster asked, suspicious of not selling out his crew, knowing Bobby had the power to crush them.

"No," Bobby responded. "I just want to march with you and your friends, peacefully."

"One second," the youngster said, running over to a group of young blacks who were about one hundred meters ahead. Before long, he returned with them, about 50 in total, and they all began shaking Bobby's hand and marching in lockstep, before thousands joined them too, all in a matter of minutes, in an amazing display of Bobby spontaneously leading his first-ever civil rights march.

Making their way down the streets, with Bobby singing the Freedom Songs he heard King and other civil rights workers sing over the years, they spotted a group of heavily armed military agents, decked out in battle gear. Like King had done marching his way through Selma toward the Dixiecrat police three years earlier, Bobby marched his way toward these federal military agents too.

"Stop immediately!" the federal army agent said with a bullhorn, guns drawn alongside thousands of other military agents, "or we will deploy force!"

Bobby, still acting like he was King himself, remembering those television images he saw from the slain Preacher years earlier, didn't stop, but instead moved forward with his group, step-by-step. The military agents quickly put on their gas masks, indicating they were about to shoot heavy tear gas at the rioters. But before they could launch their weapons, the army agent with the bullhorn said, with as much surprise on his contorted face as was in his crackling voice as he saw Bobby starting to kneel and pray , "Senator Kennedy, is that you?"

SEVENTY NINE

"This is Walter Cronkite from the CBS Evening News," the television screen blared, in a homemade VCR tape running on a replay loop. "And, I have good news to report: Senator Robert Fitzgerald Kennedy is okay, suffering no injuries when he joined a march in Washington with thousands of blacks to protest Martin Luther King's violent murder, with riot police dropping their weapons and letting him and his group pass through unscathed after they were held at gunpoint."

A dark skinned hand, not of the American type, then pressed fast-forward on the VCR, in a small home in Pasadena, California. "There is still no word on when, or if, the FBI will catch Dr. King's killer. However, Bobby Kennedy, in an act of love, attended King's funeral, which was eulogized by King's Father Martin Luther King Sr., and attended by over 100,000 mourners, where Senator Kennedy was seen weeping and hugging Corretta Scott King, Dr. King's children, and even pulling a rosary out of his pocket and giving it to Martin Luther King III as a gift, a gesture that brought the young son of the civil rights leader to tears."

As the dark-skinned man continued to watch the screen, he fast-forwarded again, seeing images of Bobby Kennedy at the funeral and also King's body lying in state at Spelman College in Atlanta, and then images of Bobby with his family at Hickory Hill, playing with his kids, and even playing with his brother's kids, wrestling John Kennedy Jr.

to the ground. He watched as Bobby won primary after primary in the Democratic Party, and the groundswell of support he had generated in the two months since King's assassination. "And tonight, on June 4th, 1968," the Anchor continued, "Kennedy is expected to be at the Ambassador Hotel in Los Angeles, to address his supporters in his quest to be the first President to be elected as the brother of a former President in what now looks like a clear path to The White House."

The dark-skinned hand then clicked off the television and glanced around the room. There was Kennedy memorabilia everywhere. Buttons. Posters. Newspaper clippings. The works. And there was even a journal he had been keeping, devoted to the Senator and would-be Commander-in Chief, in which he had just written the words:

"Robert Fitzgerald Kennedy Must Die!"

The man, with dark hair and eyes, and standing at just 5 feet, 5 inches tall and weighing 120 pounds, then reached for his .22 Revolver. He studied its features carefully, rubbing the weapon as though it was a sacred object, and kissing it with his lips. Before long, the phone rang.

"This is Sirhan Sirhan," the dark-skin foreign-born man with a double-name said, listening to whomever was on the other end of the line. "Don't worry," Sirhan teased, "it will be done tonight."

Continuing to listen to the voice, Sirhan grew impatient, telling the man on the phone that he could accomplish his services without the help of any other men who would also be planted in the Ambassador Hotel this evening. He said, "I don't need to work with the CIA, I've already been through their MKUltra program, and I don't need to work with anybody else. I can do this on my own."

The phone then hung up.

About 50 miles away in Malibu, Bobby was enjoying a peaceful day with Ethel, and several of his kids and nieces and nephews, who had accompanied him on this leg of the campaign. It was a rare occasion for them to all be together, especially with Bobby's schedule, but the kids were out of school and this was California, and they couldn't pass it up, especially staying at a beach house.

"Uncle Bobby," 10-year old Caroline Kennedy said, "you're going to be the next President of the United States!"

Smiling, Bobby replied, "Well honey, it's still a few months before the general election."

"Richard Nixon can't beat you!" Caroline blurted out, matching Bobby's wide faced grin.

"What makes you say that? Because your dad beat him?" Bobby said, still smiling.

"No, not because of that. I say it because nobody likes Richard Nixon!"

"He has a lot of support in the country," Bobby responded, referring to the innovative dog-whistle campaign Nixon was running to secure racist whites in the South who opposed civil rights, to combine with his support in the North.

"Doesn't matter," Caroline said, "he's mean and calls everybody a son of a bitc—"

"Watch it," Bobby interrupted, laughing, as Ethel came up behind him, wrapping her arms around him, and Caroline skedaddled outside to play with her cousins on the beach.

"You know," Ethel said, jubilee in her eyes, "at first I was nervous about you running."

"And now?" Bobby replied back, glancing down at a newspaper headline which showed him with a commanding lead in the polls.

"I'm still nervous," Ethel said. "But I believe with everything inside of me that you are the man to lead this country. I'm proud of you not just because you are a hero to so many in this nation, blacks among them, but because you are a good person who has grown so much these past few years."

"Thank you, sweetie," Bobby said, "that means a lot. Especially because you and Jackie were so dead set against me running."

"I know we were, and still are on a personal level," Ethel continued. "Because we love you. But on a political level, on a social level, on a historical level, how can we be against you? You're sincere and you have learned to put other people ahead of yourself and your own self-interests, something other politicians just don't do. Something most people don't do. You've given a voice to the voiceless and hope to the hopeless, just like Martin Luther King did. Just like your brother did."

Bobby looked into the eyes of his wife, taking in these beautiful and kind words from the woman he loved unconditionally, and gave her a smooch on the lips.

"Who knows," Bobby said with irony in his voice, "maybe what I said about us not getting to decide our own fates will turn out well? Maybe fate will smile on us and our country, and maybe we can actually accomplish the work Martin still had to finish and that Jack still had to finish?"

"Who knows indeed?" Ethel said, giving a smooch back to her man. "That's why you're running."

"Okay," Bobby replied, cutting the conversation short as he looked down at his watch, "we should probably be heading to the hotel now."

With those words, Bobby put on his coat, Ethel grabbed her purse, and Bobby said goodbye to the children. They hopped in the motorcade outside of the rented Malibu estate, and began making their way down the Pacific Coast Highway, taking in the sights of the white-sand beach, of the glistening ocean, and, their favorite of all, of the fading sunset.

The motorcade pulled up to the Moroccan-themed Ambassador Hotel at 3400 Wilshire Blvd, which had served as host to over a half dozen Academy Award ceremonies, and a premier destination for Presidents, dignitaries, and celebrities of all sorts, none of whom were as big as Bobby had become. Getting out of the vehicle, Bobby was hounded by press, with blinding bulbs flashing, as he and Ethel entered the grand lobby to the 1,000 suite deluxe venue, which had gorgeous crystal chandeliers and decadent accoutrements everywhere, fitting especially for a Kennedy, and made their way into the ballroom, where Bobby gave a celebration speech for winning the California Democratic primary by a huge margin over his opponent today.

Listening to the speech over the PA system in the kitchen, however, Sirhan, Sirhan hid behind an ice machine, looking at a map of the hotel he had sketched out two days before on his planning visit, and waiting for Bobby to enter its paths once his talk was over, hoping that what he had heard on the news about how candidates typically enter or exit big venues, usually through their backways and kitchens, proved fatally true.

Bobby finished his speech and was grabbed by the arm by an aide, who advised him that he needed not to linger with the people any longer, but instead to go to the kitchen, where the poor workers and cooks and busboys and waiters and waitresses, the people he championed, wanted to meet him.

Sirhan held tightly onto his disguised rifle, spotting the handsome young candidate ten feet away, surrounded by a mass of people. *Come closer*, he thought to himself. *Just a little closer.*

Shaking hands with what seemed like an endless number of staff, Bobby was being pulled left and right, becoming somewhat discombobulated by not just the amount of people, but because it was just past midnight, and he was starting to feel a little tired. As he walked toward the ice machine, he went to reach for the hand of a worker but heard a loud bang. Looking down, he saw that it had hit his body, with blood starting to pour out everywhere. Winching, he heard another bang, with blood starting to spew from another part of his body. Then he heard two more bangs ringing in his ears, as Sirhan Sirhan, at point black range, fired at him indiscriminately, with a smirk on his cold-blooded assassins face, hitting Bobby and multiple people around him.

Bobby collapsed to the ground, with his eyes rolling to the back of his head, lying in a puddle of heavy blood, struggling to breathe, to see, and to make out what was happening, a psychedelic whirlwind captivating his senses in a haze of gut-wrenching light. He looked at the young man next to him, who was tending to him and who took the rosary he happened to have and placed it in Bobby's hands. Without thinking of himself, Bobby asked, "Is everyone okay?" But the look in the young man's eyes, the look in everyone's eyes, said it all.

EIGHTY

―

"Mission accomplished!" roared the Imperial Wizard to his Klansman, in a vile celebration as wicked as the men who were gloating were, to clinks and clanks of beer bottles. "The nig*er-lover is dead!"

"Serves him right," an arrogant Klansman responded who was a state judge and former prosecutor, as he stumbled, tipsy, in the KKK's Georgia Church headquarters, which had just been renovated with funds from a slew of new financial donations that surged after King's, and now Bobby's, assassination. "Ha!"

Another Klansman, a local school teacher, pulled out the *Daily Mirror* newspaper, which had a headline of "God Not Again" above an image of Bobby's slain body, which was pronounced dead at Good Samaritan Hospital 26 hours after his shooting, and started to burn it, tossing the paper to the ground. Three other Klansmen began dancing around the paper in a circle, like demons encircling a hellfire, chanting, celebrating, congratulating themselves on their teamwork, resilience, smarts, and ability to outwit the man and system, maintaining a bond of destruction through thick and thin, against multiple enemies.

"So Boss," the state judge Klansman said as he approached his serpent-like leader, both of whom were not wearing their traditional white pointy hats or fascist white robes, "you heard from your Contact since the news broke of Kennedy's death?"

The Imperial Wizard, with a look of exalted ecstasy on his face, responded, unconcerned, "No, he seems to have disappeared out of the blue."

"Probably a good thing, don't you think?" remarked the state judge Klansman, somehow functioning despite the amount of alcohol he had imbibed in celebration.

"Absolutely," said the Imperial Wizard. "His work is done. Besides, they arrested that dumb son of a b*tch Sirhan Sirhan, just like my Contact said they would, and they will fry that foreign asshole like an egg."

"True, dumb ass fall guy," the state judge Klansman responded, knowing that who he believed the front killer to be would likely get the death penalty by electrocution or the gas chamber, in a speedy trial to satisfy the public's need for immediate closure, and to close off any ties to himself or his group. "But what about King's assassin, James Earl Ray, who's still on the run?"

"It's only a matter of time before they get him too," the Imperial Wizard replied confidently. "He's used 17 aliases and is trying to flee to South Africa or Rhodesia last I heard."

"But those countries won't extradite him?" the state judge Klansman asked, worried that this could leave the case open longer than it should be, and possibly implicate him, and the Klan, in a conspiracy if things weren't swiftly wrapped up.

"Yeah, they won't extradite him if he can get to either place," the Imperial Wizard said, gulping down some more liquor. "But I can't see J Edgar Hoover not getting him because the FBI will come under fire if they don't, given the size of their supposed manhunt."

"Speaking of Hoover," the state judge said, shifting the conversation, "one of my friends who works at the FBI overheard his reaction to the nig*er and the nig*er lovers' deaths. And I think you'll like it."

"Oh yeah, what was that?" the Imperial Wizard asked, delighted and intrigued by the gossip.

"Apparently Hoover said, quote, 'Nobody is going to miss those stupid nig*ers,'" the state judge Klansman responded, with a bright smile on his face, and vile laughter coming out of his mouth, before stating that Hoover had revealed his FBI informant source who, in addition to all of the wiretaps and bugs, told him where King would be at all times throughout the 1960s: King's personal civil rights photographer, the double-crossing Ernest Withers, which delighted the judge even more.

"Here, here!" the Imperial Wizard said back.

"But not to sound like a cynic during a time of celebration for us," the state judge Klansman continued, suddenly worried again, in the dramatic whims alcohol took him, his legal mind always calculating political risks and realities, "but do you think their deaths will generate sympathy from the public for coons? America loves nothing more than famous martyrs, like JFK and King and now Bobby, and their dumb ass causes."

"I do," the Imperial Wizard said gruffly. "But that's why we have to adapt, be smarter, stay ahead of them. We can't keep using the word nig*er, nig*er, nig*er when we talk about King, or the Kennedys, or civil rights, or blacks. We've got to get more subtle than that given public opinion shifting on the issue, especially for Northern white moderates who are now more sympathetic to blacks."

Of course, the Imperial Wizard was referring to the oft-used play-book White Supremacists had been employing for years each time public opinion turned against them—first in the Civil War and now Jim Crow—perfectly summed up by the President of the Confederate States of America Chairman Jefferson Davis who said, "The principle for which we contended is bound to reassert itself, though it may be at another time and in another form," and by author of the 1868 'Lost Cause' narrative Edward Alfred Pollard, who concluded, "The Lost Cause needs no new war to regain it. We have taken up new hopes, new arms, new methods."

"So are you saying we should use coded language instead of how we normally talk about coons to stop them from passing any more civil rights bills and from trying to enforce their rights, which they clearly should not have?" the state judge Klansman asked, curiosity illuminating his gaze.

"Yes," the Imperial Wizard responded. "Dog whistle politics allows us to speak out in the open without anyone knowing what we're saying, unless they're in on it. Like what Nixon is doing to bring in all of the former Dixiecrats to his campaign. He saw that he lost coons in 1960 to JFK and he's just abandoning them, like the Republican party recently has, at least for now."

"By appealing to the new language of States Rights, and saying things like we're for a colorblind and merit-based society, knowing white men will always have more merit than black nig*ers, invoking 'reverse-racism' whenever blacks continue to demand their rights, and that sort of thing?" the state judge Klansman asked.

"Absolutely," the Imperial Wizard agreed.

With this strategy, the Klansmen knew that "colorblind" and "merit-based" language could be easily sold to Northern white moderates and blacks of all types on the surface more so than "nig*er" and "states rights," with the idea that America should not see color and only give preference to people based on their "qualifications." While nice in theory—just like the Declaration of Independence stating all men were created equal while the country was simultaneously and hypocritically importing millions of slaves—in practice this colorblind and merit-based language would mean that, because all of the political, economic, educational, and social power structures are overwhelmingly run by white men, both nationally and in every state in the country, these white men could still pick and choose who they let in the "club." Because these white men had exclusively given themselves a several hundred year legal and financial head start on blacks, a de facto white affirmative action—accumulating trillions more in wealth, hundreds of thousands more in total number of political offices, and the right to define history and social structures and perceptions for the last 350 years—saying "there is now an equal playing field" will seduce Northern white moderates into thinking that the game is being played fairly between the races. In reality it will be played with white men starting 5 yards from the finish line competing against black ones who are, in most cases, still being denied tickets to the stadium because they can't afford entrance fees, much less the training or opportunity to compete in the first place. Sure, you might have the occasional black that breaks through like Jackie Robinson in this color-blind and merit-based system, these Klansman thought, but by stating things are now fair and square between the races it will allow the white moderate's conscience to be appeased without the underlying social and political system changing at all. Except for the most rare and exceptional black people, probably just in things like sports and possibly entertainment, but not in the thousands of other industries that exist like law and medicine and finance and business where real life is lived for the majority of everyday black people. It will also allow the white moderate, including those born into poor or middle class means, to continue believing the myth that his individual success is exclusively because of his own hard work and not also due in significant measure to the advantages of the de facto white affirmative action system he was born into that he has been blinded from seeing that affords him success while it denies most others of a different skin hue—who have the same talent and work ethic as the white moderate—their success, which all statistics of the time have proven damnably true.

"If we use this language of color-blindness and merit, and claim reverse racism whenever our whiteness is invoked to create doubt and controversy when blacks demand their supposed rights," the judge Klansman continued, "and if if we use this dogwhistle strategy, we can keep our country in tact, with white men on top, where we deserve to be, and coons, Catholics, Jews, wet backs, women, and faggots on the bottom, where they deserve to be, without these Northern white moderates even knowing what we're saying, what we're doing, or in many cases unknowingly speaking these things themselves."

"You hit the nail on the head," the Imperial Wizard said in complete agreement. "And what's great about this new coded language we'll be using is that it just allows us to put lipstick on a pig, the same pig we've been riding high on since the great days of the Confederacy, keeping us at the top."

"Makes sense. We just have to let this moment of sympathy fade from the public's mind for these nig*ers," the state judge Klansman said, "and it will be business as usual, with no more talk of marches and protests and justice and all of that bullsh*t. We just have to stand strong with colorblindness, meritocracy, and reverse-racism and have our undercover politicians and media spokespeople and school teachers convince white moderates and even black people everything is okay now. We need to make them believe that White Supremacy ended with the I Have a Dream speech and the enactment of the Civil Rights Acts of 1964 and 1965, to convince them that these things magically created true equality between the races, which we know they did not. And once the white moderate is convinced, this ideology will need no reinforcement and will perpetuate itself over and over again in the name of fairness and common-sense, and will become so widespread and self-evident it will never be questioned by another white person again, at least for a long time."

"Exactly," the Imperial Wizard said. "We just need to get through Robert Kennedy's funeral tomorrow and we, and America, will be golden, even if some blacks make marginal gains. As long as most of them are put in their place, well, then, that's good enough for me, for right now."

"Here, here," the state judge Klansman said before asking, "speaking of that coon-lover's funeral: is his wife giving the eulogy?"

"Ugh, yes," the Imperial Wizard replied, swigging some more beer. "Along with John Kennedy's old lady and King's too apparently."

"Oh well," the state judge Klansman shrugged. "Nobody cares what a couple of Catholic b*tches and their nig*er counterpart has to say anyway."

EIGHTY ONE

Ethel Kennedy's tears bellowed out of her like an apocalyptic battering ram, as the "Air Force One" plane was landing that President Johnson specially commissioned to bring Bobby's body back from California to the east coast. Jackie Kennedy and Corretta Scott King, who both accompanied her after meeting one another for the first time, were equally devastated, along with the rest of America. What had been one tumultuous American tragedy after another for this 1960s nation had been one continuous personal fight with the devil for each of them, a fight they did not want to have, but one they still could not refuse, given the vision of equality they had supported even in the midst of their husbands' blood—despite the midst of their husbands' blood—of an America where all people, blacks and whites alike, could live together in peace and harmony once and for all.

The widows, the women who were equal parts grace and agony, could barely move as the flag-draped casket carrying Bobby began to be lifted by United States military personnel, and escorted out of the back.

"Ethel, Ethel!" Corretta said, as Ethel started to collapse to the ground, nearly passing out from the suffocation that grief had ravaged her body with, asphyxiated by the haunting image of her husband's body lying lifeless on a cold hotel floor the night of his assassination, an image she kept replaying over and over again in her mind.

Looking up, with mascara smeared, Ethel screamed, "They took them from us! How could they take them from us!" in a moment that was all too similar to Jackie's reaction to her husband's death, and Corretta's reaction to hers.

Jackie quickly came over to comfort Ethel. But as she did, she started weeping too. "They didn't deserve this," she said, her entire body shaking. "They just wanted to heal our country and those bastards took them from us!"

The U.S. military personnel, watching this scene unfold, didn't know how to react. The three most famous women in America, who always stood so perfectly composed and quietly beside their men, were actually people, with real emotions, real feelings, real heartbreak, and with a hopelessness that was as palpable as it was calamitous, and this was shocking to people who expected, who assumed, public figures were supposed be emotionless robots, not real humans just like them. Nevertheless, as they observed they remained respectful, not moving Bobby's body anymore, until the three de facto First Ladies of the United States somehow summoned the strength to compose themselves.

Corretta started to dry Ethel and Jackie's tears with a handkerchief, and then reached into her purse to pull out some lipstick and eyeliner, for them to share. Eventually, after they got as calm as they could under these circumstances, they made their way out of the makeshift Air Force One and into the hearse processional that was first to take Bobby's body to lie in mass at a Cathedral in New York and, shortly thereafter, to lie in State in Washington, D.C., before his final burial.

On the ride to mass, the First Ladies hardly spoke to each other, or to anyone else. How could they? First Jack was taken five years before. Then Martin two months before. Now Bobby in the blink of an eye. What could be said of this? What could be said of an America that had fought a civil war over slavery, and now a civil war over civil rights, that could respond with such vicious hatred to the men who dared to try to make things right between the races? What could be said of Jack, who knew Abraham Lincoln was signing his own death warrant by supporting the first Emancipation Proclamation a hundred years before, nevertheless following in his footsteps by eventually backing King's Second Emancipation Proclamation, knowing he would probably get the same death wish in return? What could be said of Martin, who knew he would die if he didn't stop his struggle, either by heart failure or worse, who had proof of his inevitable demise by the cross shaped scar on his chest, but that he nevertheless pushed forward anyway? What could be said of Bobby, a man who was so ruthless and practical about civil rights in the beginning, a man who only wanted to opportunistically seize political wins and protect his brother, who nevertheless transformed and was willing to become a martyr because he came to believe so deeply in the cause of freedom and equality and dignity for blacks, and for all people? What could be said of these men? They were warriors. They were heroes. They were statuesque demi-gods, regardless of the many human flaws they carried. But, more than that, to the women that loved them most, they were the men that they had married, bore children to, lived life with, supported through thick and thin, and gave up everything for. And now, despite all of these things that their husbands unequivocally were, there was something more that they definitely weren't: here. They were gone. Inescapably, tragically, horrifically gone. And what could be said of this? Of being punished for doing good, for being good, for trying to do the right thing, for trying to snuff out the darkness with light, of being rewarded with wicked mens' vengeance?

After Ethel, Jackie, and Corretta made their way to the first mass, at which they didn't give any public eulogies, and after they began to depart for the second mass to watch Bobby's body lie in state, they started to talk. This time, on this second and final leg of their journey, they took a train along the eastern seaboard from New York to Washington, D.C. Somebody had arranged this moment for them to go by train with Bobby's casket instead of by plane so that everyday people could watch the locomotive caravan go by, to pay their respects, to say goodbye to the man—and the women representing him, and their husbands—one last time.

On board the train, Corretta reached into the travel belongings she had brought with her. She looked over to Ethel and said, "I hope this is okay, but can I share something with you, from my son Martin Luther King III?"

"Of course, Corretta," Ethel said, her face a little more flush, her flesh a bit more alive than it had been earlier, though she still was emotionally wiped out, and raw.

"Well," Corretta said, searching for the words to say, "when Bobby came to my husband's funeral a few weeks ago he did something so kind for my son."

Eyes widening, Ethel responded, in a whisper, "Oh, what's that?"

"Well," Corretta continued, "Bobby gave my son his personal rosary from his pocket, one that he always carried with him, which I know in the Catholic tradition is very important."

"It is," Ethel said tenderly, Jackie shaking her head in agreement.

"That deeply touched my son, even as a little Christian that he is," Corretta responded. "So he gave this personal item to me to return the favor to your family."

Corretta then reached into her bag and pulled out Martin Luther King III's special teddy bear. "This teddy bear, which was the first and most important gift ever given by my husband to my son, is named 'Love.' And my son wanted to give it to your husband, Bobby, to bury it with him."

"Wow," Ethel replied, startled and awe struck, at the offer of the young boy who was the heir to MLK's legacy, and deeply moved.

"This way," Corretta said, "the Love of the Kings can be forever shared, forever linked, forever bound up with and to the Kennedys."

Ethel started to cry again and reached for Corretta's hand, grabbing it tightly. "Thank you," was the only thing she could say. "Thank you."

They all got up to make their way to Bobby's casket, to put Martin Luther King III's "Love" inside of it. They began moving from car to car in the train caravan. As they did, they looked outside of the windows. There were millions upon millions of people—black and white and Asian and Chicano and rich and poor and able and disabled and Christian and Catholic and Muslim and Jewish and Hindu and atheist and agnostic alike—as far as the eye can see. People were holding large and small American flags. Some were holding signs with quotes from Bobby like "Only those who dare to fail greatly can ever achieve greatly" and "Few will have the greatness to bend history, but each of us can work to change a small portion of events." And some were even holding pictures of him and Jack and King and lit candles and flowers and all sorts of other arrangements of blessings and honor.

One smattering of people caught both Ethel and Corretta's eyes as the train entered Washington. It was a few of the Black Panthers decked out in their uniforms, some of the same ones who had been with Bobby months earlier for their late night meeting, as well as a few of Martin

Luther King's Freedom Riders who had also been at King's funeral, including Carol Davis, John Lewis, and James "Big Duck" Smith who had originally given Bobby a piece of his mind about civil rights years earlier. The Black Panthers had their hands over their hearts, standing in solidarity, showing their respect for the man they voted for for President. The Freedom Riders, tears streaming down their faces, simply saluted Bobby's train, with "Big Duck" struggling to hold back his emotion.

In the car containing Bobby's body, Ethel got permission to open the casket from the traveling mortician. The lid lifted and revealed Bobby's still handsome face, and motionless body, decked out in his favorite blazer, that of his brother Jack's, along with his favorite quote from Aeschluys about the awful grace of God. She and Corretta jointly held the teddy bear and lowered it in, placing Love near Bobby's heart. They then closed the casket, slowly, carefully, ruefully.

The train finally arrived to have Bobby lie in state. Shortly thereafter, he was taken to Arlington National Cemetery in the dark of night, in a private ceremony that was invitation-only. Standing there, as the casket sat next to JFK's grave, in a special burial plot of land, the wives' minds swirled, next to King's top friends and family, like Ralph Abernathy and Daddy King and his wife Alberta, and Bobby's, alongside his other living family members, including his incapacitated Father Joe, brother Ted, mother Rose, and his nieces, nephews, children, and beloved dog Freckles, who all looked like death-turned-over. As the casket began lowering into the ground, the three wives thought, collectively, and without saying anything to each other or anyone else, what would history eventually say about their husbands?

Jackie wondered, would Jack be remembered only for his looks, his charm, and his murder, or would he be remembered for something more, like standing up for blacks when push came to shove? For being a profile in courage?

Ethel wondered, would there ever be another white man of Bobby's stature who would willingly forsake his own interests, and the interests of his ethnicity, and of his own power and resources, just to deploy them on behalf of a despised group because it was the right thing to do? To courageously and humbly see the world through their eyes, and not through the eyes of advancing only their own one-sided point of view, their own privilege, and their own will? Would there ever be another white man who would take the time to understand people not like himself, take genuine interest in befriending them, and risk it all not only in the name of justice, but in the name of love too?

Corretta wondered, studying Bobby's casket inching near the nadir of its ultimate resting place, would there ever be another black man like her Martin, who spoke like he did, marched like he did, loved like he did, organized like he did, dreamt like he did, and endured the kind of self-sacrificial pain and suffering like he did, demonstrating the best of what it means to be an American, to be a man, and to be the purest form of a child of God?

Bobby's casket finally reached its end, only a few feet from the eternal flame that had been lit on behalf of his brother's grave. As Ethel, Jackie, and Corretta looked upon it one last time, they then turned to each other, tears gripping their faces. Jackie asked them, "Will this country ever produce men like our husbands again?"

"No," Ethel said gently. "It won't. But it can produce men, and women, of all colors and backgrounds and orientations, who can grow into the best versions of themselves, and who can fight for love and peace and justice like they did."

"Amen to that," Corretta replied, hopeful. "It can certainly do that. America will only become what she is called to become if its future generations, the courageous and selfless among them, will step not into the shoes of our husbands, but who will step into what they believed in."

"I like that," Jackie said, smiling, wiping a tear from her right eye. "America will only become what it is supposed to become if it steps into what they stood for."

"Yes, Ethel finished, as she turned to look one last time at the eternal flame burning bright in the night sky, "America will only become what it is supposed to become if it steps into the legacy of Kennedy and King."